MOUNTAINS WANTED

MOUNTAINS SERIES #1

PHOEBE ALEXANDER

To Mike, without whom this book would never have been born. You have been the driving force behind all of this. You have always believed there is greatness in me, and I love you for that, among other things. You will always be my mountain, and I will never stop wanting you.

1

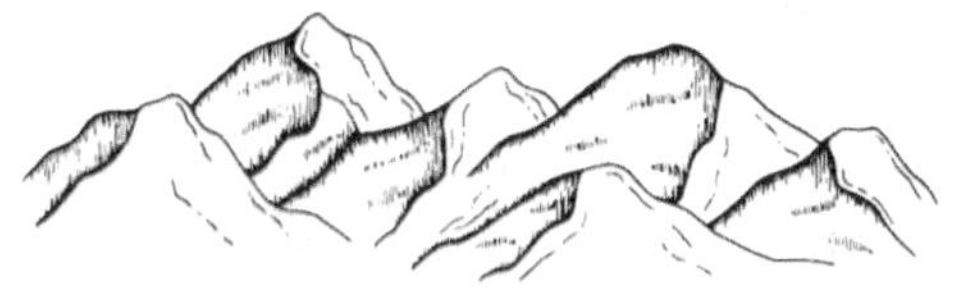

"Make it a six-inch, please," directed the young man standing at the counter.

Sarah stifled a giggle. *Thirty-six years old and I still have such a dirty mind.*

Her gaze swept up and down the man's body. He was dressed in camouflage, and though his ass was mostly covered by his uniform, his thick, sturdy legs promised it would be equally spectacular.

She bit her bottom lip as she turned to study the young woman behind her. She had soft doe-brown eyes and auburn curls, and on her feet were kitten heels in a deep crimson shade. She seemed too young to be a fellow faculty member, too well-dressed to be a student.

"I love your shoes," Sarah gushed, eliciting an embarrassed smile from the woman, who quickly averted her eyes.

The man in front of her spun around to have a look, and Sarah caught a glimpse of the nametag on his uniform: *McAllister.* He grinned at her before turning to tell the sub shop employee what he wanted on his six-inch on wheat.

Wow, he's gorgeous. The woman is gorgeous too, but she doesn't seem to be into women. Pity.

Too much time had passed since Sarah had indulged herself with either sex, and both men and women seemed to be catching her eye more and more often these days.

I've been working too hard. She placed her sandwich order and watched the soldier push his way out the glass door. *A seven-inch would be perfect for me.* She stifled another laugh at that thought.

Sarah stepped out into the hot September sun with her lunch. She trekked across the quad toward her office in the Art-Sociology building, reviewing the remaining items on her to-do list before her afternoon lecture. No matter how hard she tried to focus on work, thoughts about ending her dry spell crept in. The phone buzzing in her pocket jolted her back to the present.

It was her son Owen's school calling. He was sitting in the nurse's office with a fever. *Shit, how am I going to accomplish both eating and running to get him before my 2 PM class?*

Only slightly daunted, she rerouted to the parking lot where her car blasted its pent-up heat into her face as if there were a burning inferno inside. Sarah turned the key in the ignition, cranked up the A/C, and crammed a bite of sandwich down her throat before backing out of the parking space. It was all part of being a single mom.

OWEN HAD PERKED up quite a bit by dinnertime. Sarah presented her two children with a colorful stir-fry with just the right amount of spice. Owen gulped his portion down while Abby picked at hers. Sarah shook her head at this phase her teenage daughter was going through: too much eyeliner, wearing skinny jeans and baggy t-shirts with scraggly uncombed hair, begging for a nose piercing, and not eating dinner—only to gorge on potato chips at midnight.

Sarah snapped out of her reflections on Abby to hear Owen ask, "What's an erection?

Abby looked mortified. "Eww, Mom, there he goes again with the gross questions! Make him stop!"

"Oh, Abigail, it's a perfectly reasonable question." Sarah was used to her younger child's inquisitive nature, which she heartily encouraged. By this point, she was completely unfazed by his questions and actually prided herself on the matter-of-fact scientific answers she provided him. "An erection happens when blood flow is increased to the penis, and it grows bigger and harder."

Abby promptly left the table shaking her head. Owen looked satisfied. It was always difficult to tell if Owen was actually curious or just wanted to annoy his older sister. Sarah figured it was probably a combination of the two.

"Abby, put your food in the fridge in case you get hungry later," Sarah called after her as she started up the stairs in a huff. "I don't want you eating junk food late again!"

Sarah heard her cell phone ringing on the kitchen counter. *Rachel.* "Hey, lady!"

"How was class today? Is Owen alright?" came her best friend's concerned voice.

News sure travels fast. Sarah assumed Rachel's son, Thomas, who was also in fifth grade, had told his mother Owen went home sick. "Yes, he's fine. It's probably another one of those 24-hour viruses that's going around. He just scarfed down his dinner as if nothing is wrong. I don't have a class till twelve tomorrow, so I'll just see if my mom can watch him in the afternoon. What's new with you?"

"I want to do something this weekend! I'm insanely bored. And I need to get laid."

Sarah laughed. There was only one woman on the planet as blunt and open about her sexuality as she was, and that was her best friend, Rachel Brock. They were kindred spirits, destined to meet and become lifelong friends. They had been together since their Lamaze class, gave birth to boys within days of each other, and when Sarah moved to Maryland, Rachel followed. It was almost like having a spouse except they didn't live together.

"Girl, you always need to get laid," Sarah giggled. "I heard there's a new club in DC... I've kinda been wanting to check it out.

"Or, you could come with me to this house party I was invited to at the beach," Rachel suggested.

The beach. Ugh, that's a three-hour drive. "I don't know, Rachel, that's pretty far. I have a lot of work to catch up on this weekend. My senior seminar has their annotated bibliographies due on Friday."

"Work, schmork," Rachel retorted. "I swear, Sarah, your girly bits are going to shrivel up and fall off if we don't get you some cock soon! Speaking of which, any cute students in your classes this semester?"

Actually, Rachel might be more blunt and open than I am, Sarah recalculated. "How many times do I have to tell you that my students are off limits?" She heard Rachel start to protest. "When is this party?"

"It's on Saturday night."

"I have a big lecture on Friday evening. Let's see how I feel after that, okay?" Sarah conceded.

"Why are you giving a lecture on a Friday night?"

"Oh, it's really more of a panel discussion than a lecture. It's part of the university's fall colloquium series: Current Issues in American Politics. This one is on the military's Don't Ask, Don't Tell policy. I'm going to talk about sexuality and the military."

"That sounds hot," Rachel laughed. "Sex and military men. Two of my faves!"

"Why am I not surprised you think it's hot?" Sarah said sarcastically. The memory of McAllister from the sub shop immediately flashed in her mind. "Okay, listen, I'm going to go clean up from dinner. Text me later, okay?"

"Will do, Sugarlips," Rachel replied.

A house party, Sarah thought as she began to clear the dishes from the table. *It's been a long damn time.*

ON FRIDAY, Sarah was relieved when she finally arrived home after her long day. Her cozy bungalow with the warm golden and amber walls and the beautiful wood floors felt like an embrace when she crossed the threshold. She loved having a sanctuary away from the craziness of the beltway traffic and the noise of campus.

She wanted to raise her children in a nurturing atmosphere, so she had done everything possible to make her home feel like a nest for her two baby birds, even though they were hardly babies anymore. She had also done research about how a child's environment impacts their behavior and ability to learn. She was the crazy mom who stood at the paint counter at Lowe's debating whether Cinnamon Apple or Nutmeg Spice would be the "homier" color for the kitchen walls.

She hurried to change her clothes, hating that she had to leave again as soon as she got dinner on the table for Owen and Abigail. Otherwise, she'd be late for her Don't Ask, Don't Tell panel event. She didn't imagine it would be very well attended. *I mean, seriously, how many students are going to voluntarily attend on a Friday night?* she pondered.

An hour later, she shuffled down the sidewalk toward the auditorium. The sun was sinking in the west, and the trees silhouetted against the glowing clouds created a little stinging tear in the corner of her eye. Sarah was generally optimistic, but every once in a while just a bit of melancholia crept in, no matter how hard she fought it. Beauty often stirred those passions inside her, leaving her wishing she had someone to share it with.

She shrugged away the tear, trying to clear her head to focus on her lecture notes. Several uniformed military types were milling around outside the hall where the lecture would take place—relatively unremarkable due to the proximity of the university to several military bases as well as the topic of the lecture.

Sarah had more than a passing curiosity about military life and particularly the sociological aspects of it. She'd never really been close to anyone who served, but she had studied deployment-related post-traumatic stress disorder, and as part of her research into homosexuality and bisexuality, she had examined the Don't Ask, Don't Tell Policy. That was the focus of the panel tonight.

Sarah hoped for a lively but civil debate. It always surprised her how heated discussions about human sexuality could become. *Why did people care so much about what others did behind closed doors?*

She fired up her laptop and watched the audience file in. Most of the military-type people sat near the front of the auditorium. One young man caught her eye and chose a seat within spitting distance. He was nearly six feet tall, sported sandy brown buzzed hair, broad shoulders, and piercing blue eyes. *Well, if he isn't the quintessential All American, clean-cut Army guy,* Sarah mused. *I think I will call him GI Joe.*

Suddenly his eyes met hers, and she was busted for staring at him. Recognition dawned immediately—he was McAllister from the sub shop. He smirked a little in return and then quickly glanced down at his program where Sarah's picture and a brief bio fell on page two.

The panel moderator adjusted the microphone, initiating a bit of feedback, which signaled the audience to quiet down, then proceeded with the introductions. Each panelist presented the findings of their research on the topic, taking fifteen minutes or so apiece, and then the moderator opened up the floor for questions from the audience.

There was quite a bit of passion and fire in the voices of those who asked questions, but civility was maintained. Sarah was relieved. She was particularly proud of her response to one older, retired veteran who was adamant he wouldn't want to serve alongside a gay man in combat.

"With all due respect," Sarah remarked, "let's say your life is on the line in the heat of battle. Would you rather have a gay soldier who is one hundred percent focused and loyal to his fellow soldiers by your side, or a straight soldier whose mind is nowhere near the battlefield? The truth of the matter is people have the ability to be professional and put their recreational and sexual desires aside when needed. This ability has absolutely nothing to do with sexual orientation. It has everything to do with integrity and work ethic."

There was applause when she finished.

The discussion wrapped up around 9 PM, and Sarah

began to gather up her belongings. Some of the panelists were sticking around to further debate with audience members, but she wanted to get home to her children. She walked down the stairs and began heading up the aisle when GI Joe—McAllister—stepped into her path.

"Dr. Lynde," he said formally, apparently not recognizing her from earlier in the week at the sub shop, "I appreciated your response to the vet earlier, but I wondered if you have any personal experience serving in the military? I have found when hunkered down in close quarters with my fellow soldiers that I don't want to be distracted by thinking one of them is checking me out."

He seemed as if he was prodding her for a specific response, testing her. As the corners of his lips turned up into a fuller version of the smirk he'd given her earlier, she realized how incredibly good-looking he was. He was definitely older than her traditional-aged students, but still young, perhaps late twenties? He projected an air of confidence. A presence.

"No, I haven't had the honor of serving." She honestly couldn't recall what else he'd said, she was so distracted by his full lips and straight white teeth, not to mention the mischievous gleam in his icy blue eyes. She forcefully gained her composure. "Please, call me Sarah." She extended her hand.

He firmly shook it. "I'm James McAllister, nice to meet you. I'm an instructor in the ROTC program, and I required my students to attend tonight. I was interested in the research you did on homophobia among military personnel. I have heard a lot of that bullshit throughout my years in the service." He suddenly looked a little embarrassed. "I'm sorry, please excuse my language," he added sheepishly.

She wondered if he meant her research was bullshit or the homophobia itself was. "No need to censor yourself around me," Sarah offered. "I'd love to talk to you about your experience sometime, not to mention hear your own thoughts about the Don't Ask, Don't Tell policy. It's a hot topic these days, and the media is having a field day with it." She gave him another once-over, which set her wheels turning, "Maybe over coffee or something?"

James flashed his all-American grin, even more broadly than before. "That would certainly be interesting."

"Interesting good? Or interesting bad?" Sarah's eyebrows rose as she leaned toward him expectantly, a posture that showed interest and openness. Her fascination with nonverbal communication would often cause her to stop mid-thought to analyze the position, angles and gestures her body was exhibiting. She couldn't help but notice how close together they were standing.

"I believe things are good if they're interesting," James explained with a wink.

"I like the way you think." Sarah smiled and fished through her bag for a business card. She scrawled her cell phone number on the back and handed it to James, this time studying his hands as he tucked the card into the pocket of his uniform, his eyes never leaving hers.

At that moment a flash of lightning struck her mind: a brilliant image of those broad, tan fingers gliding over her, gripping her...

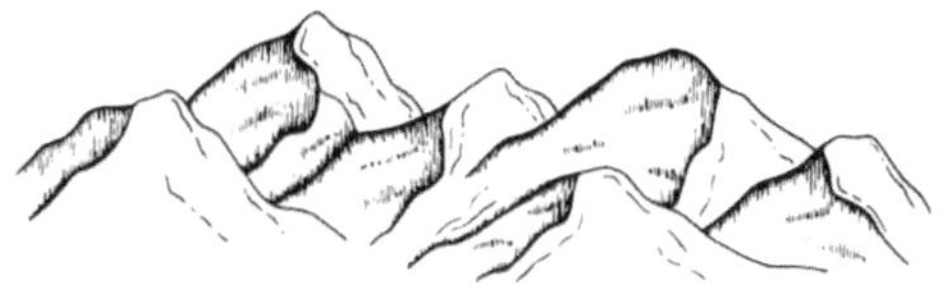

Sarah slept restlessly, in and out of dreams. She awoke to the sound of Owen tearing through the house with Abby chasing after him screaming, "Mom! Mom! He took the batteries from my Wii remote and won't give them back!!!"

Sarah sighed. *First world problems.* "Give your sister her batteries back, Owen," she called half-heartedly from her bed.

Both of their young faces appeared in her doorway. "There aren't any other batteries, Mom," Owen explained, his long-lashed brown eyes wide with innocence.

Sarah shifted her gaze to her daughter just in time to catch an in-progress eye roll. "Abby, are you playing the Wii right this minute?"

Her daughter shook her head slowly, her face scrunched up in a snarl.

"Fine, just let him borrow the batteries until you want to play again, alright? We'll get some more at the store later today."

"Whatever," Abby retorted and slinked away. Owen

beamed. Sarah hated the feeling of choosing one kid over the other during a disagreement. She liked it better when they could work out their own differences, but she was too tired to listen to them bicker over something so trivial.

The green light on her phone was flashing with a text message.

Rachel: *How did last night go? You going with me tonight or what?*

She glanced at the clock. *8:04.* Rachel had sent the text at 4:52, which could mean a couple of different things: insomnia or her friend had late night company that she kicked out before the sun came up this morning. She decided to text back rather than call so she wouldn't wake Rachel up if she were still asleep.

Sarah: *Last night was great. Met an interesting guy. What time do you want to leave?*

She headed down to the kitchen, where she started the coffee pot and cleared cereal bowls from the counter. Her phone buzzed again.

Rachel: *I'm thinking like 3 pm? What are you going to wear?* And then: *New guy?! Awesome, gives us something to discuss on our 3 hour drive.*

Fortunately Sarah had given her mother a heads up about her potential plans earlier in the week. It was such a blessing to have her mother nearby to help with the kids.

Kathy Lynde had raised Sarah and her younger brother Adam back in the 70s and 80s, and she knew firsthand how difficult it was to be a single mother. Now her daughter's life seemed to parallel her own. Having retired from her career as an elementary school teacher just a few years before, she insisted on moving to Maryland with Sarah so she could help whenever she was needed. Sarah's children were her only grandchildren, and there was no place she'd rather be than with her darling Abby and Owen.

Sarah began preparing a to-do list. *Call Mom. Groceries. Batteries for Owen. Finish the laundry. Try to get at least a few of the annotated bibliographies graded. Find something to wear to the party. Oh...I have some...um...shaving to do.*

She plodded through the items on her list. First the phone call to her mother, then she took the kids to the store and out for lunch, which much to her relief did not involve a battle. Everyone seemed to agree on Mexican; a consensus was so rare. They were angling to see a movie, but she knew she needed to get back in time to get ready for the party. "We'll see the movie tomorrow afternoon when I'm back," she promised.

After they returned home from their errands, she struggled through about five of her students' assignments, growing increasingly frustrated by the cardinal sins of improper citation style, incorrect grammar and spelling errors.

She noticed her shoulders had grown extremely tense. She sprawled out on the floor to do a couple of stretches. *Mmmmm...downward dog...that feels nice.* She savored the burn in the back of her legs. *I should have gone to the gym today. Why is it so hard for me to make time for myself? I'm supposed to be Super Woman.*

Super Woman was her ex-husband's nickname for her. The mere thought of him caused Sarah's head to start pounding, so she scrambled to her feet and headed to her closet. It was as if changing her activity would banish the thought of him from her mind, not to mention ward off the threat of a migraine.

She sipped a long drink from her water bottle and shuffled through a few dresses at the back of her closet. She hadn't gone out for a few months now. *Ah, I remember the last time...to celebrate the end of the spring semester. Holy shit! I didn't go out all summer? What the fuck is wrong with me?*

She recalled getting entirely too drunk when she bar-hopped with a group of her colleagues from the theatre department as if they were the students finishing up their finals instead of the faculty who were grading them. *Damn, those theatre people sure know how to party,* she mused. Against her better judgment, she'd gone home with a man she met that night who later turned out to not only be a lousy lay but a pretty big jerk as well.

She hated that she'd been treated like that, and she wondered if she'd unwittingly stayed in all summer to punish herself for making a mistake with the asshole she hooked up with. *Well, that's over now,* she conceded. *Wonder who will be at this party?* Even though she was going in with a little bit of hope but no firm expectations, anything could happen at a house party—and she knew how wild Rachel's friends could be.

So which of these dresses maximizes my potential of getting laid? she joked to herself. She pulled out a red dress, a black dress, and a purple dress and laid them on the bed. She started to slide her yoga pants down when she heard her phone ringing in the bathroom where she'd accidentally left it earlier.

She ran for it in case it was Rachel with an issue about the evening plans and accepted the call without even looking at the number. She was positive it would be her friend, possibly confirming her wardrobe choice for the evening. "Hello?" she managed with more air than voice.

"Well, hello to you too, Dr. Lynde," came the smooth, deep voice, clearly amused by her breathy greeting. He cleared his throat. "This is James McAllister. We met last night?"

"Oh, yes, of course." Sarah attempted a deep breath, but this turn of events seemed to decrease the air in her lungs rather than restore it. *Talk about getting caught with your pants down!*

"I know it's sort of short notice, but my afternoon freed up, and I wondered if you might want to grab that cup of coffee?"

"Oh," Sarah replied before really thinking, buying some time while her brain processed the four million things vying for her attention. "I'd love that."

"Excellent," James responded evenly. "Is four o'clock too soon? There's this place near campus..."

"Four will work fine," she answered, at last finding her professional voice. "Oh, do you mean Java the Hut?"

James laughed. "I take it you're familiar?"

"I'm an addict," Sarah admitted. I'll see you there at four!"

Holy shit. What did I just do? I better call Rachel and rethink my wardrobe options.

She dialed Rachel's number while she put the dresses back in the closet and started to review her jeans and nice top possibilities. "Uh, hey, Rachel, I'm not going to be able to go tonight after all," she confessed.

"Why the fuck not?"

"Well...remember that guy I was going to tell you about? He just called and asked me to have coffee with him!" After she finished, she chided herself for not trying to rein in her excitement.

"You're going to give up a house party at the beach for coffee with some guy?" Rachel asked incredulously.

"Right. I know it sounds crazy," Sarah conceded, "but I also have one of my crazy feelings about this guy!"

"Holy shit, I'm scared now." Rachel laughed. "You and your feelings are well documented! Okay, I'm not happy about going alone, but I had this feeling you might renege, so I've already been in touch with Mark to see if he minds going." Mark was Rachel's longtime friend with benefits, a young, good-looking single man in "refuse to grow up" mode, for which Rachel played "enabler" at every opportunity.

"You know me too well, darling," Sarah replied. "Okay, have a good time and we'll have to compare notes tomorrow."

"Yep, sure thing, Lovechop!"

Rachel hung up, and Sarah glanced at the clock on her nightstand. *2:42. Yikes, only one hour and eighteen minutes to get dressed, get the kids to Mom's, and get to Java the Hut.* She slid a pair of faded jeans up her thighs and hips then reached for a sleeveless purple paisley blouse that would expose just the right amount of cleavage. A few dots of makeup, a brush through her thick brown waves, and the product of a last-minute change-of-mind: she opted to ditch her librarian-ish glasses and pop in her contacts.

She loaded up the kids and dropped them off at her mother's house with a minimum of chit chat. She didn't actually need an overnight sitter now that she wasn't going to the beach, but she didn't want to change the plan and deal with questions, plus she was thinking about all the grading she could get done without the kids in her hair. It seemed like the prudent thing to do.

She whipped her little red Toyota into a shady parking place and took a deep breath to quell the butterflies forming in the pit of her stomach. *Why am I so nervous about this?* she asked herself. *It's just coffee.* But she couldn't ignore the instant attraction she felt toward James as they stood in the crowd at the auditorium. And she couldn't deny her intrigue about what was going on behind those piercing blue eyes.

She tried to walk down the sidewalk to the coffee shop as nonchalantly as possible, meanwhile her mind was spinning: *Just be yourself... This is no big deal. It might lead to some new research...maybe on the ROTC students or program? Maybe I should take notes. No, that would be weird...right? I wonder how old he is...can I ask him that? Would that be wrong? Maybe it will come up. Okay, shut up and let's do this... It's just coffee!* She glanced down at her watch: *4:07. Only running a few minutes behind. Fashionably late.*

She immediately spotted him on the far side of the café, looking down at a newspaper with a slight frown, or maybe it was just a serious look. She had a moment to study him while she made her way to the small table he'd claimed adjacent to the windows. He wore baggy khaki pants that were a bit frayed at the cuffs, brown leather sandals and a navy polo shirt. Those rugged hands gripped the paper firmly as his eyes scanned the gray columns. He glanced down at his watch at the exact moment Sarah arrived at the table.

He immediately stood up and extended his hand. "Dr. Lynde, I'm so glad you could join me."

"Oh, please call me Sarah," she reminded him as she took a seat. She crossed her legs, going for the prim and proper look until things relaxed a bit.

He folded the paper up and leaned back in his chair. "Alright, Sarah, would you like some coffee?"

Sarah nearly blushed when she considered that coffee was probably the furthest thing from her mind, but she quickly recovered and nodded. They headed toward the counter to order. "How long have you been teaching in the ROTC program?"

"This is my first semester," he replied. "How long have you been at the university?"

"I'm in my second year here after a year's post-doc work in New Mexico," Sarah said. "I think I may actually get the hang of things this year!"

James laughed. "Well, based on what I heard last night, I'm sure you're a great teacher," he said confidently as he paid for their drinks and led her back to the table. "How did you decide to become a professor?"

"I have always wanted to teach, since I was a little girl," she reflected. "I thought I wanted to teach high school, but after my first sociology class in college, I was hooked. What about you? Are you new to teaching?" She couldn't imagine he'd been teaching long with as young as he looked. *He can't be more than thirty*, she decided.

"I'm brand spanking new," he admitted with a grin. "I haven't the slightest clue what I'm doing, but I've had some good teachers to emulate. Imitation is the sincerest form of flattery, right?"

"I definitely had some extraordinary mentors, too," she agreed with a laugh. "So where are you from?"

James smiled and looked down for a second as if he had to access the answer from some deep cavern in his mind. "I'm an Army brat," he stated. "I've lived all over, but I guess you could say I spent my formative years in the Midwest. And that's where my parents settled down after my dad retired from the military and bought a farm."

Ah. The Midwest. This is all seeming cliché. The All-American good looks, the Midwestern sensibilities, the military service. He really is GI Joe...or...GI James.

She didn't usually find herself attracted to wholesome, farm-raised, military types. Her gaze swept from his eyes to his feet and back up again. *He's quite the specimen, though. Maybe this is just a physical attraction?* She had recently dated a long string of academic and artistic types. And she'd completely given up on corporate types following her failed marriage to Daniel, the man who still made her shudder when she so much as thought his name or envisioned his face.

Wait, is this a date? The question bounced around her mind like a rubber ball. *Or is this a professional thing?* Her excitement when she received his phone call and anxiousness to see him had felt date-ish, but his serious demeanor and the interview-like conversation seemed to indicate other-wise. Disappointment surged through her. *Maybe I should have gone to the house party?*

She had let the conversation lapse, which was the last thing she wanted. "I'm from Colorado originally," Sarah offered. "It's been an adjustment getting used to the East Coast. I never thought I'd be particularly well-suited to this region, but I seem to be managing."

James nodded, his expression relaxing ever so slightly. "I've found I can thrive pretty much anywhere. Even in the desert."

"Oh, do you mean Iraq?" *This conversation might finally be going somewhere.*

"Affirmative." He smiled as a flash of pride crossed his features. "Although, I've been back home for two years now from my last deployment. I sometimes consider accepting another overseas assignment but wonder if it would be a lot harder now that my body is older and my brain is wiser."

"You make it sound like you're so old!" She laughed but instantaneously regretted her tone. *Way too patronizing.*

"Well, it's different when you have a choice to go..." He pursed his lips. "Well, at least right now I have a choice. You never know when Uncle Sam will change his mind."

"Oh, so you'd go voluntarily?" She didn't mean to sound incredulous, *but why would someone want to go back to a war zone?*

James didn't miss a beat, clearly familiar with this response. "I know it's hard for civilians to understand, but there are pros to serving in a war zone," he replied, still sensing the confusion on her face. "It's okay, my mother doesn't get it either."

"You don't have to defend yourself," Sarah recovered and redirected the conversation. "So, back to the original topic from the other night. I thought you might talk a little bit more about the Don't Ask, Don't Tell thing?"

He cleared his throat. "Of course." He took a long sip of his coffee and thoughtfully set his mug down on the table. She studied his hand and the way his elbow grazed the wooden tabletop. She caught a slight inkling...very slight...that he might be disappointed the conversation had already shifted back to a professional track so quickly.

"Being deployed in a war zone, it's obviously not like everyday life," he began. "In order for the men to stay focused, accomplish their missions and stay alive, it requires —more than anything else—mental discipline. If an individual loses focus and doesn't see something they ought to have seen, it may not only get them injured but the person next to them as well. It's imperative to keep distractions to a minimum. It's focus and discipline that make the difference between frightened boys and professional soldiers who get the job done. That's also why drinking and sex are discouraged while deployed."

He looked at Sarah to gauge her reaction. When she nodded, his tone relaxed a bit as he continued, "I'm just thinking what it would be like to have a flamboyantly gay soldier in my bunk going on and on about hair products or something like that. Or wiggling his ass in front of the guys. Or having a lisp over the radio..." His voice trailed off.

Sarah's expression betrayed that she was trying to formulate a diplomatic response to something she passionately disagreed with. "You seem to know a lot of gay stereotypes."

His blue gaze widened, but he didn't reply.

"You asked me last night if I'd ever served in the military, but I have to ask you," she paused for effect, "have you ever known anyone who is gay? And do you really believe that— considering all the people you've served with—that not a single one was gay, lesbian, or bisexual?" She crossed her arms over her chest and leaned back in her chair to await his response.

James was quiet for a moment before he sucked in a deep breath. "No, I haven't ever really known anyone who was openly gay."

"Well," Sarah said gently, with no trace of judgment, "my brother is gay, and he is one of the most masculine men I know. You'd never know it just by looking at him or talking to him." An image of her brother Adam popped into her head: tall, well-built, shaggy brown hair, slightly slouchy posture and a way more casual wardrobe than many gay men would find acceptable. He had a deep voice and a really quiet way about him. He was the antithesis of flamboyant or effeminate.

"I see," James responded.

"If openly gay men were allowed in the military, do you think they'd be beating down the recruiters' doors to enlist? I mean, it's quite a commitment, and I would think anyone who joined would be serious about serving their country. I can't imagine someone enlisting just to flaunt their sexuality —or to hook up. God knows there are *much* better places to do that."

James smiled. "Yeah, I suppose you have a point, and boot camp does have a way of weeding out those who are unfit for military service."

"How many times has your sexual orientation impacted your ability to do your job?" Sarah questioned.

"Never." A bit of an uncomfortable silence followed. "So your brother is gay, Dr. Lynde," he finally said. "Care to tell me something else about yourself?"

The air between them seemed to shift as she leaned forward in her chair and set her coffee cup down on the table. "Let's see if I can manage an executive summary." Sarah smiled as her eyes bounced between his. "I'm divorced; I have two kids. I love to read and write. And one of my legs is longer than the other. I'm extraordinarily klutzy, yet I love rock climbing. I guess I have a bit of a reckless streak sometimes. I have a lot of strong opinions. I'm probably not someone you'd enjoy arguing with unless you don't mind losing."

James obviously took that as a challenge. "I don't have to win…all the time…"

A suggestive flash emanated from his blue eyes as he leaned back against his chair, his posture open and inviting. Sarah was pretty certain he didn't mean a *verbal* argument.

"So, speaking of rock climbing, you said you were from Colorado," he redirected the conversation. "My dad was stationed at Fort Carson for a little while when I was young, so I lived in the Springs for a while. I've done some rock climbing as well."

"Oh, wonderful!" Sarah exclaimed. "Colorado Springs is beautiful... Pikes Peak, Garden of the Gods... What's not to love?"

"It's easy to miss the mountains when you're out here on the East Coast. I go up to Pennsylvania in the winter sometimes to ski, but it's not the same as the Rockies," he admitted. "So you ended up out here for your job?"

She nodded. "It's pretty typical for us academic types to search nationally for positions. You have to find a college hiring in your specialty. I got lucky to land such a great tenure-track position even after the economy tanked."

"Well, I'm sure it speaks highly of your credentials...and abilities," James noted. He looked at her so intensely that she could feel his eyes boring through her. "Smart and beautiful," he summed up his findings. "I'm sure you would be at the top of the pack for any position you applied for."

She couldn't help but smile at his flattering statement.

Maybe this is a date? she oscillated again. His demeanor seemed to have changed, relaxed. Perhaps it was her strategic just-enough-cleavage blouse. Maybe it was that sultry look she had a habit of casting from her dark eyes.

She flushed, her head spinning with wild thoughts...envisioning those fingers grazing her skin...those intense eyes caressing her body in a more private setting. *It's been too damn long.* She remembered her empty house, her empty bed, and all of her damn rules she had just reviewed earlier that day... *Is James McAllister worthy of breaking the rules?*

It's like he read her mind: "So what are you doing tonight?"

Her heart started racing as her eyes met his again. Her responsible adult self kicked the wanton slut she'd tried so hard to repress out of the way. "I've got a ton of papers to grade," she blurted out before she could change her mind. "In fact, I should probably wrap this up and get home soon, as much as I'd like to stay and get to know you better."

Despite that, additional conversation flowed easily between them. She finally got the answer to the age question: he was twenty-nine. He was the oldest of three with two younger sisters. He had a soft spot for country music and, surprisingly, classical. But mostly he remained a bit on the mysterious side. He was a puzzle she wanted to take her time solving. *After all, a puzzle isn't quite as fun after all the pieces are in place.*

James walked her to her car another hour past when she said she needed to go. Then there were twenty more minutes that slipped away as she leaned against her red Toyota, suppressing moderate concern her backside was getting filthy. Then there were the last few minutes before parting, when he leaned in so close that she could feel his breath on her cheek.

"I hope I see you again," he said before brushing his lips against hers, light as a feather.

A shudder rocked through her body as she regretted her decision to grade papers instead of putting a few more pieces of that puzzle into place...namely the ones that could be pieced together between the sheets.

When he walked away, the sun was starting to sink behind him.

3

Sunday evening Sarah was scrambling to finish up her grading. The extended coffee date coupled with the half bottle of wine she consumed Saturday night, plus the movie outing she'd taken Abby and Owen on that afternoon had really cut into her work time. She sat in her armchair with the pile of papers on the end table, her red pen getting a workout. She was listening to the music and sounds of the video game her kids were playing and found her mind wandering again and again to nowhere in particular. She finally decided to call Rachel and get the scoop on the house party.

Rachel sounded even more tired than Sarah felt. "We didn't get back until noon today, and I haven't really been to sleep yet except an hour or so in the car. I'm so glad Mark drove!"

"See, it worked out better without me going, cause you know I would have wanted you to drive if I'd consumed a drop of alcohol in the preceding eight hours," Sarah joked. "But the real question remains: did you get laid?"

Rachel deadpanned, "Seriously? It's me...of course I did."

Sarah was shaking her head at her friend's predictability and waiting, more or less patiently, for details. "Oh, don't make me beg! Spill it, woman!"

"There was this couple, mid-forties, really hot," she started, as if the details were about to explode under pressure. "We were in the hot tub, and I noticed Mark had moved really close to her. Then her husband started inching toward me...and, well, we started there and then ended up taking things inside to one of the bedrooms. He was pierced!"

Sarah smiled, glowing in her friend's happiness. "Nice!"

Rachel divulged all of the juiciest nuggets from her and her boyfriend's encounter. Some might have accused her of over-sharing, but this was Classic Rachel, and Sarah loved her for it.

"So..." Rachel finally wrapped up her story, "how was your date?"

Sarah considered what details she wanted to share, not being quite as forthcoming as her best friend. Especially when meeting new people, she didn't particularly like to share until she knew if it would go somewhere. She wondered if that was a fear of rejection thing. If it didn't work out, she'd have to admit to her friend he wasn't interested, or whatever the issue was.

"Well," she knew she wouldn't get away with silence on the matter, "his name is James, and he's twenty-nine. He's an ROTC instructor at the university. He seems really bright—and good-looking." Obviously Rachel would focus on the latter.

"Young. Hot. Military," Rachel summarized. "I like where this is going. So did you fuck him or what?" She always cut right to the chase.

Sarah laughed. "Seriously, Rachel, you know me better than that. It was just coffee. Nothing more. Although I'm considering asking him to dinner next weekend," she admitted, a vision of James's intense blue eyes popping into her mind.

"Go for it," Rachel encouraged. "I probably want you to fuck him as much as you want to!" She laughed so hard at her own comment that the chuckle morphed into a minor coughing fit.

"Haha, I bet you do," Sarah replied once her friend's coughs settled down. "Yikes, hope you're not catching a cold, honey." She paused for a moment, then, "Alright, listen, I have to get back to grading. We'll have lunch on Tuesday, okay?"

"Sure thing, Babydoll!"

SARAH COULD COMPOSE a treatise on patience—or lack thereof. She was thinking about how, a few years ago, if two days passed after a date, and she didn't hear anything, she would have given up hope and written the guy—or girl—off. Now, she was calmer, more rational, and realized it really was okay if a) if she didn't hear from the individual at all, and b) if she initiated that contact herself.

She reflected about how much she had matured throughout the past few years as she strolled across campus, her sandaled feet getting wet in the morning dew. She loved this time of day, just prior to 8 AM classes, gazing across the quad at the earliest risers whose coffee-infused arteries were just beginning to circulate enough energy to stir their weary souls from slumber. It was September, too early to witness a cool mist rising from the warm ground, but Sarah imagined what the scene would look like in two more months when fall began to creep into central Maryland.

She felt a sudden pang of homesickness for Colorado and the enduring backdrop of the Rockies that had sheltered her during her childhood. It had been nearly two years now since her eyes stared up, awestruck, at their snowy peaks, since she watched the purple mist gather in their valleys. It had been almost two years since she hiked up a rocky canyon and picnicked on the edge of a cliff. She never thought she'd be away from the mountains so long.

My soul is aching for home, she finally admitted to herself.

Am I being ungrateful? My home is here now, in Maryland, with my beautiful children and devoted mother. She'd learned to appreciate things about this place: proximity to the beach and major cities such as Washington DC, Philadelphia, and even New York City. Everything was close by on the East Coast. The weather was milder than in the mountains. She had even learned to love crab cakes.

She considered the painful memories she left in Colorado, and even in New Mexico, where she'd spent her first post-doc year. There were things she left unprocessed, packed away, all boxed up where she couldn't access the memories. She had come to the East Coast for a fresh start. *And that's what I've gotten, right?*

Still, she longed to look up at those mountains and not feel a pang of regret or a sigh of discontent. *Those rocks are my roots, my genesis.* She didn't want to have her Motherland tainted by the bad memories she associated with her last few years there.

You know what they say: you can never go home.

Sarah's mental meandering was interrupted by a knock at the door. She saw the sweet young face of Emma Knightley, one of her favorite students and her most trustworthy research assistant. "Hey, Dr. Lynde," she said brightly. "Can I talk to you a second?"

"Of course, Emma. Please, come in!" Sarah greeted her warmly.

"It's about my senior seminar research project," Emma began, helping herself to a seat and tossing her bag on the floor next to Sarah's desk. Sarah wasn't used to students being so relaxed in her office, but Emma had spent a lot of time in that chair and considered Sarah to be her mentor. Sarah couldn't help but remember her own undergrad days hanging on every word her mentor, Dr. Sharpe, spoke. It seemed fitting that she could now pay it forward with her own little protégé.

"Did you settle on a topic?" Sarah questioned.

"Well, actually, yes. At least I think so." Emma smiled. "I wanted to write something about the recent explosion of bisexuality. It's all the rage now, girls in clubs showing off, walking around campus holding hands, making out in front of drooling guys. Like, what is the deal with that?"

"Interesting observation," Sarah remarked, though she was well aware of the phenomenon. She was always very careful to keep her private life and non-traditional beliefs under wraps. She would bet money that Emma would be shocked to discover her mentor, her beloved Dr. Lynde, identified as bisexual. "What else do you know about this trend?"

"Not much, really," confessed Emma. "But I want to do some research, obviously. Get started on my literature review. I was thinking of making an appointment with the reference librarian we met with last year for our research methods class."

"Wonderful idea," Sarah encouraged her. "I think it sounds like a great topic, particularly if you can come up with some sort of observational tool or survey. Don't forget you'll need to allow enough time to get your methodology approved by the IRB, okay?" She hated it when students waited till the last minute, and the institutional review board didn't have time to approve their research requests.

Emma nodded. "I was thinking of gathering up some articles this weekend and coming back next week to show you what I found."

It was hard not to beam with pride about a student this motivated and invested in her learning. "Perfect! See you soon!" And she knew Emma would follow through. Sarah could always tell which students would follow through and which would drop the ball.

After Emma left, Sarah glanced down wistfully at her phone. It was as silent as death. *Fuck it,* she conceded. She thought about James walking into his classroom of ROTC students across campus, setting up for his lecture. She would have given almost anything to be a fly on that wall to see how he interacted with his students.

She sent a simple text, hoping to create a spark of communication.

Sarah: *It was nice seeing you on Saturday. Hope you have a good week :)*

His answer came much later that afternoon, around 4 PM.

James: *I had a good time. Worked the rest of the weekend. This week is already sucking.*

Her patience lost out to her impulse to text right back.

Sarah: *Oh, why is that?*

James: *Picked up some new duties. Victim of my own success.*

Feeling slightly impulsive, she went for broke.

Sarah: *I see. Well, you could come hang out with me on Friday night.*

James: *Sounds like a plan. Did you have a place in mind?*

Sarah: *Sure. My house?*

Sarah's mind was racing, and that paled in comparison to what her heart was doing. *Well, I guess I just invited him over?*

SARAH WAS DISTRACTED. She hadn't been able to think of much else but her date with James all week long. Those piercing blue eyes. That strong jaw. His thick arms. Her head was filled with visions of what it would be like to be in those arms.

She had fallen behind in grading, in some committee work, and had also delayed confronting Abby about something she'd found in her room while putting laundry away. But since she needed to shuffle the kids off to her mother's house with as little drama as possible, a discussion would have to wait.

In addition to being distracted, she'd also felt restless all week. Maybe it was just her hormones surging as her body inched closer and closer to ovulation.

"Being a woman is such a challenge," Sarah had told Rachel during their Tuesday afternoon lunch.

"Damn Eve! She ruined it for all womankind! Stupid

bitch!" Rachel had commiserated. They'd both laughed, and then even harder because the waiter had definitely overheard them.

Then Rachel encouraged her to be forward with James, to very directly tell him what she wanted. "Women suck at asking for what they need, you know? Don't be like that."

Sarah aspired to be the type of woman who knew what she wanted and wasn't afraid to go for it. She'd already been plotting how to approach James regarding her views on relationships.

Now that he was across from her, and there was candlelight and soft music filling the room, she was almost ready to chicken out. She poured herself another glass of wine as she tried to gauge his interest in her.

I invited him for dinner, Sarah considered. *What if he has no clue what he's getting himself into? What if he has no idea what this is about?*

But there was that kiss at the coffee shop...

Her usual assertiveness had picked a fine time to desert her. *How do we get from the table to the bedroom?* She'd have to figure out some sort of segue way. She took a deep breath, pushed her chair back from the table and started to clear some of the dishes.

"All finished?" Her gaze swept over him as a satisfied smile spread his full lips.

He patted his stomach. "That was amazing." He drained his second glass of wine, then helped carry his dishes to the counter.

"I'm glad you enjoyed it! It's an old family recipe." She gave him a wink and bolstered her resolve.

For the first time that evening they were both silent for a few beats. The conversation at dinner flowed freely with laughter, insight, and valid points and counterpoints. One moment James would make some profound statement, sounding brilliant and mature. Then the next minute he'd cast Sarah a boyish look, and she would remember he hadn't even seen his thirtieth birthday yet.

She gave up hope she'd find a way to transition to the bedroom, so she decided not to say a word. She simply walked down the hallway and up the stairs. He followed. No discussion, no invitation, no words.

Sarah stood for a moment beside the bed and watched as James stepped through the threshold of her bedroom, taking in his surroundings, ever-observant. This is what she'd tried so hard to picture all week.

She turned to him, studying his features for clues he was comfortable with where this was heading. "Do you mind if I light some candles?"

"That sounds nice." His voice was gravelly as he stood with his hands behind his back, feet slightly spread. *At ease,* she recognized the military posture.

After lighting the two jasmine-scented candles on her dresser, she caught a glimpse of the candlelight dancing in his gaze, which was warm but inquisitive as he studied her outline silhouetted against the wall across from the bed.

I think that was a flash of desire that just flickered through his eyes.

He took a step toward her, his lips curling into a smile. *He knows,* she realized. It wasn't terribly awkward, but the question of *who starts this?* lingered in the space between their two bodies as they stood next to the bed, close but not touching.

Why am I so nervous? she thought. *I never get this nervous.*

As he leaned toward her, she took a deep breath, her body flooding with anticipation. *God...this is it. It's been a while since someone new has been in my bed.*

"May I kiss you?" Now his voice floated out like a feather, merely a whisper.

Her answer came in the form of a gentle stroke down his

jaw. But all her thoughts melted away as soon as his lips found hers.

Wow...they're so soft. It was a stark contrast to the strong hands that cupped her chin as his mouth explored hers. She felt something electric race up her spine as her fingers ran through his buzzed hair, then brushed the slight stubble appearing on his jawline. Those restless feelings she harbored all week disintegrated beneath his touch, his fingers delineating the outline of her hips, his mouth making a trail down her neck. The first-time awkwardness evaporated like steam.

Sarah remained completely clothed...sweater, cami, jeans...feeling constricted as her flesh burned to press against his. She lifted his shirt up and over his head, tossing it across the room. Unclasping her bra, she freed her breasts from the three layers of fabric preventing their chests from making skin-to-skin contact.

After they'd slowly backed up to the bed, he pushed her down onto the mattress where her fingers traced his well-defined triceps as he lowered himself onto her. Her panties dampened as his body pressed against hers and his lips explored her flesh.

I don't know how much longer I can wait to get those pants off you and free your cock, she thought, feeling his erection pressing against her pelvis. She pushed against him, urging him to turn onto his back so she could work her magic and make the rest of their clothing disappear.

He watched her fingers work her button and zipper, sliding her jeans down her thighs, followed quickly by her panties, which were soaked with desire. She paused, letting his eyes absorb their first glimpse of her nude figure, her curves bathed in the candlelight. After climbing onto the bed, she took his face into both hands, her lips meeting his again and eliciting a deep moan. Her hands began to wander, touching and stroking his well-developed arms and shoulders, feeling the tight mounds of muscles under her fingertips, her scientific mind listing off the names she'd learned in her college anatomy class: *biceps, deltoids, trapezius*. He was a specimen worthy of close study.

She leaned over him, her long, wavy brown hair covering their faces like a veil, kissing his lips again, then his neck and down his chest and stomach to his thighs. She wanted to devour him completely, but she tried very hard to pace herself, to slow down and savor this perfect and gorgeous model of masculinity spread out before her.

He was a masterpiece, Michelangelo's *David* in the flesh. She'd nearly forgotten how wonderful it was to feast upon the supple flesh of a twenty-something-year-old, especially flesh broken down and built back up by the U.S. Military. *Damn. There is something to be said for bodies built by Uncle Sam,* she mused as she glanced up at his face, gauging his response to the fact she'd nearly reached his manhood.

His eyes burned into her with white-hot intensity, stretching her lips into a wicked grin as he quickly ripped his pants and boxer briefs off and flung them aside. She lingered over his thighs and the crevice between his legs and groin, letting him feel her warm breath seep into his skin. As patient as she wanted to be, she couldn't ignore his swollen cock any longer as it lifted its head toward her, saluting her, needing her touch, needing attention.

Her tongue circled his balls and licked up his shaft as a soft sigh escaped his lips. The sigh transitioned into a moan as she spiraled the head of his cock. "Fuck, Sarah," he gasped out as she teased him, making him rock hard under the tip of her tongue.

This is like unwrapping a present for me. I can't wait to see how you respond.

She took his length into her mouth, sliding him deep into

her throat and holding him there as she studied him with her dark eyes. His head tilted back, his eyes closed, lips moist and slightly parted. *Mmmmm...I'm going to enjoy this as much as he will.* Her hands and mouth began to work in concert, slowly at first and then gradually increasing the pace. She teased his rock-hard cock until he could take no more and pulled her on top of him.

She kissed him again, straddling his thighs, her hot, moist mound radiating heat against his thigh.

"It's your turn now," he decided, turning her over onto her back with his strong arms.

Her eyes half-closed, she felt his lips on her breasts, teeth gently raking against her nipples, feeling them harden against his mouth.

James gasped when he reached Sarah's sex, finding her dampness had spread to her inner thighs. "You're so wet," he whispered as his tongue slid up her labia, first one side, then the other, sending a tingly shock throughout her body.

She could feel how hungry his mouth was as he eagerly lapped up all her juices. She was already close to climax, the kissing and touching alone having pushed all her buttons, and considering how long it had been... But once he slid one of his thick, tan fingers into her slit and worked his tongue on her clitoris at the perfect tempo, she knew for certain she was about to lose control. The tension mounting, her thighs clenched his head. Her fingers tangled in his hair, her pelvis lifting toward his mouth. Without warning, she soared off the edge, trembling underneath his face as he savored every spasm against his lips.

She caught sight of a wide grin spreading across his face as he emerged from between her legs and slid up her body. "Kiss me," she demanded, taking his face in her hands, her own scent filling her nose as she pressed her mouth against his again. Her hands stroked down his body to his firm backside, his hardness pressing against her leg. He repositioned himself as her hands grasped the muscular mounds of his ass, moving his erection closer to her pubic bone.

Oh my god...so close...my pussy is throbbing.

"I need to feel you inside me, James." Her desperation rendered her voice nearly inaudible, but her mind continued speaking without making a sound. *I know you're feeling it too... Letting the anticipation build is killing us both.*

Her synapses fired bolts of electricity through her body. *Finally, finally...it's time...*

James murmured, "Oh my god," as he slowly worked his cock inside her, holding it there, adjusting to the feel of her walls clenching him tightly.

Sarah sighed as he began to thrust into her ever so slowly, her hips grinding against him in rhythm, her hands on his ass, feeling him reach her very depths, her legs wrapped around him.

James's lips found hers again, and she gasped at the thought, *I can't believe we've never done this before... It feels so natural.*

Sarah's vantage shifted, leaving her feeling as though she were observing the scene from above the bed, feeling all the physical sensations but processing the events in a different dimension. Completely overwhelmed by their powerful sexual connection, she couldn't remember ever feeling this intensity the first time with anyone else.

She narrated the scene from her disembodied vantage: *your cock stroking in and out of me, my back arching. Taking me into your arms, holding me close to your chest...trying hard to hold back, make it last.*

I love the sounds you're making, the moans, the little phrases... Oh fuck...oh god...just listening to you is going to make me come... You start to thrust into me harder and faster... just...at...that...exact moment... I'm falling over the edge... I'm coming...tensing... releasing...contracting...my pussy milking your cock, and then you must *slow down...savor a bit more...feeling those last spasms gripping you, taking deep breaths as you keep control of each deliberate thrust.*

She came down from her orgasmic high as her mind joined her body again in the present. She watched his face again, their eyes locked together. She mentally granted him permission, telling him with her eyes *I want to see you come,* and at that precise moment he moaned, "Oh, god, Sarah..."

She felt his body tense and his breath quicken. His cock throbbed and hardened inside her while she waited for his release. She watched his orgasm overtake him, capturing him in its powerful spell.

I absolutely love watching a man climax, she thought, *knowing I'm making it happen...giving it to him, a gift.*

Afterwards, she lay in his arms, her hands caressing his chest, aware of the fact they were both breathless and speechless. Until finally James whispered, his voice soft and iridescent in their afterglow, "Is it normal for the first time with someone to feel so natural?"

She didn't have to look at his eyes to know he was as awestruck as she was. She sighed in response, continuing to stroke him, answering with her touch instead of her voice.

All while her mind cried out, *Oh...that was anything but normal... There's never been a first time like that in the history of first times.*

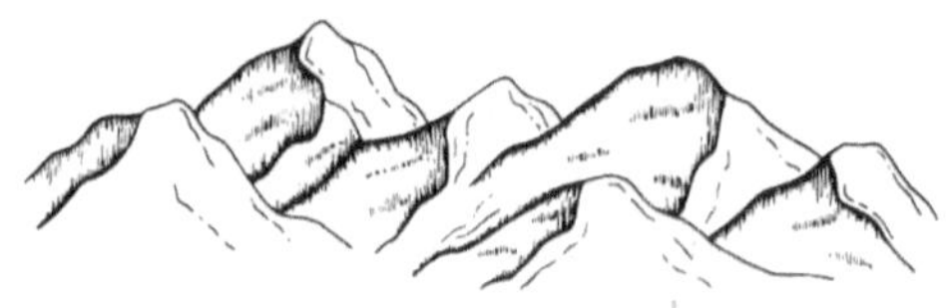

James had left Sarah's house early the next morning just after the sun came up. They'd slept with their limbs twisted together like pretzels. Sarah sent this a few hours later:

Sarah: *One word: Amazing.*

She released those three simple words like shiny balloons out into the atmosphere and watched them float into oblivion, hoping they'd return in another form.

The first day, it didn't bother her that she hadn't heard back. She was sure he'd gotten busy with work and hadn't had time to reply. The night after he'd visited, she lay in bed alone, pillows strategically surrounding her so it gave the illusion of less space, less emptiness. *How can my bed feel even emptier after someone has shared it than it did before?* It was a paradox for which she had no explanatory theories. And she was rarely lacking in theories.

Two days after his visit, it was Monday and the rat race was back on. Sarah was mildly irritated she hadn't heard back from James, but she wasn't overly worried. Even so, she continued to periodically glance at her phone, willing it to chime, but there was nothing. She went to bed that night hopeful that tomorrow would be the day.

After three days, on Tuesday, she felt silly, like she had completely misread everything. She made a living reading people and understanding behavior and motivations, yet she had been dead wrong about his interest in her, about their connection, about everything. That night in her lonely bed she reexamined the ridiculously strong sexual chemistry she felt with him. Or at least what she thought she had felt.

"How long do you usually give a new lover to text you back after you have sex the first time?" she asked Rachel.

"Man or woman?" Rachel waggled her eyebrows. She was bisexual too.

Sarah couldn't stop her smirk. "Whichever. Does it matter?"

Her friend shrugged and pursed her lips as if in thought before answering, "I don't hesitate to text back after a day or two if I don't hear from them. I mean, if the sex was good."

Have I been out of the game so long that I no longer know what good sex is? Why did I let my expectations get so out of control?

Rachel trained her gaze on her best friend. "Well, how did it go, anyway?"

"I'm not chasing a twenty-nine-year-old guy," Sarah resolved with an eye roll.

Rachel laughed. "Well, if it hadn't gone well, you wouldn't be asking me about how long I wait to hear back…so I guess we'll leave it at that." She knew better than to push Sarah into revealing more. Then her face brightened. "I have an idea! Come out with Mark and me this weekend. We're going to the new club!"

"You're right, a distraction is in order," Sarah agreed. She couldn't believe she was letting his lack of communication affect her.

And not only from the ROTC instructor who had been pure magic between the sheets…

"So, James isn't my only problem," Sarah revealed.

"Oh yeah?"

Rachel was usually the one with problems, but this time Sarah was monopolizing the therapist's couch. "I found condoms stashed under Abigail's bed when I was putting away her laundry."

Rachel's eyes widened as she shook her head. "I'm so glad I don't have a daughter. I've got *one* penis to worry about. You have *every* penis to worry about."

"Well, just the ones in the greater DC area, I guess," Sarah corrected. "I don't want to be like that, you know? I'm supposed to be all sex positive and stuff!"

"But she's only fifteen…" Rachel's voice trailed off.

"Exactly." Sarah let out a long, deep sigh. "And I guess I always thought she would trust me enough to talk to me first before becoming sexually active. I thought we would have that type of relationship…like my mom and I do…"

"Have you talked to her?"

Sarah shook her head, her mind still replaying the memory of the discovery in her daughter's room. "Two were still sealed in their packaging. The third was all stretched out…but empty. Thank the gods!"

Rachel tried to stifle a giggle but couldn't.

"I'm not upset—concerned would be a better word. Or shocked because it seems so out of character for Abby. Every time Owen asks me one of his questions—you know how he does—Abby is mortified. She seems really grossed out by anything sexual."

Rachel's laughter was still bubbling out of her mouth. "Exactly how is she your daughter?"

"I'm assuming she has some of her dad's genes in there somewhere," Sarah fired back. "But where did she get them?

Is she just experimenting or does she have a reason to need them?"

"You're going to have to talk to her," Rachel encouraged her. "But I'm so glad it's you and not me!"

ON THAT MUNDANE TUESDAY NIGHT, Sarah asked Owen to clear the dinner dishes and invited Abigail to come talk with her in her bedroom. Abby snarkily declined her invitation, but once Sarah adopted her more insistent tone, her daughter hesitantly complied. She marched down the hallway to her mother's room with heavy footsteps, a performance capped off by hurling her 115-pound body onto the bed in protest.

Sarah took a deep breath. *Was I this obnoxious when I was her age?* She pleaded with the gods to grant her patience. She found her calm voice and broached the subject as gently as possible. "Abby, I found something in your room I want to ask you about."

"Oh, so you're going through my stuff now?" came her indignant reply. "That's just great. Thanks, Mom, for valuing my privacy!" The sarcasm was so thick, Sarah could cut it with a knife.

"Sweetheart, I'm not angry, and I *do* value your privacy. I just want to know why you have condoms in your room." She witnessed her daughter's face turning various shades of red, half with embarrassment, half with anger. "They weren't exactly hidden from view," she explained. "I was putting away your laundry and saw them under the bed."

Abby rolled her eyes. "Well, you can stop freaking out, 'cause it's no big deal. It's not like I'm...having sex." She seemed to have a hard time saying the *S word* in front of her mother. "We have to learn how to put on a condom on a banana in health class, and, well, I was nervous about it. I thought I'd practice."

Health class? That threw Sarah for a loop. "Your teacher is showing you how to use condoms?" She had never been happier to teach college instead of high school. She took another deep breath and continued, "Abby, listen, I'm not mad; I just want to know the truth, okay?"

"That is the truth, Mom. I can show you a note from the teacher," Abby said matter-of-factly, her defensive tone fading. "Some kids' parents wouldn't let them participate, but I knew you wouldn't care, so I didn't bother showing it to you."

Sarah considered her next step very carefully. Should she accept Abby's explanation or probe more deeply? *Choose your battles wisely.* Maybe it was best to show trust. Perhaps if she didn't force Abby on the defensive, she'd drop the attitude. "Well, I guess I have to commend you for being so well prepared for class, huh?"

Abby's mouth configured into something that looked vaguely like a smile. It was so unfamiliar to Sarah at this juncture, she almost didn't recognize it. "Sorry, I probably should have shown you the note," Abby conceded.

"Sweetheart, you know you can come to me about anything, right?" she reminded her daughter. "I'm not one of those close-minded, judgmental parents. I'm supportive, and I really do want you to be your own person. I just want to make sure you're safe, physically and emotionally, okay?"

Abby nodded, and Sarah thought there might have even

been a tiny tear stinging at the corner of her eyelid. *There might be more she's not telling me,* Sarah guessed, *but I think I have to let her come to me at this point.*

Abigail surrendered to her mother's outstretched arms for a close embrace. Sarah couldn't remember the last time her daughter had willingly hugged her.

Ah, letting people come to me. That seems to be the theme of the week.

SARAH WAS NOT AS EXCITED for her night out with Rachel and Mark as she hoped to be. She convinced them to postpone the excursion to Saturday night instead of Friday so she could catch up on sleep and, feeling like Cinderella, she had also committed to grading a certain number of exams on Saturday afternoon before she would allow herself out of the house. *Work before play,* she reminded her friend, whose priorities often differed.

She sat in her favorite armchair, warmed by the strong rays of the September afternoon sun streaming through the panes of the French doors that led to the deck. Her cat was basking in a solar-drenched spot as Sarah completed grading the requisite number of exams plus a few more for good measure. The rest could wait till Sunday.

Abby and Owen were both staying with friends for the weekend, leaving the house eerily quiet. The shadows cast by the trees onto the back lawn seemed to be whispering to each other. It was so quiet, Sarah caught herself audibly voicing her internal dialogue a few times, just to break the silence.

She got up from her armchair and stretched, moving into the sunlight and startling the cat, who scampered off down the hallway. She stood on one foot and grabbed the other ankle, pulling it up behind her and leaning forward, feeling her core muscles engage as she heard the twinkly chime of a new text message.

James: *Thanks. What's up?*

Three words. Seven days later. It seemed as if he'd just now read her three-word text, the one she'd sent a week ago.

Damn, my heart is racing.

She set her phone back down while she continued to stretch.

Must. Calm. Down.

She tried to focus on the pose again, but her concentration was busy debating her response, throwing off her balance.

I don't want to sound too eager. Or desperate. Patience is a virtue.

Two hours later when she was getting ready to venture out for the night with Rachel and Mark, she settled on a simple, casual reply.

Sarah: *Not much. Going out tonight.*

This time his reply came immediately:

James: *Oh yeah? Where does a sexy professor go for fun on a Saturday night?*

Sarah felt like playing coy, but she found her lips almost painfully spread into a huge grin to be interacting with him, the biggest smile she'd mustered all week. Teasing him seemed to be the way to go.

Sarah: *Wouldn't you like to know?*

James: *Actually yes. Yes I would.*

She half-considered inviting him to come along. Then she

remembered the venue. And that he hadn't texted her back for a week.

Sarah: *Um, in DC. Sorry, adults only!*

James: *Haha WTF does that mean? I thought I proved my adulthood the other night.*

Sarah giggled like an adolescent girl, her thumbs flying fast and furiously on her phone's keyboard. Oh, he had proved something, alright!

Sarah: *True, but you didn't prove your ability to return texts in a timely manner LOL.*

She wasn't going to let his lack of communication slide.

James: *Ah. Sorry. Hope you have fun.*

Sarah decided to just leave things there. It was all a little game, right? Advancing, retreating, a dance, a game that men and women played. *I'm sure gay folks play it too. Hmmm...new research idea!*

She pulled the same dresses out of the closet that she had considered before the house party two weeks prior, and after a minimum of internal debate, she slipped the purple one over her head, smoothing it down around her ample hips.

Purple for passion, she thought as she swiped her lips with a burgundy lipstick, grabbed her purse, and headed out the door.

THE CLUB WAS LOUD. Sarah could feel the music pulsating in her bones, making it almost impossible to avoid swaying her hips in rhythm while Mark and Rachel checked their liquor in at the bar. That was the way these swinger clubs worked. Guests brought their own alcohol, and a bartender was provided to serve it. Defraying the cost of drinks balanced the entrance fees for couples and single men, but single women were in demand so they were admitted for a nominal fee. Single women—especially bisexual ones like Sarah—were nicknamed "unicorns." That's how rare and special they were.

I'm feeling neither rare nor special tonight, she thought as she caught her reflection in the glass doors to the hot tub area. She felt like playing the role of observer rather than participant.

The bar area looked like a typical night club with low lighting, barstools, and tables with chairs. A few black leather couches lined the walls and the parquet dance floor, which was swirling with colored lights and twinkling disco ball reflections. A dance cage at the far end featured a few scantily clad ladies grinding against each other while the metal casing rocked back and forth in time to the music. But that's where the resemblance to a "normal" club stopped.

Huge television monitors mounted high in all four corners of the room projected scenes from a biracial porno. There was a stripper pole set up to the right of the dance floor, currently unoccupied. Down the hallway from the nightclub area was a large, steamy room featuring a sixteen-person hot tub, and beyond that were twenty-four themed rooms, their doors lining each side of two parallel hallways. The themes ranged from a dungeon-style BDSM room to a 70s theme, a cowboy theme, and a doctor's office. There was a theme for every roleplay scenario one could imagine.

There were strict rules about appropriate behavior, open and closed doors, as well as protocols for watching or joining the activities in the rooms. Hosts explained all the rules to first-time visitors during an extensive tour of the facility. The club had security guards who strived to keep things clean and safe for all participants.

"So, what do you think?" Rachel asked as she and Mark rejoined Sarah on the other side of the bar. Mark glanced around, taking in the sights and sounds.

"You know it's not really my scene," Sarah answered. "But I guess it's okay. The dance floor is nice."

"I know, I know. You like to talk a lot before you fuck," Rachel teased her, rolling her eyes. "Whereas I just like to fuck."

"Mmm, I like that about you, baby!" Mark stepped behind Rachel, grabbed her hips and pressed his pelvis into her backside.

"I just hope this one isn't clique-y..." She sighed as she studied a table of blondes with two bearded, tattooed men in the corner.

"Try not to be so much fun, Sarah, geez," Mark chastised her.

She pursed her lips. "Well, even with all that, it's still nice to be around like-minded folks."

"That's the spirit!" Rachel cheered, raising her glass. She'd already had the bartender pour her a cocktail. "What do you want to drink?"

After giving Rachel her drink order, Sarah surveyed the crowd, searching to see if anyone piqued her interest. For a Saturday night, it wasn't as crowded as she imagined it would be. "I thought there'd be more people?"

Rachel nodded. "It's only nine o'clock, though. The night is still young."

There was a table near the dance floor occupied by a group of fit, gorgeous people in their early- to mid-twenties who collectively emitted an unapproachable vibe. *Ah, yes, the requisite clique,* Sarah identified them. Going to a swinger club was a sociologist's dream come true.

Near the bar there were a few prototypical single men, trying to appear as though they weren't gawking at every woman in the place, but failing miserably. And, of course, there were several couples of all shapes and sizes, young, old, and everything in between. Even standing in foursomes or larger groups, Sarah could easily discern who went with whom. Body language always gave it away.

She briefly studied a few of the more attractive couples, but her eyes couldn't help but gravitate to the fiery redhead dancing in the cage with a tall, slim dark-skinned woman. Her pale skin glowed under the lights, and her full breasts bounced playfully in her black leather bustier as she grinded her ass into the other lady's pelvis.

Sarah found redheaded women with luminescent skin rather alluring. If she had a "type" for women, the redhead closely resembled it. She imagined raking her fingernail over a pink nipple, then pinching it lightly before tracing the outline of blue veins crisscrossing underneath the creamy flesh of her breasts.

Sarah tried to imagine what James would think if he were there taking in the scene beside her. *I'm sure he's way too conservative for me. He'd never come to a place like this.*

Sarah's eyes widened as the dark-skinned woman whipped the redhead around and gripped her rear end, pushing her pelvis against her upper thigh. Even in her heels, the redhead only came up to the other woman's chin. The taller woman bent to kiss her. The contrast of their skin colors was lovely, but what titillated Sarah was the flash of tongue she witnessed darting between the redhead's full berry-pink lips. The dark hands pulled a creamy breast from the black bustier, and her tongue flicked the nipple like Sarah had just imagined doing.

Rachel noticed the scene too. "Damn. That's fuckin' hot." She always verbalized what others were thinking.

Mark had been rendered speechless by the display and therefore had nothing to contribute to the conversation, although his eyes spoke volumes about the impact it was having on him. Rachel moved closer to her boyfriend and ran her fingers over his six-pack abs through the thin material of his black button-down shirt.

"Either of you wanna go dance?" she offered, peering at both of them through smoky eyes.

Sarah slowly nodded, still entranced by the scene in the cage. She managed to stumble only slightly ungracefully onto the parquet dance floor beside her friend while Mark opted to observe from a nearby table.

Sarah enjoyed watching her best friend in her element. Rachel was the most social creature Sarah had ever met, maybe even to the point of being co-dependent, she hated being alone so much. She was petite with blonde, heavily highlighted hair, deep-set hazel eyes always rimmed in thick black liner, and toned, shapely legs she loved to flaunt. She was a bit top heavy, carrying most of her weight in her ample bosom and around her waist. Tonight she was wearing a three-tiered black lace skirt, shiny patent leather platform sandals and a silky low-cut crimson red spaghetti-strapped camisole. She moved with confidence and unapologetically radiated what she called her "no bullshit" attitude. While she fully admitted that not everyone "got her," Sarah had discovered the sensitive, caring, generous spirit carefully buried underneath all her bluntness and flamboyance.

Rachel was partially responsible for opening Sarah's mind to new ways of approaching sex and relationships. After they bonded through the birth of their sons, Sarah spent a lot of time with Rachel when it became clear Daniel had no interest in fatherhood and even less in Sarah. Rachel and her now ex-husband frequented swinger clubs and other gatherings of like-minded folks, and Sarah began to tag along, discovering what fun it was to be a "unicorn," even if she didn't fully participate at first. It was with Rachel that Sarah first began to explore her attraction to women. Throughout the years, Sarah had experienced quite a few firsts with Rachel by her side.

The redheaded woman from the cage had stepped out onto the floor, and Rachel was dancing close to her, mere inches separating their torsos. Their breasts barely brushed together, their hips shaking in time to the beat. Sarah observed Mark conversing with a tall dark-haired man—*presumably the redhead's date?*—and pointing at the two ladies. She could almost feel the wheels turning in their four brains, plotting the possibilities. Rachel looked at Mark and winked right before she ran a finger between the redhead's cleavage, which was again popping out of the bustier.

"Hey, we're going to the 70s room," Rachel shouted in her ear, still barely audible over the music. "Do you wanna come?"

"I'll watch, but I don't think I'll play," Sarah answered.

"Whatever you feel comfortable with." Rachel smiled first at Sarah and then at the redhead, who giggled with anticipation as she grabbed the dark-haired man's hand and began to lead the way down the hall to the themed rooms.

A few moments later, starting to buzz from the second drink she'd gulped down, Sarah stepped onto the plush lime green shag carpeting and took a seat on the fuchsia pink loveseat covered in furry green, pink, orange and yellow throw pillows. There was a huge orange light fixture dangling from the middle of the room with its amber glass-covered fixtures dimmed. The corner was occupied by an oval-shaped bed flanked by two nightstands with lava lamps, one oozing with teal lava, the other purple. The doorway was obscured with a green and orange beaded curtain. A corner cabinet held wipes, tissues, condoms, and towels.

Soon she became a fixture in the room, part of the décor. The foursome had nearly forgotten she was there, but she was happy to be a spectator.

Rachel eased the redhead onto the oval-shaped bed and unhooked the black leather bustier, exposing her glorious milky-white breasts that nearly glowed under the black lights over the bed. She had the most delicate-looking rosebud nipples perched on top like cherries on a sundae.

The men flanked her on the bed, patiently watching and waiting to see what Rachel would do with this unwrapped gift stretched out before her. First she kissed one nipple and then the other, eliciting a breathy moan from the redhead's lips. Rachel planted a soft kiss on top of the moan, leaving Sarah to wonder if the redhead's lips were as sweet as they looked.

Rachel straddled the half-naked woman, lifting her chin to her mouth to taste her, one hand tangled in her auburn waves. Sarah noticed how their hips locked together as Rachel's tongue continued to explore the redhead's mouth and neck. More moans. The redhead stroked Rachel's bottom, pushing her harder against her pelvis, grinding up against her. The men looked eager, salivating at the scene unfolding between them.

The redhead's partner was a man in his mid-forties with a tall, wiry build and a hint of salt and pepper beginning to emerge in his goatee. He stood and slid his partner's skirt down around her ankles and then over her high-heeled boots, letting it fall onto the floor. Rachel took the hint, slipping her black lace skirt off and pulling the red cami over her head. Both women were now completely nude save for their footwear. Rachel knelt on the shag carpet floor, her hands stroking down the redhead's hips and thighs, parting them gently. Sarah could tell her friend's mouth was watering, anxious to taste the sweet pink flesh now exposed between the redhead's legs.

A small crowd had gathered behind the green and orange beads. With the curtain drawn, they were not allowed to enter, but Sarah could sense their anticipation and arousal. It was palpable. The whole scene: the shag carpeting, the amber and black lights, the lava shape-shifting in its plastic cylinders, the rustling of the beads at the doorway... Sarah absorbed all the dizzying sights and sounds as Rachel buried her face in the redhead's sex, spreading her lips with one hand, the other reaching up to the creamy mounds with their cherry-pink nipples.

Mark's gaze fell on her and specifically her hand, which had absentmindedly slipped between her legs. She'd become aware of her own arousal, her damp panties, her need to be touched. Mark's eyes were dark and lustful as he stripped off his shirt, revealing his sculpted abs and sprawling tattoos. Sarah had never really studied them before but now she recognized a tribal design, something with a skull and flames...*and was that a Chinese symbol?*

She had been with Mark before... It would be so easy to offer herself to him, to have her craving satisfied, but she resisted, not even bothering to analyze why. She shook her head, almost imperceptibly, and turned her attention back to the scene before her, hoping he'd take the rejection politely. He turned away from her and bent down to taste the redhead's breast.

The other man stood behind Rachel, stroking his erect cock and watching his partner's hips writhing under Rachel's mouth as her moaning intensified. The redhead continuously murmured, "Oh, fuck...ohhhhhh...fuuuuuuck..." drawing out the vowels as she grew closer and closer to climax.

Sarah watched him unwrap a condom and roll it down his shaft. He began to rub himself in the cleavage of Rachel's ass, then teased the head against the opening to her sex, slowing working his way inside her, gripping her hips as he buried his cock to the hilt, making Rachel gasp in delight. Mark followed suit, removing his pants and kneeling beside the redhead's mouth, eventually quieting her moans by stuffing his throbbing member down her throat, his hands laced through her hair, guiding her head up and down his cock.

Sarah closed her eyes for a moment and breathed deeply. She'd been holding her breath this whole time. *Would James watch? Would he be turned on? Would he want to fuck me while they watched us?* All of her questions involved him, and none of them had answers. She couldn't turn the James Channel off. It had infiltrated her mind.

Late that night she crawled into bed, feeling the dull ache the scene in the 70s room created. She reached between her thighs, sliding a finger up her lips, marveling at how wet she still was. She lightly touched her clit, the tingle reverberating throughout her body, her need for release renewed. She took her glass dildo from the drawer beside the bed, plunging it, cold and hard, into her warm, yielding wetness.

When she came, in her mind, it was around him instead of the glass toy.

SHE JOLTED awake after one of those dreams where it felt like she'd been awake all night instead of asleep. She yawned and stretched, grabbing her phone from the nightstand to check her texts and emails.

James: *How was last night?*

Sarah felt a bit victorious—*he's still thinking of me*—as she swung her legs over the bed and onto the floor. She carried her phone downstairs, glancing at the clock on the mantle from the staircase. *9:04.* The kids wouldn't be back from their friends' respective houses till late afternoon. She filled the coffee pot with water and considered how to reply.

She checked to see what time he'd sent it. *Five in the morning? Holy cow! Why so early?* She turned on the coffeemaker and opened the French doors to step out into the cool fall morning.

She studied two birds flitting back and forth in the maple trees at the edge of the property. The metaphor of their little dance was not lost on her. She stretched again, another yoga pose, filling her lungs with the crisp air. She had a few flashbacks from the club the night before and decided to be purposely vague with James about her evening. She didn't want to scare him. Would he cut and run if he found out what a freak she was?

Am I a freak? She wasn't a big fan of labeling herself, even though her job was dependent on labeling others. She realized that most didn't understand the inherent relativism in sexuality. *Most people think of labels in black or white. You are or you aren't.* There was a spectrum of bisexuality, of kinkiness, of inhibitions. Compared to Rachel, she was rather inhibited, but compared to the average prude, not so much.

Is James the average prude?

She grabbed her phone and impulsively punched in a reply.

Sarah: *I had fun. :-)*

James: *Come have coffee with me this morning and tell me all about it.*

TWO HOURS later she was sitting across from James at Java the Hut. He looked relaxed, his blue gaze sparkling as it bounced between her own dark eyes. Sarah wished she could say the same, but she felt a certain amount of tension nagging at her. She was debating whether or not she should mention him taking so long to text her after their dinner the weekend before. She decided to let it go, for now. *Choose your battles wisely. Parenting advice sometimes works for dating too.*

"So where did you go last night?" He took a sip of his coffee.

Sarah responded vaguely, as planned, "Out with my best friend Rachel and her boyfriend Mark."

"Someplace local?" His eyes were picking up the light from a nearby window and nearly glowing aquamarine.

She was starting to feel like he was interrogating her. "A club in DC. What did you do?"

"I shot pool with a couple of buddies, then turned in early. It was a busy week," he explained, as if otherwise he would have been engaged in any number of debaucherous activities.

Busy week, huh? Is that why you didn't text me back? she wanted to ask but refrained. She was not the type of person to beat around the bush. *Why is this conversation so strained? Ask for what you want,* she heard Rachel's voice in her head. *Cut to the chase.*

Sarah swallowed the coffee in her mouth and took a deep

breath. "Um, what are we doing here?" The words floated out into the still air like bubbles waiting to pop.

James shot her his all-American smile, apparently relieved she was willing to confront the elephant in the room. "I wanted to ask you the same thing," he admitted. "I'm not good at this stuff."

I am supposed *to be good at this stuff.* Sarah reflected on all the different relationships and understandings she'd nurtured in the past, different levels, different attachments, all along a spectrum from casual sex to committed monogamy. She studied him, his straight nose, his clean-shaven chin, his full, slightly upturned lips, trying to decide how to articulate it in a way that wouldn't turn him off.

"I enjoyed our night together," she finally said. "*Really* enjoyed it."

He nodded as one eyebrow rose, beckoning her to continue.

"I would like to explore our dynamic," she tested the waters, deliberately adding, "with no expectations for a commitment." She let that sink in for a moment before adding, "At least...for now...."

James looked perplexed for a moment, but then under-standing dawned. "You just want to fuck me?" he asked so softly, the F word was barely audible.

Sarah laughed. "I don't want to complicate your life, James. I know we're both busy. I enjoy your company, but there's no pressure for any strings." She was gauging his reaction to her words before she let the next sentence fly, "I believe it's called...'friends with benefits'?"

If he was shocked, he managed to hide it well. "Friends with benefits," he repeated. "I like the sound of that."

5

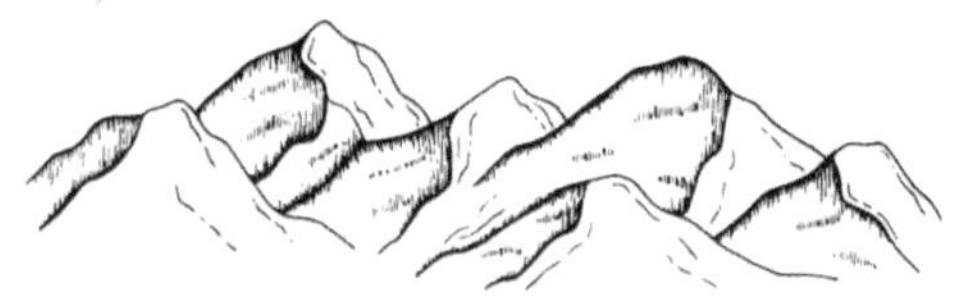

Then, Thursday afternoon:

James: *What are you doing this weekend?*

Sarah found herself shaking her head, but she was at least used to him compartmentalizing her by now. Clearly he didn't fully grasp the "friends" part of the friends with benefits arrangement.

Checking in from time to time, asking how my day was, finding out if I'm okay. Not making me feel like a human sex doll. Is that asking too much?

Lucky for him, Sarah was feeling so frisky and wanton, she was willing to sacrifice formalities to be on the receiving end of some "benefits." She made a mental note to clarify what a friends with benefits arrangement entailed.

She was feeling bold in her reply:

Sarah: *You?*

James: **evil grin**

Friday was a long day of lectures and committee meetings. Sarah firmly believed that committee chairs who scheduled Friday afternoon meetings should have their toenails violently ripped off and their eyes stabbed with needles. She was having a hard time sitting still when she knew there was a bottle of wine chilling in her refrigerator and a black satin chemise eagerly waiting to slide over her smooth skin. Unfortunately, the rumbling of a headache was tapping at her temple, so she downed a cup of coffee, hoping the caffeine would quell the pain. She just needed to get home, get the kids fed and off to her mom's...then get ready for him.

As if she needed any more distractions, images of James from their first night together persistently popped into her mind: his smoldering, half-closed eyes; the flickering flame of the candle highlighting the contours of his chest muscles; his hands, thick and tan, grazing her curves. She remembered how he looked the next morning when they awoke, limbs still entangled. When he finally stumbled out of bed, he was bleary-eyed as he pulled his boxers over his bulging calf muscles and up his taut thighs.

She remembered how they stood pressed against each other at the door, their bodies resistant to the layers of fabric separating their bare skin. She'd rested her head on his shoulder as he embraced her, kissing her softly as he turned the door handle, whispering goodbye. Last week at this time, she thought that goodbye was final. She'd given up hope of ever seeing him again, but now she was expecting him to arrive at her house in just a few hours. She felt like she was stepping off a roller coaster: disoriented, but thrilled.

Sarah snapped out of her daydream just in time for a committee vote. She wasn't sure she even knew what the vote was for, but she decided to diplomatically join the majority. *Gotta love academia; can't even go to the bathroom without putting it to a vote.* She glanced at her watch: 3:45. Fifteen minutes till adjournment, also known as freedom.

When the time arrived, she avoided idle chit chat with her colleagues and hightailed it across campus. She hustled to the parking lot, hopped in her Toyota and braced herself for navigating the always-snarled Friday afternoon traffic in the metro DC area.

Three hours later she was showered, freshly shaven and alone in her quiet, candlelit house. In all the times she'd had male company, she didn't think she'd ever felt this degree of anticipation; her thighs were quivering and her heart thundering in her ribcage. She looked in the mirror, running a hand through her long, dark tresses and adjusting her breasts in her chemise to maximize cleavage. She loved the way her pale skin contrasted with the silky black fabric. She slid on a pair of three-inch peep toe high heels in a sultry red to complete her look.

All dressed up and only going to bed. Did men really appreciate this sort of effort? More specifically: *would James appreciate this effort?*

His silhouette appeared against the sheer curtain that obscured the door to the back porch. She unlocked it, turned the knob and was greeted by a flash of his incorrigible, boyish grin. But his grin immediately dissolved as soon as he soaked up the image of Sarah in her black satin gown.

"You look..." he struggled to find the right words, "amazing..." was what he settled on. His voice was barely a whisper as he drew her into his arms.

She lifted her chin and caught a glimpse of his blue gaze before her eyes closed and her lips brushed against his, gently parting for his tongue to have his first taste of her. She heard him deeply inhale her scent. *I think my question of him appreciating my efforts has been answered,* she thought victoriously.

She stumbled backwards a bit, forgetting her heels for a

moment. "Oops, sorry!" She burst out laughing at her own clumsiness, which in turn made James laugh, and then they were standing there, mutual laughter ringing through her empty house.

"Well, that's one way to defuse the intensity," she said as she led him up the stairs to her bedroom, which had been prepared with just the right amount of candlelight, scent, and soft music. "Or it killed the mood."

James pulled Sarah into his arms. "It didn't kill the mood… Trust me." His gaze landed on her nipples jutting out against the edges of the fabric. Their dark pink flesh peeked through the space between the black lace flowers. He bent and ran the tip of his tongue lightly over one nipple and then looked up at her expectantly.

She was still trying to figure him out. *Is he experienced? Is he dominant? Is he skilled?* All of those attributes had been concealed, perhaps overridden by the sheer power of the connection she felt with him. It was as if their bodies were learning each other during their first encounter, and now was the time for their minds to follow. During their first night, she felt they had connected on a completely subconscious, visceral level, but now consciousness had seeped in, and Sarah wanted to know where his mind could take her.

"If I forget to tell you later," he whispered as he peppered kisses to her neck, "thank you for inviting me over tonight."

Her lips curled into a smile as her fingers threaded through the longer sandy brown hair on top of his head. He was only twenty-nine. She had no idea of his previous lovers, either quality or quantity. She didn't even know if he'd ever been married or had a serious girlfriend. He'd asked very little about her past, and she never boasted about her experience. Sometimes it intimidated less experienced partners.

Now her mind was reeling; she was barely concentrating

on his tongue flicking her other nipple. The nipple was responding perfectly, but Sarah was left thinking *what if last time was just a fluke?* A twinge of nervousness accompanied a slight somersault in her stomach.

There it is again, that expectant look. Is he expecting direction? Sarah taught for a living. She didn't want to teach in the bedroom. *Maybe that's why I've never been into younger men. I want someone who can take control. And, let's face it, I'm strong-willed; not every man has that capacity.*

She met his eyes with smoldering intensity and delivered one, simple instruction: "I want you to take me."

That was all he needed to hear.

James pressed Sarah up against the wall next to the bed, his body weight pinning her. He began to devour her, starting with her lips and then moving down to her ears, neck, chest before returning to the nipples that had captivated him moments before. All the thoughts swirling in Sarah's mind vanished as blood rushed to other parts of her body. His ravishing left her weak in the knees and unsteady on her high heels.

In an attempt to regain her balance, she opened her eyes to find him staring back intently, waiting for her to meet his gaze. Once their eyes locked, he undid his belt buckle and unfastened his pants. Unable to tear her eyes away from his, she heard the rustle of his pants hitting the floor, his eyes never leaving hers.

He took her hand and pressed it against his groin so she could feel his erection bulging through his boxer briefs. "This is what you do to me."

Sarah slowly dropped to her knees before him and slid her thumbs under the waistband of his underwear, pulling it down to the floor on top of the pants. His thick, rock-hard cock sprang out from the material into her face. She kissed along his inner thigh and testicles, then with agonizingly slow strokes of her tongue, she licked up his shaft and around the head till she'd covered every inch of his manhood with her hungry mouth.

"Fuck, Sarah…"

She glanced up long enough to see his eyes roll back in his head as she took him as far as possible to the back of her throat, nearly gagging herself on his engorged flesh. She slid her mouth back up his length, and then, after a torturously long pause, abruptly plunged back down again on him, eliciting a guttural moan. She teased the tip with her tongue until she thought he might come unglued.

His need had grown so urgent that he grabbed her head and plunged deep into her throat, his hands laced through her hair. She braced herself by grasping his muscular calves as he thrust in and out of her mouth until she could no longer fill her lungs with enough air to breathe.

He released her head, and she pulled back several inches, stroking him with her hand. She watched his glistening shaft disappear in and out of her clenched fist while glancing up at his lusty eyes. A drop of pearly fluid appeared at the tip of his cock, which she savored on her tongue.

His thighs trembled beneath her fingers as she took him into her mouth yet again. He was clearly holding back. She had half a mind to suck him to completion, but before she could commit to it, he pulled her to her feet. He ripped the chemise from her body, whipped her around and pushed her down onto the bed face first.

"So, just to clarify," he growled next to her ear, his gravelly voice rattling all the way down to her clit, "you still want me to take you, right?"

She gasped as he fisted her hair and pulled, forcing her to arch her back. She eked out, "Yes…" and that was all she could manage to say in response.

In seconds, she felt his warm body slide against hers. His

hand traced down her spine and gripped her ass cheeks as the other hand held his throbbing cock between her legs. Feeling him so close to spreading her lips, brushing up against them but not quite penetrating, was driving her absolutely wild.

Although he had yet to touch her there, she knew without a doubt she was soaking wet with desire. *This is what you do to me,* she thought as he groaned. Some of her juices had dripped onto the head of his cock, and he was feeling her silky wetness against his searing hot flesh.

He stroked down her back all the way to her bottom, caressing and kneading her ample curves with his strong hands. She could barely concentrate on how amazing his hands felt massaging her flesh because all of her blood had pooled in her sex. The totality of her energy was fixated on his hardness being so close to penetrating her, but yet so far away. She pushed back against him, eager to feel him inside her, but the passage was still tight and closed.

Eager is an understatement, she corrected herself. *I'm fucking impatient. I'm impatient to fuck. PLEASE FUCK ME!!!*

Yet now he was the one in control. *Which I asked for,* she reminded herself. *How ironic.*

He twisted her long, wavy locks in his palm and wrapped the thick, dark band twice around his knuckles, pulling her back into an arch again. With his other hand, he repositioned his cock so the head rested between her soaking wet lips.

"James, please..." she moaned, conflicted over the pain radiating from her scalp mixed with the anticipation burning against her throbbing slit.

"Is this what you want?" he demanded, pushing only the tip almost imperceptibly inside her.

She was silent except for her heavy panting. He pulled back harder on his makeshift rein to force a reply, and she cried out, "Yes!"

He was still not satisfied with her answer and left his cock suspended, the tip still barely grazing the entrance to her pussy. He was winning the battle of their wills. She could not imagine wanting anything more desperately at that moment than she wanted him inside her. He seemed to be taking his sweet time putting the condom on.

He gripped her ass again and commanded her, "Tell me what you want, Sarah."

"I want your cock inside me," Sarah moaned. "Please...please, James, please...."

Without another word, he plunged hard into the depth of her, causing her to scream out as she bucked against him, impaling herself on him as fast as he would allow. Her climax was half-built before his first thrust. Her breathing was ragged and punctuated by moans.

James continued to grip her by her hair and held steady, letting her push back against his pelvis until he decided he'd had enough and forcibly took back control. Without warning, he released her hair from his fist and pushed her face down onto the mattress, forcing her ass high into the air. He firmly grasped her hips, his fingers pressing into her soft, feminine flesh as he drilled into her relentlessly.

Even muffled by the mattress, her cries still pierced the air. The sensation of her pussy clenching his cock was so overwhelmingly intense, he began to moan as well. Both found their release at precisely the same exquisite moment, their bodies violently shuddering against each other with each spasm.

As the waves slowly dissipated, James dropped his head to rest on her back, his heaving chest pressed against her bottom. Their racing heartbeats slowly wound down to normal rhythms as they struggled to catch their breath. She was frozen, not wanting to move and possibly miss the last lingering moments of her climax. He made a trail of gentle kisses down her back which starkly contrasted with the pounding he'd delivered just moments before.

They shared two more sessions that evening, going late into the night and rendering both parties exhilarated yet exhausted. After the third, she lay with her cheek pressed against his chest, his wiry hair tickling her nose as his ribcage rose and fell with each deep breath. Just when she thought he was asleep, his fingers raked through her dark tresses that had cascaded over his arm. Lightly gripping the base of her neck, he tilted her head up to meet his, pressing his lips against hers and murmuring softly, "Goodnight, beautiful."

The way he'd shown the full spectrum of his passion that night...from tender to commanding and back to tender again...Sarah was reeling. He was so much more than she had thought.

As she drifted off to sleep, a very clear, lucid thought rang out through her mind: *This man is going to break my heart someday.*

THE SOUND of the phone ringing startled Sarah from her slumber. James was still there, spooning her with his arm around her waist and his hand resting near her thigh. Sarah scrambled for the phone as soon as she realized it was Rachel calling.

Rachel would never call at seven o'clock on a Saturday

morning if there was not some sort of crisis. Sarah's heart pounded, her mind busily churning out all the different potential catastrophes that might be afoot.

"Hello?" Her vocal cords were raspy from their workout the night before.

On the other end, she heard nothing but sobbing—deep, uncontrollable sobbing. Sarah could count on one hand how many times she'd heard her best friend cry in the decade she'd known her. James began to stir as Sarah reviewed her options for calming Rachel down.

"What's wrong?"

Rachel's voice was shaky and riddled with more sobs. "Mark...left...me..." came her punctuated-between-sobs reply.

Sarah had never heard such anguish from Rachel: not when her son needed emergency surgery, not when Rachel's husband filed for divorce. Never.

"Oh my god, Rachel," Sarah managed. "I'll be right there, honey. Give me twenty minutes."

James sat up in bed and rubbed his eyes for a moment. "What's going on?" he asked wearily.

"It's my friend," Sarah replied. "I need to go to her." She raced to the bathroom, grabbing clothes on her way and forgetting to close the bathroom door as she started to empty her bladder. *Whatever. He's half-asleep anyway.*

Sure enough, she emerged half-dressed, her hair in a lopsided bun, glasses on and teeth brushed, but James remained in the same half-upright position, his eyes closed again. *Apparently he is not a morning person.*

She was slipping on her flip flops when his eyes flickered open. He looked mildly shell-shocked. *Am I supposed to just leave him here or what?*

"I'm so sorry I need to go," she said gently. "You can stay as long as you want. My kids won't be back till four this afternoon." She kissed him on the cheek. "See you soon...I hope..."

The last words floated in the air as she hurried down the stairs and out the door. Fortunately, James's truck wasn't blocking her Toyota. She sped off to Rachel's, hoping she could console her friend.

The door to Rachel's modest blue vinyl-sided ranch with black shutters was ajar, so Sarah let herself in, removing her shoes in the foyer. She headed straight for Rachel's bedroom, where her friend was curled up amongst a pile of fluffy purple pillows and used tissues.

"Can I bring you anything?" Sarah asked immediately, thinking of how dehydrating all those tears must be.

Rachel shook her head but then meekly requested, "A valium?" She almost managed a smirk through her puffy lips and red, swollen, bloodshot eyes. "A shotgun?"

Sarah sat on the bed and took her friend into her arms. Rachel felt small and childlike in her embrace. The lamentations started again, and Sarah tried to absorb her friend's violent sobs into her own body, letting her tears soak into her shoulders and fall into the wisps of hair slipping out of her haphazard bun.

She just kept whispering "Shhhh...shhhhh." Finally, like a music box winding down, the sobbing ceased.

Rachel pulled back and sniffled a bit, blowing her nose into yet another tissue. Her cheeks were streaked by the trails of tears that had traced their way down her face. "I can't believe it's over." She stared out the open window, momentarily distracted by a little wren that had hopped up on a nearby limb.

"Can you tell me what happened?"

Mark and Rachel had been dating, although non-exclusively, for two or three years. They started off as friends with benefits while Rachel's divorce was being finalized, but then their friendship grew into something a bit more regular and *relationship-y*, for lack of a better term. But not once had Sarah ever heard Rachel say the "L" word to describe her feelings for Mark, and not once had she ever heard them make plans to spend their future together. It was a very "live in the moment" type of arrangement.

"A few months ago he started seeing some chick he met on a dating site," Rachel began, now seeming clear-headed and detached. "Get this! Her name is Ashley Silver. That's a porn star name, don't you think?" She very nearly laughed when she said it. It was good to see the real Rachel break through the storm clouds that surrounded her, even if it was only a glimpse.

Sarah patted her friend's back, encouraging her to let it all out. Rachel continued, "So they'd gone on a few dates, and finally Mark told her he was seeing me too. And Ashley got all bent out of shape about it. She just flat out refused to see him again as long as I was in the picture."

Rachel paused and blew her nose again. She glanced down at the bed littered with crumpled tissues and shook her head in disbelief. She ran her fingers through her blonde hair and considered her story, as if she was trying to make sense of it as she told it. "I really thought that would be it, you know. Mark has never had any trouble blowing off girls who have an issue with him seeing me...but apparently Ashley is *different*. He has *feelings* for her," she said, her emphasis making the word "feelings" sound like the other F word.

Sarah reflected for a moment on the word "feelings." That was probably what upset Rachel most of all. She didn't have a problem sharing Mark physically; after all, she'd shared him with the redhead at the club the weekend before and seemed to enjoy it immensely. It amazed her in all the studies she'd done on human sexuality that no matter how good people were at separating sex and emotion, they were still regularly conflated, even by the most well-intentioned parties.

"So he's leaving you to be with her exclusively?" Sarah summarized.

Rachel nodded as the tears began to well up again in the corners of her hazel eyes. "I guess I knew in the back in my head this day would come eventually," she admitted. "He's twenty-eight, after all, never married. I knew he wouldn't wanna be with me for the rest of his life."

"Is this Ashley chick going to support him?" Sarah questioned, knowing full well that Mark practically lived at Rachel's, even though his "official residence" was his mother's address. He'd bounced between warehouse and retail jobs the past six months, only recently landing a bartending gig at a local bar.

Rachel managed a little laugh. "Well, Porn Girl is twenty-four and an even bigger mess than Mark. I think she's a full-time student, actually. So, yeah, there's definitely a negative cash flow there."

Sarah patted her friend's leg. "He'll be back." Mark would miss the stability Rachel provided, but Rachel deserved so much more than Mark could give her. She qualified her original assessment: "He'll be back, if you'll let him."

"What's that supposed to mean?" Rachel retorted with more than a twinge of defensiveness.

"Well," Sarah searched for the diplomatic phrasing required by Rachel's delicate emotional state, "don't you ever think about being in another relationship? Settling down and trying it again someday with a man who loves you and supports you?"

Rachel grew a little pale at the sound of the word *settling*. "I think part of me thought we would be settled someday..."

her voice trailed off as her mind drifted far away. "I don't think I knew how much I loved him..."

Sarah's mind flashed to an image of James propped up on the pillows in her bed this morning as she was scrambling to leave for Rachel's. *Fuck, what am I doing?* Was she setting herself up for the same stark realization Rachel was now facing? She wanted to encase her heart in steel, weld it shut, add a lock for good measure. She had no desire to experience the emotional upheaval and turmoil she was witnessing.

She'd grown much too independent to deal with that mess. She spent the last three years finishing her PhD, launching her teaching career, and settling into single motherhood. For the first time in her life, she felt like she had control of herself and her future. The last thing she wanted to do was to surrender that control to a man—or a woman, for that matter.

If she did fall in love again, it would be with someone equally stable, equally equipped to return her affections, and, by all means, someone who was capable of contributing to a healthy relationship.

The premonition she'd had late last night as she drifted off to sleep in James's arms came back to her...that he would break her heart someday. *He can't break what he can't open,* she resolved. She'd just riveted the lock and hidden the key away.

When Sarah returned to her house later that afternoon, James was gone. No note, no text, no trace of him except for the crumpled sheets where he had lain. Sarah felt a sudden pang of sadness stab at her when she thought about how amazing it felt to be in his arms the night before. She felt so safe nestled against his chest with his warmth enveloping her. He'd remarked that she seemed to fit there perfectly.

Like I belong there, she'd added silently.

It was a scary thought. How could she feel so connected to him when they were together but so disconnected when apart? That had never bothered her before about a friend with benefits, but something felt off here. She wasn't sure it was going to work out, after all.

Sarah still felt a little melancholy when her kids returned from their friends' houses. "Let's order pizza and watch something on Netflix," she suggested to the kids, who were both in favor.

After pouring herself a glass of wine, she realized she and James had been so eager to devour each other the night before, they'd never even cracked open the bottle she had chilling. Just when she thought she'd sufficiently distracted herself from thoughts of him, she felt another punch to her already tender heart.

Why am I so sad? she chided herself. *I have made a new friend, and we had great sex. There is no reason to be upset. I think I'm still sad for Rachel.*

She texted her friend and asked if she and her son would like to join her brood for movie and pizza night. Rachel seemed relieved for the invitation—she certainly wasn't one to wallow in self-pity for very long.

That night Sarah sat in her living room with her favorite people, her heart full of warmth. *See, I don't need a man. I have everything I could ever want right here in this room.* Even the cat had joined in and was sitting on the arm of the sofa.

Sarah looked at the beaming smiles of Abby and Owen as they watched the comedy Owen chose and stuffed their faces with the rare treat of junk food. She spied Rachel from across the room, and, despite some dark circles and puffiness under her eyes, she looked amazingly peaceful curled up on the couch sharing a blanket with her son.

I'm a lucky woman to have a friend like Rachel and two smart, healthy, happy kids. I'm truly blessed.

THE ADMITTANCE

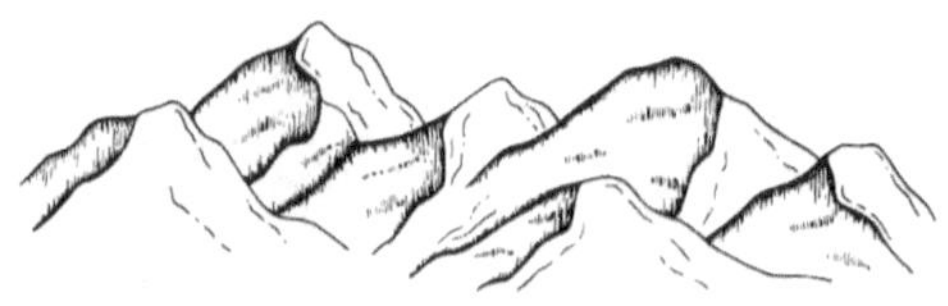

6

The next two months were a whirlwind of lectures, grading, committee meetings, journal article editing, and soccer games...punctuated by playdates with James. She'd been so absorbed in all her duties, she'd nearly missed the changing of the leaves. When she'd finally acclimated to fall, winter was starting to nip at its heels. The leaves she shuffled through on her way to her office every day were becoming increasingly brown and brittle. November was bringing something else in addition to a chill in the air. It reminded Sarah she needed to slow down and take stock of what was happening before she felt out of control.

Sarah had collected a mental scrapbook of images from the fall. Scarlet and gold leaves raining down on campus beneath cloud-wisped skies. The thrill and exhilaration she and Owen shared when he made his first goal in a soccer game. A photo from the Halloween party she and Rachel attended as Laverne and Shirley, right down to the curvy "L" embroidered on Sarah's shirt. A candlelit still of James's muscular frame hovered over her, propped up on his wrists with his triceps bulging, her nails dug into his back as he buried himself inside her so deep, she cried out his name.

"How's it going with James? You seem to see him at some point every weekend," Rachel observed from the sidelines as their sons battled the other team for the soccer ball.

"He does seem to pop up…and for some reason, when he texts me, I'm still surprised!" Sarah shook her head. It was silly for her to feel that way, but she did.

"When do I get to meet him?" Rachel pushed.

"It's not like that," Sarah insisted. "I feel like I know his body a lot better than the rest of him. So I guess it's just a physical thing…"

Rachel's eyes narrowed as she pursed her lips and studied her friend's expression. "You sound disappointed."

Here was a man she was wildly physically attracted to, moderately intrigued about intellectually, and she was finally at a point in her life where she craved a deeper level of intimacy with someone. Everything had converged to a peak, and yet conditions didn't seem right for climbing it.

"It's too late for more now," Sarah conceded. "And besides, he is too young. It would never work."

Rachel was still recovering from her breakup with Mark and was extremely vocal in discouraging Sarah from forming an emotional attachment to James. "He's military," she reasoned. "That means he's not staying."

Sarah couldn't disagree, but every time she was with him, she felt the pull a little stronger. Sometimes it was so strong, she considered just quitting while she was ahead, moving on before there was no turning back. But something compelled her to stay the course and she couldn't quite put a finger on what it was beyond the amazing sexual chemistry they had. She was fascinated by a story yet told. It was only a matter of time before she discovered why it was that James McAllister had come into her life.

JAMES SEEMED LESS like a stranger the more she learned about him during their pillow talk. Most nights he visited, they enjoyed two or three romps before finally collapsing from exhaustion and surrendering to slumber. He loved catching her off guard with a deeply philosophical or scientific question like "Do you think it's ever acceptable to kill a fellow human being?" Or "Do you believe in evolution?" Their fascinating exchanges on myriad topics struck Sarah as odd because communication during their time apart continued to be a challenge for him.

"So you *can* communicate," she teased him one night after he'd spun a long yarn. "Do you just save up all your words for when you see me in person or what?"

James gave her one of his trademark smirks in response. "I'm not much for phone calls or texting," he explained. "I guess I just like the real thing so much better." And with that, he lifted her chin and pressed his lips against hers, wrapping his arm around her waist and pulling her down on top of him.

"As usual I'm right! See how much better this is?" he asked.

She pursed her lips and shot back, "How can I possibly argue with that logic?" before brushing a soft kiss against his neck.

That particular night as she nestled into the deliciously comfortable spot in the crevice of his arm, her cheek pressed against his chest muscles, she started to probe a little more deeply than she had before about his family and background. "Have you ever done anything else besides the Army?"

"I wanted to," he responded. "I always wanted to be an engineer. As a matter of fact, that's what my degree is in."

Sarah sensed a "but..."

He stroked his thick, sturdy fingers down her thigh as he answered, "My dad really wanted me to go into the military. There was quite a bit of pressure, to be honest. It's kind of family tradition...and, well, my family is all about tradition."

"Oh yeah?" Sarah smirked. Her family was about the least traditional she'd ever known. She loved it when James let his guard down and allowed himself to be vulnerable. She was putting his puzzle pieces together. "How else is your family traditional?"

James sensed the hint of sarcasm in her tone that she'd meant to disguise. "Well, Dr. Lynde, not everyone has a hippy-trippy-love-child, gay-son-loving mom like yours." He laughed.

He remembered my brother is gay. Interesting. Good thing I'm not easily offended, she thought regarding his description of her mother.

"My family is Irish Catholic," he continued. "I went to Catholic school—that should explain a lot right there."

Sarah nodded, her hands running up and down his back, her fingernails gently grazing his skin.

"My mom stayed home and baked cookies. Dinner was on the table every night at 6 PM sharp. We moved around a lot, but wherever we went, things were the same. I think because of the constant uprooting, my parents felt the need to have a lot of consistency and stability at home."

"Well, there's nothing wrong with that," Sarah agreed.

"Kids need routines. So how is it now, with your family? Are you close?"

James looked thoughtful for a moment, trying to come up with the right phrasing. "I love my family, but I'm my own person. I'm sure my mom would have me married off with a slew of kids by now if she had her way. That's kind of how it went with my sisters."

"Really? Tell me about them." She propped herself on the pillows and pulled him down to rest his head on her breast. She would play the therapist, and her bed was her couch. Something told her the therapist is not supposed to be in bed with the patient. *Ah, but I'm not much for keeping with tradition, right?*

"I'm the oldest, as you know," he started. "Patty is the middle child. She did have her wild days after high school, and she dropped out of college, but then she got really religious and married this guy named John. He's military too, and they have four kids."

"FOUR?!" Sarah's eyes grew wide. If she was younger than James, she couldn't be more than twenty-seven or so.

James laughed at her reaction. "Yes, we like big families in the Midwest! She got married at twenty, so in seven years she's popped out four kids—despite my brother-in-law being deployed so frequently. Yeah, four kids, that sounds about right for the Bible Belt, doesn't it? Wouldn't be surprised if they had another before it's all said and done!"

"What about your youngest sister?" Sarah was growing more intrigued by the moment. She considered her brother Adam, his stance on kids, and how he was unlikely to give her children any cousins. It was hard to imagine a big, traditional family when she'd never been part of one.

"Allie is twenty-five. Married. One son, a daughter on the way around Christmas."

"So you're the black sleep?" she observed. "The rebel who

won't settle down."

He was quiet for a moment. "Yeah, I guess you could say that," he replied, his voice sounding distant. "I never really thought of myself that way, though."

Something about that stuck with Sarah. There was a lot more he was holding back. Maybe someday she would get to uncover it. She could unearth, a little at a time, chipping away at his story.

But it's James, she rationalized. *He's always holding back. Unless it's sex. And then I get all of him.*

"MOM, WHAT DOES AN ORGASM FEEL LIKE?" Owen asked matter-of-factly as Sarah cleared the table of breakfast dishes on a sunny Saturday morning.

Abby rolled her eyes but said nothing. She usually balked at any question her brother posed about sex or bodily functions. Sarah took instant notice of her silence on the subject.

As for Owen, Sarah was used to her son's queries and didn't seem the least bit shocked. She delivered the most sensible and non-erotic answer she could think of, "You know how it feels when you really need to sneeze, and then you finally do? And it's like 'WHOA! I feel better?' Kind of like a sense of relief but way, way better. Your whole body feels pleasure that comes in waves, very intense and close together at first, and then fading out after several seconds."

"Oh," Owen replied thoughtfully, his dark eyes twinkling. "That sounds nice."

"It is," Sarah assured him. She caught a glimpse out of the corner of her eye of Abby smirking from behind her laptop. It had been a few months now since Sarah found condoms in her room, condoms supposedly for a health class assignment, but she remained skeptical, especially considering Abby and Tyler seemed to be quite the item. But since that discussion, her daughter's smart mouth had taken a (possibly) temporary —but wholeheartedly welcome reprieve. She was dressing more femininely, and her grades were higher than ever. *If she is having sex, at least she knows how to put a condom on a banana, right?*

Rachel was on her way over for a girls' day out which entailed pedicures while Abby watched the two younger boys. Rachel was all aglow over a new love interest and hardly mentioned Mark anymore, although she'd heard through a mutual friend that things had quickly fizzled out with Ashley AKA "Porn Girl," as Rachel had dubbed her. Just as Sarah had predicted, Mark made a couple of attempts at reconciling with Rachel, but her wounds healed and her resolve strengthened, she'd just ignored him.

They'd gotten settled in their chairs, letting them massage away their stress while their feet soaked and they awaited their turns with the aesthetician. "So, Owen asked me about orgasms today," Sarah reported.

Rachel didn't bat an eyelash. "That sounds about right. And Abby cringed?"

"Not exactly." Sarah blew out a breath. "I still think there's more going on with Tyler than she's letting on."

"Your kids are a trip." Rachel laughed before popping a piece of gum into her mouth.

"They ask sex questions, but they don't ask about the really hard stuff—like their dads..." Sarah hadn't meant to sound so wistful when she said it, but it was too late to change her tone.

"They're perceptive kids." Rachel reached over to pat her leg. "They probably sense it's a difficult subject for you."

"Well, Abby's dad in particular." Sarah looked over to see her best friend nodding in agreement. "I will tell them everything when they get older."

"They'll probably ask when they're ready."

"I can't believe it's been three years since they've seen Daniel." The wistful tone was back in Sarah's voice, despite her attempts to disguise it. She needed to change the subject—and change the subject fast. "How's it going with New Guy?"

Rachel giggled. "He has a name, you know!"

"No, we're calling him New Guy until you're sure he's the right fit for you," Sarah teased.

"He's definitely more established than Mark," Rachel shared. "His daughter is four, and he dotes on her. It's so cute!"

"I can't wait to meet him!" Sarah offered, leaning her head back against the massage chair and soaking up the vibration in her sore neck muscles.

"I invited you out last weekend, but you said no!" Rachel protested.

"You wanted me to bring James—"

"So?"

"Well, it's just not like that with us..." *Nope, wistful again. Damn it.* "We've only been out the one time. For coffee."

"You guys sound more like fuck buddies than friends with benefits," Rachel accused. "No offense."

Sarah rolled her eyes. "It is what it is."

"What are you so scared of?" Rachel pinned her gaze on Sarah, who could feel it even without seeing it. "Just ask him out. You've fucked his brains out, Sarah! This doesn't have to be so hard."

The aesthetician who'd just arrived to take her place at

the foot of the chair nearly lost her balance. Her eyebrows were in her hairline, and she seemed completely befuddled by Rachel's brash statement.

"I don't know what I'm scared of," Sarah answered, this time her voice barely more than a whisper. "Pushing him away. Losing him." She swallowed hard. "Him deploying again…"

Rachel conferred with the pedicurist about what color she wanted while Sarah resolved to change the topic of conversation. She'd recently met someone new, and she was ready to let the cat out of the bag. It had all began very innocently and platonically with a visiting professor spending a lot of time hanging out in her office, shooting the shit with her, which in academia involved words like "paradigm" and "microcosm" and names like "Foucault" and "Kafka."

She had been on three dates with Pawel so far, and none had conflicted with time she spent with James, so she hadn't told him. They weren't exclusive, and she assumed during all that time he wasn't texting her back, he was probably seeing other people too.

Rachel turned back to her. "We're eating lunch after this, right? I'm starving."

Sarah nodded before biting her lip to suppress a smile. "Hey, so, guess what?"

Rachel's eyes widened. "I know from that look…it's something exciting. What?"

"I also met someone new recently, and we've been out a few times!" She enjoyed watching Rachel's expression morph from surprise to annoyance that she'd been kept in the dark. Rachel hated it when Sarah didn't overshare, but Rachel was the oversharer in the relationship, not Sarah.

"Well, don't just sit there! Tell me about him!"

"Well, his name is Pawel Kowalczyk, and he's a visiting professor from Poland. He couldn't be any more different than James if he tried!" She pulled out her phone and showed Rachel some photographic evidence.

"I see what you mean. He has really nice eyes," Rachel observed.

He did have nice eyes—warm, kind brown eyes deep set behind thick, perpetually smudged lenses. And he had long gray-streaked hair he was always pushing off his forehead. When he took off his glasses, there were red marks where they'd rubbed the bridge of his nose, and he was so near-sighted that he looked a bit like a mole when his glasses were off.

She didn't know whether to be exhilarated or exhausted from trying to keep up with Dr. Pawel Kowalczyk's mental acrobatics. Not that James was simple—he was far from it—but being younger and having no letters after his name made him seem so much different than someone so worldly and educated as Pawel.

"So…how is he…you know, in bed?" Rachel pushed. She was always way more interested in hearing about Sarah's sexual escapades than the minutia of her partners' professional or personal lives.

"I don't know yet," Sarah answered, trying to stifle a smile. "So far he's only pecked me on the cheek."

"What?" Rachel made a *tsk-tsk* sound. "Well, I hope you're not wasting your time just to find out he sucks in bed." She laughed. "Reverse dating all the way, Sarah."

Rachel was a big believer in sleeping with a guy first, and then if that went well, she could figure out if she liked him enough to get to know him. Sarah went on a case-by-case basis. Obviously with James, she was exploring their physical dynamic first—but she doubted they'd ever move beyond that.

Her cheeks glowed as a sheepish grin spread across her lips. "Well, there's no hurry… It's not like I haven't been…"

"Really well-fucked by one hot Army officer?" Rachel laughed. Now the pedicurist was full-on blushing. "So maybe your new guy is just intimidated by you. A lot of men are, you know."

"James isn't," Sarah fired back. As if he was her exemplar for everyone now.

"How do you stand all those stuffy academic types?" Rachel questioned, choosing to ignore the remark about James.

"Am I stuffy?" Sarah retorted.

"Touché," replied her friend, studying the picture a bit more closely.

"Pawel texts me a million links to articles to read, sometimes in the middle of the night. It's obvious he gives up sleep to work. He's so passionate about his research, and, you know, he gets me on a different level. We're both students of human culture—there's a camaraderie there I'd never have with James or another guy."

Rachel glanced back down at Pawel's photo. "It *would* be nice to run your fingers through hair like his. So, you've got your G.I. James and your Dr. Smart Guy." She laughed. "The best of both worlds!"

"Amen to that!" Sarah concurred as her pedicurist took a seat and began to inspect her toes.

"Want to do dinner with me and Jack next week for my birthday?" Rachel questioned, Jack being "The New Guy's" name. Knowing the answer would be yes, she quickly added, "Do you think you could bring a date with you? Pawel or James, whatever."

"So, in other words," Sarah laughed, "I should just bring someone with a Y chromosome?"

Rachel giggled. "You can bring a woman, if you want, but since you're dating two men—either one will do, I suppose, since I haven't met either one yet," she replied. "Bonus points if he's hot and into foursomes."

RACHEL'S BIRTHDAY dinner was the following week, and Sarah first invited Pawel to join, but he was slated to be in Chicago for a conference where he'd be accepting an award for some research he recently published. Undaunted, Sarah decided to broach the subject with James that night during one of their intermissions.

Her heart palpitated when his familiar broad silhouette appeared against the back door. Within seconds she was in his arms, their tongues tangling. He pinned her against the wall, pressing his growing bulge into her soft flesh. He had her bra unhooked and shirt unfastened in a heartbeat, and when she opened her eyes, she took his hand to lead him to her room, not saying a word.

He wasted no time throwing her onto the bed and sliding her panties off. He dropped to his knees on the floor and pulled her by her calves so her bottom reached the edge of the mattress. After spreading her thighs, he ran a finger up the inside of her legs from her feet to her slit, slipping just the tip inside to gauge her wetness. The slight hint of penetration elicited a sigh as she arched her back, thrusting her pelvis toward his face. She already craved more, remembering how amazing he'd felt inside her during their last encounter.

He seemed to enjoy making her wait, intensifying her

desire, and for the next few seconds, his hot breath fell on her flesh, his lips mere inches away with no actual contact. Her desire flared, moans throbbing up her throat as he finally let the tip of his tongue part her labia and slide nearly up to her swollen clit but deliberately stopping short. She breathed deeply as she settled into what was shaping up to be a lengthy, torturous tease.

The sound of his zipper lowering and the heavy fabric thudding against the carpet filled the room. Even though she couldn't see his hands, she knew he'd taken his stiff cock out of his boxer briefs and was beginning to stroke it slowly as he made a trail of kisses up the crevice between her vulva and her inner thigh. She was lying on her hair, so she sat halfway up to gather her thick brown locks, then fanned them out all around her head before closing her eyes, anticipating his next move.

With one hand stroking his cock, he began to tease the opening to her sex with his other hand, just one finger lightly traveling from her anus to her clitoris, almost imperceptibly penetrating her labia on each trip back and forth. Then his tongue took over, tracing the same path, once again lightly entering her just enough to taste a hint of her sweet nectar. All of this teasing and her clit was soon throbbing with an urgent need for attention. She wanted to pull his face closer, to lift her hips and grind against his mouth.

Patience has never been my strong suit, particularly not when it comes to matters of a...carnal nature...

He parted her lips again with his free hand, holding her open, and finally allowed his tongue to encircle her swollen rosebud. Her thighs began to quiver as the sensations surged through her body. Her orgasm slowly built under his tongue as his finger slid inside of her and arched to find her G-spot. He took her entire clit into his mouth, gently sucking it as his fingers massaged her deep within her sex, slowly thrusting in and out of her, deliberately strumming that magical bundle of nerves behind her pubic bone.

She felt the walls of her sex swelling as if a dam were about to break. The intensity rendered her fingers numb as all her blood pooled in her core. She no longer had control of her voice or her hands; her escaping moans sounded only vaguely human. Her fingers firmly gripped James's head, his buzzed hair tightly, holding him in position as if the fate of the world rested on his mouth maintaining contact with her pussy.

Just as the floodgates were literally about to open, she shouted, "Watch out!"

He was watching, alright, but it was the "out" that caught him by surprise. His entire face was drenched by a huge gush of fluids emanating from her sex, a display the likes of which he had only witnessed in internet porn.

"Holy fuck!" he whispered as her thighs closed around his neck, preventing his escape. The sweet, hot juices dripped down his chin and chest, quickly cooling in the chilly night air. For minutes afterwards Sarah lay convulsing beneath him, maintaining her death grip around his neck until she slowly released, her thighs lazily falling to each side as if she were completely limp and lifeless.

As she came to, she realized they had not spoken one actual word of greeting. Nothing had been said at all except her warning to watch out and his exclamation of surprise.

Complete silence continued as he pushed her back onto the bed and filled her still dripping pussy with his swollen cock. His intense gaze landed on hers as he stroked slow and deep within her, his need for release so great that, any faster, and he would come undone. The wet spot she had created seeped outwards on the sheet under their bodies, a reminder of the powerful orgasm that had claimed her under the direction of his mouth. The momentary rewind of the scene occurring just minutes prior prevented him from being able to hold back any longer. A few more long, deep strokes and he exploded inside her so forcefully, she felt his cum hit her cervix.

That was when she realized he hadn't worn a condom.

SARAH LAY in James's arms in her special spot for several minutes after he finished and rolled off onto the bed beside her. The warm, sticky semen dripped from her sex and onto her thighs, adding to the wetness of the sheets from the earlier oral activities. *I'll have to get up and change the sheets. How many times have I been with James now...is this our tenth night together?* He'd never failed to produce a condom from his pants pocket or to grab one from the drawer beside her bed. *What made this time different?*

He was still and silent, like he was about to drift off to sleep. They had talked about so many things during these quiet post-coital moments, but never their experiences with other lovers. She still had no idea about his past, and he had no idea about her lifestyle. Guilt for not being upfront with him permeated her pores, and she couldn't shift the blame to him for not asking. *It's time. Now is the time.*

"So...no condom this time?" she broke the silence, causing his eyes to jolt open. The muscles in his arms and chest tensed at the abrupt sound of her voice.

"Oh, god, Sarah… I was so caught up in the moment..." He huffed out a breath as he lifted himself to a seated position.

"My tubes are tied; I'm not going to get pregnant or anything." She turned to him, fighting the panic welling up inside of her. It didn't seem like he was the player type...but he always went days being *incommunicado...who knows what the fuck he is doing when he's in his own little world?*

"Whew!" he sighed and laughed a bit. "Good, we're good then, right? Why didn't we talk about this before?"

"Are you seeing anyone else?" she asked pointedly.

"Not right now." He didn't hesitate, which put her at ease. "Are you?"

She sat up so she could look him in the eyes. "There's probably something you should know about me, James."

His face bore the signs of stress and confusion—an expression she'd never seen him wear. He was always so confident and relaxed. She patted his leg a bit, trying to reassure him as she began her story. He looked as if she was about to tell him she was dying of some rare disease or something.

"I don't know where to start exactly..." She cleared her throat. "When I met you, I hadn't been with anyone for a long time."

He relaxed a bit and urged her on with his eyes. "But?"

"Right...there's a but..." She smiled when his eyes narrowed ever so slightly. "I...I haven't really had a traditional relationship since my marriage... I actually prefer having multiple partners," she explained, carefully gauging his reaction.

"That's why I suggested a friends with benefits arrangement. I thought maybe my situation might be too complicated for you. I wanted you to know that I just started seeing someone else, and although I haven't had sex with him yet, I expect we will at some point."

James looked confused, as if he couldn't decide whether he should be relieved or shocked. "What, are you like a swinger or something?" He made it sound like it was the punch line to a joke.

Sarah laughed at the way he said the word, as if it was dirty. "I don't particularly like that term. I actually consider myself to be polyamorous."

"Polyamorous?" he repeated. "I'm sorry, I'm not familiar with that term."

She smiled and took a deep breath, hoping she wasn't going to freak him out. "Polyamorous means forming romantic attachments to more than one person."

"Being in love with more than one person at a time?" he clarified, one eyebrow arching.

She nodded. "Yep, that's the gist of it. And if we're going to forgo condoms, we need to be on the same page about it."

"So I guess I don't understand what this means," he admitted. Sarah looked into his eyes—he looked so young, so naïve all the sudden. "What does it mean for me?"

"Well, it's definitely something I should have told you from the beginning, and I'm sorry I didn't," she apologized. "It's been a long time since I've seen someone who isn't in the lifestyle too, so it's my fault for not broaching this topic sooner. But we've known each other for a while now, and we should be open about any other partners we have. I just met someone else, and I haven't...been with him yet, but I would have told you...when we did. It's better to have this talk now, though."

The words tumbled out like water from a broken faucet, in disjointed spurts. "I just didn't want to scare you off..." She swallowed harshly. "I really like you, James..." She took his hand into her own and laced her fingers through his. "Maybe too much..."

Regret slapped her in the face when she added those last three words. *When will I learn those words are probably scarier to a man than finding out how many partners I've had?* She looked down at how small and delicate her pale fingers looked intertwined with his thick tan ones. She studied the way the hair on his knuckles grew and listened to her last words hang in the air.

She nervously glanced up to find James smiling. "I might like you a little too much too," he revealed, squeezing her hand in his. He leaned down and kissed her on the cheek. "I know you think I'm an unenlightened simpleton, but you may be surprised at what I'm open to."

"Really?" Sarah questioned, relief washing over her. She found it hard to disguise the beaming smile spreading across her face.

He laughed. "Try me," he dared her.

"Alright." *Wow, this is the perfect segue way.* "My girlfriend Rachel, who is even more wild and uninhibited than me, believe it or not, has requested that I bring a date to her birthday dinner next weekend. You game?"

He nodded. "Girlfriend, huh?" His blue eyes were glittery with all manner of devious ideas.

*Why am I not surprised that *girlfriend* was the word that resonated with him?* She didn't know if she was more interested to find out what he thought of Rachel or what Rachel thought of him. "Just for the record, I don't think of you as an 'unenlightened simpleton,' not at all," she clarified, patting him on the leg, then adding as a word of warning: "But, oh baby, you have no idea what you're in for...."

James just smiled, brushed her hair out of her face, and lifted her chin to his. Once his lips were on her again, nothing else mattered.

7

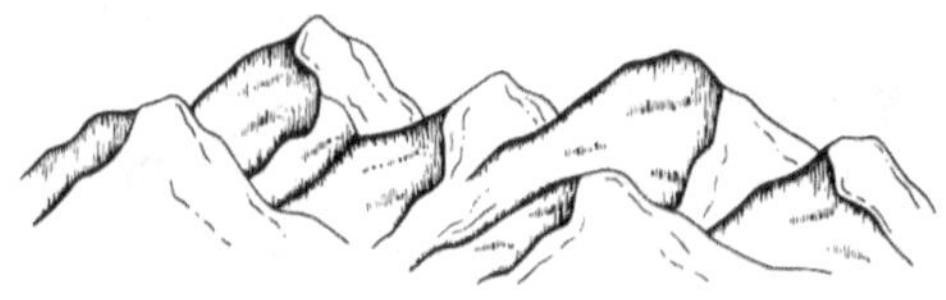

*H*er whole body felt weak and damaged, and then there was the pounding, the incessant pounding in her skull. She smelled coffee and...*bacon? Were the kids using the stove?*

Her eyes jolted open, and she found herself in a strange bed covered in gray and blue sheets. She wanted to call out, "James?" but she was languishing. Her vocal cords felt sewn shut.

She heard footsteps in the hall followed by a perky Polish morning greeting. *Oh, it's Pawel,* she thought, not even trying to disguise her disappointment. She thought her lips would crack if she forced them into a smile.

"How are you feeling?" the good doctor asked, laying his palm on her forehead. "You still feel a little warm."

It all came back to her now. She and Pawel had gone to dinner the night before, and she'd begun to feel bad around 10 PM, so ill she wasn't sure she could drive home. *Oh yuck...*a vivid flashback to the contents of her stomach being violently spewed onto the concrete sidewalk was unleashed in her brain. Food poisoning, she was pretty certain. She felt like she'd been hit by a truck.

"I don't think you're ready for coffee yet," Pawel determined. "I'm going to give you some ginger ale, okay, darling?"

Sarah pulled the sheets around her and realized she was wearing one of his t-shirts, and her clothes were neatly folded on the chair beside the bed. *Four dates, he finally sees me naked, and I wasn't even awake to enjoy it.*

"I feel so weak," she moaned to Pawel, who was opening the curtains on the other side of the room. The space was filled with sudden bright light that made Sarah squint and want to hide under the covers.

"Well, I think you evacuated your entire digestive tract," Pawel explained.

Oh my god, thought Sarah, *I don't even want to know what he means by that.* She didn't embarrass easily, but she cringed thinking about what all his statement might entail. "Thanks so much for taking care of me," she managed weakly as Pawel took a seat on the bed beside her. "You have a really nice bedside manner!"

Pawel smiled graciously. "It's easy when the patient is as beautiful as you are." He grinned before his demeanor grew serious. "It's an awkward time to bring this up, but…we've leveled up, is that what they call it? Not because of you getting sick, I mean. I actually aimed to have this conversation before you stayed the night, although I never imagined your first time staying would have these circumstances!"

He reached under the covers and drew out Sarah's hand, which was ice cold. He rubbed it a little between his palms.

She felt even less at ease now after hearing that they needed to have a "conversation." *I don't know that I'm ready to explain my freaky side to my colleague,* she worried. She started to mentally prepare a speech about how she was just dating around and didn't want to get serious with anyone. *Why would he want to do this while I'm so sick?* she wondered, annoyed.

"I don't know exactly how to say this to you," Pawel began.

Funny, Sarah thought, *that's usually how I begin these conversations. Like with James. Just a few days ago.* She just nodded and let him continue, too tired to argue.

"I'm married, actually," he stated matter-of-factly. "My wife remains in Poland and doesn't prefer to travel."

Sarah's expression remained unchanged as she dissected his English-as-a-second language sentence structure, but he must have sensed a judgmental undertone. "Oh, it's not an… affair!" he quickly clarified. "We have an open marriage. We opened it up several years ago, actually."

She smirked a little bit at his overuse of the word "actually." He was visibly nervous to broach the topic, but his admission couldn't have made Sarah happier. She kept her poker face and simply replied, "Oh, that's wonderful," without very much inflection.

"Seriously?" Pawel seemed incredulous that Sarah would be so calm and nonchalant.

"I'm poly," Sarah admitted, finally smiling to let him know she really was perfectly alright with his situation. "I'm dating someone else too, just so you know." *So there, things are out in the open. Why do people keep these secrets when it is so much easier to just put things out there?*

"Yes, poly, that's the term." Pawel squeezed her hand. "I just knew you were a kindred spirit, Sarah."

ON THE WAY to her house, Pawel recounted the series of events that happened the night before. Sarah had gotten sick, thrown up, and passed out. Pawel knew she was expected home but was in no condition to go, so he took the liberty of finding her mother's number in Sarah's phone and calling to explain the situation. Kathy Lynde came over right away to take care of Abby and Owen and got them up and ready for school the next day. The next morning, Pawel called Sarah's department chair and managed to send word to cancel Sarah's Friday classes.

Sarah was stunned by his initiative and kindness. "I really don't know how to thank you," she said as he kissed her on the cheek goodbye.

"Promise me the next time I see you naked, the circumstances will be improved." He laughed and waited for her to get inside her house before giving a wave and backing down her driveway.

Sarah was welcomed home by a very concerned mother, daughter, and son. Kathy took one look at Sarah's pale skin and dark under-eye circles. "Just go to bed, sweetheart. You look exhausted!" she told her daughter.

Sarah offered a weak smile of gratitude and nabbed a stack of papers to grade and her phone. As she'd gotten settled in her bed, all propped up with pillows, Rachel called.

"You still going to be able to make it tomorrow night?" she asked bluntly.

Sarah rolled her eyes behind the safe disguise of her phone. She knew her friend was concerned, but she had a funny way of always making things about her.

"Of course," Sarah replied. "I'm fine. I just need some rest and rehydration."

"Alright, Muffin," Rachel said, relieved. "I'm glad you are okay. Wow, Pawel is quite the hero, huh?"

After they hung up, there was a little knock at the door, and Owen appeared, a huge smile lighting up his face and his hands full of a crystal vase with a variety of blooms springing out the top in purples, pinks and whites. He carried it to the nightstand and set it down triumphantly. "These came for you!"

Sarah sighed and reached for the little card attached. "Get well soon, Professor Lynde," she read the note from Pawel. She didn't read the "xoxo" afterwards out loud to Owen.

"Oh, that's nice!" Owen cooed, his brown eyes gleaming. "Why do we send sick people flowers, Mom?"

"Oh, it's just a nice gesture," Sarah explained. "If you're stuck in bed sick, having bright, colorful flowers in your room is supposed to cheer you up."

"Oh," Owen replied. "That makes sense. You gonna be okay, Mom?"

"Of course, sweetie," Sarah comforted him. "Here, sit down and tell me about what you did with Grandma last night."

As Owen began to recount his tales of adventure from the night before, Sarah heard her phone chime, and a quick glance revealed the incoming text was from James. It was pretty unusual to hear from him out of the blue.

She pushed James out of her mind and focused on Owen's animated face. She loved watching his eyebrows move up and down and how his lips curled so readily into a smile as he spoke. She saw so much of herself in her son, and that was a good thing. Looking into his dark eyes was like looking into a mirror. She wasn't sure if she could handle having the soulless blue-gray eyes of his father staring back at her.

Abby heard all the commotion and came to see what she

was missing. She sat down at the end of the bed and listened as her brother told their mother more of the plot of the movie they'd seen the night before. "Did you like the movie too, Abby?" Sarah asked.

Abby shook her head. "I thought it was entirely too juvenile," she critiqued, wearing a very serious expression.

"Oh, whatever," Owen retorted. "I heard you laughing in some parts."

Abby chose to ignore her brother's remark. Her expression changed in a flash, the seriousness disappearing completely and anticipation taking its place. "Mom, Tyler is having his birthday party tomorrow night. Do you care if I go? I was planning to stay at Chloe's house afterwards. She's going too."

"That's kind of last minute, isn't it?" Sarah questioned. "Are his parents going to be there?"

"Of course they are, Mom," she replied, trying not to sound too defensive.

"Alright, that's fine. I hope Chloe's parents have a reasonable curfew for you girls. You shouldn't be out too late."

"They're picking us up at eleven," Abby reassured her mother.

Sarah smiled. Abby's attitude had improved remarkably since the "condom incident." She wasn't sure if it was all due to Tyler's influence, but she was confident that Abby having a boyfriend would encourage her to do everything in her power to avoid being grounded.

The kids scrambled off to the living room to play video games, and Sarah grabbed her phone to check out the waiting text from James.

James: *You ok? What time tomorrow?*

He was always straightforward over text. Sarah shook her head at his brevity, then started to wonder why he asked if she was okay. Did he have a sixth sense something was wrong with her? Should she tell him about the food poisoning crisis?

Sarah: *I was sick last night but I'm ok now. Can you meet me at the restaurant at 6pm?*

James: *You don't want me to pick you up?*

Sarah's mind started spinning. She was reticent to have him come to her house because of the kids, but they would both be gone by six. She hadn't said much about her kids to James and didn't know how he'd feel about meeting them. She wasn't sure how she felt about her kids meeting him either, for that matter. *You're getting ahead of yourself. Meeting the kids is a long way off. If it ever happens.*

Sarah: *Alright, that's fine. 5:30 at my house then.*

Wow, this is like a real date. How strange it would be to go out in public with James for the first time since their coffee date...to actually be out and about with him. Going together, leaving together. Having people evaluate whether or not they made an attractive couple.

Do I look seven years older than him? Will people wonder what a gorgeous man like him is doing with me? This seemed totally different than the two times they'd met for coffee. *This is very couple-y.*

No matter how hard she tried to convince herself that it was no big deal, her heart was still a little fluttery.

JAMES WAS RUNNING LATE. The kids had dispersed to their respective friends' houses hours ago, and Sarah was puttering around the kitchen, straightening the pile of mail that had accumulated on the counter and wiping down the countertops once again.

Sarah: *He's running late. Please don't be mad!*
Rachel: *No worries, Apple Dumpling. You feeling better?*
Sarah: *Yes. Much!*

She'd chosen a simple, low-cut black dress for the evening and added sparkly silver jewelry and her red heels. She did a once-over in the mirror and was pleased with the way the fabric hugged her curves, concealed her tummy and accentuated her creamy décolletage. Her heels clicked on the tile floor as she walked back to the counter once again. She had a birthday gift for Rachel tucked inside a card she'd signed with only her name. *Should I have signed James' s name too?* she pondered, not really knowing the appropriate etiquette. *No, no, that would make us seem like a couple. And we're not.*

She'd just started to score a few more of her students' tests when she heard the familiar rap at the back door. She grabbed her jacket from the back of the couch and went to let James in. He looked a bit discombobulated, not his normal relaxed and confident self.

"What's wrong?" Sarah felt the tension rising off him and evaporating into the chilly November air.

He gave her a quick kiss on the lips. "My mom called right as I was leaving," he explained. "My sister's water broke, and she's at the hospital. She's about five weeks early."

She wasn't surprised to see such concern for his loved one carved into his facial features. The more she'd gotten to know him, the more compassion she'd found in his personality. His furrowed eyebrows had produced two fine lines she'd never seen before, and she wasn't used to seeing him agitated, either. Little by little, she was peeling away his layers, seeing what made him tick. She took his hand and squeezed it. "You going to be okay to go to dinner?"

Without hesitation, he smiled. "Of course. There's nothing I can do anyway but wait. They have to induce labor." She could tell by the way those words tumbled off his tongue that they were foreign.

"Both of my labors were induced," Sarah reassured him. "Everything will be fine, and five weeks is not that early these days."

He looked genuinely grateful for her confidence that all would be well. They headed to his truck, and he chivalrously opened the passenger side door for her. The moonless sky was layered with thick gray clouds, and a bit of icy drizzle had started to fall. Sarah thought about Abby heading to the party and whipped out her phone to send a text.

Sarah: *Let me know when you get back to Chloe's house tonight.*

Tonight was a new milestone in her relationship with James. They were on a date. Although she had never been in his vehicle before, it felt comfortable and familiar somehow. She took advantage of his attention being on the road to study his profile, the serious cast emanating from his icy blue eyes, topped off by those furrowed brows. His phone was on standby in the drink holder inches away from his hand on the gearshift. She hated that he was so distracted, so on edge. She silently sent his sister Allie easy labor vibes and wondered if she would be creeped out by a strange lady six hundred miles away wishing an easy passage down the birth canal for her newborn.

She slipped a little further into reflection mode, traveling fifteen years into the past to her first time in the delivery room. She was in her early twenties and thought by virtue of having read every piece of literature known to mankind about childbirth, she was fully prepared for anything and everything that could possibly happen. She'd sailed through childbirth classes and stood staunchly and vehemently opposed to any type of pain-relieving intervention. She was going to do it drug-free or not at all.

Then she'd gone over her due date. A week passed and she was so swollen and uncomfortable that when her OB suggested inducing labor, she didn't think twice. No amount of idealism could ease the discomfort she was feeling and her desperation to evict the little one who had taken up what seemed like permanent residency in her womb.

She settled into her suite in the child birthing wing of the hospital and braced herself for what was to come. Little did she know that the evil drug Pitocin had a reputation for making contractions hard and painful from the beginning, giving her no chance to ease into labor. She was about ten hours into the grueling ordeal when she succumbed to the siren lure of the anesthesiologist who was pushing epidurals.

In the end, it was the right choice. She ended up taking another ten hours to fully dilate, and she wasn't sure that she could have made it without the pain relief. It was just another example of stubbornness resulting in Sarah having to eat her words. But at least she had a beautiful newborn daughter to show for her efforts!

She thought again of James's sister, surrounded by her husband and perhaps other family members, everyone supportive and rooting her on. Sarah had mostly labored alone. Her mother had arrived at the hospital by delivery time, so at least someone had been by her side to share in the joy of bringing a new life into the world.

She remembered staring into her daughter's tiny, precious, scrunched-up newborn face, marveling over her impossibly pinchable cheeks and delicate nose and lips. Her eyes were tightly closed and fully dedicated to the business of sleeping. Sarah was seized by an overwhelming sense of love and responsibility. All she knew was that this tiny bundle in her arms was completely hers to take care of, to guide and teach and protect.

"You okay?" James startled her from her fifteen-year-old flashback.

"Oh, sure," Sarah replied. "Sorry, I was thinking about your sister and remembering the day Abby was born."

"Oh yeah?" He glanced over at her briefly but then turned his eyes back to the road. They had nearly reached their destination.

She was still unsure how he felt about her being a mother. Plus she didn't want to remind him any more than necessary about his sister's situation. She reached over and touched James's hand, and the corner of his lips curled up at the feel of her skin against his. He steered the car into the parking lot, turned off the ignition and stroked Sarah's cheek with his finger. "You look beautiful tonight."

There was something about receiving a compliment from such a handsome man that made it more meaningful than hearing it from someone else. They walked hand in hand into the restaurant, and after pausing briefly at the hostess station, Sarah caught sight of Rachel waving at them in her usual boisterous, vivacious manner. They headed for the table, where introductions were made all around. Sarah handed the birthday card over to Rachel, whose hazel eyes lit up with excitement.

"Oooh! I love being the birthday girl!" she squealed in a high-pitched voice. Sarah studied James's reaction to her. She'd never been around James with other people before, and she had no idea what he would think of her best friend.

Rachel tore into the envelope, and as soon as she opened it, a plastic gift card to the local adult store fell out with a click onto the table. Rachel's eyes became even more animated, if that were possible. "Oh my god, Sarah, you are the best girlfriend ever!" She slid out of her seat and over to Sarah in a flash, practically sitting on her lap, throwing her arms around her in a tight embrace. "Thank you so much! You have to come with me to pick some stuff out!"

Sarah was relieved to see that James was amused by this display. He was grinning at Rachel, and the tension he'd worn on his face earlier in the evening had dissolved.

"It's so hard to find a vibrator that can stand up to vigorous use, you know?!" she ranted.

James seemed rather entertained, and Jack looked on with a wicked grin, clearly adoring his girlfriend's fetish for being the center of attention. Sarah loved watching how her friend could captivate men so readily with her over-the-topness. *Over-the-topness, yes, if you look it up in the dictionary, there's a picture of Rachel.*

Although Sarah was quite gregarious and open in her own right, she always played the "straight man" to Rachel's antics. They really made a good team, complementing each other perfectly. She thought for a moment about all the times they'd hit the town as single women and played "wing woman" for each other. They never failed to leave a swath of smitten admirers wherever they went. *Looks like Jack and James are just two more of the fish we've easily hooked,* Sarah joked to herself.

Dinner was a roaring success. That adjective was all the more appropriate because Rachel had the waiter roaring in laughter. Every time he came by to refill drinks and check in on his guests, she was in the middle of some erotic tale. He overheard quite a display of vocabulary, including such gems as "cocksucker," "dripping wet pussy," "perfectly sober orgy," and James and Jack's personal favorite of the evening: "gold medal winner in the kink olympics." The waiter, who, much to Sarah's relief looked too old to be a college student, confided in the foursome that they were the most fun table he'd ever had the pleasure of serving. And he wanted them to know he had been waiting tables for over five years.

Two hours later, Sarah and James headed back to his truck, James sober as the designated driver, but Sarah a wee bit tipsy after three glasses of wine. "Where to, milady?" he asked, grinning ear to ear.

"My house, and stat!" She plopped down into the seat and slammed the door as if time was of the essence. "Take me to bed or lose me forever!" she exclaimed as James revved up the engine and peeled out of the lot.

They made it back to Sarah's house in record time. Sarah had sobered up a little and was starting to think of James's sister again. She hadn't heard his phone go off, and he hadn't looked at it. *Should I remind him or wait a little longer? I'll remind him after the first time...*

He came around to her side of the car, opened the door and scooped her out into the brisk night air. After sweeping her into his arms, his lips, warm and wet, pressed against her own. His tongue darted into her mouth as his hand grasped the small of her back, drawing her even closer to him. His musky scent filled her nose, and her insides quivered at the thought of him stripping her black dress away and running his hands down the length of her torso and legs.

He took the house keys from her hand and unlocked the door for them. After all the times of her leading him up to the bedroom, this time, he led her.

Sarah's dress was the first thing to go as soon as they passed over the threshold. James was unbuckling his pants and stripping away his shirt all at the same time. *Wow, I didn't realize he was so good at multitasking,* Sarah noted.

"I've been dying to feel your body against mine all night," James whispered as he gently lowered her onto the mattress.

Sarah heard the chime of her phone from within her

purse that she'd haphazardly tossed to the other side of the room. *Oh, that's Abby, telling me she got back to Chloe's house.* Relief came and went as James's mouth found the sweet spot on her neck that sent a thousand tingles up and down her spine when activated. Her face buried in his shoulder, she once again breathed in his delicious masculine scent.

A sense of urgency arose from nowhere, but both James and Sarah felt it. He slid his cock into her just moments after they became horizontal. She wrapped her legs around him, gripping his ass cheeks to push him to the depths of her pussy, her nails buried in his flesh, thrusting her hips up to meet him.

"Oh my god," she breathed into his ear, "I can't believe how fucking good you feel," as he stroked slow and deep inside her.

James pulled back and grabbed Sarah's legs, placing her ankles on his shoulder, which changed the angle of entry and forced her to cry out in response to the intensity. He braced himself with his hands on either side of her, and she ran her fingers down his bulging triceps as his pace began to quicken.

Holy fuck his arms are amazing! she observed, her fingertips stroking up and down his muscle fibers. She looked up into his eyes, which were completely devoted to the task at hand, namely sending her over the edge of sanity. Her climax bubbled up deep within her, shooting ripples of pleasure from the epicenter of her pelvis and radiating out to her extremities and back again in waves.

Sweat beading on his forehead, James released Sarah's ankles and spread her thighs wide. "I'm not going to last much longer," he warned.

She felt him grow impossibly hard before he abruptly pulled out, stroking his cock with his hand three or four times until a spurt of fluid erupted, the first hitting Sarah along the collarbone, the second coating the bottom half of her breast. She studied him, his eyes closed, his hand still squeezing and releasing his seed onto Sarah's abdomen, his body vibrating with pleasure.

She was so turned on watching him that her fingers instinctively migrated to her sex. James opened his eyes and watched Sarah touching herself for just a moment before he kneeled between her legs and put his mouth to work where her fingers had just been.

"Oh, god," Sarah sighed at the feel of his hot tongue against her clit. "Oh god, don't stop!" He sped up his tempo as she began to buck against him, splashing her juices all over his face, holding him steady while her orgasm shook through her.

"I think we made a mess," James observed as he lay down beside her. His face was wet; the bed was wet, and Sarah's body from her neck to her navel bore the evidence of James's release.

"I got a pearl necklace—and then some!" She swung her legs over the side of the bed and stood up. "My sheets never last very long with you around," she teased him.

"Tell you what," James bargained, "you go start the shower, and I'll strip the bed. Deal?"

Sarah giggled and nodded. As she glided across the hall to the bathroom, she was struck by a singular thought: *In this moment, I am so happy. I'm completely full of joy. And it's HIM. He makes me feel this way.*

She returned to the bedroom where James was bent over the bed, lifting the fitted sheet from its grip on the corner of the mattress. She studied the musculature of his back before he realized she was standing there admiring him. She must have worn a peculiar expression because as he whipped around, he questioned, "Are you staring at my ass?"

Sarah sheepishly laughed. "Well, now that you mention it,

you do have a very nice one!" She moved behind him and gave him a playful smack. "The water is ready. Go ahead and get in. I'm just gonna grab my robe and check my phone. Oh, maybe you should check yours too?"

He nodded and fished his out of his pants pocket, taking it with him across the hall to the bathroom. She dug into her purse and pulled out her blinking phone. There was a text from Rachel and two from Abby. The latter one read, "On my way home," and the timestamp was twenty minutes ago.

SHIT!!! Sarah screamed inside her head. *Why is she coming home?* The first text was vague and only said, "Leaving the party." Sarah glanced at the clock on her nightstand and back at her phone. *She should be here anytime.* She threw on her robe and ran into the bathroom.

"Hey." She peeked around the shower curtain.

"What is it?"

"Issue with my kid. Apparently she's coming home."

His immediate reaction was clearly one of disappointment. "Oh. What should we do?"

"Go ahead and shower, and then you can either wait in here for me, or you can go home if you want. It's totally up to you. Did you hear anything about your sister?"

"Not yet."

How quickly they had both come crashing back to reality, and how deflated they both felt. Sarah was furious at the thought of not getting to spend the night curled up in her lover's arms. *Abby better have a damn good explanation for this.*

Sarah threw on some jeans and a t-shirt and headed downstairs. She saw lights flashing in the driveway and assumed it was Chloe's parents bringing home an under-the-weather Abby.

Instead of Abby opening the back door with her key like Sarah expected, the front doorbell rang, echoing through the silent house. Sarah's heart began to pound as she considered all the different reasons Abby wasn't letting herself in the house. *I hope she just lost her key.*

She rushed to the door, opening it to reveal Abby and two adults she didn't recognize. She knew they weren't Chloe's parents, whom she'd met on multiple occasions.

"Dr. Lynde?" the man addressed her as soon as Sarah shoved the storm door open. Abby looked tiny next to the 6'4" silver-haired man and his tall, thin, elegant-looking female companion.

Sarah nodded. Her spine was tingling. *Nothing about this seems good.*

"Sorry for disrupting your evening. We're Tyler's parents, Steve and Jessica. I'm sorry we aren't here under better circumstances."

Sarah looked from him to his wife and then down to Abby, who was teary-eyed and pale. "Call me Sarah. Please come in and tell me what's going on."

Abby entered first, and Sarah noticed she was trudging along slowly, a little off-balanced. The grandfather clock in the dining room was chiming midnight with long, slow, ringing notes as Sarah ushered her company into the kitchen.

"Would you like something to drink?" she offered as they all took seats around the table.

Both adults declined with a head shake. Abby looked pale and forlorn as she stared at the same apparently captivating speck on the tile floor.

"We were out at a party tonight," Tyler's mother began to explain. "We'd told Tyler we would be home around one or two. He's sixteen, and we didn't see any problem leaving him alone. He's always been a responsible kid."

His father took over the story, "We came home early because my wife was feeling ill, and we found your daughter half-naked and drunk in our living room. They'd broken into our liquor cabinet."

Oh my god, are you fucking kidding me? Her blood began to boil thinking of how Abby had lied about the party, about going to Chloe's house, about Tyler's parents being home. *Not to mention the thought of James still upstairs in my bedroom, where I should have been getting my brains fucked out.*

She glared at her daughter. "Go up to your room, Abigail. We will discuss this in the morning."

After Abby left, Sarah got a few more details about the evening's debacle from Steve and Jessica and thanked them profusely for safely returning her daughter home. Then she apologized and promised Abby would be appropriately punished. They pledged to do the same with Tyler. She said goodbye and closed the door, shutting out the cold night air.

Her face flushed, her head pounding, she tried to collect her thoughts before heading upstairs to check on James. *I figured something was going on with that girl,* Sarah thought. *I should have trusted my instincts when I found that condom in her room. I should have pushed her for more information.* Myriad "should haves" bombarded her mind as she climbed each stair, hurrying to see if James was lying in bed, awaiting her return.

He had already left.

8

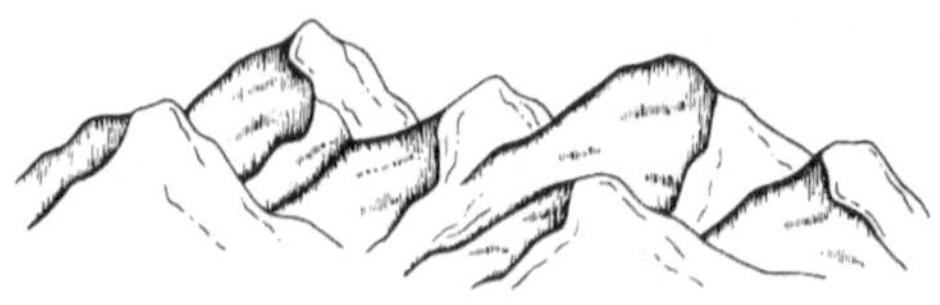

Sarah tossed and turned that night, her body missing James and the feeling of him curled against her. She was so angry at her daughter that even when she finally succumbed to slumber, she'd rouse in tiny fits of rage, remembering the events of the preceding night all over again. With any luck, Abby was not sleeping peacefully down the hall. Hopefully she was considering her actions and growing increasingly repentant. Finally, Sarah jolted awake for good at 6:45 AM and reached for her phone, thoughts of James and his sister foremost in her mind.

There was no text from James waiting for her, but there was one from her best friend:

Rachel: *OMG! Well done, Lovechop! He's a catch! Xoxo*

She wished she'd had a chance to review the evening with James. She was wildly curious what he thought of Rachel and Jack. That conversation probably would have happened in or after the shower, if they hadn't been so rudely interrupted by a drunk and deceitful fifteen-year-old. *Ah, there's the ire again.* She threw her robe on and marched down the hall to Abby's room, where she threw open the door and subsequently aroused a very groggy teenager from slumber.

Abby sat up in her bed and rubbed her eyes, which might have been a covert move to conceal a snippet of eye-rolling. Sarah took a deep breath and attempted to formulate a speech that didn't involve blowing a gasket.

"What happened last night?" she finally chose an approach. *Non-judgmental. Open-ended. Best I can do under the circumstances.*

Abby managed to look relatively contrite. Her small voice offered, "I screwed up, Mom. I'm sorry."

"That's it? That's all you're going to say?" Sarah couldn't believe that Abby, who had the cunning argumentative skills of a defense attorney, wasn't going to offer some sort of excuse for her behavior.

"Well, I was caught," Abby explained. "What else can I say? Go ahead and ground me or whatever other punishment you're gonna give me. I know I deserve it."

Sarah was not expecting her daughter to concede so easily, which made her suspect more was going on, and Abby was pleading down to a lesser crime. She decided to cut to the chase: "Are you and Tyler having sex?"

Silence.

"Abby?" Her daughter's gaze shifted straight ahead. "I'm not going to judge you, Abby; I just want to know the truth."

Sarah had not forgotten what it felt like to hide her sexual exploits from her mother. She remembered the lies. The justifications. She also remembered when her mother discovered the truth, she was understanding and kind...and there was something about it being all out in the open that made sneaking around to have sex much less appealing.

Abby hesitated for a moment, fisting her long honey-colored hair and twirling the ends before nodding.

"Alright." Before Sarah could devise her next move, Abby burst into tears.

Overprotective maternal mode flipped on, and the anger she'd harbored since the night before faded, replaced by concern. "Oh my god, Abby, did he hurt you? Did he force you?"

Abby's body was shaking with sobs. "No, of course not," she managed.

"What's wrong, then?" Sarah asked gently, smoothing her daughter's hair out of her face and wiping away a tear that had rolled down her cheek.

"I just hate disappointing you," Abby confessed.

"Oh, baby," Sarah held her daughter tightly in her arms, "I'm not disappointed. I just want you to be safe and happy, that's all." She rocked Abby back and forth for a few moments, remembering what it was like to hold her when she was small and had skinned her knee or had a bad day at school. Sometimes she wondered how this could be the same child as that bright-eyed, compliant little girl with pigtails and freckles.

She'd have to confront Abby about the alcohol consumption, the lying, and give her the safe sex speech again, but that could wait. She still wasn't entirely sure Abby's remorse wasn't a ploy to help her achieve a lighter sentence, but Sarah wasn't going to delve more into that now. Right now she just wanted to hold her little girl.

PAWEL CALLED that afternoon to make sure Sarah had completely recovered from her illness on Thursday night, and he wanted to invite her out for drinks after work the following Friday. Sarah was happy to hear from him but couldn't help but feel somewhat wistful that it wasn't James calling.

Maybe I should just call him later. To check on his sister.

When Owen came home from his friend's house, it was as if he sensed something had happened between his mother and sister in his absence. Sarah noticed how chatty he was and thought he might be trying to defuse the tension. She couldn't believe how perceptive her son was sometimes. *A chip off the old block*, she laughed.

Abby retreated to her room shortly after Owen's arrival, when he began to recount his entire weekend to Sarah, even the parts she was there for—*it's obviously necessary to recap because maybe I missed some of it when I was sick, right?* Satisfied his mother was completely up to date on his activities, he ambled off to his room to finish up homework for Monday.

Sarah nervously shuffled through the contacts in her phone until she came to James McAllister. She hadn't spoken to him on the phone since the day of their first date, way back in August. Her heart was pounding as the phone rang. *Holy shit, what is wrong with me?* she scolded herself. *I feel like I'm in the eighth grade phoning a boy for the first time.*

"Hello?" came his husky voice, sounding like he'd been asleep.

"Hey, James...what's up?" she tried to sound casual. "I didn't get to say goodbye to you last night."

"I know, I'm sorry," he replied. "My mother called, and I didn't want to take it in the house where your kid might hear, so I decided to go."

"Ohhhh." Sarah let the syllable float out across a long pause. "Is everything okay?"

"Everything is fine," he reassured her. "My sister gave birth to a healthy baby girl at around 2 AM. Her name is Annalisa Katherine. Five pounds, three ounces. She's a little premature, so they're keeping her in the NICU for a few days, but she seems fine so far."

"Oh, I'm so glad!" Sarah exclaimed. "Wow, that's quite a big name for such a tiny girl! My middle name is Katherine too. And my mom's."

"Really?" James asked. "That's my grandmother's name."

"Nice." *Awkward silence. Shit, this is what I didn't want to happen.*

"I'm sorry I couldn't stay. Is everything okay with your daughter?"

"Yeah, it will be. Teenagers, ugh. When will I see you again?" *Might as well cut to the chase.* Her body was already longing for him, and she couldn't help but feel cheated out of several more rounds with him the night before.

"Actually," his voice rang with a hint of excitement, "I was going to ask if you'd like to come to my place next weekend. For dinner."

Her heart burst like a firework, raining down glittery gold sparkles all around her. "I would love that."

They worked out the details before she disconnected, still feeling giddy. She now had a date with Pawel Friday night and James Saturday night. *Am I the luckiest woman on the planet or what?* she wondered as she dialed Rachel's number.

She spent the next hour on the phone with her best friend, picking apart in intricate detail every nuance of the dinner conversation the night before. Then she updated Rachel on the Abby situation and the two of them conferred about Thanksgiving plans. Jack would be joining them this year, along with his four-year-old daughter Gia.

Rachel and Sarah traditionally celebrated holidays

together, with Sarah's mom joining them. Oftentimes, they invited current boyfriends, lovers, or sometimes colleagues who had nowhere else to go. Sarah had debated asking either Pawel or James to join them for Thanksgiving dinner, seeing as they were both away from family, but she couldn't ask both of them—*Pawel would probably be fine with it, but James might be weirded out*—plus she still wasn't sure about introducing either man to her children, so she decided to leave them both off the guest list.

Phone calls behind her, Sarah gritted her teeth and headed for Abby's room. It was time to deliver the bad news: the punishment.

THANKSGIVING MORNING STARTED at 6 AM when Sarah went out to the sun porch to turn over the turkey in the brine. She decided to sit out on the wicker loveseat to enjoy her coffee and a novel she had just begun reading. It was so rare for her to read something other than student papers or academic journals. *Coffee and pleasure reading as the sun rises. It doesn't get any better than this.*

There was a tart crispness in the air and a shroud of bluish mist in the trees behind her property line as the sun began to flirt with the horizon. It was one of those days that felt exactly as it should. Across the field at her neighbor's house, formerly raked piles of leaves had lost their roundness after children jumped and played in them. Her other neighbor had a dazzling display of mums, cornstalks and pumpkins lining the porch steps. Sarah felt a sense of peace as she closed up the sun porch and headed to the kitchen to start the rest of the preparations.

Rachel arrived at 8 AM to commence the cooking. Together they peeled potatoes, rolled out dough, seasoned the vegetables, frosted the cake, and baked the pies. The kids, including Rachel's son, made frequent stops into the kitchen to solicit samples whenever possible. Sarah was glad to see that even Abby was still interested in making regular public appearances, even if she still felt a little raw over her punishment.

"So what happened with Abby?" Rachel asked as she dumped the cut potatoes into the boiling water.

"Well, we had it out Sunday night after Owen went to bed. Abby was not quite as remorseful as she had been in the morning. It's like she spent the entire day bolstering her defenses," Sarah answered.

"Uh oh. So what did you do?"

Sarah chopped celery and carrots as she continued the story, "I reminded her that underage drinking is illegal. I lectured her about how lying to your mother is a good way to destroy the trust we've spent fifteen years establishing. I spoke about being sexually responsible and about unintentional pregnancy and STIs. She broke down and cried again when she learned she was grounded for a month."

"A month!" Rachel's lips pursed. "Have I mentioned lately how glad I am that Thomas is a boy?"

"Well, at least her attitude has improved since our discussion. That's a victory, at least." Sarah shook her head as she used the knife to transfer all the vegetables she'd chopped into a bowl. "Growing up is tough. Sometimes it hurts. I don't want her to think I've always been perfect or made the right choices. It's all a learning process."

"Why? Did you tell her--?"

"I'm not ready to tell her about when I got pregnant with her yet. But I will—probably sooner rather than later."

At high noon, Jack arrived with his adorable daughter Gia, and shortly after, Sarah's mother Kathy made her appearance with her famous oyster bacon dressing and sweet potato casserole. Soon everyone was seated around the candlelit table set with the fancy china and silver. All the guests' stomachs rumbled at the delicious aromas wafting through the room. As Sarah brought the centerpiece into the room, all eyes fixated on the turkey, golden and juicy, ready to be carved. Sarah sat at the head of the feast, electric knife in hand, so happy to see her loved ones gathered around her.

Later, after the festivities wound down, and people were starting to pass out in tryptophan-induced comas on every available horizontal surface, Sarah retreated to her bedroom to have a moment of peace and to check her phone for messages.

James: *Happy Thanksgiving*

She felt a pang of sadness that he wasn't there. Maybe it was time to see if he wanted to meet her family—it seemed like a big leap in their relationship. She didn't know how to label their relationship. He wasn't just a friend. He wasn't quite a boyfriend. Yet, she felt he was becoming an increasingly important part of her life. There had certainly been a shift since that day they discussed their arrangement at Java the Hut. Things weren't that simple anymore.

Sarah: *I'm thankful for you.*

A few hours later:

James: *Me too. Miss you.*

EVERY YEAR SARAH questioned why she let Rachel talk her into Black Friday shopping. *The earliness, the crowds, the traffic, the headaches.* "What about this is supposed to be fun?" she asked her best friend as they pulled out of her driveway at approximately 5:02 AM.

"It's not supposed to be fun," Rachel educated her. "It's the thrill of the chase. It's about the hunt! The sweet victory of bargains!"

Sarah rolled her eyes, glad it was still too dark for her friend to see. "I think I need more coffee."

"We'll hit Starbucks right after Target. That's where we're starting." As always, Rachel had their entire conquest mapped out, including coffee and bathroom breaks and culminating in a victory lunch around one in the afternoon.

If I last that long, Sarah thought after seeing the proposed itinerary.

The two managed to make better time than Rachel had imagined. She was pushing for IKEA.

"Are you nuts? IKEA on Black Friday? It's bad enough on a regular weekend," Sarah complained.

"Thomas wants this stuff for his bedroom," Rachel explained, "and it won't be so bad. Besides, we're running ahead of schedule!"

"I'm starving, though," Sarah argued. "Let's eat lunch first, and then we'll go, okay?"

Rachel agreed, and soon the pair was sitting at a quaint little cafe ordering soup and sandwiches. "So, how are things going with James?"

Sarah nearly blushed at hearing his name. *How can he make me blush when I'm not even a blusher?* The physical response the mere thought of him elicited blew her away. She couldn't recall any other lovers from her past having that sort of power over her. "Things are going very well," Sarah admitted. "I've even thought about asking him if he would like to meet the kids."

"Whoa, really?" Rachel seemed surprised. "I thought this was a casual thing! When did that change?"

"I'm not really sure." Sarah took a sip of her iced tea. "It's the weirdest thing. When we're apart, we're apart, but when we're together, it feels like we are together. *Together-together.* You know?"

Rachel laughed. "Um, no, you're gonna have to explain that to us non-sociology professors. Is that some sort of jargon?"

Sarah smirked at her friend's reaction. She took a deep breath before divulging this: "When we have sex, Rachel..." She paused for effect. "It feels like we're making love."

Rachel's hazel eyes grew wide. "Oh my god, Sarah, you've fallen in love with him!"

Sarah was in full-on blushing mode now, her brown eyes sparkling. "No, I wouldn't say that. I just feel something...deeper for him than I should, well, I mean, considering how long I've known him. I feel... almost a visceral connection to him."

"Visceral? What do you mean by that?" Rachel looked skeptical.

"Like beyond the conscious, like on a molecular level?" Gauging her friend's facial expressions, she realized she needed to elaborate. "I don't know, Rachel; I can't even articulate it, really. I still feel like I'm getting to know him in many ways, but I also can't believe how drawn I am to him. I want to discover him. I feel pulled. Like a magnet."

"Well, he's fucking hot," Rachel laughed, "I want to discover him too!"

Sarah joined in the giggling. Rachel had this amazing way of lightening serious conversations with sexual interjections. *Although, this particular interjection has some merit*, she realized as a new thought gripped her attention.

As usual, her friend was reading her mind. "Alright, out with it, does he know about us?"

Sarah smiled. "Sorta." She let about two beats pass before broaching the topic: "So...do you think a threesome would be possible? Wouldn't that be the best Christmas present ever?"

"I can't think of a better way to celebrate the holidays! You know what they say: 'the more the merrier!'" Rachel agreed. "Could we both wear big red bows?"

"Why, of course! What else do you get for your Not Really Boyfriend?" Sarah laughed at the image of her and Rachel totally nude save for two huge red bows. "Would Jack mind? I'm certainly willing to return the favor sometime for the two of you!"

Rachel's eyes darkened as her smile faded. "Well, I'm not sure what's going on with me and Jack, to be honest."

I've struck a chord. How did I miss that something was awry when I saw them yesterday? "Oh no! What's wrong?"

Rachel shook her head. "I don't know, maybe nothing. I can't decide what to do exactly."

"Well, don't be vague," Sarah admonished her. "What's the problem?"

Rachel's voice softened, which was out of character for her. "It's actually a sexual matter," she finally confessed. "He's having some difficulties...reaching climax."

Sarah considered that for a moment. "You mean recently? Like before he was fine, and now all of the sudden there are issues?"

Rachel shook her head. "He's always had some issues, and

it's weird. I mean, he's only thirty-four. Sometimes he has to do it himself, like it doesn't matter how long we fucked, he just can't get over the edge. But it seems like things have gotten worse lately."

"Well, stamina is nice," Sarah consoled her, not so sure she would be complaining if the shoe were on the other foot.

"Of course, but come on, I want my partner to get off on me, you know?" Rachel explained, and Sarah nodded in understanding. "Now we'll have sex two or three times over the course of a day or two before he finally comes..." Her voice grew even smaller, then: "I'm afraid it's me, Sarah."

"What makes you think that?" She remembered a couple of similar circumstances where there were issues, and she felt she might be to blame. *Insecurity*, she remembered. She'd been there.

"Well, maybe he's bored with me," Rachel considered. "Maybe he isn't really attracted to me. Maybe it doesn't feel that good to him."

"Have you asked him what he thinks the problem is?" Sarah saw how Rachel's whole demeanor had changed having delved into this topic. She looked so small and down-trodden, her eyes filled with worry. Sarah wasn't used to seeing this side of her friend, who was ordinarily the most confident woman she knew.

"Sort of," Rachel admitted. "He thinks he watches too much porn. He thinks he's a little desensitized."

"Oh," Sarah replied. "Well, there is a growing body of research supporting that idea. Some studies show that porn can have a negative impact on sexual performance and rela-tionships."

Rachel seemed a bit relieved to hear that. "God, I should have known you'd be able to cite some research about it." She laughed before her prior seriousness returned. "But I still feel pretty shitty about it."

"How much does he watch? The studies show that porn stimulates the dopamine system in the brain. It basically acts like a narcotic." Sarah scanned her memory for a citation to the most recent article she read on the subject.

Rachel looked half-relieved there might be an explanation that didn't involve her, and half-worried it was too big of a problem to deal with.

"How is he with other partners?"

"I don't know; it's been a while since we've been with anyone else." She picked at some food on her plate. "It's just weird because we haven't even known each other that long. It just seems like if there's this big of a problem so early on...then I don't know what that says about our future...you know? And I don't want to play with others if we can't even get our own shit straight."

She understood Rachel's reticence to add others to the mix. *It's hard to surrender that control and to trust your partner is really "yours" when there are unresolved issues, especially sexual issues.* "Maybe he senses you're stressed out by it, and that's stressing him out even more? You know, a vicious cycle type of thing."

"Yeah, maybe," Rachel responded, but she was still clearly upset by the situation.

"You aren't considering dumping him over this, are you?" She knew her best friend all too well. She had broken up with lovers for less than this. Sometimes it was easier for her to cut ties than to have to deal with the emotions.

Rachel smiled sheepishly. "Well, I don't know. I don't want to...but..."

"Rachel," Sarah said seriously, "give him a chance. Take the pressure off. Enjoy the sensations and worry about your own orgasms, not his. Just stay in the moment."

"Alright, alright," Rachel conceded. "Although, I will say

it's funny how you jumped all over my issue so you could avoid discussing yours."

Sarah smirked. "True. It's just one of my many talents." They knew each other's M.O.'s all too well.

To say that Pawel seemed both excited and nervous about their date would be an understatement. *Tonight is the night,* Sarah realized. *That's why he's being so crazy with all the plans.*

She couldn't believe they had dated for a month and had never consummated their relationship. He had already called her three times throughout the course of the day to ask questions about what kind of wine she preferred and whether or not she would eat lamb or asparagus or a chocolate torte.

"Pawel," she finally assured him during the third phone conversation, "whatever you make will be wonderful; I just know it. Relax! It's all going to be fine!"

While Sarah thought it was adorable how attentive Pawel was being, his behavior also reeked of insecurity. Lack of confidence was a trait she found exceedingly unattractive. It took her years to realize her ex-husband compensated for his insecurity by being a pompous asshole... *Douchebag is the word I prefer. Asshole is too refined for him.*

Sarah donned her simple black cleavage-baring dress again, the one she'd worn to dinner with James, Rachel, and Jack the weekend before. *I need to go shopping. If I'm going to have two boyfriends, I need a nicer wardrobe!*

Pawel answered the door in jeans and a striped button-down shirt, the cuffs rolled to his elbows. This was the most casual she'd ever seen him, but he still emitted a sexy erudite vibe. He pulled her close, his lips plump, soft, and delicious against hers. His skin was velvety smooth, and his wavy salt-and-pepper hair was still damp as she ran her fingers through it.

"You look absolutely stunning tonight, Sarah," he remarked as he closed the door behind her, his eyes sparkling with excitement. "You're simply breathtaking!"

Soft jazz filled the air, and candlelight flickered throughout his apartment, which was very bookish and cozy. There were oriental rugs in every room and real paintings on the walls, all abstract-looking stuff featuring geometric shapes and designs. "My father was an artist," he explained when he caught Sarah studying the picture above the mantle.

Her attention shifted to the west wall where she found a picture collage of Pawel's family. His wife was older-looking, with wispy gray hair and kind eyes. She was tall and willowy in a family portrait that also included Pawel and two grown sons. "What a beautiful family!"

Pawel smiled without saying a word as he led her into the dining room, which featured a very traditional cherry dining room set, complete with a sideboard and hutch and ornate chairs covered in an emerald green chintz.

"I love the way you combined old world-looking furniture with modern art throughout the house. You have really good taste!"

"I want to just accept your compliment," he responded, "but I should probably confess that I'm actually apartment sitting for another faculty member who is on sabbatical. The furniture is hers, and the artwork is mine."

Sarah laughed. "Well, you've brought it all together flawlessly."

Pawel's dinner was exquisite. Sarah had dated a chef

or two in her time, but Pawel's meal rivaled the best her former chef boyfriends had created. She couldn't believe how relaxed she felt, sitting in this beautiful space with this beautiful man, thinking of nothing else other than enjoying the moment. She didn't waste a second thinking of work or worrying about the kids. She sipped her wine and relished the conversation and the dessert, the most scrumptious chocolate torte to ever pass her lips.

After dessert, Pawel guided her, wine glasses in hand, to the living room, where they continued their discussion about evolutionary biology and whether or not humans were designed to be monogamous. An eavesdropper would have picked up on words such as "Darwin," "bonobos," and phrases such as "anthropologically speaking."

Pawel reached out and stroked Sarah's cheek with his long, elegant fingers. A smile spread across her face, and she looked down for a moment at how their bodies were positioned increasingly closer, before glancing back up into his deep brown eyes. Without another word, his lips found hers, and he pulled her into his arms so she stretched across his body, his hands stroking down her back to the curve at her hip.

He stood and lifted her to her feet, bare since she'd kicked off her heels earlier in the evening. She felt light and glowing, enveloped in a wine-induced aura. He led her down the hallway and spun her around to face him again as they stood beside his four-poster cherry bed.

He kissed her neck, then his lips lingered around her collarbone, sending a shiver down her spine. He unzipped the back of her dress and slowly, sensuously slipped it off her shoulders until it slid down her body to the carpet below. She stood in only her black lace bra and matching panties, the dark fabric contrasting with her creamy ivory skin, her dark, wavy hair cascading across her back, just past her shoulder blades.

He caressed her shoulders and down her arm so reverently that her body lightly quaked under his touch. "My god, Sarah," he whispered, admiring her nearly nude form before him, "you are a goddess."

He reached behind her to unfasten her bra and gently stripped it away, watching her round, full breasts succumb to gravity and fall to rest on her ribcage. He tenderly took her rose-colored nipple into his mouth, teasing it with his tongue and feeling it grow hard between his lips.

Sarah sighed as the electricity raced through her body. She started to unbutton his shirt to reveal his sleek, wiry body, his chest nearly hairless save for a trail leading down to what was still covered by his jeans. She deftly unbuckled his belt, unfastened the button and slid the zipper down, releasing the fabric so his pants fell down his hips and thighs. He stepped out of them and stood pressed against her, her soft, supple flesh contrasting against his lean frame, the thinnest of material segregating their respective sexes.

He coaxed her down to the bed and kissed her lips, followed by each breast, before moving down her body to nibble at the roundness near her navel. He traced her hips again and hooked his fingers under the black lace panties to slide them down her thighs. His eyes feasted upon her totally unencumbered form stretched out before him. Gently parting her thighs, he paused to breathe in the scent of her, the scent of a wanton woman. He groaned when it filled his nostrils, as if he were overcome with desire and compelled by irresistible forces to delve into her sex with his tongue.

Foreplay with Pawel was just as Sarah expected it to be: deliberate, slow, tender and thorough. Sarah was quite sure not an inch of her flesh had been missed by his lips when finally, finally he slid his cock deep inside her. He was so long, he very easily struck her cervix with the first stroke, and Sarah gasped in shock at the welcome intrusion. He reined in his thrusts, letting her acclimate to his generous length.

Surprisingly, after the long, slow foreplay, Pawel was quite the opposite when he began to truly fuck her. Once he felt assured that Sarah was ready, his speed intensified. He lifted her legs and pushed them toward her head, thrusting so deep that she cried out with every stroke. She wasn't sure how long she could handle the sensation; it was right on the very fine line between pleasure and pain. Fortunately, Pawel couldn't handle the sensation very long either, because after only a few minutes in that position, he moaned loudly and was spent.

He pulled out of her, still gasping for air before immediately apologizing for his lack of stamina. "It's been a few months for me," he confessed.

Sarah smiled. She tried to take it as a compliment, and besides, she had climaxed twice due to his talented tongue. She reassured him that she was fine and all was well.

Later they snuggled, Sarah wrapped in Pawel's arms, head against his pec. Both were quiet, lulled by the rhythmic rising and falling of their chests as air moved in and out of their bodies. But when it came time to fall asleep, Sarah turned over onto her side.

When she awoke in the morning, there was a foot of space between them.

THE NEXT MORNING as Sarah was packing up her things to head back home, she messaged James.

Sarah: *What time do you want me tonight?*

By four in the afternoon, he had yet to respond.

Sarah: *Is everything alright?*

By five o'clock, she had still not heard back, and she began to worry. Something seemed wrong.

9

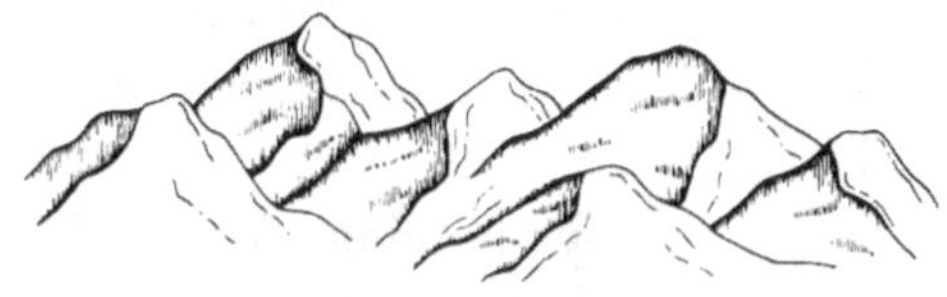

Sarah woke up in a cold sweat.

The kids were off to her mother's house for the night, and she'd been waiting to hear from James. *I was only going to sleep for twenty minutes...* There was something so disorienting about falling asleep in the dusk and waking up to complete darkness.

She rubbed her eyes and reached for her phone, which had gotten shoved under the pillow on the other side of the bed. *Surely he's contacted me by now.*

Nothing.

James was not a stellar communicator, a fact of which Sarah was painfully aware, but it was unlike him to go radio silent when they had plans. She tried not to panic as she reviewed the possible explanations. *I'm sure something came up at work.* Slightly blinded by the brightness emitted from her phone, she fumbled for the switch on the lamp next to the bed. Even before the light filled the room, she noticed the clock said 8:08. She'd been asleep for over three hours.

A loud banging echoed up the stairs. Her heart leapt in her ribcage as she thundered down to see what was going on.

The sound was coming from the back door, and there was a figure outlined against the light-colored curtains. *James.* A sense of relief washed over her as she quickly unlocked the door and let him inside.

"What's going on?" Sarah shrieked, so surprised and happy to see him. She threw her arms around his shoulders and hung on tight. His frame felt stiff and unyielding.

He backed away from her a bit, his expression devoid of his trademark grin. "I'm sorry, my phone is out of commission; that's why I haven't been in touch."

"Oh." She'd worried for nothing. "That's okay, I'm glad you let me know, though. I was starting to wonder about you."

He kissed her on the cheek. "I can't stay, unfortunately; something came up at work, and I need to go in. I just didn't want you to worry about me."

The smile vanished from her face. "On a Saturday night?" She took a step back and found herself butting up against the smooth, cold wall.

"The US Army doesn't care what time it is." He smirked. "I'm really sorry."

He wouldn't make full eye contact. *Something else is going on.* A wall had sprung up. She could sense it in his body language, in the way he deflected her warmth and energy.

He read the disappointment on her face and looked away again. "I'll get my new phone next week, and I'll be in touch then." He kissed her on the cheek, then turned and left without another word.

Sarah stared at the empty doorway as if he would return any moment, and they'd start over again. But when he didn't, she began to wonder if she'd imagined the whole encounter. After all, she had just awakened from a horrible nightmare. *Maybe I'm still dreaming?*

She shook her head and rubbed her eyes, feeling the stark, cold reality seep in. *I appear to be pretty lucid. Shit.*

Sarah tried to coax herself into the kitchen to make something for dinner, but she'd lost her appetite. The dark silence of the living room greeted her as she stiffly seated herself in her wingback chair. She felt suspended, numb as she processed the scene that had played moments before, the tiny details bursting into her mind all at once like popcorn popping.

There was more going on than a broken phone and a call to duty. Sarah always trusted her gut in situations like this; after all, her intuition had served her quite well in her thirty-six years. She would have never survived single parenthood or her divorce if she hadn't trusted herself. Not to mention grad school. *That was a leap of faith.*

Every fiber of her being was screaming at her that something was awry, something had changed. Her thoughts began to take shape. The one conclusion she had vehemently tried to deny for weeks was now ringing throughout her mind: *I'm in love with him.*

They never talked about their relationship, not since she suggested the friends with benefits arrangement. She claimed she didn't want to complicate his life. Rachel constantly admonished her to keep her feelings in check. A flashback struck of their first night together, when she'd lay in his arms and sensed with startling clarity: *this man is going to break my heart someday.*

Maybe it's already started. But why? What has changed?

She curled her feet up under her thighs in the wingback chair and wrapped her arms around herself. She started to rock back and forth, ever so slightly, as the tears began to trickle down her cheeks.

I've fallen in love with him, but he doesn't feel the same. I'm just this woman he can hang out with from time to time, who takes care of his needs, holds him for a while and then sends him back out into the world. I'm this older woman. A mom. I'm a toy he takes out of the box and plays with once a week, and then he tucks me away till next time.

She was heaving and sobbing now, her head in her hands, trembling with despair at this stark revelation. *He would never consider an actual relationship with me, and here I am pining away over him like a fool.*

Sarah stood up and pulled her hair, damp and sticky from her tears, off her face. She took a deep breath and walked into the kitchen where she poured herself a glass of wine.

I can do better than this. I don't need James McAllister.

After two more glasses of wine, her resolve was fortified. She took out her phone and deleted his number, his picture, and all of his text messages.

SARAH SPENT a considerable amount of her Sunday grading papers from her Sociology of Gender class. The more papers she read about feminism, the more strongly she felt about her decision to let James fade out of her life. *I am not defined by my relationships,* she repeated a mantra she had adopted several years ago. *My happiness is dependent on me, not a man.*

It was a lot of fun while it lasted, but it's better to stop now while the heartache will be minimal. She wouldn't say anything to Rachel just yet. She just wanted some alone time to focus on getting through the rest of the semester and trying to make the holiday season fun for her kids. *Ah,*

Rachel will be disappointed that there won't be a threesome in her future.

"Hey, Mom, can we put up the Christmas tree today?" Owen's voice interrupted her thoughts.

She sighed as her eyes bounced between his. "I need to get through this week at work, sweetie," she explained. "But next weekend, okay? It's not even December yet!"

He looked disappointed but accepted her answer and went off to torment his sister. That naturally drew the teenage beast from her lair and into the public space of the house to prowl. Sarah could tell immediately from Abby's heavy, plodding footsteps down the stairs that she was in a mopey, crabby mood.

She heard the refrigerator door open and slam shut. The heavy footsteps worked their way into the living room where their maker stood with her hands on her hips, wearing an exasperated look. "There's nothing here to eat," she whined.

"Sure there is," Sarah replied. "There are leftovers from dinner the other night. There's frozen pizza. There's salad. There's frozen yogurt."

"Yuck, that all sounds gross."

Sarah didn't even look up from grading. "I'm sure if you're hungry enough, something will eventually sound good."

Abby plopped down on the couch and let out an Oscar-worthy dramatic sigh. She propped her feet up on the coffee table and sighed again, in case the first one had somehow escaped her mother's notice. Sarah had a feeling the drama was only going to escalate until she initiated a conversation and addressed whatever issue was plaguing her daughter.

"What's going on?" she asked as neutrally as possible, setting her red pen down to show she was serious, and gave her full attention.

Abby looked down at her feet, which were covered in

brightly striped knee socks. She took a deep breath and then softly uttered, "I'm sad that I won't be able to go to the Christmas dance." She twisted her long honey-colored hair between her index finger and thumb and awaited her mother's response.

Sarah had to suppress the urge to roll her eyes. She could see that Abby had taken on the role of Contrite and Pitiful Teen, hoping to gain clemency. Sarah thought the month of grounding was a fairly merciful sentence considering the egregious crimes of lying and underage drinking.

She smiled sweetly at her daughter, whose gaze was dejected and downtrodden. "I'm sorry, honey, but I think you should have thought about the dance before you made the choice to get drunk and lie to your mother and your boyfriend's parents."

The contrite façade abruptly vanished as Sarah witnessed the anger boiling up from deep within her daughter, her face reddening and her posture stiffening. An explosion was imminent, this was the perfect opportunity to teach her daughter that using drama to manipulate her mother's emotions was an unequivocal fail. "You needn't get angry with anyone but yourself, Abigail," Sarah said sternly. "When you make bad choices, you must live with the consequences."

The magma was soon to reach the mouth of the volcano. Sarah could feel it rising, bubbling from within her daughter's core, her body starting to tremble with venomous rage. "Yes, obviously you've always been the perfect human. I'm sure you've always made brilliant choices and never had anything go wrong!" Abby finally erupted.

"I think you know full well that I've made both good and bad choices in my life, and when I've made a bad choice, I've learned to cope with the fallout. That is a life lesson that everyone must learn," Sarah said as calmly as she could.

"Oh, that's right," Abby's voice grew louder and deeper,

bolder. "You did make a mistake..." She paused for effect, then screamed at the top of her lungs: "ME!" She was no longer able to contain her tears. They began to spew out of her face along with her words: "I know you were drinking the night I was conceived. And you don't even KNOW who my father is!!!" With that, Abby stood up and began to turn toward the steps, preparing to return to her lair.

Sarah was seething now. Abby had been told her father was Sarah's college boyfriend who decided he was too young to be a father and chose not to be involved in his daughter's life. She had no idea where Abby's rage was coming from, let alone the accusations she was making. "Get back here, Abigail. You are not leaving the room in the middle of this conversation."

Abby reluctantly turned around but didn't step back into the living room. Sarah glared at her expectantly, but she was stiff like a statue. She took a deep breath and found her calm voice again. "Sit down so we can talk this out."

Abby complied.

"Please tell me why you said that just now," Sarah requested gently.

Abby rolled her eyes and crossed her arms but kept her focus straight ahead, avoiding her mother's eyes. "I heard you talking to Rachel about it a long time ago."

"A long time ago?" Sarah felt a knife stab through her heart, cutting deep. *Abby has been carrying this burden for a long time?* The weight of it seeped into her body like droplets of lead.

Abby nodded. "At least a year ago. You guys were in here talking, and I don't think you realized I could hear you from the kitchen. Rachel was a little drunk, I think."

"Tell me what you heard," Sarah said. "Please."

"Well," Abby began, "first you were talking about Dad."

Sarah visibly stiffened at that word. She'd almost

forgotten Abby had called her ex-husband Dad, even though he'd never formally adopted her, despite years of promises. "You were talking about your track record with men, and Rachel was teasing you."

Sarah gasped as the conversation popped into her memory bank. Rachel had said something like, "Well, I may have awful taste in men, but at least in college I didn't get drunk and high and fuck all my boyfriend's friends."

Those words rang in Sarah's ears like the sound of a fatal collision echoing miles down the highway. She tried to imagine how those words would sound in a fifteen-year-old's ears. They'd gone on to discuss the camping trip where Abby had been conceived and everything that went on that night, at least what Sarah was able to recall.

"Oh god, Abby," she finally said before her daughter could relay any more of the story. "I'm so sorry you had to hear that, especially in that way, and especially not coming from me."

Abby looked up at her through teary blue-gray eyes. "So you really don't know who my father is?"

Sarah clasped her daughter's hands into her own. "I made some bad choices, and I was older than you and should have known better. My group of friends during college...well, we were very open with each other. We also smoked a lot of pot. We drank a lot of beer. We were good students, but sometimes we had more fun on the weekends than we should have," Sarah confessed.

Abby's eyes were so wide, Sarah thought they might pop out of her skull. *I don't think she ever expected me to confess to smoking pot.* She considered toning down the story, maybe sharing a euphemistic, sanitized version, but she had gotten this far, and, ultimately, she *did* want her daughter to know the truth. *With any luck, I can make this a learning experience,* Sarah hoped, ever the educator.

"So, that summer, about a month before we headed back to campus, a bunch of us decided to go camping up in the mountains," she continued. "I went with Matt, my boyfriend, a few of his friends and a couple of their girlfriends. There were seven of us altogether and only two tents. Well, the other girls were drinking pretty early, while the guys and I were hiking and rock climbing. The other girls didn't want to go, and I think one of the guys stayed behind too. The three of them passed out at like eight o'clock that night in one of the tents. They were sick and hungover. Probably had alcohol poisoning."

"Eww," Abby interjected, engrossed in the story.

"The other guys, my boyfriend and his two friends, and myself...we were drinking a little, but we were also smoking pot. Matt had his guitar, and we were just all sitting around the campfire singing and talking and just having a good time under the canopy of stars, mountains all around us. They were making fun of me because I was jumping at every sound coming from the rocks. I kept saying we were going to get eaten by mountain lions." Sarah laughed just remembering it all; it was such a crystal-clear memory, she could nearly hear the crackle of the fire and the echoes of laughter.

"So, eventually," Sarah continued, "the guys convinced me to go into the tent, saying they were going to distract me from the mountain lions. I was drunk and high, but I knew what was happening, and, looking back, I don't feel like I was coerced. I mean, I had as much of my faculties as they did, maybe even more so because Matt was pretty messed up at that point." Sarah paused, searching for a way to tell the next part of the story. Abby was completely engaged, sitting on the edge of her seat expectantly, her tears dried up and taken over by intrigue.

More memories flooded back to Sarah just then, visions of body parts, sensations she had never experienced before, six hands on her flesh, moving her, taking her, three cocks releasing their seed into her orifices. And that, that was how she was certain Matt was Abby's father. He was the one who came inside of her. Besides, Abby looked like Matt. She had his light hair, skin and eyes. She had his disposition and build. Sarah took a deep breath and explained the rest of its story in its entirety, but as delicately as she possibly could.

Abby sat in silence absorbing the information, until she asked, her voice small and thin, "So then what happened?"

"We never talked about that night again, not explicitly," Sarah remembered. "We didn't even tell the other guys what happened. After that, Matt went to visit his grandparents in Florida for a couple of weeks, and when we got back to school, things had changed. I never could figure out exactly what went wrong between us. I missed my period. I remember telling him, but he just shrugged and said...I will never forget...that 'a slut like me probably didn't even know who the dad was.'"

Abby leaned closer to her mother and put her hand on her knee, an uncharacteristically tender gesture coming from her.

"He'd lost all respect for me after that night," Sarah explained. "I was angry. So angry, Abby. I didn't understand why men could go out and sleep with anything that moved, and they'd be considered a stud, but in one night of drunken, stoned debauchery I'd earned my slut card? And trust me, that word did *not* have any positive connotations back then."

Sarah cleared her throat and found the teachable moment. "Having sex doesn't make a person good or bad. Our bodies were designed to give and receive pleasure. If we make the choice to have sex, it doesn't reflect poorly on us just because we're women. We should feel empowered by our decision to use our bodies in the way they were designed. The important things are making good choices, being safe, and choosing partners who respect and care for us. That was obviously my mistake," she admitted.

A tiny shred of time passed while Abby internalized her mother's words. Then she asked, "So he didn't want anything to do with you after you told him?"

Sarah shook her head. "I think he really convinced himself that you weren't his. He severed all ties with me, and we both went about our senior years. I was living with some girlfriends off campus, and he was living with his guy friends. Our paths just didn't cross. When he saw me at commencement, I had just reached my due date. He didn't even speak to me. His eyes were as cold as ice."

Sarah was instantly transported back to that day. Her mother sat in the audience with her brother Adam. The whole of Sarah's support system was taking up two seats in the vast auditorium. Nine months pregnant, her black robe flowing out over her protruding abdomen, she marched in with her classmates, her feet so swollen she could hardly wear shoes. Her honors cords bounced against her heavy breasts with each step, and she caught sight of the eyes, the hundreds and maybe thousands of pairs of eyes that seemed to fixate on her girth. It took more strength and determination to walk across that stage to receive her diploma than it took to enter the delivery room a week later to have her labor induced.

"Abby, I know Matt is your dad. You look like him. You *know* you don't look like me! You have his blue eyes and light hair, his freckles, his slight build, his stubbornness. I have no doubt. Trust me, this isn't a *Mamma Mia* situation," she laughed.

Abby nodded. She had seen pictures and the resemblance. Her mother had kept some memorabilia from her college days, and there were shots taken of them together, Matt with his guitar and his arm around Sarah, looking young and vibrant and happy. "What if I wanted to get in touch with him?"

Sarah visibly stiffened. "I'm not sure that's a good idea." She didn't disclose that she had long ago tracked Matt down on Facebook and had even contemplated sending him a friend request so they could catch up. In the end, she decided it had more potential for harm than good. *What if he wanted custody of his daughter?*

Abby returned to the kitchen to fix herself a snack. Sarah went back to grading. She'd never been able to envision having that discussion with her daughter. And now it was over. Her conscience felt light and airy as she contemplated how this new information would influence the path Abby would journey in life.

On Tuesday, Sarah sat in her office, her Pandora station cranking out "November Rain," which was all too appropriate given that the skies were clenched with tight gray clouds and spitting out rain so cold it was on the verge of becoming ice crystals. The last few hours of the month were fading into the history books. She was working on a proposal for a new book, a departure from the normal heavy academic and theoretical stuff she typically wrote. This book would be for the masses, a book about dating, relationships and alternative lifestyles on college campuses based on all the interviews and research Sarah had compiled throughout the years. She was contemplating how to phrase a certain idea when her phone chimed.

Unknown number: *I'm back in commission.*

She knew it was James when her body physically responded to the thought of him before her mind could command it to be still. Her trembling fingers erased the text, and she went on with her thoughts.

10

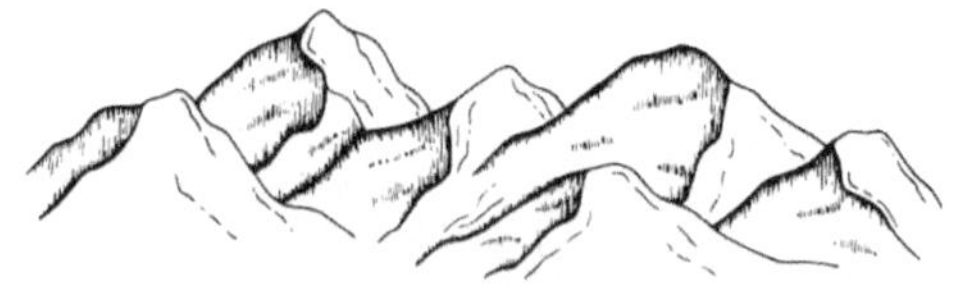

There were no more texts from that number. Finals were on the horizon; Sarah's book proposal was due to her editor by December fifth, and Pawel was preparing to spend the holidays in Poland. He'd been a bit clingy, wanting to see her several times a week. She might have been annoyed, but under the present circumstances, she found it nice to be wanted. Some nights they would just sit in the stillness of her living room grading papers by the light of the fireplace while Abby and Owen slept upstairs. She had finally introduced him to the kids as her colleague Dr. Kowalczyk, and having met so many of her colleagues through the years, they were completely unfazed.

Ah, there's nothing more romantic than grading papers together by the fire, she joked to herself one night from her armchair, a plaid fleece blanket thrown over her legs for additional warmth. Her hand was cramping from all the comments and suggestions she crammed into the margins. She was particularly pleased with Emma Knightley's research on bisexuality that they had discussed earlier in the semester. She noticed

Emma had cited an article Sarah published on the topic the prior year.

Reveling in that warm sensation she felt when students managed to impress her, she glanced over at Pawel, who was sprawled out on her couch. The book he was reading was on the verge of slipping out of his hands as he began to doze off, his black plastic-rimmed glasses sliding off the bridge of his nose.

Sarah studied him as he drifted further and further into a REM cycle. She could see his eyes twitching beneath their lids. His face looked so peaceful. His wavy graying hair had been pushed behind his ear, and stubble was starting to emerge. His nose was long with a slight bump, and his bottom lip was fuller than the top. It was one of his most striking features and always made Sarah want to nibble on it. When she kissed him, she liked to draw his bottom lip between her teeth and gently chew on it.

Pawel was one of those people who stayed in amazing shape without ever setting foot in a gym. He had long, lean limbs and sinewy muscles. As much as she hated to compare lovers, she couldn't deny she preferred James's thick frame and bulky muscles. Something about James's size made her feel so delicate and feminine, even though she was quite sturdy in her curvy 5'5" 175-pound frame. Next to Pawel's tall, lithe body she always felt much too short and Rubenesque.

Before she could do any more comparing, her phone rang with Rachel on the line. "Hello?" Sarah answered, trying to sound perky for 11:32 PM.

"You never returned my calls!" Rachel wasted no time reading her the riot act. "What the fuck is going on with you, woman?"

Sarah inadvertently let out a sigh. "Well, it's just my crunch time, you know. Grading. Exams. Yada yada."

"Bullshit," Rachel accused, over-pronouncing the T at the end. "Come on, out with it, lady. Is it the Smart Guy or GI Joe? Which Y chromosome is giving you trouble?"

Sarah had to laugh. *This woman knows me better than anyone on the planet, so I might as well confess.*

"Alright, it's James," Sarah admitted. "It's over. And honestly, Rachel, I think it's for the best, so I really don't want to dissect it all right now, okay? It's late. I should be going to bed soon."

Rachel grunted her disapproval. "Come on, just give me the executive summary. And for the record, I was looking forward to our threesome!"

"How are things with you and Jack?" Sarah inquired, trying to divert Rachel's attention away from the James Situation.

"Oh, come on," Rachel replied. "You don't seriously think I'm going to fall for that, do you? That's like the oldest trick in your book!"

Sarah was defeated. "Okay, fine," she conceded. "Last weekend he was supposed to have me over for dinner, and I waited and waited and heard nothing. Finally, he showed up at my house late acting really weird and telling me he couldn't stay... something about his phone was broken, and he got called into work."

"Go on..."

"Okay, so I sensed there was really something else going on because he acted so weird," Sarah explained. "Anyway, I just started thinking about him after he left, and how disappointed I was to see him go. Like, it physically affected me... I felt hollow and broken."

Sarah noticed Pawel had begun to snore, so she walked into the kitchen as Rachel said the words Sarah didn't want to hear, "Oh my god, you really fell for him, didn't you?"

Those words brought the emotions flooding back to her, along with tears stinging at the corners of her eyes. She had forced herself to turn off the waterworks three days ago. *Why am I starting this up again? It's like I have absolutely no control over my body's response to him. His power over me is so. fucking. scary.*

Rachel's tone changed as she transitioned into empathetic, comforting friend mode. "Oh, honey, I'm so sorry. So that was it? You never heard from him again?"

Sarah grabbed a paper towel from the dispenser near the sink and dabbed gently at her wet cheeks. "He texted me on Tuesday."

"So did you guys try to talk things out?" A tiny ounce of hope rose to the surface of Rachel's voice.

"No. I never texted him back."

"WHAT?!" Rachel shrieked. "Why the fuck not? What's wrong with you?!"

Sarah nearly laughed at her friend's response, it was so dramatic. *How do I make her understand this?*

She took a deep breath. "I know he doesn't feel the same way about me, Rachel. He's just hanging out with me to have someone to play with," she explained. "I'm a toy he takes out once a week, plays with, and then puts back in his toy box till next time."

"Whoa," Rachel balked at that description. "You are so far off base!" Sarah could nearly see her friend shaking her head in disagreement through the phone line.

"Whatever." The energy required to argue had been depleted. "You met him one time. What do you know?"

"I saw the way he looked at you," Rachel said. "And he didn't look at you like you were just a toy to amuse him. Trust me, there is something more there. Something deeper."

A tingle crawled up Sarah's spine. *What if I made a huge mistake?*

THAT NIGHT, despite being curled up with Pawel, Sarah's willpower lost out to the desire to broadcast The James Channel throughout her mind. She remembered the day she spent at Rachel's consoling her over the loss of Mark, who had, without much foresight, decided to abandon Rachel to pursue a relationship with "Porn Girl." Sarah knew Mark would come crawling back, and her intuitions were confirmed. Then she remembered how she left Rachel's house that day promising to guard herself against falling for any men who weren't right for her, for men who lacked the depth, maturity and stability to enter into a healthy relationship with her. *That oath sure went out the window.*

Her worst decisions in life were the result of not having a plan. Therefore, she found it crucial to always formulate a rock-solid plan. One firm tenet: *don't fall in love with jackasses.* She had made that mistake with both Abby's father and Owen's father, and although she had made a lot of progress toward recovery, she was still paying for both mistakes emotionally. Since then she had developed fond feelings for several men but had never quite jumped the hurdle to the L Word with any of them.

That's probably why it freaked me out so much to realize I had L-Word type feelings for James. He's is the wrong type of guy, isn't he?

He's young.

He's military.

He's never been married.

He doesn't have kids.

All excellent reasons to avoid serious involvement. When she first met him, one of the things that made him so appealing was that he seemed "deliciously unripe." He was so opposite of the men she typically dated that he seemed safe. But it was easy to make the leap from a physical to an emotional connection when all the right ingredients were there. *Talk about a recipe for disaster.*

THE WEEKEND IS RAPIDLY APPROACHING, she thought as she lumbered up her building's concrete steps. Her joints felt stiff —it had been a long time since she'd worked out any more intensely than hoisting a basket of laundry up the stairs. Her calendar was surprisingly free for the rest of the day, her 10 AM class being the last on the docket for the week. She could leave campus early before the nasty beltway traffic wrapped its sticky tentacles around the metro area.

She'd stashed her gym bag in her office earlier in the week when she'd vowed to make an appearance at the university fitness center. She would make that happen today, her last opportunity before the weekend. After class, she didn't even bother to check her email or voicemail. She simply snagged the bag off the chair lodged between her bookcase and filing cabinet and headed back out the door.

It was a cloudless, nondescript early December day. The trees were nearly bare, the sky almost completely colorless. *I would really prefer a more inspiring landscape,* she thought as she crossed the quad. She imaged the great mountains rising in the west. She couldn't see them of course, but she imagined them there, looming in the smoky mist at the horizon. She remembered how homesick she'd been at the beginning of the semester, wishing for her homeland, missing her mountains. She'd pushed those feelings aside so she could concentrate on the semester, but now that things were winding down, those desires were welling back inside of her.

March, she thought, *I have a conference back home in March. Three more months to go.*

She changed in the locker room, filled her water bottle, and settled herself on the elliptical overlooking the free weights. She did love to ogle the weightlifters and their rippling muscles as she felt the burn in her quadriceps, hamstrings and glutes. *Besides, the elliptical can be quite monotonous if you don't have a good distraction.*

She felt zero guilt for fixating on a particular young man whose back faced her. He had strong, well-shaped legs and a solid build. He was bent over one of the benches doing some work on his triceps. She watched his arm extending, the muscle bulging through his skin and then retreating again.

Wow, he really reminds me of James. A memory of running her fingertips down his triceps as he hovered over her, sweat beading on his forehead flashed before her eyes.

As she continued to study him, it became alarmingly clear that the object of her fixation actually *was* James. Adrenaline surged through her, activating a fight or flight response. She glanced down at the display on her machine, and she'd managed to complete exactly three minutes and twenty-eight seconds of her work out.

Shit, I can't just walk away. I'll just have to hope he doesn't turn around. Or recognize me.

She continued to examine his hindquarters, though, the memory of kneading his firm glutes as he pumped his cock deep inside her too delicious to resist. She couldn't tell if she was blushing or just flushed from her workout.

He put down his weights and moved on to a different machine, his back still turned to her. Feeling relieved—*right now in all my sweaty glory is not exactly the time I'd choose to figure out what's going on with us*—Sarah buried her nose in her magazine and continued her workout, punching the button to increase the resistance on the elliptical a couple of times for good measure.

Her phone began blinking from the little plastic holder beside her water bottle, so she unlocked her screen and went to retrieve the new text.

Unknown number: *I can see you in the mirror. Having a nice workout?*

Shit! Sarah immediately felt exposed. *Shit. Fuck. Damn. Shit.* She tried to keep her face expressionless because she knew his eyes were on her now. Her blush extended from her cheeks down onto her collarbones and breasts, spreading far beneath her sports bra and tank top. *So now what? I can't exactly ignore someone who is in the same room as me, can I?*

She found him in the mirror and smirked. He got up from the machine and made his way over to her. "Why are you ignoring me?"

"I'm not sure this is the time or place to discuss it," she replied nonchalantly.

"Oh?" He looked genuinely confused. "I guess I'm out of the loop, 'cause I thought everything was cool."

"You would," Sarah retorted, thinking about how James had just conveniently opened up his little Sarah Toy Box and wanted her to come out and entertain him. The weekend was upon them, after all. Just the thought of that made her furious.

I'm supposed to be a Friend With Benefits. Not a Toy You Play With When You Feel Like It.

He continued to stand beside her as she moved up and down on the elliptical, her grip on the handles tightening. He wore an expectant look, his blue eyes like arctic pools. "So you're really not going to talk to me?" he asked in disbelief.

"Not at the gym," Sarah replied coolly. "How much longer will you be here?"

"Thirty minutes?"

"Can you walk me back to my office?"

He nodded. He took one last look before turning to walk back to the weight machines. She finished up her workout, completely distracted by thoughts of him the entire time, took a quick shower and met him in the hallway outside the gym. As they exited the building into the colorless day, the sun struggled to peek through the strata of cool gray.

Just feeling the heat coming off his body and catching a whiff of his masculine scent was making her weak in the knees. The wild feeling he inspired in her was at once thrilling and terrifying. But she decided to just be honest with him. She really didn't know how else to be.

"The other night when you stopped by, your phone was broken, and you had to go to work," she began. He nodded in recollection. "Right, well, I don't think that's all that was going on."

He was still looking straight ahead as they crossed the quad. "Yeah," he admitted. "There was some other stuff, but it's worked out now, and it's really no big deal."

They climbed the steps to her building. *"Some other stuff,"* she repeated to herself. *"No big deal."* She was tired of his elusiveness. Maybe that's why she'd grown so frustrated and felt so trivialized. *His inability to open up is driving me crazy!*

She had already walked away from the relationship in her mind, so she would go for broke and tell him why it wasn't going to work out. She was silently plotting her words as they turned down the hallway to her office. She fished her keys out of her gym bag and fumbled with the lock while he leaned against the cement block wall and watched her through wide blue eyes.

He had never been in her office before. He took in his surroundings as he stepped inside: the full bookcases, the plants representing various stages of life and health in all sorts of different pots and containers, the walnut-framed diplomas and awards, the large colorful Van Gogh print, the velvety purple throw with amber and gold beads slung over the chair in the corner between the window and the book-case. She closed the door behind her and turned to face him, waiting for him to finish examining her space and turn his eyes toward her.

She went to deliver the speech she'd formulated, but her heart balked. She didn't want to chastise him; all she wanted to do was collapse into his arms. She needed to avoid touching him, or else her resolve would be completely destroyed.

"Look," she began, her tone reflecting her seriousness, "I know we're not in a traditional relationship, but I feel a huge disconnect when we're not together."

He appeared genuinely surprised. "What do you mean?"

"There have been so many mixed messages," Sarah explained. "When I'm with you, I feel really close to you, really connected. Then we part ways, and I feel like you compartmentalize me until you're ready to bring me out to play again. I just can't reconcile the feelings I have for you when we're together with the emptiness I feel when we're apart. Maybe you don't understand what friends with bene-fits really means?"

He reached out and took her hand, the warmth of his flesh absorbing straight into her soul as his eyes examined her. His voice was soft and yielding: "What do you want?"

She shook her head. "That's the problem. This isn't about what I want. It's about what you can give, and I really don't think you're capable or willing to give it."

His hand enveloped hers, mitigating the silence that had gathered around them. "You're the one who said you didn't want to complicate my life. I enjoy your company, Sarah, and I thought I was a good 'friend with benefits.' What did I do wrong?"

She saw his passion flare and his pupils widen, revealing his sincerity. "Maybe I was wrong about what I wanted," she admitted. "Maybe I thought I'd be more integrated into your life? I don't know what my problem is."

She squeezed his hand, unsure if this conversation could possibly close the chasm she felt. She felt a bit of her resolve returning. "When we're together, it's magic," she tried to explain again. "When we're not together, I feel like I don't even exist to you. I'm a toy you box away and only bring out when you want me. And it's my own silly fault for thinking you would want anything else with me."

Her forced brusqueness had given way to a stray tear rolling down her cheek. She'd lost the battle to stay in control. He seemed to have that effect on her.

He pulled her so close to him, her face smushed against his shoulder. He kissed the top of her head and held her tightly against his body as she surrendered to the flood of emotions that had been walled off behind her eyes. As the tears broke the dam, she could feel the fabric of his shirt growing damper as she sobbed into him. She never thought she'd let him see her so vulnerable. *Maybe he's not the only one who has put up walls.*

Finally, he lifted her chin till their eyes met again. "Sarah, you are one of the most beautiful, intelligent, amazing women I have ever met. Why in the world wouldn't I want you?"

She melted. Those were the words she needed to hear.

THE NEXT WEEKEND, on the eve of finals, she found herself lying on her bed next to Rachel, both wearing tiny red bows on each nipple with bigger red bows affixed further south. It was a surprise. James had been instructed to let himself in and come straight to the bedroom. The candles were lit, and the wine was chilling. She and Rachel were giggling like schoolgirls waiting for a boy to call on the telephone, only they were completely nude, save for the bows and red heels adorning their feet.

After James had kissed her in her office that Friday afternoon, they didn't really cover any more ground in their discussion. Instead, they'd succumbed to the fiery passion that had reignited between them, kissing and groping each other until James bent Sarah over her own desk and showed her how much he'd missed her.

A switch had flipped inside her as soon as his lips met hers—she felt euphoric. Feeling his arms around her again, and even just the simple words he expressed, were more than she'd ever hoped for.

On the other hand, maybe she'd let him off the hook too easily. All she knew for certain was that her heart had never been ready to give up on him completely.

Soon she was on the phone to Rachel conspiring about how to give James the best Christmas present ever. After all, he was leaving in just a week to visit his family back in Ohio, and her time was limited. Rachel agreed that a night with two beautiful women would be at the top of any man's Christmas wish list.

When they heard footsteps on the stairs, Sarah leaned over and dramatically put her finger to her mouth in a silent "shush," while tossing her hair back like a naughty librarian. Rachel stifled a giggle just as James turned the corner to enter the room. The sight met his eyes in flashes: dark hair, light hair, pink flesh, red lips, red bows, red shoes. It was a fantasy come to life.

"Merry Christmas to me!" he exclaimed with his trademark smirk as he eagerly climbed onto the bed and sandwiched himself between the two women. "I must have been a very good boy this year!"

"Oh, baby, quite the contrary! You have been a very naughty boy this year," Sarah cooed in her sultriest voice, playfully shaking her finger at him, "but, fortunately for you, the elf we work for rewards naughty boys, not nice ones."

"Sounds like my kinda boss." James bent to kiss Sarah's ripe red lips. Then he turned and lightly brushed his lips against Rachel's cheek. "It's nice to see you again, beautiful," he added.

In typical Rachel fashion, she gripped his chin with her shiny red manicured nails and pulled him closer, opening her mouth against his, her tongue darting between his lips.

As she went to work kissing him, Sarah began the task of clothing removal, starting with unbuttoning his pale blue oxford. She knelt behind him, her breasts and stomach pressed against his muscular back, her arms reaching around him to deftly unfasten each button.

James's hands wandered down to cup Rachel's full

breasts. He hesitated before revealing what was underneath the small red bows, taking his time to unwrap his gifts. Sarah moved on to the waistband of his pants, loosening his belt and waiting for him to shift so she could get the right angle on the button and zipper. He obliged her by standing up and sliding his pants down before returning to the bed fully nude, resuming his position in between the two bow-adorned beauties.

Rachel's eyes traveled down his beautifully built body, admiring the contours of his muscles, and, naturally, his stiff cock standing at attention, saluting them both. "I see what you mean about bodies made by Uncle Sam," she remarked, running her finger down his sternum between the two firm raised mounds of his pectorals and then down the line separating his taut, sculpted abs.

Sarah knelt over his manhood and began to lick up his shaft, watching approvingly as Rachel reached down to caress his balls. She re-positioned so they flanked him, perpendicular to his body but facing each other, their tongues running up the length of his cock in tandem, their lips meeting together over the tip. Sarah engulfed him down her throat, sliding her lips back up to the tip before surrendering him to Rachel's ravenous mouth. They continued like this, back and forth, their mouths occasionally kissing with his hardness between them, their tongues tangling around his glans.

James propped his head up on the pillows so he could watch the show. Every few moments, the changing pressure or rhythm elicited a deep groan. He began thrusting his hips up into Sarah's mouth, the muscles in his thighs tensing. Wanting to prolong the show, she slowed down, and Rachel descended so her tongue could tease his testicles. Sarah was certain Rachel's skilled tongue covered every square centimeter from where his shaft met his balls, all the way to his ass. Now James's eyes were half-closed, his head tilted back as if he'd never experienced such a state of agonizing ecstasy.

"If you don't stop," he choked out, "I'm gonna come."

Rachel's eyes flickered with a devious glint as Sarah's face brightened with a new plan. "We'll give you a tiny break," she told him and motioned for Rachel to lie down on the bed.

Sarah moved between Rachel's legs, parting her thighs and planting a trail of kisses from her knee inward toward the smooth triangle of flesh at the top. James lay beside Rachel, quickly removing all the shiny red bows and tossing them aside. As the tip of her tongue gently teased open Rachel's labia, Sarah softly sighed at the first taste of her friend's salty-sweet juices, leaving James nearly breathless as he absorbed the scene.

Sarah shifted to her knees, her dark hair falling around her face as she began to penetrate Rachel with her tongue. James inverted his body to lie on his side with his face near Sarah's so he could witness her ministrations up close and personal. He brushed her hair out of her face, gathering it into a thick ponytail while he murmured, "Good girl, good girl..."

Rachel began to writhe her hips under Sarah's mouth.

"I'm not sure this is helping me last any longer," James said with a smirk and moved again, this time directly behind Sarah. She was so wet, his cock easily found passage into her sex.

She groaned as he found the absolute depth of her, slowly stroking in and out so as not to disturb her rhythmic sucking on Rachel's clit. Slowly, until he balanced on the edge of losing control and was forced to pick up speed. Gasping, Sarah arched her back and lifted her head, the intensity of his strokes causing her to lose focus on Rachel, but her friend grabbed ahold, forcing Sarah's head down to meet her rising hips.

Rachel opened her eyes long enough to lock gazes with James, and the sight of his huge throbbing tool drilling into her best friend as her mouth worked her pussy over was evidently more than she could handle. She screamed, "Oh god, I'm going to come," and clenched Sarah's head with both of her hands while she drenched her face with her juices.

Watching Rachel's body begin to shake, James could no longer hold back. The final straw was when Sarah began to come as well, her pussy milking his cock until he had no choice but to release his seed deep inside her.

The trio of naked bodies collapsed breathlessly on the bed, James's arms outstretched so both ladies could rest their heads on his solid, muscular chest. He held them close as their breaths slowed and softened against his chest hair. No one said a word. It was too perfect of a moment.

The best part was when Sarah looked up at James's closed eyes, his features set in a state of bliss. He seemed to be in awe.

After a while, Rachel stroked up his thigh toward his cock, which was still oozing cum. She dabbed it with her finger and touched it to her lips. "Mmmm, James, you taste delicious," she broke the silence.

James smiled. "If you like it so much, you should go straight to the source."

Rachel slid down the bed. "I have a better idea." She tapped Sarah's leg to coax her into turning over, then adjusted so her chin rested on the mattress directly under Sarah's dripping pussy. She began to lap up the remnants of James's load.

"Oh fuck, that's hot," James observed, his cock beginning to swell again.

Sarah moaned softly as James stood up and leaned down

next to her on the bed, his lips close to her ear. "Can I fuck Rachel?"

Sarah nodded, her breath ragged but managing to produce a convincing "Of course."

He grabbed a condom from Sarah's nightstand drawer and rolled it onto his erection. This time he approached more gently and patiently, stroking Rachel from her blonde hair down to her rear, which he rubbed, petted and caressed for a few moments before asking if he was allowed to fuck her. She moaned, "Oh, yes, please...I want your cock inside of me," before returning her attention to Sarah's throbbing clit.

Permission granted, he began to rub the head of his cock against the opening to her sex until she was rocking back onto him, attempting to take him inside of her. A slight thrust of his hips, and Sarah opened her eyes to watch both his expression and her friend's as he buried himself balls deep inside her.

"Oh god," her mouth broke contact with Sarah's quivering sex. Sarah watched Rachel's head tilt back as James began to thrust in and out, adjusting to his thickness. Then she continued to suck the rest of his fluids out of Sarah's opening before traveling back to her clit.

James pumped away, his glutes contracting as his pelvis worked against Rachel's full, round ass. Rachel arched her back again, momentarily losing her ability to continue her oral obligations, her hips rocking back to meet James's pelvis. She slid two fingers into Sarah's wanton sex and began to fuck her hard, matching James's rhythm. When he saw Rachel's mouth was neglecting his lover's clit, he pushed her head down between Sarah's legs and held it there as he began to pound her mercilessly, her screams muffled against Sarah's slippery wet mound.

The sound and vibrations of her friend's moans against her pussy combined with the look of pure concentration of

James's face as he held himself back from his second climax were enough to send Sarah's body over the edge into orgasmic convulsions. James slowed down so Rachel wouldn't drown in Sarah's juices, holding her head back by her hair.

"I'm not done with you yet," James said as he withdrew and flipped Rachel onto her back. He entered her again, pulling her legs up onto his chest.

"Fuck, I'm still coming," Sarah moaned as she repositioned herself at Rachel's side, bending down to take each of her tender nipples, one at a time, into her mouth to suckle.

"Fuck, I'm going to come again!" Rachel announced while Sarah caressed her breasts.

Sarah slid down the bed and pressed her lips to James's, her mouth still tasting of Rachel. On her knees, her body molded to his side as he continued to bury his cock again and again in Rachel's spasming pussy.

Finally, James slowed down and commanded the girls to get ready. "I'm going to feed you my cum," he commanded.

They complied, Sarah lying down beside Rachel, leaving room so James could position himself between them. He pulled the condom off and began to stroke his cock. The girls turned toward him with their mouths open, eagerly awaiting his pearlescent nectar. His fingers slowed and squeezed, his balls visibly tightening under his throbbing shaft.

Without any more than a slight moan, his semen shot out into the space between them, each spurt hitting different facial features: cheeks, tongues, lips, and chins. When both women were virtually coated in his fluids, he backed away to watch them kiss, cleaning each other's faces and carefully ensuring that not a drop was wasted.

James sank down onto the bed again, his legs quivering as if made of jelly. "And that," he said at last, pulling both women back into his strong arms, "was the singular most wonderful night I've ever had in my entire twenty-nine years."

The three curled together savoring the delicious afterglow. "Merry Christmas, darling," Sarah whispered and sealed it with a kiss.

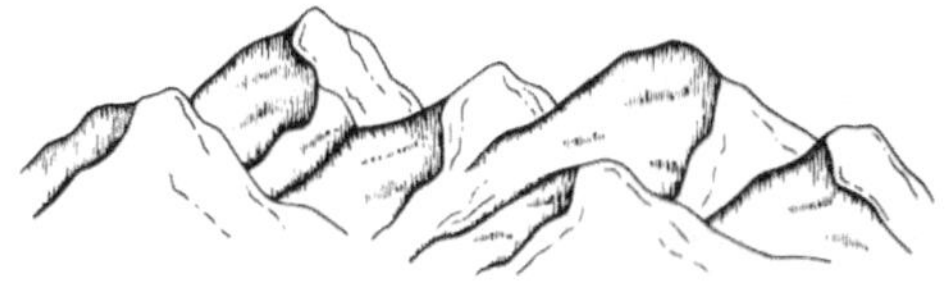

There was lots of breathing. Deep, relieved breathing. Lungs full of chilled December air, exhaled into puffs of white, quickly absorbed into the atmosphere.

Sarah couldn't imagine a crazier or more demanding semester, and it was finally over. She submitted the last of her grades to the registrar and headed home, her car loaded down with a stack of articles and books she needed to read over winter break, plus a couple of plants that wouldn't get watered during her three-week hiatus.

Her kids had already started their break and were no doubt lounging around the house in their pajamas, if they'd even managed to get out of bed. Sarah declared this first day of the holidays to be a Day of Vegetation. No real clothes. No chores. No obligations. Just eating, sleeping, and entertaining oneself.

Sarah arrived home to find Owen making himself a peanut butter and jelly sandwich in the kitchen and leaving bread crumbs all over the counter. *Guess it's not a day of no chores for me.* She sighed, brushing them off onto her hand

and then dumping them in the trash can. She tousled Owen's dark hair as he carried his sandwich and milk into the dining room and then went to see what Abby was up to.

Sarah found her pajama-clad daughter sprawled out on her bed, her laptop in front of her, completely absorbed in an instant messaging conversation with Tyler. Her grounding sentence was finally over, and so was his. She'd been in an uncharacteristically cheerful mood ever since her punishment lifted. Sarah assumed she'd be asking permission to see him soon.

Sarah grabbed the novel she'd picked up at the library and snuggled into her armchair. Out the French doors past the deck, the wind was picking up some stray leaves on the ground and swirling them around. The sun was high in the sky and gave the illusion it was warmer outside than it really was. A wistful longing for summer enveloped her as she flashed back to that night in early September, when it was still warm and muggy, climbing the stairs to the auditorium, having no clue her life would change later that night when she met James McAllister.

Her heart was full of thoughts for him. Some warm, some confusing, and some were downright troublesome to her. He'd left for Ohio just a few days before and had only texted her to let her know he made it safely.

Since then she'd had little visions of him at his parents' house. Playing with his nieces and nephews, maybe holding his newborn niece for the first time. Watching football with his dad and brothers-in-law. Eating his mother's home-cooked meals. She felt a warm, content vibe radiating eastward from him, which helped ease her disappointment at the lack of communication.

She picked up her phone and sent him a little token: *Thinking about you xo.*

How very little he would need to give to make her feel

like she was integrated into his life. Just the tiniest of gifts. A few words. She didn't need much.

After running into him at the gym, she'd introduced him to the concept of a *holistic* relationship. His lack of communication made her feel like she wasn't important to him. She hated feeling like she only existed to him when they were together, and she made it clear she wasn't asking or a commitment or any promises, just to be a whole person to him.

He laughed when she said those exact words to him. "Of course I think of you as a whole person!" he defended himself. "How else would I think of you?"

"Then act like it," Sarah instructed. "Don't send me one-word texts. Ask me how I am. Act like you care what is going on with my life."

She had a feeling the military had taught him to compartmentalize all the different aspects of his life. How else could soldiers survive deployment?

He'd nodded as if he understood. Then he questioned her about her relationship with Pawel. "So, what about that other guy?"

Sarah had stared at him blankly.

"You know the one: 'I intend to sleep with him eventually,'" he did a little impersonation of her. Sarah had to laugh at the way he over-enunciated his words and raised his pitch in an effort to sound like her.

"Ah yes," she'd replied after she got past the giggle at his impression, "Pawel." James nodded. "We are still friends, and yes, seeing each other on occasion. He is from Poland, and he'll be there over the holidays with his wife and family."

James's eyes widened. "Poland? He's married?"

Sarah sometimes had to remind herself that James was...*how do I put this without sounding elitist?* she questioned. *Unenlightened? Unexposed? Hmm...how about just...new at this?*

"He and his wife have a special arrangement when he's traveling," Sarah explained.

James had rolled his eyes. "Oh, sure they do. Come on, don't tell me you really buy that bullshit!" He laughed at her.

Sarah did not appreciate his tone. "Well, you know what? Pawel is an adult; he's almost fifty years old, and I really don't think he has any reason to lie to me, whether his MO is to get in my pants or not."

"Whatever helps you sleep at night," James replied coolly, still unconvinced.

He didn't ask if they'd consummated their relationship. How would he feel about it? Would envisioning her with another man bother him, especially considering their threesome with Rachel? *After all, what's good for the goose...*

Sarah had changed the subject by running her fingers through his hair and pulling him close to her for a kiss. Overall, he did seem a little annoyed by her seeing Pawel. *I shared my best friend with you,* she could have argued. *But I'm a lover, not a fighter!* That little thought made her puckered lips spread into a smile against his open mouth. He opened his eyes and asked what was wrong, but she quickly distracted him with kisses down his neck.

Pawel had also wanted to dissect their relationship and clarify their boundaries before leaving for Poland. *Oh, men,* Sarah thought, *they are so damn territorial.*

"I know you're poly, and you understand," he'd begun, "so you're probably not surprised to hear I have special feelings for you."

"Special feelings" seemed to be code for the L Word. She hadn't averted her eyes or reacted in any way, just waited to see what else he had to say.

"Are you still dating the Army guy?" he'd questioned, his voice wavering ever so subtly.

"Yes, we're still seeing each other," she answered. "Not exclusively, of course."

Pawel seemed to be looking for a sign, some encouragement to put himself out there, like when he'd tried to kiss her for the first time. His initial attempts were always weak until she gave him positive feedback. Then he would be emboldened. She didn't grant him any signs this time.

She enjoyed Pawel's company; he was brilliant and refined and was absolutely gifted at courting her. She always had an amazing time no matter what they did together, but that intensity, that passion she felt for James was absent. What she felt for Pawel was a very mild chemical reaction, not the fireworks she felt when she was with James.

But that's okay. Pawel was the type of man she usually dated and found they made good boyfriends, but not always the best lovers. While she loved the attention and doting she received from men like Pawel, the fiery intensity that came from more confident, secure, and yes, perhaps even aloof men such as James was so much more sexually appealing to her.

"Why do I like that so much? Do I want a challenge? Do I want someone I can't really have?" she'd asked Rachel when her best friend tried to force her to choose one man over the other—just a little game, of course.

Rachel had shrugged, her hazel eyes gleaming. "Isn't it nice that you don't have to choose?"

"Definitely," she'd agreed. "Being a free agent is the only way to go..." Her lips curled down into a frown. "And besides, even if I chose James...it's not like I could actually have him."

She would continue to be open and honest with both Pawel and James. That was the only promise she was making.

And with that final thought, she cleared her mind and cracked open her book. An unabashed bibliophile, Sarah absolutely adored the sound a new book made when the cover was first opened. Judging from the singular due date stamp in the back, she was the inaugural reader of this particular title. Settling into the first chapter, which was full of colorful, juicy description that read like a seven-course meal, she was tantalizingly absorbed in the narrative...until the doorbell rang.

Owen appeared from nowhere, running for the door and turning the handle before Sarah could get up from her chair. It was the UPS delivery driver with a small brown package. Beaming, he brought it to his mother, excitedly yelling, "What is it? What is it?"

Sarah laughed. "You'd think it was Christmas around here or something!" She turned the package over in her hands and saw it was addressed to *Dr. Sarah Lynde*. She shook it a bit, but there was no sound. She couldn't remember ordering anything, and she didn't see a return address.

She walked into the kitchen to cut the seal with a knife. After prying the tape away from the edge of the box, she opened it up to find burgundy and gold tissue paper wedged inside. She carefully unfolded the many layers, and inside was a thin silver strand with a sparkly diamond pendant in the shape of a teardrop surrounded by smaller stones.

Sarah audibly gasped. She didn't even notice that Owen had followed her into the kitchen and was standing with his mouth open, his eyes fixated on the glittering gems. "Who's it from, Mom?"

There was no accompanying note and no return address anywhere on the package. Sarah didn't know whether to be ecstatic or disturbed. *Who sends a gift with no note?* She decided she couldn't wear it until she knew who sent it, so she carefully folded the necklace back into the tissue paper and set it on top of her chest with her other jewelry.

The first thought that sprang to mind was James, but she

was certain he couldn't have sent it. They had agreed not to exchange presents, and, furthermore, a surprise of that caliber just wasn't in his character. It had to be Pawel, of course, who was en route to Poland that very moment. She sent him a text right away.

Sarah: *OMG it's beautiful! Thank you so much, darling! Have a safe trip xoxo*

Later that night, she received an email:

Dearest Sarah,

I have arrived safely in the Motherland. All seems well here. My wife has asked a lot of questions about you. I showed her your picture, and she said you are beautiful! So happy you received the necklace and like it. I can't wait to see it gracing your lovely neck.

Yours,

Pawel

SARAH WAS TRULY at a loss for words. She would have to think of a special way to express her thanks. Pawel was such a beautiful soul. She felt a bit of relief that he had told his wife about her. She assumed he had, or he would, but the conversation she'd had with James still echoed in her mind. She went to bed that night with the pendant fastened around her neck, thinking about how cherished she felt. Her heart was full of happy feelings, and she was more content than she had been in some time.

THE NEXT DAY, Sarah and Rachel took the kids into Washington DC to visit the Smithsonian museums. There was a new exhibit in the natural history museum Sarah wanted to see, and Rachel had volunteered to take the two boys over to the Air and Space building so Abby and Sarah would have time to linger over the new exhibit without two antsy ten-year-old boys asking when they would get to see the airplanes and rockets four million times.

It was a chilly morning in the nation's capital and quite the contrast to the stuffiness in the Metro. They got off at the Smithsonian stop and rode the long, steep escalator out onto the National Mall. Sarah hadn't been down to the Mall since cherry blossom time the spring before. She observed how gray and stark the monuments and Capitol looked against the cold December sky. It was a bleak, austere scene, especially in contrast to the softness of her last visit, with the frilly white and pink blossoms framed by wispy clouds under a cerulean blue sky.

Sarah and Abby crossed the Mall to the natural history museum and Rachel, Thomas and Owen headed toward the Capitol to get their air and space fix. They walked up the steps, through the security check and into the marble rotunda, circled by stately columns and reigned over by a large African elephant. The museum was celebrating its 100-year anniversary and had a special exhibit to commemorate the event. Sarah was also anxious to see the exhibit on evolution.

She and Abby lingered over those two exhibits and then made their way upstairs to the gems and minerals, which were Abby's favorite collection. She ooohed and ahhhed over the Hope Diamond and some of the other jewels, which reminded Sarah that she was wearing her pendant from Pawel and had completely forgotten to tell Rachel about it. She wasn't sure about showing it to Rachel and confessing

Pawel sent it with their mixed company—it might be better to wait until they were alone.

Sarah and Rachel texted to make lunch plans and settled on a restaurant a few blocks away on Pennsylvania Avenue. Once everyone was seated, Owen announced in a bubbly voice, "Hey, Rachel, did you see the necklace my mom got in the mail yesterday?"

Sarah's cheeks erupted with a light pink flush. *Leave it to Owen to spill the beans.* The pendant was tucked under her sweater, but in a microsecond, Rachel reached across the table and lifted it out to put it on display. "Oh my god, Sarah, that's absolutely gorgeous! Who gave it to you?!"

"Pawel sent it before he left for Poland," Sarah answered calmly, nonchalantly, as if she received precious gems from men every day.

Rachel's eyes widened, but she seemed to get the hint that further conversation on this topic needed to be out of earshot of the kids. After lunch, she grabbed Sarah's arm and almost dragged her to the ladies' room while Abby begrudgingly kept an eye on the boys and listened to one too many fart jokes.

"What does this mean?" Rachel demanded as soon as they were in private...or as private as a public restroom could be.

Sarah shook her head. "It means nothing. He's just being generous. It's the way he is. He's married, you know."

"Do you wish it was from James?" Rachel always knew right where to slice.

"James will never buy me a necklace," Sarah replied, refusing to answer the question. *On the grounds that it is so ridiculous.*

Rachel smirked. "You are so fucking lucky. Men never buy me jewelry," she complained with an exasperated sigh. And with that, they went to rescue Abby from the pre-pubescent male humor she'd been subjected to for the preceding five minutes.

I am lucky, Sarah thought as she collected her things. *I hope I never forget how lucky I am.*

THE NEXT DAY Sarah drove to BWI airport to pick up her brother Adam, who was flying in from Seattle for the holidays. Their mother and the kids were waiting at home, cooking up Adam's very favorite meal. "For a gay guy, I sure suck at cooking," he always joked. He didn't get to see his mother and sister often, but when he did, he very much relished their culinary expertise.

Sarah waited in the cell phone lot for Adam's call. Sure enough, at 12:07 on the dot her phone rang.

The deep voice of her baby brother came through on the other line, "Hi, I can tell I switched coasts. I feel a little disoriented!"

Sarah laughed too. "I'll be right there!"

The security guard was shooing the pair away from the curb after a prolonged *Welcome to Maryland* hug. This was Adam's first trip to visit his mom and sister since they'd moved for Sarah's job. She stepped away and took a good look at him: taller than she remembered, same old flannel shirt, maybe a few pounds heavier, and he'd let his hair grow out. "Oh god, Adam, you have a beard? What's up with that?"

Adam nearly blushed. "A certain someone happens to like

the scruffy mountain man look!" he gushed as he climbed into Sarah's Toyota.

Sarah drove away amid a nasty stare from the guard who'd shooed them. "A certain someone? Oh, for fuck's sake, you don't need to be all elusive with me!"

Adam laughed again. Sarah loved his laugh; he bellowed deep from his diaphragm, like he was expelling gold. She'd missed that laugh so much since she'd moved out east. She hadn't seen Adam for a year now. They'd gone back to Colorado to visit him for the holidays the previous year, but since then he'd moved to Seattle for a new job, and apparently had acclimated quite well to the Pacific Northwest.

"Okay, okay," Adam relented. "His name is Brandon, and he's twenty-seven and gorgeous. He's a software engineer. We just moved in together!"

"Oh my god, Adam, that's awesome!" She was beaming with happiness for her little brother, but a little taken aback that he had yet to say anything during their long phone conversations. "I can't believe you didn't tell me, though! I trust you'll share pictures when we get back to my house. Why didn't he come with you?"

"Well, we talked about it, and he wanted to go see his family in Cali, and, of course, I wanted to see you guys. We thought this year we should go see our families separately, and next year maybe we can go together," Adam explained. "There is one problem on his end, though."

"What's that?" Sarah had a feeling she already knew.

"He's not really out to his family yet."

Sarah could hear the disappointment in his voice, and, glancing over, even in the fraction of a second her focus left the highway, she could see it in his dark eyes.

They caught up on Adam's life, and Sarah heard probably more than she ever wanted to about Brandon. Even though there was a bit of wistfulness that they couldn't be as open as

Adam would like, Sarah still got the impression he was very happy. They pulled into her driveway, and the kids and Kathy ran out to meet him. Soon Adam was covered in Lyndes and one Taylor, all embracing their favorite son, brother, uncle.

That night at dinner, Sarah's feeling of gratitude was so immense, it swelled up inside her like a dam about to burst. *My family may be small,* she thought, imagining James gathered around a huge table with his parents, sisters and their families, *but it's totally awesome.*

ON CHRISTMAS MORNING, Sarah glanced at the alarm clock and was surprised to see the green numbers read 7:04. *Since when do my kids sleep this late on Christmas morning?* They had been up late the night before playing board games with her, her mom and Uncle Adam. *Maybe this means they are growing up,* she thought with a bittersweet twinge. She grabbed her phone off the nightstand and saw she had three texts.

Pawel: *Merry Christmas, sweetheart! Going to call you later! *kisses**

Rachel: *OMG!!!! Big news! Might drop by after the kids open presents.*

James: *Merry Xmas! :-)*

She replied in the order she received them:

To Pawel: *Same to you darling! Talk to you soon xoxo*

To Rachel: *Wow, sounds exciting! Come over whenever!*

To James: *Merry Christmas, handsome. I'll call you later. Xoxo*

Well, James is sending texts with emojis, she observed. *I guess that's a step in the right direction.* She shifted her focus to wondering what was going on with Rachel as she made her way downstairs. Stirring from the upstairs bedrooms filtered into her ears. The house felt cold, so she turned up the thermostat and headed into the kitchen to start the coffee.

That was when she heard the thunder of ten- and fifteen-year-old feet thumping down the wooden stairs. "You two sound like a herd of elephants!" Sarah exclaimed, glad to see the happy and expectant grins of her children appearing in the kitchen.

"Is it time yet?" Owen prodded.

"We need to wait for Uncle Adam and Grandma," Abby admonished her brother, and Sarah nodded. Owen ran off to see if Uncle Adam was still asleep on the futon in the den.

Kathy wandered in just as Owen ran out. Abby threw her arms around her grandmother and kissed her cheek. "Merry Christmas, Grandma!"

"Merry Christmas to you, pretty girl!" Kathy returned her kiss. She grabbed a mug from the cabinet and waited for the coffee pot to fill. Sarah was busy putting some cinnamon rolls in the oven and unloading the dishwasher.

Owen returned in minutes with a bleary-eyed Uncle Adam in tow. "We're ready!" Owen shouted excitedly and dragged Sarah's brother out into the living room. Kathy and Sarah filled their coffee mugs and joined the children in the living room as well.

Watching everyone open their presents, it seemed like Sarah was observing from a spot on the ceiling, not really in the moment as an active participant. Christmases had been hard since her divorce—she had too long retained that idyllic vision of a traditional family, complete with mother, father, daughter, son, something out of a Norman Rockwell painting. *I'm never going to have that again. Actually, I never had that with Daniel either.* She had no idea where all the nostalgia was coming from, but it wasn't welcome.

An hour later, Sarah was cleaning up the aftermath when the back door handle twisted. Sarah heard Rachel's bright voice call out, "Merry Christmas, everyone!" Thomas had an arsenal of nerf guns sticking out of a backpack strapped to his posterior.

Rachel was glowing. *Christmas spirit?* She glanced down at her friend's left hand and saw the source of her glow immediately.

"Nothing gets by you," Rachel laughed, noticing Sarah's attention was already drawn to her finger. "Jack proposed!"

Sarah squealed, "Oh my god, Rachel! That's wonderful!" She took her friend's hand into her own and bent to inspect the diamond solitaire set in white gold with three ruby baguettes arranged like flower petals jutting out from each side. "Wow, it's stunning!"

"Mark your calendar now," Rachel warned. "We're getting married in Colorado in June!"

Sarah was overwhelmed. Rachel had known Jack for less than three months. She couldn't believe they were close enough to already be talking marriage. *I've known James for at least a month longer,* Sarah considered, *and I can't imagine even saying the L Word, let alone the M one.*

But she was happy for Rachel. Jack was a good man and such a step up from Mark. *I guess they worked out those problems that we discussed on Black Friday.*

Sarah took a deep breath and pushed thoughts of James out of her mind. "So, I'm the maid of honor, right?"

Rachel threw her arms around Sarah. "Don't be ridiculous! Of course you are! And I'm making you wear a pink dress with poufy sleeves," she joked.

Sarah laughed, trying to imagine Rachel choosing anything pink or frilly. Her pick was much more likely to be revealing and slinky, maybe in red or deep purple. "Wow, you only have six months. I guess we better start planning. So, Colorado, huh?"

"Yes, in the Springs," Rachel replied, which was where her family was from. "I want to get married in Garden of the Gods."

Two trips home in the coming year. She wouldn't even have a chance to get homesick between the two trips! The thought of seeing her mountains instantly made her smile. She grasped Rachel's hand and squeezed. "What an incredible Christmas this has been!"

12

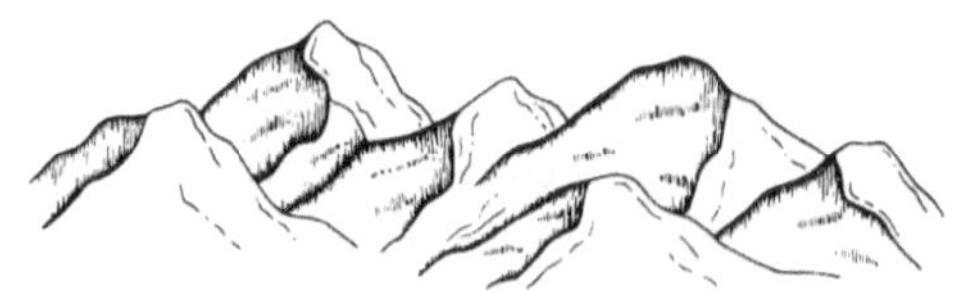

James had issued Sarah a raincheck for the dinner at his house that never came to fruition. On New Year's Eve, she decided to cash it in. He'd just returned from Ohio, and she was missing him fiercely.

Fiercely is not too strong a word. Too many nights now she'd lain in her empty bed feeling such a deep longing, it was like a vacuum in her soul. And it wasn't Pawel she was thinking about on those lonely nights, although she missed him for different reasons. Her longing had a trigger—and it was James. There were times she'd toss herself from one side of the bed to the other, abruptly awakened by a flash in her memory: him hovering over her…the way his long eyelashes kissed his cheeks when he slept…or the cleft of his spine delineated between the hemispheres of his muscular back.

On her drive to his house in Laurel, she had plenty of time to think. It was a thirty-minute trek. She couldn't believe she hadn't seen him for two weeks. She spoke to him on the phone on Christmas, and that conversation still echoed in her mind, particularly the part where she shared that Rachel and Jack got engaged.

"Wow," he'd remarked, then fell silent. Sensing his discomfort with the topic, she changed the subject quickly.

"How's your newborn niece? Did you hold her?"

James had laughed, the tension instantly defused. "Oh, she's really cute. Doesn't do much yet at this age. I held her for a minute, and my sister took a picture."

Sarah envisioned his strong hands cradling a tiny baby. "Oh, I want to see!"

Her GPS said she was getting close. As much as they'd revealed about themselves, she still hadn't shared very much with him about her children. *Does he think of me as a mother?* The whole MILF fantasy didn't seem to be his thing —after all, he rarely mentioned her children. Was that part of the compartmentalization? She was just Sarah the Sex Goddess—and he had called her that—and perhaps Dr. Lynde, the sociologist. But the other huge part of her identity was motherhood.

The night was cold and drizzly, with temperatures right on the verge of freezing, but not quite cold enough to push the rain over the edge to solid precipitation. The car had gotten all toasty warm just in time for her to venture out into the brutal elements. She slowed down, reading the house numbers and searching for the right driveway, very nearly missing her turn. Her night vision was failing her, the black pavement was so shiny and reflecting.

Squinting, she started to wish she'd worn her glasses. *Maybe I need a stronger prescription.* She was momentarily blasted with feelings of self-consciousness. *Fuck, I'm getting old!* In the back of her mind, anxiety lurked. *What in the world does a man like James see in me?*

Her mother said she'd keep the kids as long as Sarah wanted, but she'd insisted she only needed the one night. The prospect of having a whole weekend with James had a powerful effect on her body. *Would he think I'm overstaying my welcome if I didn't leave right away tomorrow?*

The damp, cool night air was saturated with promise. The thick layer of clouds concealed the moon and stars, but she wished on an invisible star anyway just as she heard him unlock the door. It was sheer moments before she was caught up in his arms, him bending down slightly, his breath on her neck as he whispered, "I missed you..."

This. This is what I needed.

He tenderly stroked her cheek and brushed his lips against hers, his other hand still encircling her waist. After several seconds, he pulled back, and she had another look at him, her eyes tracing a line from his face, across his broad shoulders and down his front. He was wearing sweatpants and a t-shirt. He was also barefoot. *I guess he feels comfortable not dressing up for me at this point.*

He led her into the kitchen, where there was an assortment of pots and pans all steaming and sizzling away. "What are we having?"

"Stir fry," he replied. "And there's a pie in the oven."

Wow. James McAllister makes pie? Homemade pie? Surely not.

"Everything smells delicious!" Sarah reassured him as she took in her surroundings.

She felt like she was studying a wild animal's natural habitat. The kitchen was tidy, almost clinically so; she noted the cutting board already soaking in the sink. She peered through the opening to the living room and the first thing she saw were books, zillions of books.

She transitioned through the archway and surveyed the living room: a recliner, a loveseat covered with an antique-looking afghan, and books. The idyllic scene was warmed by the amber glow of a lamp on the end table. There were books on shelves and books on the coffee table. There were books stacked in the corner and beside the loveseat and floor lamp. Her eyes grew wide at the sheer numbers of volumes.

James had followed her and was grinning at her reaction. "I like to read," he explained in his classic, understated way.

"I see that." *I clearly underestimated his nerdy side.* She scanned the titles. Lots of science fiction. Some fantasy. Tons of nonfiction: politics, history, a huge collection of Civil War and WWII, biographies, scientific-type stuff.

She turned around to see him still smiling. *He looks like such a jock.* She admired the outline of his chest muscles pressing against the cotton fabric of the t-shirt. *So much more than meets the eye.*

"All these books," she confessed, laughing, "these are making me wet. Did you set this up just to seduce nerdy chicks?"

James laughed and shook his head. "No, I genuinely like to read. I don't watch TV except sports and movies. I really prefer reading."

Who knew that James McAllister would turn out to be a pie-baking intellectual? The man is full of surprises.

James headed back into the kitchen, and Sarah heard the clattering of china as he withdrew plates from the cupboards. She looked over a few more titles, then peeked around the corner down the hallway. There were three closed doors. *Two bedrooms and a bathroom.*

"Hey, Sarah," he called from the kitchen. "What do you want to drink?"

She loved the way her name sounded in his deep but soft voice. She crossed back into the kitchen and eyed the wine glasses on the counter. "Ah, you know me too well," she smiled. "Why even ask?"

He uncorked the bottle and began to pour a generous glass of Riesling, her favorite.

James's stir fry was surprisingly good: spicy, but not too

spicy. Sarah had to keep reminding herself to slow down and savor the meal because all she could think about was skipping ahead to the part where she was running her fingers over his chest muscles and her tongue up his shaft. But he was extraordinarily relaxed and conversant, like he sensed her urgency and wanted to make her wait for him.

Later he led her to his bedroom and they lay on their sides on his bed facing each other, continuing the conversation from the dining table. James was finishing up his tales of the holiday and his trip to Ohio.

"So where's this photo of you and the baby?"

"Oh, right. Here it is." He took out his phone and showed her the picture of him holding his newborn niece, the tiny pink bundle cradled in his strong, massive arms. Sarah had never seen a sweeter picture. *There is something so moving about seeing strength subdued, harnessed into a gentle tenderness.*

"Oh, you'll make such a great daddy someday," Sarah remarked, her eyes a little glassy after seeing the picture.

James beamed. "I hope so."

His eyes were a little distant. Sarah had wanted to tear his clothes from his limbs the moment she saw him, but the tone had changed. She saw an opening. "So why is it you've never married and started a family?"

James hesitated, looking away for a moment before meeting Sarah's expectant gaze. "I was married a long time ago."

Sarah internally gasped. She had known James for five months. *How can I just be learning this?*

"Well," he began, "I went to Alabama for boot camp fresh out of high school, and that's where I met her. She followed me to Florida for EOD school."

Sarah's eyebrows rose. "EOD?"

"Explosive Ordnance Disposal," James explained. "I was there for nine months, then I got orders for Iraq." He paused, searching for the right words. "I kind of freaked out, to tell you the truth. All I could think about was not coming home. And even if I did, not having someone to come home to."

Sarah could feel the tension growing in his voice as he struggled to stabilize his pitch. She felt the memories creeping up on him, threatening to ambush. "So you married some chick from Alabama?"

He nodded. "Her name was Becca. She was very cute, very manipulative, and very crazy."

Sarah laughed at his description. "How so?"

"She was insanely jealous. I'm off fighting a war, and her only real concern was whether or not I was fucking anybody else. 'Cause, you know, a Middle Eastern war zone is the best place to pick up chicks." He shook his head and sighed.

"Oh!" he exclaimed, a memory snagging hold. "How about this for crazy: she stopped taking her birth control pills so she could try to get pregnant without me knowing! Fortunately, that didn't work."

"Oh my god, James, really?" Sarah asked, incredulous. "And you still married her?"

James shook his head. "Hey, I was nineteen years old. Give me a break."

Sarah could see that talking about Becca had riled up some other memories. His hands were just slightly trembling as his eyes searched the wall behind her. She instinctively placed her palm on his knee and squeezed, hoping he wouldn't clam up, hoping he'd feel her trust.

"So what happened?" she asked softly, hoping she could get him to continue opening up.

His limbs stiffened under her hand as the memories rocked through him like an earthquake. "It's a pretty long story." He bristled, like he was unsure he wanted to expend emotional energy in reliving tales of his deployment.

Sarah didn't want to make him uncomfortable, but she

couldn't help but push just a little. He was on the verge, right on the edge of letting his guard down, showing her his vulnerable side. "You don't have to tell me if you don't want to," she assured him, "but I would like to hear about your experiences over there. I've never heard about war first-hand...and, well, I think it would really help me understand you."

If you want to be understood, she added silently, realizing a man like James—who was so capable of compartmentalizing a person—was probably even more adept at compartmentalizing feelings and memories. *His response will tell me a lot about his trust in me and his willingness to invest in our relationship.* Her heart was pounding realizing how pivotal of a moment it was.

He nodded and breathed deeply. She could almost see the box marked "Iraq" open up in his mind. "I had a couple of close calls," he shared, looking away again, "and I lost some friends."

She squeezed his knee, and when he turned toward her, his eyes had illuminated, glistening with emotion as he began to spill the contents of that box at her feet.

"I saw a lot of the country during my time over there, but most of it was spent in the north around Mosul. This was the area where many foreign fighters came through and was also a main corridor for smuggling weapons. One of my responsibilities was to detonate weapons caches that were discovered."

Sarah tried to listen neutrally, but her eyes were growing too wide to disguise her concern. She repositioned herself slightly so they were no longer touching and pretended she was hearing the story from a stranger. Thinking about him...*fighting a war...at age nineteen...my god.* She couldn't even fathom how scared he must have been.

"One night I was called out to detonate a cache that was

buried under the floor of a house where IEDs were being made. The bad guys knew the weapons would be detonated if found, so they started to booby trap the weapons caches. One of the less experienced guys asked to go in my place. He was full of piss and vinegar, very ideological and patriotic." James smiled as he conjured up the image of his fellow soldier. "Yup, that was Will. He'd take a hill singlehandedly with only a Swiss army knife if asked to do so."

Sarah smiled hesitantly, but inside she was afraid of where this story was headed. She urged him on with her eyes —she could feel his energy bubbling up, needing release, like these words had a need to be spoken.

He continued, "It was a small cache, and I was nearing the end of my tour so I agreed to let him go. So Will gets to the site, and, probably due to his excitement and lack of experience, he ends up setting off the booby trap. The trap was likely designed just to harm the person entering, but the bad guys aren't exactly experts. They can be really unpredictable."

He shook his head for a moment, his eyes fading into the distance, transporting his brain back to the desert. "In some ways, that's really the most dangerous type of enemy. The small explosion ended up setting off the rest of the cache, which consisted of the material equivalent to two VBIEDs designed to take out Iraqi Police checkpoints."

Sarah shrugged at the unfamiliar acronym. "Vehicle-Born Improvised Explosive Devices," he explained.

She nodded in understanding. *Is the story over?* He had drifted away—maybe she'd lost him.

He finished his story matter-of-factly, "Will died. His folks were really religious. There weren't enough of his remains to send home, so they couldn't have a proper burial."

Tears stung at her eyes thinking of a mother who would never see her son again, dead or alive. She couldn't watch war movies or witness other tragic events portrayed because the emotion would well up inside her so strongly, wrenching her heart, overwhelming her. She didn't have that switch others did, the one that could shut off the effects of tragedies that were not their own realities.

"Another kid was badly injured but lived for a while, and a third, who was the first to respond to the blast and tried to pull Will out...well, they both ended up dying from inhalation of chlorine gas. Chlorine is an additive sometimes used in IEDs—cheap, plentiful and deadly," he explained, his voice unwavering.

Sarah was wiping away the tear that had slipped down her cheek. "It could have been you," she said so softly it was a whisper.

He nodded. "It was supposed to be simple. Textbook." He shook his head again. "But over there, things have a way of getting complicated."

"Are you okay?"

"Yeah," James answered, "of course. It's my job. It's what I signed up for. I have to be okay. Although if I'd been there, I would have probably gotten the job done right...because I had more experience...but it's just the way it worked out."

He looked calm again, the sad memories having evaporated. "Other shit happened while I was there for that deployment, and I did another tour a few years after that. But Will sticks out in my mind, I guess because I still see his face sometimes. And if it hadn't been only a month till I came home, I probably would have gone in his place."

She wasn't entirely convinced he had come to terms with it all, but she wanted to know more. "So what happened when you got home?"

James laughed. "Well, what do you think happened?" The tension from his earlier story had fully dissipated. "That fucking bitch I was married to, the one who was so afraid of me looking at some burqa-wearing Iraqi woman, had gone and gotten herself knocked up. And, no, it wasn't mine."

"Really?"

"Yeah, some nerve, huh? I'm off fighting a war, and she's home fucking everything with two legs and a dick. So, uh, yeah, we divorced."

He was quiet again for a moment, as if he were still processing all he had shared. "You know, I grew up that year. I got married; I went off to war; I saw some buddies get blown up, and I came home to a cheating bitch and got divorced. It was like a whole lifetime of living condensed into one year." He smirked and placed his hand on Sarah's thigh. "After that, everything else seems pretty damn easy."

She'd had some pretty tumultuous years in her life too: getting pregnant right before college graduation, trying to care for a newborn and work full-time, her first year of grad school, and she'd had her own experience with cheating spouses. *We're both survivors. We just had a moment of understanding.*

Sarah stretched back out beside him, placing her head on his chest again. He wrapped his arm around her instinctively. *This explains a lot. Why he seems older than his age. Why he's so elusive. Why there seems to be a barrier. Why it was hard to let me in.*

They lay there for a little bit in silence, their bodies meshing before Sarah lost all track of time. Finally, she looked over at the clock on his nightstand, and it read 12:37 in bold red numbers. They had missed ringing in the New Year, the Ball Drop, the kiss at midnight. *Oh well,* she thought, *I'm here with him, and every moment feels like the stroke of midnight on New Year's Eve.*

SHE PEELED AWAY the covers and perched on her knees between his legs. The expression painted on his face was one of blissful slumber, but a body part further south had already begun to stir. It had not escaped her notice under the thin sheet that loosely shrouded his hips and thighs. She moved the fabric aside and stretched before him, bowing to his rising manhood, which was beginning to wave, a little more than semi-stiff with morning wood.

She brushed the edges of her lips against the tip and felt it instantly swell against her soft skin. She took the head into her mouth as her fingers gently caressed between his legs and around his balls. Soon his shaft was rigid, and she slid her mouth down it, feeling it glide to the back of her throat.

She glanced up to see if his expression had changed. His eyes remained closed; his arms were stretched above his head, highlighting the definition of the muscles in his shoulders. The only thing that had changed was that his breathing had grown a little heavier.

Now that his cock was hard and ready, she straddled him, a thigh on either side of his hips. "James, are you awake, darling?"

He murmured something that was a cross between a moan and a groan.

"Can I fuck you?" She reached between her legs, her fingers dexterously encircling his throbbing cock. She teased it against the opening of her sex and gasped at discovering her slit was already dripping with desire, ripe and wanton for him. She'd been waiting to feel him inside her again for two weeks now.

"Mmmmm," he moaned in affirmation, and she watched his fingers clench the sheets on either side of him.

She guided the head inside and then very slowly slid her pelvis down to take him deep inside her. She started to rotate her hips, grinding against him ever so slowly at first, her breasts just barely brushing the prickly stubble on his chin with each thrust downward. She moaned at the sensation of the rough hair against her nipples, then gripped the metal headboard as she began to slam her pelvis down to meet his more forcefully.

He let a gasp escape as his cock was fully engulfed by her warmth, and intermittently a moan would find its way from his lips. Her orgasm built steadily as she sat almost straight up, perched on his cock, her palms bracing her weight against his muscular chest. She watched his eyes twitch a bit under his eyelids, noticing how long his lashes looked brushing against his cheek. She ran her fingers through his hair, pulling his mouth to her breast. Instinctively, his lips parted and sucked her nipple inside, raking his teeth against its firmness.

Without warning, he bit down, and the intense spike of pain reverberated through her core, driving her completely over the edge and sending her pussy into strong spasms around his cock. She suspended her motion to feel each contraction squeeze his shaft, and with each one, she let out a soft, "Oh my god, oh my god," the exclamations becoming further and further apart as the climactic waves gradually faded.

She finally opened her eyes to witness a smile curling his lips, though his eyes remained closed.

She dismounted his still-hard cock and slid back down his body to inspect it. It was coated in white cream from her pussy, which her tongue tingled at the prospect of tasting. She cleaned up his cock thoroughly, taking it deep into her mouth to get every drop of her juices just as he lazily opened his eyes to say, "Good morning..."

"I don't want to go home," Sarah whispered, not knowing if he was really awake enough to hear her.

He drew her close to his body again, burying her face in his chest hair. "So don't."

AFTER DOZING for another hour or so, this time James woke first. He reached over and smoothed Sarah's hair away from her face and stroked a finger down her cheek. "Sleep well?"

"Mmmmm," Sarah moaned, turning over to face him. "I did. It's so nice waking up next to you."

James smiled. "So...coffee? Breakfast? What is on tap for you today?"

Sarah shrugged. "No real plans. How about you?"

"Hoping to fuck you again directly," James admitted, winking at her.

Sarah laughed. "I think I can hang around for that."

"You can stay as long as you'd like," James offered generously and ran his hand along her thigh, across her stomach and up to her breasts where he tweaked her nipple between his fingertips. Sarah felt the energy surge through her body, traveling from her head and her toes toward her core at lightning speed. "You are incredibly responsive," he observed. "I love it." His hand stroked down her stomach, teasing his way toward her sex, which was beginning to throb in anticipation of his touch. He stopped short, and she sighed with disappointment.

He chuckled at her reaction, but then his normal intensity returned, and soon his eyes were bearing down on her as he moved between her legs. She felt his stiff cock press against her thigh as his mouth grazed on the flesh where her neck met her shoulder. She shuddered beneath his weight, yearning to feel his cock sliding into her. She really hoped he wasn't going to torment her too badly. He didn't orgasm during the earlier episode...*so hopefully he feels a sense of urgency*.

As if reading her mind, James shifted his pelvis, repositioning his cock so it pressed against her labia, parting them slightly and slowly easing its way inside her. Once he felt the resistance diminish, he pushed more forcefully, and she gasped as her body struggled to accommodate him.

"You are so fucking tight," he remarked, slowly withdrawing and then thrusting into her again.

"Mmmmhmmmm," Sarah moaned breathlessly. "That's 'cause you didn't warm me up properly first!"

"Well, I'm sorry you're just too alluring to resist, lying there all half-asleep. I had to have you. And besides, didn't you get warmed up an hour or two ago when you practically raped me?" James questioned, then picked up his speed, leaving Sarah too breathless to answer.

"It's my turn now," he added, beginning to drill into her faster and deeper.

He had rendered her speechless. She grabbed his ass and ground her hips into his thrusts, feeling the pressure on her clit and causing her orgasm to build. He tensed just then, slowing momentarily as if trying to hold back his release but quickly realizing it wasn't possible.

"Oh, god, Sarah," he apologized, unable to control himself

any longer, which was enough to drive her over the edge as well, precipitating an explosion that reverberated through her body in intense spasms that milked his cock, draining him of all his seed.

Later, after a long, hot shower together, she picked up the phone to call her mother. She was feeling so giddy with all the endorphins and adrenaline pumping through her veins from their earlier romps that her mother almost didn't recognize her voice.

"What's wrong?" Kathy Lynde questioned, concern evident in her tone.

"Nothing's wrong, Mom. I just wondered if I might get a little more time away?"

"Oh," Kathy replied, relieved. "Are you with James?"

"Yes, I am," Sarah admitted, a sheepish grin on her face. She felt a little guilty asking for more time away from her kids. This was the part of motherhood she found most challenging: balancing her own needs against those of her children. The latter always won out. But she'd been with them for the entirety of Christmas Break, she knew she shouldn't feel bad about having some adult time.

"Oh, good, honey, that's fine! You haven't had more than a single night away from the kids in ages," came her mother's reply. "Why don't you just pick them up tomorrow afternoon?"

"Oh, thank you, Mom, that would be great." Sarah looked at James with a wide smile on her face and flashed him a thumbs-up sign.

"So, how long can I have you?" he asked, pulling her into his arms.

As long as you want me. "Till tomorrow afternoon."

James grinned and pulled her into the kitchen to go over their lunch options. The rest of the day was a whirlwind. They went for a hike on the frozen tundra of a nearby park.

They picked up groceries for dinner, and it was now Sarah's turn to show off her culinary skills, settling on lasagna, which upon tasting, he was duly impressed. When the sun set on the first day of the new year, she found herself curled up with her head on his lap on the sofa, surrounded by his plethora of books.

He sighed, running his fingers through her dark tresses, untangling the knots that came from hiking in the cold January wind. "This has been nice."

"Very nice," Sarah agreed. *This feels like a moment, a moment for us to discuss where we are. I want to be bold. To ask for what I want.*

"What's up?" Maybe he sensed the wheels turning in her head.

"Well," Sarah started, choosing her words carefully, "I guess I'm a little confused."

"Oh yeah? Why's that?" He barely moved, his words were smooth and calm.

"I don't really understand what we are," she admitted, a tiny voice urging her on while a stronger one told her she was making a mistake rocking the boat.

James didn't miss a beat. "Well, we are *homo sapiens...* I am of the male variety, and you, the female." He laughed.

Sarah sighed. *I didn't realize he was going to make a joke out of this.* "How do you think of me?"

James stiffened and sat up, forcing Sarah to rise as well. She scooted to the other end of the couch and pulled her knees up, wrapping her arms around her legs and pulling them in close to her body. He was clearly uncomfortable; the humor had faded and was replaced with ambivalence. Her heart was pounding in her chest as she instantly regretted saying anything at all.

Why can't I just leave well enough alone?

"I don't know what you mean, Sarah. I think of you as a

friend. And a lover." His whole demeanor had changed in a flash.

Patience, she chided herself. *Don't make him get defensive.*

"I feel really close to you sometimes, James," she confessed. "I've started thinking of you as a big part of my life. But when I think about you, when I talk about you...I just don't know what kind of label to give you. I don't know where our boundaries are."

He looked at her, his eyes softening, and pulled her hand into his. "I thought you didn't do labels."

There were a few awkward beats of silence while *that* L Word hung in the air. But it wasn't the L Word Sarah had been toying with.

And then: "Why do you need a label? We enjoy each other's company. Why do we need anything else?" he questioned, the sharp edges shaved off his voice.

It made no sense. She'd told him she didn't want a label or any commitments, and now here she was defying her own words. "I'm a sociologist," Sarah rebutted, scrambling for some sort of logic when she knew everything in her heart was completely illogical. "It's my job to define relationships and social interactions. I can't help it."

I can't help it, alright. That much was true.

"I see," came his reply.

She could see him accept defeat; his shoulders fell. He was going to have to talk about his feelings. *I bet he thought after last night's conversation, he was off the hook for a while. But seeing that glimpse only made me crave more of him. And not his body. His heart.*

"I'm sorry," she apologized. "I'm not trying to pressure you or upset you in any way. I just want to know where you see us...where I fit into your life." She searched his eyes for some sort of understanding, a portal into his heart. "I thought it was a fair question... After all, I've known you almost five months now."

He leaned in toward her and ran a finger through her hair, tucking it behind her ear. "I care a lot about you, Sarah."

She sensed a "but."

He stood up and crossed to the other side of the room, facing the fireplace, his back to her. "I'm just at a different place in my life right now than you are. I'm not ready to settle down at the moment...but someday I hope to meet a woman I can fall in love with and start a family." His voice trailed off. "You know, the American Dream."

The facetiousness was back in his trademark smirk. *So easy to deflect seriousness with humor.*

She remained seated, motionless. *This is what I expected him to say.* "I'm not asking you for anything like that," she explained. "I just want to know how I fit into your life. Where you see this going."

"Oh. I didn't mean to jump to conclusions."

She stood and walked to him, putting her arms around his waist and leaning against his back, her head almost reaching his shoulder. "I feel a strong connection with you is all," Sarah said wistfully, "and I enjoy having you in my life. I don't want what we have to end. I know we don't have any strings or commitments, but—I don't want to lose what we have, either."

He turned toward her and pulled her into his arms. "I'm not going anywhere," he promised. "Don't worry."

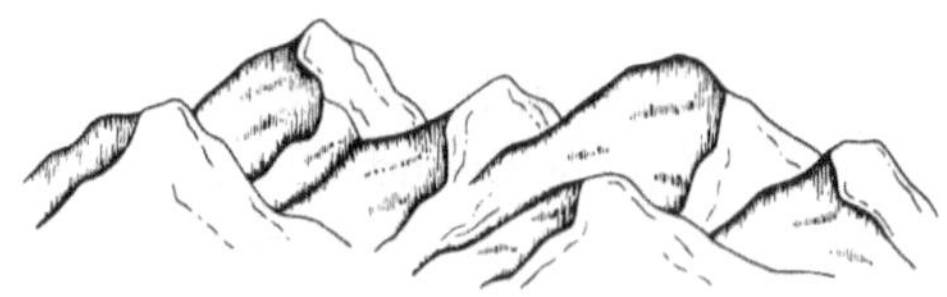

13

It had been an excruciatingly long day of wedding dress shopping. Sarah's feet hurt, and her nerves were frazzled. She envied Abby being at the house watching two pre-adolescent boys despite the accompanying gross humor, not to mention foul odors, she would endure. Kathy Lynde, acting as the honorary Mother of the Bride, as the real one was hundreds of miles away, was usually Miss Congeniality, but even she had lost her patience by the end of the day. The only person who still seemed to have any energy left at all was Rachel. *And it's not exactly a positive energy,* Sarah observed.

The ladies did manage to agree on a Japanese place for dinner and spread out comfortably around the table. Sarah was the first to break the silence. "So, we've covered every bridal shop in Baltimore; does that mean DC is next?"

"There are a few places in Annapolis," Rachel replied with more than a hint of exasperation. "Is it just me or was that sales lady at the last shop a total bitch?" She had a talent for delivering expletives in an even louder volume than her normal speaking voice, and usually just as the waitstaff was making their rounds. The petite Asian server who was about to take their order turned and scurried back to the kitchen at the utterance of the "B word" like a mouse running away from a cat.

"Well, you just scared off the waitress," Sarah laughed, trying to inject a bit of mirth into the tense mood that had wrapped its tentacles around the table.

"I don't care what that hideous cow said, I'm not ordering a dress that big," Rachel continued, unfazed. "For fuck's sake, I'm only 5'1"... That dress would be as wide as it is long! What kind of fucking racket are they running?"

Kathy put her hand over Rachel's soothingly. "Now, honey, you know it's all a conspiracy, right? They're in cahoots with the tailor they employ. They order the dress extra big, and then you pay extra to have it taken in!"

A look of realization spread across Rachel's face, unfurrowing her brow. "Ah, that makes perfect sense."

Yes, a conspiracy theory! Way to go, Mom. Sarah shot her mother a congratulatory wink.

Satisfied with her newfound understanding, Rachel changed the subject. "So how was New Years with James? You've barely said anything about him all day!"

Sarah shrugged. "There's not really much to say," she confessed. "I spent the weekend with him, and we had a fabulous time."

"Oh, come on, that's bullshit. We want details!" She looked across the table for support. "Don't we, Kathy?"

Sarah's mother nodded vigorously. Sarah had often discussed the details of her relationships with her mother, and often with Rachel while her mother was present. *I'm sure they're puzzled about why I'm being so secretive this time.*

Sarah straightened in her chair as if poised to divulge a deep, dark secret. She laughed at the way they hung on the edges of their seats like they were about to receive a juicy morsel of gossip. "Okay, here's the deal…" She drew in a sharp breath. "I'm afraid I like him more than he likes me."

Another epiphany raptured Rachel's face. "Oh, I get it now. You aren't in control, and that's something you hate."

Kathy nodded in agreement. "I think you totally figured her out, Rachel. Well done!"

Sarah felt exposed. "I'm okay with not being in control all the time. I think…" she paused to consider her choice of words, "I'm afraid of losing him and maybe never feeling this way again."

"Is it because he's in the Army?" Kathy wondered.

Sarah shook her head. "It's not that. I'm afraid he's going to meet someone he likes more. Someone younger. Someone hotter. Someone without kids. Someone less complicated. And he's not poly…so if he meets someone else, then…" She made a throat-slitting gesture with her finger. "I feel like I'm just temporary."

Laughter bubbled out of Rachel's mouth. "Dramatic much?" She shook her head, still giggling. "If he loves you, he will accept all those things about you: your age, having kids."

"Well, I don't think he loves me," Sarah said bluntly.

"Has he met the kids yet?" her mother asked, defusing the tension left by her daughter's last admission.

"Nope," Sarah replied. "And he's not going to. I'd prefer he just go on thinking of me as the sexy professor and leave Owen and Abby out of it."

Rachel burst in, "At first I thought you *should* keep the kids out of it, but now I think that's a big mistake. Your kids are a huge part of who you are. You can't expect him to fall in love with a part of you. He has to know the real you…and maybe that's held him back. Maybe he's scared of the unknown… You know, kids are scary to people who don't have them."

"Another brilliant point by Ms. Brock," her mother

praised Rachel. "Hanging out with a sociologist all the time has certainly worn off on you, sweetie!" She turned to her daughter. "Why don't you invite him for dinner with you and the kids sometime this next week?"

Sarah groaned, unsure if she was ready to open the doors between those two worlds just yet. "I don't know, guys...." She couldn't even picture it. "I will think about it. That's all I can promise for now."

SARAH WAS in her office the next week working on her book. Owen and Abby were back to school, but the university's classes had not yet resumed. Sarah always felt like that week or two between the end of the kids' Winter Break and the start of her spring semester was a treasure. No meetings, usually no deadlines, no papers to grade, just time to catch up on loose ends and prepare for another semester. The only better time was summer.

Her train of thought jumped off the tracks at the sudden sharp knock on her door. She had it locked, so she jumped up to open it and revealed Pawel on the other side. "Oh my god!" she exclaimed. "I didn't know you were back in town!"

"I wanted to surprise you!" He smiled, taking her into his arms. The first thing she noticed was not his warmth or smell, but how slight he felt compared to James. She shook that thought away and looked up into his face. He kissed her gently and then guided her inside the door so she could shut it behind them.

"When did you get in?" Sarah asked. "How was your flight?"

"Last night. And everything was perfect." He was still drinking in the image of her. "Is it possible that you're more beautiful than when I left?"

She laughed. "Pretty sure I'm just 'more.' Might have eaten a little too much candy and junk over the holidays." She patted her stomach. "I'm going back to the gym this week. You know, with the other hordes of resolution makers."

"I love your body," Pawel said, smoothing his hands down her frame, gliding over her hips. He had sat on her soft, over-sized chair and pulled her toward him. She clasped her hands behind his neck and hugged him tightly.

She remembered the pendant he sent her for Christmas and pulled it out of her sweater with her index finger. "Pawel, I still can't believe you sent this! It's absolutely stunning!"

"Yet it still pales in comparison to the loveliness it graces," he retorted with an adoring smile.

"Wanna grab some lunch?" Sarah suggested, and he nodded. She gathered up her purse and keys, and they headed back out the door and around the block to a little sandwich shop just off campus.

Pawel caught her up on everything in his homeland. His oldest son had gotten engaged, and like Rachel, was planning a summer wedding. "It means I can't stick around the States for a few weeks after the semester ends like I planned to."

"Oh," Sarah remarked, sensing his disappointment. "Well, you'll only see your son get married once! Hopefully…"

"True," Pawel agreed. "But I was going to sweep you away on a western adventure. I wanted to see some sights while I'm here. I've been up and down the coasts and I've been to

Chicago and Texas. I wanted to go to your mountains...see where your people come from."

The sweetness of that statement slowly sank into Sarah's soul. "Well, maybe you can come back and visit sometime," she consoled him. She wanted to run her fingers through his wavy hair and push his glasses back up the bridge of his nose. His hair had grown out even more since he'd been away, and he had the beginnings of a beard poking through his chin and cheeks. He pulled off the erudite professorial look to a T.

He looked a bit disappointed by her suggestion, wishing she'd proposed something more adventurous, but then he brightened. "I plan on making the most of the time I have left here," he promised.

She smiled back. *Maybe juggling two relationships isn't the best idea,* she considered, thinking of her book and how much work her classes were going to be this semester. *But I get something I need from both of them. I'll just make it work. I always do.*

TONIGHT IS THE NIGHT. How do I make this seem casual when I feel so much pressure to make sure everyone likes each other? Sarah debated as she drove to pick up the pizzas. *Pizza is a symbol of "casual," not a complicated dinner cooked from scratch.* She had also fretted over what to tell Abby and Owen. They already knew she hung out with Pawel quite a bit, but she always referred to him as her "colleague." Her kids were intuitive. *They'll sense I feel something more for James.* She just knew it.

She'd decided against inviting her mother over for dinner too. *That would just be too overwhelming.* Her mother could be quite outspoken at times, and who knew what kind of intellectual sparring match she might try to start with James. *Heaven forbid he share any of his thoughts about homosexuals serving in the military!* Sarah shuddered, remembering their very first conversation over coffee.

Simple, relaxed, and casual. That's what I'm going for here. Like a walk in the park.

She arrived home, pizzas in tow, and went immediately to the kitchen to get everything prepared. Abby slinked in and quickly observed, "Why are you rushing around? Are you nervous or something?"

Sarah turned around to face her daughter, her skin warming. "I...I'm not, I've just been rushing around all day. I guess I haven't gotten out of work mode yet." She laughed and made a mental note to tone down her energy level. "How was school today?"

"Ugh." Abby offered up one of her classic eye rolls.

"That bad?" Sarah questioned.

"Geometry test," she explained, shaking her head. "Not my finest moment."

Sarah patted her daughter's shoulder sympathetically just as she heard the knock at the door. "Don't worry, I'm sure you did fine."

She had started to head for the back door, but then James appeared in the kitchen, having let himself in. He nodded at Sarah but turned his attention to Abby immediately. "You must be Abby," he said confidently. He shook her hand, pumping it so vigorously that her tiny frame moved up and down.

Sarah could already see Abby's eyes light up just to have a

handsome man's attention on her, calling her name. Her face glowed, and the commotion sent Owen running into the kitchen at full speed. He stopped short right at James's feet and looked up with his wide brown eyes. "I'm Owen!" He'd very nearly crashed right into him.

That's one way to make a first impression. Sarah shook her head, biting her lip to keep from chuckling.

James stepped back with his hands out as if to protect himself, but he was smiling. Even in January, he was still wearing sandals, his usual baggy khaki pants and a gray sweater. He turned to Sarah. "I could have picked Owen out of a crowd of kids as being yours. He looks just like you!"

Sarah smiled. "Yeah I've heard that a time or two!" Owen had already grabbed James's hand and dragged him off to another room, probably to look at LEGO creations or his comic books.

As soon as they were alone, Abby nudged Sarah on the arm. "Wow, he's really cute, Mom. How long have you been seeing him?"

She never hesitated to tell her kids the truth, or at least a version of it they could handle. "Since September," she replied. "Five months I guess?"

In a few minutes she had all the drinks poured and paper plates—still going for that effortless vibe—set out for their casual dinner. She called everyone back into the kitchen, and soon plates were heaped with slices of pizza and breadsticks. They all gathered around the dining room table, and Sarah marveled for a moment at how surreal it felt to have a man joining her and her children for dinner once again. But the mood was so different than when her ex-husband sat at the table. Despite the awkwardness of the situation, the mood was light and jovial.

Sarah tried not to let a certain thought take hold in her mind: *this could be a vision of my future.*

What she thought she'd never want again was knocking on the door of her mind, begging to be let in, to warm up by the fire, to take root in her garden of ideas. To be watered and have a chance to wind its way around her heart.

After dinner, they played a board game. Sarah watched James carefully as he interacted with her children. He had an ease about him and a magnetism that drew Abby and Owen to him. Their laughter echoed throughout the house. At nine, she sent them upstairs to bed and looked at James expectantly for his assessment.

He grabbed her hand and pulled her down onto the sofa beside him. "Your kids are awesome," he pronounced.

Sarah couldn't help but beam. *Of course they are!* She squeezed his hand gratefully. "I'm so glad you got to come and meet them. I think they really liked you."

"Was this some sort of audition?" James questioned, smirking a bit.

Sarah laughed. "Of course not." There was only a touch of defensiveness in her tone. "It's just that being a mom is a big part of my life, and you don't really know that side of me. I thought you might like to see me in my natural habitat."

"As with everything else in your life, I can see you also excel at motherhood. They're smart; they seem happy, evidence of a job well done," James congratulated her.

Relief washed over her, and for a moment she basked in the resounding peace she felt. Just sitting there on the couch, the kids off to bed, in the quiet stillness of the house, it was enough. It felt like all she could ask for.

SHE STARED at her phone in disbelief. Two days had passed and James had fallen silent. *Back to his old ways—after I thought he'd made so much progress.*

She put her phone in her purse, tired of looking at the screen, willing the little messaging symbol to pop up. She should be soaking up the last day of freedom before the students returned, and she'd promised herself she would return all the emails that needed to be returned, schedule a phone meeting with her editor, and start getting her presentation together for the conference in March.

As hard as she tried to concentrate, her thoughts kept returning to the words she'd sent two days before.

Sarah: *I'm so glad you liked my kids. What are you doing this weekend?*

She rubbed her eyes and wished the work on her computer screen could hold a fraction of the interest James did. *Did I scare him off? Is he mad? Did something happen to him?*

She was going to Pawel's for dinner. She hated to admit that she was in no mood to see him. *I'm sure I'll be fine when I get there. After all, he'll distract me and take good care of me. I should really not be thinking of James all the time anyway.*

Why does this man hold such power over me? How can we feel so much, so strongly when we are together and then poof, he's so elusive and distant?

Moments later she pulled her phone back out again and sent him another text.

Sarah: *Are you okay? It always worries me when I don't hear back from you.*

SARAH ENDED up going home early. Her mind was too cluttered to concentrate, and sitting in her office chastising herself for her lack of productivity seemed unproductive. She sent Pawel a text to say she wasn't feeling well and hoped to reschedule dinner. Then, in addition to feeling angry at herself for pining away for James, she also felt guilty for bagging Pawel.

I am a mess. She sat by the French doors and watched a couple of winter birds sampling the seeds Owen had put in the feeder. Sipping her tea and trying to shake the pervasive feeling of discontent, she heard the screech of the school bus's brakes and then the handle on the back door turn.

"How was your day?" Sarah faked cheeriness as her children ambled in, searching for an after-school snack. "There are apples," she reminded Owen as he grabbed a bag of chips from the cupboard. He momentarily looked defeated, and then a big smile spread across his face. "What?"

He thumbed through the papers in his folder and handed her one. At the top was an A circled in green ink. "I got an A on my science test!"

"Oh, that's fantastic!" Sarah affixed the test to the refrigerator with an Empire State building magnet they'd gotten on a summer excursion to New York.

Sarah noticed Abby was standing at the refrigerator, the doors spread wide, as if the contents were going to morph before her eyes. "What's up, Abby?"

She shook her head nonchalantly and reached for a yogurt. "What's for dinner?"

Dinner, ugh. She hadn't eaten all day. "Tacos?" she hypothesized. *Assuming I can find the energy.*

Abby looked satisfied and began to walk away just in time to hear her mother sigh and glance down at her phone again, which was projecting its emptiness from the cold, hard countertop.

Abby turned around before she reached the archway to the hall. "Are you okay?" she asked, concern growing in her eyes.

Something inside Sarah broke. The tear she'd been battling slipped down her cheek before she could will it back inside. Her sinuses stung and burned as she struggled to get herself under control. "Oh, Abby, I'm sorry...just having a rough day." She gave a little shrug and fully expected her daughter to nod and flit up the stairs to her bedroom to do whatever teenage girls do after school to avoid doing their homework.

Abby looked surprised enough to be knocked over with a feather and even jumped when her mother's phone came alive and began to buzz from across the room. She watched as her mother's eyes glistened with hope.

Sarah crossed the room toward it, getting close enough to see who was calling. "It's Rachel."

"Don't you want to talk to her?" Abby inquired, clearly confused.

Sarah pulled a chair out from the table and with trembling fingers sat, placing the phone face down against the smooth wood. She didn't want to talk to Rachel. It would just be "wedding plans this" and "wedding plans that." As much as she wanted to be happy for her friend, she could not deny there were pangs of jealousy taking little bites out of her, like a parasite.

Great, more guilt. Sarah cringed. *God, I wish I knew what was wrong with me today.*

"How are things with Tyler?" Sarah changed the subject—her go-to tactic whenever she was on the verge of showing emotional weakness. *Turn the tables. Get the other person to talk instead.*

"Things are good." Abby's eyebrows furrowed. "Mom, is this about James?"

Sarah sighed again; she had almost forgotten the cat was out of the bag. Abby had met James, so there was no denying his existence. The tears welled up inside her eyes again as she thought about what a risk she'd taken introducing him to her children.

Mom and Rachel were wrong, she realized, *I shouldn't have done it. There was no need to. It scared him away. I fucked every-thing up.*

Abby pushed a little harder, "So...it's James, right? You know, I really liked him. What did he do?"

There were times, little flashes, when Sarah could see herself in Abby. This was one of those times. Abby took a chair next to her and set her spoon on top of her unopened yogurt container as if listening to her mother's answer was more important than snacking.

"I haven't heard from him since he was here the other night," Sarah admitted, her walls crumbling. "I'm afraid having him over to meet you guys was a mistake."

Abby looked sad, her blue-green eyes wide and full of empathy. She placed her hand on her mother's. "I'm sorry, Mom. Maybe he's just been really busy?"

Sarah nodded. "Maybe. I don't know, sweetie. He's so hard to understand sometimes."

A little smirk lifted the corner of Abby's lips. "You mean guys in their thirties don't make any more sense than sixteen-year-olds?"

Sarah laughed and turned her hand so it was on top of Abby's, patting it a little. "I wish I could say they do," she admitted. "Relationships are tough. Sometimes it's hard for people to be honest with themselves and with others. I don't think James really knows what he wants. He's several years younger than me, you know." *Which I sometimes fail to take into account when it comes to getting frustrated with him.*

"Really?" Abby remarked. "He doesn't look that much younger!"

Sarah smiled at her daughter's unintentional flattery. "He's actually only twenty-nine. And thanks for the compliment," Sarah said with a teary laugh.

"Go, Mom! Does that make you a cougar?" she asked innocently.

"Oh, Abby! Where did you hear that term?" She shook her head. "And, no, it doesn't make me a cougar, silly girl! Cougars are women in their forties dating guys in their twenties or younger. It's like a twenty-year age difference, not seven. Give me a few years, alright?" She laughed again, already feeling her heart lighten.

"James seems like a great guy," she said. "I'm sure if he really cares for you...if it's meant to be...you'll hear from him soon."

Words of wisdom from a fifteen-year-old...

She squeezed her daughter's hand again, the maturity she'd just displayed taking her breath away. A little vision of Abigail's pixie face framed by long honey-colored pigtails and a smattering of freckles flashed across her mind. She could barely reconcile that vision with the half-grown woman sitting beside her. *Why didn't anyone tell me how bittersweet motherhood is?*

And with that thought, the tears started again. She mouthed the words "thank you" to her daughter and squeezed her hand again.

"You should call Rachel back," Abby suggested. "She worries about you, you know."

It was hard for Sarah to accept the idea of anyone worrying about her. As hard as she tried to be independent and self-reliant, she didn't like thinking there was a crack in the veneer. Now she had three people, if she counted her mother (what mother didn't worry about her children?) and possibly four if Pawel was included, worrying about her—and all because of one man. She shook her head, still not understanding why James had this effect on her.

Later when she finally had the energy to tackle taco preparation, she felt a dull ache in her lower abdomen. *Ugh, my period.* She rummaged through her cabinets for the box of tampons she had shoved to the back at the end of her last cycle. *I should have known my hormones played a role in this.*

As she went to find the bottle of ibuprofen, she noticed her phone was flashing with a text.

James: *hey...everything is fine...been busy. miss you*

THE PROMOTION

14

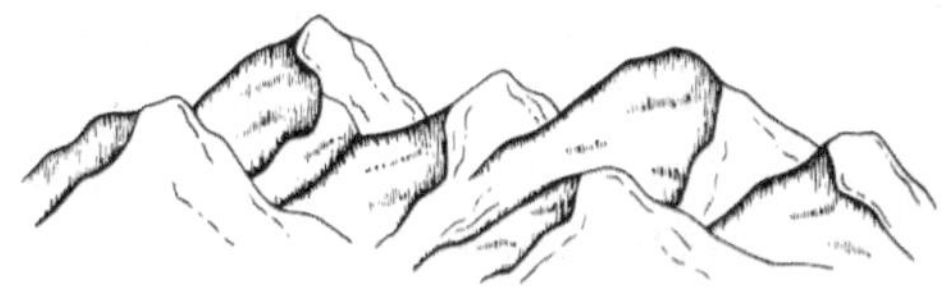

She awoke to a body pressed against hers, an arm draped around her waist, and a leg slung over her hip. She felt warm breaths falling against her neck and wanted nothing more than to sink back down into the pillows, but her bladder had other plans. She tried to maneuver her body out from under the other one, but his limbs were like lead. She slowly shifted her hips while grabbing his calf, attempting to lift it, foiled by its weight. She wiggled and gradually slid out from under his leg, then had a slightly easier time freeing herself from his arm.

She still wasn't used to navigating James's house in the dark. She'd driven over very late that night after a strained text conversation and never really got her bearings, she'd been so upset over his inability to muster any consideration for her hurt feelings. She made the forty-minute drive because her heart ached so badly she knew she wouldn't be able to get to sleep. She hated the tension, the uncertainty.

Are we breaking up? The question hung in the air like a wave reaching its crest.

The conversation was still ringing in her ears. "I don't

understand what you do all day," Sarah had complained. "I don't understand why it's so challenging to take ten seconds to respond to a text." She didn't even care that her tone was cold and accusatory. She was tired of his bad behavior and of feeling like she was riding an emotional roller coaster of his design and operation.

"What do you mean 'what you do all day?'" he had retorted. "I work a full-time job, same as you. I get up at 0515, I'm ready to go by 0545, PT at 0630. I run four miles, and then at 0800 I'm in the office. I accomplish more in those first two hours than most people do all day. At 1000 I have class, so I have to drive to campus. After class, I hit the gym." His blue eyes had glared at her like they had shards of ice buried in them. "Is that enough of a breakdown, or do you need to know when I use the restroom too?"

"I don't need your itinerary," Sarah had argued, her voice still cool, but the emotion was swelling, threatening to surge. "I just feel like I'm an afterthought to you. I don't like going two days without hearing from you. I think about you all the time. Do you ever think about me when we're apart?"

By the last sentence she was trembling. And she hated the need in her voice. *Hated it.*

"Of course I do," James had replied, softening, his body gravitating toward hers. He pulled her into his arms, and she immediately yielded, strong sobs jerking through her shoulders, and the tears erupting onto his chest.

He'd kissed the top of her head and held her tightly, his voice barely more than a whisper, "I'm not sure why I have these walls up, Sarah. I'm sorry. I'll try to do better."

Later, after they'd both calmed down and shared about their weeks, she had apologized, "I don't know why I get so emotional about you. I just feel really deeply, I guess."

"I always feel better when I'm with you," he confessed,

and the words soaked into her like raindrops into cracked, barren soil. "I don't know why I resist it sometimes."

But he didn't say he felt deeply too.

He had kissed the top of her head again and pulled her into his bedroom. That was the last thing she remembered before drifting off in his arms. Now she was tiptoeing through the stillness of his house, trying to gather her things to leave. When she reached the bedroom, he'd rolled over so his back faced her. *It's always two steps forward and then a retreat.* She saw the symbolism in his position. *This is a war I will never win.*

She fumbled for her purse and keys and managed to trip over a book he had tossed on the rug so that one corner was submerged under the bed and the other under a mound of clothes. *I thought he was a neat freak the time I was over here before. Must have been trying to impress me.*

She slipped her shoes on and made her way toward the door when his voice fractured the silence, "Where are you going?"

Her heart leapt at the sound of him. He had turned over, and now that she had adjusted to the darkness, she could feel his eyes bore through her. "I think it's better if I just leave."

He sat up, groggy and somewhat exasperated. "I thought we worked all this out a couple of hours ago," he groaned.

Sarah sighed, unsure if she had the energy to till this soil again. He would continue to make empty promises and say what she wanted to hear, but his actions would keep betraying her faith in him. *He's a baby. He doesn't know how to give.*

"Come back to bed, please?" His voice sounded smaller than usual, with a tinge of desperation. She was frozen between the bed and the door, both options seeming equally valid and equally impossible.

He paused a beat. "Sarah," he pleaded, "come lie down with me."

Those words. *With me.* They pulled. She felt his usually concealed tenderness seep out and guide her body toward him. In seconds her face was buried in his chest hair, both of his arms around her, his warmth filtrating through her like oxygen in her cells.

Why does it always feel like everything is perfect when I'm right here? And so wrong when I'm not?

RACHEL STOOD on the beige carpeted pedestal in the middle of the bridal shop surrounded by mirrors. Peering from her angle on the sidelines, Sarah saw a hundred Rachels primping and posing, hands on her hips, adjusting the veil. She could hardly believe she was witnessing her friend in a white dress.

"Well, what do you think?" she queried, her face aglow.

Sarah smiled. "I didn't picture you wearing white, to be honest," she began, "but that style is very flattering on you. I really like it."

"I didn't picture white either," Rachel admitted, "but stranger things have happened, right?" She smoothed the satin around her hips.

The dress fit her like a glove, like it was made for her, with a plunging V neckline accented with tiny pearls and rhinestones and a short train attached to the basque waist that curled around her bare feet. "This would look so much better with heels though. Oh!" she gasped, her voice quivering with excitement. "White leather lace-up boots with a stiletto heel!"

The saleslady returned with four purple dresses in a similar style. "These are the bridesmaids' dresses," she explained, handing them to Sarah.

Soon Sarah was standing beside Rachel on the pedestal, amethyst satin draped over her curves. The dress had a ruched bodice and a neckline that echoed the bridal gown's. The bodice stopped slightly above her natural waistline and was accented with a rhinestone clip where the material was gathered and then floated away from her body all the way to the floor. She liked the way the deep purple looked with her ivory skin and dark hair. She felt a little like royalty.

What would James think of it? Will James still be in the picture for the wedding? Would he fly to Colorado to be my date?

"Well?" Rachel asked expectantly. "Are we gorgeous or what?"

"And you're sure you want purple, right?" Sarah questioned, "Not the deep red we talked about?"

Rachel nodded. "I thought the red might be too clashy with the rocks in Garden of the Gods. The purple is perfect! 'Purple mountains' majesty!'" she quoted from the patriotic song, which was penned by Katharine Lee Bates during a summer she spent teaching in Colorado Springs.

Sarah laughed. "Of course. Well, I love the cut. I feel beautiful!"

As if reading her earlier thoughts, Rachel remarked, "Just wait till James sees you in that, Lovechop! Then he'll want to walk you down the aisle for sure." She winked.

Sarah could not allow herself to hope that far in the future.

SARAH WAS STILL SHAKING her head in disbelief at the text message glowing from her phone.

James: *Come to dinner with me tonight? Want to celebrate.*

She reread it multiple times to make sure it was really from James and not Pawel.

Sarah: *Sure. What did you have in mind? Can't stay out too late on a school night.*

James: *NP. I'll pick you up at 6.*

Sarah barely had enough time to grab a quick shower and throw on her slim black pencil skirt, tall black leather boots and a low-cut wine-colored sweater. She surveyed her appearance in the full-length mirror on her closet door before heading out. She felt bloated and puffy, having picked up a few pounds over the holidays. *Ugh...retaining water from my period.*

Owen called up to announce that James had arrived before she had a chance to continue fretting about her appearance. She traipsed down the stairs to see Owen showing James some of his LEGO creations. She studied him for a moment before he noticed she'd arrived. *James is either completely enthralled by Owen or one hell of an actor.*

"Ready?" she called to James, who looked startled until he drank in her image and a wide grin spread across his face.

She instructed Owen and Abby, "Be good. I'll be back before bedtime."

"You look beautiful," James said and kissed her on the cheek. She turned just in time to see Abby wink at her.

Because it was a weeknight, the Italian restaurant James

chose was fairly empty. They shared a booth constructed of rich, dark wood in the back corner. The waiter looked familiar, and Sarah was fairly certain he'd been one of her students a couple semesters back.

James waited until after they ordered and were served their wine before telling her what they were celebrating. "I want to propose a toast." He smiled, his blue eyes glinting in the soft, low lighting.

"Right," Sarah said, her nerves tingling and weary from several hours spent reviewing all the possibilities. "So what are we celebrating?"

"I have some exciting work news." He seemed to enjoy the expectant look emanating from Sarah's dark eyes as her suspense mounted. When she was nearly ready to explode with anticipation, he announced, "I got a promotion."

"That's wonderful news! What kind of promotion?" She felt warm pride surge through her for a few moments, and then...it hit her like a ton of bricks: *he's going to leave*. She tried to keep the color from draining from her face. Every intuitive fiber of her being was crying out that she was going to lose him.

He didn't seem to notice. "I'm being commissioned," he said, beaming. She'd never seen him so animated.

"What does that mean exactly? I'm sorry, I'm completely ignorant when it comes to military matters," she apologized.

"I'm being commissioned to be an officer. It's a pretty big deal. There will be a ceremony, which is what I wanted to ask you about."

Sarah's synapses were confused, unsure which direction to fire. *Relief? Is there something more?* "Ask me about what?"

"I want you to come to my commissioning ceremony." He smiled a little nervously. "If you can, I mean. You could do the pinning...if you want to."

Her head was spinning. She had no idea what he was

talking about, but she nodded. "I'd love to. I think?" She giggled, sounding as nervous as he did. "When is it?"

"Next week," he replied. "It'll be on campus, hopefully not during one of your classes. Owen and Abby can come too if they want."

"Oh, James, this is really exciting!" *It is, right?* She would have to do some research to find out what the ceremony was...what "pinning" meant.

He certainly looks as if... She studied his face... *He's glowing with excitement. Boyish and on top of the world. Like he's just been crowned king.*

"Oh! I should propose the toast!" she gushed, raising her glass, the red wine swirling with her sudden movement.

He grinned and raised his glass slowly, deliberately, his head tilted as if waiting expectantly to hear her smooth voice sprinkle a silvery shower of admiration over him. Sarah could feel his pressure bearing down on her, wrapped around his grin...*and when am I at a loss for words?*

She cleared her throat and went for it: "Here's to the US Army for recognizing talent, strength, drive and initiative when they see it. Who says 'military intelligence' is an oxymoron?" She paused for a moment to giggle at her joke, feeling her natural ease finally return. And then with her most earnest sincerity: "And here's to you, James, my officer and gentleman, with my very best wishes for a long, fruitful and illustrious career. I'm so proud of you, darling!"

She nearly felt the heat of his cheeks blushing as his wine glass clinked against hers. He couldn't even respond, his eyes were crinkled so deeply with happiness. The wine exploded against her tongue and seemed to be absorbed directly into her bloodstream. She didn't know what was more dizzying: the alcohol or the smile that radiated from his face.

He grew serious and reached for her hand, which he held

in his across the table. "There's one more thing you should know." His fingers laced through hers.

And now her heart began to pound. This time he didn't make her wait.

"I'm deploying in June."

Her face was blank as she struggled to keep the emotion from being painted across its canvas. Finally a word managed to form itself on her lips: "Where?"

She flashed back...her cheek on his chest, his arm around her... *This man is going to break my heart someday. I knew this was coming. I had no idea it would be so soon. Shit.*

"Oh, Sarah," he whispered, recognizing the emotions suspending her in midair. "Please don't." He waited for her eyes to meet his. They were round and wide with uncertainty. "Please, Sarah...this is a good thing. This is a great opportunity for me. It's only for nine months."

"Where?" she repeated, this time her voice stronger.

"Afghanistan."

THE NEXT WEEK WAS A BLUR, a cycle consisting of office, class and home, requiring very little emotion or thought. Sarah spent the night with Pawel that Friday night and stayed home and watched movies with the kids, Rachel and Thomas on Saturday night. She let Rachel keep her up all night with talk of bouquets, centerpieces, and wedding music.

She didn't see James. She didn't contact him. She reached

for the switch in her mind that controlled The James Channel and tried desperately to turn it off.

Finally it was Tuesday, the day of his commissioning ceremony, and Sarah was forced to flip the channel back on full blast. She walked across campus that afternoon in the late January chill, the sun already beginning to sink toward the horizon at four in the afternoon. Everything was washed in dappled golden rays, but it was a cold, unforgiving winter sunshine, the kind that constantly reminded one how far away summer was.

By summer, he will be gone. That thought chilled her more than the air.

She walked up to the auditorium, and the memory of trudging up the same steps the night they met crashed into her. *I would have never envisioned all this coming from that single question he posed after the panel on Don't Ask, Don't Tell.* She couldn't shrug away the butterflies that were starting to flit between her ribs.

Just a tiny moment that changed me forever. A tiny, solitary moment.

James was already there, decked out in his dress uniform, his shoulders impossibly broad, the line from his shoulders down to his shiny patent leather-clad feet impossibly sharp. Despite the stiff-looking ensemble, he looked relaxed conversing with the other officers, his superiors. There was a softness around his eyes that Sarah recognized, that the uniform couldn't disguise.

Now that she knew him so intimately, his usually well-concealed tenderness was impossible to hide from her. She looked at him through such different eyes than she had five months before. He had gone from an amorphous figure to a three-dimensional one, one that made her heart react in ways her brain was not able to control.

His peripheral vision finally picked up on her presence.

He turned toward her, excusing himself from the conversation in which he was engaged. He let her give him a chaste hug. His students were present and giving him knowing glances, which made Sarah giggle. She wondered if they had any overlap in students, but she didn't recognize any of the faces. He showed her where to sit and then rejoined the officers.

The ceremony got underway, but Sarah was so lost in thought she didn't even hear the words. She watched James cross to the front of the room. *So formal.* She tried to watch his body as if he were a stranger, but she couldn't help but dwell on what was under that uniform. How she knew every muscle, every freckle and mole, every nuance of his physical structure. How he looked with his eyes closed. The way his biceps bulged when his hands were behind his head. The shape of his navel. The pattern of his chest chair.

And then she thought about what she knew of his insides, what had taken her much longer to uncover. *His vulnerable side. The way he can be self-deprecating at times but otherwise, so damn confident, he borders on cocky. And what about the books? All the freaking books! How he spouts off some historical or scientific fact and completely catches me off-guard. What about his conviction? The fact he is willing to give up his life for our country. The way he poses philosophical questions out of the blue, the way someone else might ask if I liked a movie. How sometimes I look into those blue eyes and feel like I am staring into his soul.*

She heard her name called—she needed to proceed to the front of the room for the pinning. Rising stiffly, she walked to the stage almost as formally as he had. She was handed the pin for one side, and the officer did the other side. As soon as she touched his body, even through the thick uniform jacket, she felt his heat absorb into her flesh. He stared straight ahead, but he noticed the electricity. It was obvious.

There is something between us—call it electric, call it chemical

—something that defies logic and reality. And that is why I am here and not walking away right now.

This man is going to break my heart.

Her intuition grabbed ahold of her and shook her. She needed to be strong, to find her pragmatic side, to steel herself against the fall. She'd climbed so high...

And it would be a long way down.

OWEN'S BIRTHDAY fell that weekend. Sarah's house was full of rambunctious ten- and eleven-year-old boys, along with the accompanying stomping feet, loud voices, Nerf guns and video games. Abby had wisely escaped to Chloe's house for the evening, but Sarah's mother and Rachel came to provide moral support and a feeble attempt to balance out all the testosterone. Rachel volunteered to clean up the kitchen after the devastation was mostly complete, and Kathy and Sarah went to check for damages to the rest of the house.

Kathy was scooping wrapping paper and smashed soda cans up into the trash bag she was holding when she tossed an innocent "How are things with James?" into the space between them.

Sarah immediately bristled. She usually didn't mind sharing details of her love life with her mother or with Rachel, but lately she'd wanted to hold those details close to her heart. *Out of fear. Fear I will have to admit what he's doing to me.*

Kathy Lynde wisely sensed the answer in her daughter's

silence. "It's okay; you don't have to talk about him if you don't want to. It's been a while since I saw you affected by a man though, Sarah, and I have to tell you, if I'm being honest," her dark eyes grew wide behind her thick-lensed glasses, "I'm kind of worried about you."

"Oh, Mom," Sarah brushed her off. "I'm almost thirty-seven years old. If there's one thing I've learned from Matt and Daniel and all the other men I've dated, it's that I can stand on my own two feet. I'm my own person, and my feelings are my responsibility, not a man's."

"That's my girl." Kathy smirked, knowing full well Sarah's response was a defense mechanism.

"Mom," Sarah said after a moment, stripping down that wall she'd put up, "he's deploying." She barely got the word out of her mouth before the tears unexpectedly choked her, forcing her words back into her throat.

"Oh, honey," Kathy sighed. She put down the trash bag and gathered her daughter into her arms. The simple embrace released the floodgates, leaving Sarah sobbing into her mother's shoulder.

She finally caught her breath and was able to ease the words out, words tinged with anger and directed inward, "I don't know why I'm so upset. I knew all along this would happen. I knew from day one, Mom, from the first time I was in his arms."

"Sometimes that doesn't matter," Kathy replied soothingly. "Sometimes you must see what's behind that door; you're just compelled...by invisible forces. I've felt it, sweetheart, I know." She brushed her daughter's dark hair back from her eyes and tucked it behind her ear. Then she wiped away a stray tear that had clung to her reddened cheeks.

Kathy Lynde had more empathy in her pinky finger than most people had in their entire souls. Sarah wiped her eyes and nodded. "And it's just like that. It's like I can't help myself. I can't stay away. When I'm with him, I'm on top of the highest mountain. And when I'm not, I'm in the lowest valley."

She shook her head, irritated she couldn't articulate her feelings without resorting to metaphors. "I've never felt this way before...so out of control! I didn't even know it was *possible* to feel this way." She looked into her mother's eyes. "I'm not used to feeling irrational." She managed a laugh. "I don't much care for it!"

"I was like that with your father," Kathy revealed. "And I was too young to look at my feelings objectively like you can, to recognize I was being irrational. I didn't know I was going to get hurt. That I would lose him. But you do know, and it's okay, Sarah. There's only one thing you can do."

Sarah's eyes widened, wondering if there could really be an answer to this unending torment. "What's that?"

Kathy took her daughter's hands into her own and stared into the eyes of a younger version of herself. "Just enjoy every minute you get with him, sweetheart. Every single minute is pure gold. You may never feel this force again. I think some people go through their entire lives without feeling it." When she smiled at this thought, her eyes crinkled and creased. "To feel this power, what you feel right now for James? This is divine, Sarah. This is a gift. Embrace it. Learn from it. Relish it."

Sarah nodded and hugged her mother tightly. Kathy Lynde, wisest woman on the planet, had just given Sarah's heart the words it had been trying to tell her head for the last five months.

15

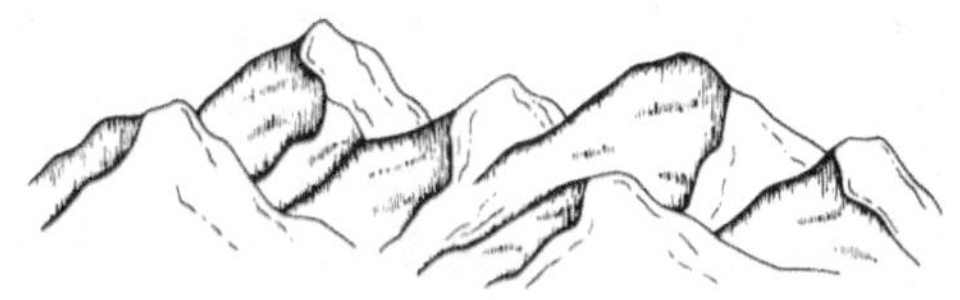

February was a wild tease, provocatively flirting with warmer temperatures, even though everyone in the mid-Atlantic region knew it would be a long while before spring settled in for good. Sarah had stuffed her winter coat at the back of the closet, knowing full well she'd have to dig it back out again. She was burning to be outdoors, to be active, to burn off the energy she'd stored during her winter hibernation. Her students seemed to share her restlessness as they counted down to spring break. Everywhere she went, Sarah noticed the masses of humankind were beaten down by the meteorological roller coaster, desperately craving stability.

Pawel and Sarah went on a bike ride and picnic one unseasonably warm Sunday afternoon. The park was deserted except for a few brave squirrels and a chipmunk or two. The trees were still bare, and the ground was firm but thawing. A dampness clung to everything, coupled with a chill when the sun hid behind the clouds.

They sat on top of a picnic table tossing bread crumbs to the squirrels and attracting the attention of a few winter birds. Sarah took off her knit cap and shook out her dark hair all around her. Her skin was starting to feel itchy in the damp chill. "I need to get home soon," she remarked, interrupting Pawel's staring contest with a nearby squirrel.

He took her gloved hand into his. "Your cheeks are flushed the most delicious shade of rose," he offered. "They look like apples, and I want to bite them."

Only Pawel could say that with a straight face. "Is that so?" she retorted. "Well, no one is stopping you!" She tossed him a teasing smirk.

He turned toward her and, with one finger, lifted her chin in the direction of his mouth. He grazed his teeth against her cold flesh, and she felt his heat searing through her, replaced by a chill as the saliva evaporated. Then his lips were on her, soft and gentle, his facial hair brushing against her. The wind whipped through her hair, throwing it into the breeze and making it flap against both of their faces like a dark veil.

He eased her down onto the picnic table and pressed his body against hers. He was so hard that she could feel his cock throbbing against her thigh through two layers of thick denim as his mouth continued to devour her. *Damn, I wish I had worn a skirt,* she thought wistfully as she considered how much better it would feel if they were naked with him sliding inside her hot wetness.

"God, Sarah, I want you so bad," he whispered against her neck, the sound tickling her ear.

She sat up and pulled him to a sitting position so his bottom was on the top of the table and his feet rested on the bench, then slid under him so she faced him. She began to unbuckle his pants, furtively glancing around the clearing to make sure no one had stumbled upon them. Satisfied the coast was clear, she pulled his cock out of his cotton boxers and immediately plunged her hungry mouth down on top of it, taking his entire length deep to the back of her throat.

He gasped at the contrast of the cold air with her hot mouth.

She felt a drop of his excitement ooze onto her tongue as she began to work his cock with her mouth and hands, stroking him faster and more firmly and swirling her tongue around his head. She felt his hips rise to meet her mouth, his hands laced in her hair, guiding her throat down so he was balls deep inside her.

"Oh, Sarah, don't stop... Oh fuck that feels amazing...just like that... I'm so close..." he moaned.

She barely had time to breathe during the upstrokes, concentrating on not choking when the tip hit her tonsils. Working over his shaft with her hands, she teased the tip with her tongue and lips until his thighs clenched. Pawel's eyes closed half-way, and she wondered if some of what he was grunting was in Polish, but she couldn't quite understand.

As she leaned forward to swallow him whole, he groaned unintelligibly, his hot, salty semen shooting deep into the back of her throat, so much all at once that it nearly gagged her. Her eyes watered as she forced herself to swallow the mouthful, his hands still firmly holding her head in place.

He sat silently for several moments, his cock still pulsating and oozing thick white fluid that she greedily licked up. Once the sensations subsided, his dark eyes opened and looked at her, full of gratitude and admiration. "That was simply marvelous. Now, what am I going to do for you?"

Sarah stood up from the bench and immediately sensed her panties were damp with desire. She pulled a still-shaky Pawel off the table and to a standing position, then guided him toward his Jeep. He took the hint rather well and folded down the back seat so there was room for Sarah to lie down. She eased her pants down to her ankles, far enough that she could spread her legs. The Jeep was cool, and goose-bumps sprang up on her milky white thighs.

Pawel knelt between her legs with barely enough room to maneuver but fully dedicated to returning the favor. He sighed as his tongue made contact with her clitoris, lapping up the juices that had accumulated between her lips. "Oh god, Sarah, you are delicious."

I can only imagine how I taste after biking and hiking, Sarah thought, but Pawel was so enthusiastic that she quickly put it out of her mind as the sensations began to envelop her, turning her mind to mush. This time it was her turn to lace her fingers through his hair as she felt her orgasm building. She pushed her hips against his mouth, rubbing her clit against his lips and giving him the hint that she wanted it in his mouth. He happily obliged as the impending climax surged through her body.

The stimulation was just right for keeping her on the edge, but a fantasy crept in of someone standing right outside the Jeep, peering in the window. Her vision was of a younger man, who after watching the action for a few moments, exhibited a noticeable bulge in his pants. A hungry look burned in his eyes, and he was soon compelled to unzip his pants and pull out his thick, hard cock. His eyes turned glossy and wanton as they peered through the glass, watching her writhe under Pawel's tongue. The thought of watching his hands sliding up and down his shaft, getting off on watching her get off...well, that was enough. She exploded in Pawel's face, drenching him in her juices, screaming and panting as the waves shook through her, her body convulsing.

Pawel had a huge grin on his face as he pulled away and grabbed a towel from the nearest seat. He wiped his face dry and handed the towel to Sarah. "Oh god, I think I made a little mess in your Jeep." She laughed, mopping up the damp upholstery.

"No worries." Pawel smiled. "It was totally worth it!"

When Sarah sat up, her little fantasy from moments before flashed back to her. Her eyes had been shut tight the whole time she'd imagined being watched. But as she glanced out the window, she saw a tall, lanky figure in a gray hooded sweatshirt and jeans retreating deep into the woods.

SARAH REALIZED she hadn't seen Rachel since they picked out her bridal gown and the bridesmaids' dresses. Days had slipped into weeks, and Sarah felt guilty for not helping more with the wedding plans. She invited her best friend to lunch on a Tuesday afternoon at the little sandwich place near her office. Rachel was energetic and bubbly like usual, but Sarah felt rather subdued, which her friend picked up on immediately.

"What's your deal?" Rachel asked as soon as they'd ordered their meals. "You seem like something is up." She had her classic no-nonsense, going-to-get-to-the-bottom-of-this look embedded in her hazel eyes.

Sarah shrugged but ultimately accepted that playing dumb was useless where Rachel was concerned. Not only did she know Sarah better than any other soul, but she was adept at dragging information out of the most stoic individual. "It's James."

A trace of empathy widened her friend's pupils. "Because he's leaving?"

"Because he has so many walls up," Sarah explained. "He's always on the verge of falling for me. I feel it in his touch; I see it in his eyes. He just can't get over that wall. I think there's something he's not telling me."

Rachel nodded. "You are so intuitive, I'd imagine you're right."

Her heart ached with longing for him that she could never seem to control no matter how hard she tried. "Maybe I should stop seeing him now. I feel like I'm getting too attached."

"What did your mom tell you the other day? To enjoy it while it lasts...right?"

Sarah felt a tear stinging at the corner of her eye. "She did say that, but I know I'm going to be so hurt when he leaves."

"You're going to be hurt whether you stop seeing him now or in June," Rachel pointed out. "And he won't be gone forever. What is the deployment...nine months? How do you know he won't want something more with you when he returns? Maybe he just needs to get this tour behind him first?"

Sarah nodded. "I know nine months is not that long in the general scheme of things, but he could get transferred someplace else when he comes back. I already feel like my heart is breaking, and he's still here."

"Oh honey." Rachel patted her hand. "If it's meant to be, it will work out."

Sarah hated that answer. She'd always hated the idea of letting fate decide her future. *My future is what I make it, what we make it.*

If we want to be together, we will make it happen through our choices.

She didn't have the energy to argue with Rachel. *She has*

her man. It's easy for her to tell me to be patient and wait for things to fall into place when she's picking out wedding cakes and flowers.

I'm not sure I can stick around and wait for fate to shine her favor on me. I think it's time to leave while I can escape relatively unscathed.

As if he sensed something was awry, James was uncharacteristically chatty over text for the next few days. He asked Sarah a few times if she was okay, to which she responded that she was busy grading the first round of exams.

James: *Let's do something this weekend. You need a break.*

Sarah: I need something *tongue out emoji*

James: There's a new rock-climbing gym over near Rockville. You game?

Pangs of homesickness for her mountains stabbed into her.

Sarah: *How can I say no to that?*

He picked her up early Saturday morning, and they headed to Rockville. Sarah was excited but nervous. It had been a while since she'd climbed, nearly five years. She'd gone a few times in graduate school with friends—on real rocks, of course—but this time she felt out of practice and afraid of embarrassing herself in front of James, for whom any athletic endeavor was second nature.

She was quiet on the car ride, looking out the window of his truck at the trees and the frost-kissed landscape rushing past. Her head was spinning with ideas about how to tell him she needed to move on. *My nerves are in a tizzy. I hope I can do this*, and by that she meant both tasks looming in front of her.

They settled in at the gym and were helped into their equipment. Sarah mustered up enough confidence to forego the instruction that was offered. *This is going to be like riding a bike...I hope.* James's blue eyes gleamed as he watched her place her foot in the first hold and reach for another.

Relief flooded her nerves as her muscle memory responded to the familiar motions. She wanted to watch James's adept movements propel him to the top, his muscles bulging and the look of concentration on his face, but she required all that mental energy for her own climb. Pulling her weight up the faux rocks sent a delicious pain burning through her muscles, but the endorphins urged her upward.

After reaching the summit, they were both laughing, and James seemed impressed by her performance. "Not bad for an old chick, huh?" she joked.

He rolled his eyes. "You're not old! Don't be silly."

When they returned to earth, he helped her out of her gear and pulled her into his arms, which were exposed in a sleeveless athletic shirt in a shade of brilliant royal blue. He had barely broken a sweat, of course. He squeezed her, his arms encircling her waist, and she buried her face in the cleft between his pectorals.

I wish this didn't feel so damn good. She wondered if she'd really be able to walk away.

They headed back to his place for a shower and late lunch. This time, they were both a lot chattier on the drive.

"So, I have a conference in Denver next month," she told him. "Maybe I'll go rock climbing there if the weather is agreeable. You never know how spring will be in the mountains. There could be a foot of snow or it might be sixty degrees. Hell, I might see both in the five days I'll be there."

He laughed. "Yeah, I remember that from when I lived there as a kid. Or how about when it's eighty degrees in the Springs, but it's thirty and snowing up on Pikes Peak?"

She nodded, thinking about the majestic view of Pikes Peak stretching across the horizon, remembering what the frosty summit looked like from the red rocks of Garden of the Gods. She thought of Rachel's wedding set against that backdrop and how James would already have left for Afghanistan. He wouldn't be able to accompany her. The thought of not getting to be with him in her mountains the way she had fantasized about carved a little wound into her heart.

James started stripping off his clothes as soon as he walked through the threshold of his house, leaving a trail behind him. First his jacket and shirt, then his shorts, next his socks, and finally his boxer briefs. Sarah giggled at his urgency to get naked and went behind him, picking up all the clothes and depositing everything but the jacket into the hamper in his bedroom.

When she met him in the bathroom, he was already standing under the shower, steam starting to rise. She surveyed his naked form with the water rushing off his flesh, drinking in the sight of him. With every fiber of her being, she wanted to be naked next to him under the running water, her soft skin turning red with the heat, and his thick fingers gripping her hips and bending her over so he could take her from behind.

He wiped the water off his face and looked at her curiously. "What are you doing?"

She couldn't find the words. The image of his cock piercing her pussy and his hands kneading her ass cheeks as the water riveted between them was monopolizing her thoughts.

"Get naked and join me, woman," he commanded, shooting her a mock-authoritative glare.

She thought about turning to leave then but was hypnotized. *He's like a drug, and I'm an addict.* She found herself mindlessly stripping off her clothes, letting them fall to the floor and stepping into the shower beside him.

"That's more like it." He pulled her close to him and brushed his lips against hers while the water beat down on them.

I guess it wouldn't hurt me to have sex with him one last time, she thought as his mouth grazed her neck. *Or I could even wait until tomorrow morning so we can fuck all night. Shit. Why does this have to be so hard?*

Later they twisted their limbs together in his bed, his arms around her and her head on his chest. They'd satisfied their hunger for each other's bodies and were now at the point of considering actual sustenance.

Sarah was about to doze off when James startled her. "You've been married before, right?"

Sarah sat straight up. He had never pried into her past, so this question out of nowhere was a shock to her system. "Why are you asking?"

James sat up too and stroked her back reassuringly. "Sorry, I didn't mean to upset you."

He can clearly feel the negative energy triggered by this topic.

"I have just been thinking about marriage lately. No particular reason, but, you know, why some last and some don't. And I realized I don't really know what happened with yours. I mean, you had two kids together and...then what? You grew apart?"

Numbness permeated her limbs. "First off," she corrected him, "Abby's father was my college boyfriend. I didn't meet Owen's dad until Abby was two."

"Oh, okay." James leaned in to express interest but gave

her a wide berth.

She sighed, recognizing his body language and what it meant. As much as she hated talking about her ex-husband, this was a positive, him asking about her past.

"I struggled when Abby was little. My mom helped, but I worked full-time as a waitress. I wanted to focus all my energy on raising her. I had this customer who came in several times a week...only a few years older than me...very charming, although 'smarmy' is the word I would use now. Daniel Taylor was his name, and he...well, as much as it shames me to admit it now, he swept me off my feet."

James was still stroking her back, listening intently. She remembered the night he spilled his guts about his former wife and his service in Iraq—that story had endeared him to her. She may have fallen in love with him that night. *What effect would this story have on him?*

"Daniel was one of those men who always had some sort of plan, some sort of scheme," she continued. "Always had a new business venture. It's not that things weren't on the up and up; he just didn't have nearly the connections or capital to leverage that he thought he did. But I didn't realize that at first. At first it seemed like things came easy to him. We were always getting new stuff: houses, cars, boats, clothes, jewelry. He wanted me to have a baby right away. We married, and Owen was born the next year. He was absolutely thrilled to have a son. It was like a status symbol for him."

"But you weren't happy?"

"I was numb," Sarah admitted. "I was going through the motions. I decided when Owen was one that I wanted to go back to school for a PhD, which meant moving. Daniel wasn't particularly supportive." Her eyes narrowed a bit as the memory of those fights fell like fresh snow on the canvas of her mind. "I had finally decided what I wanted to do with my life, and he just thought it was ridiculous."

He squeezed her to his side. "I'm sorry to hear that."

"He finally conceded. My mom moved with us to help with the kids. She'd always had bad vibes about Daniel. She tried to tell me so many times, and I was completely blind. I loved him..." Her voice trailed off as if the wound reopened right before their very eyes. She shook off the pain and shared more, "So we moved; I started my PhD program, and I saw Daniel less and less. He was always away on 'business,' and that was when I started doing my own thing."

"Your 'own thing'?" James's eyes widened. "What do you mean by that?"

"Well, I'm not stupid. It was pretty obvious he was cheating on me. And not with just one woman. Little things didn't add up. I looked at emails, phone numbers; I found receipts. He had three or four women spread all over the country. I stopped having sex with him because I was afraid I would get an STI."

James nodded. "I don't blame you for that."

"And I started hanging out with Rachel more," Sarah explained. "I knew she and her husband were into some...unconventional stuff, but she invited me to come along to a party one weekend. So I went." She paused as a tiny smile turned the corner of her lips upward. "I didn't look back after that."

"Wow, that's awesome." And his tone was genuine, which still surprised her.

She'd never shied away from identifying as polyamorous in front of James. As traditional as he was, he didn't seem to have any ethical issues with it. And he hadn't minded being involved in that threesome—rather, he seemed to enjoy it very much—but Sarah had the impression it was something he'd only entertain or approve of for someone who was single—not for someone who was married, who had committed to one person for the rest of their lives.

Nevertheless, she continued, "I started researching. I was looking for a dissertation topic, so I started looking into alternative lifestyles and interviewing different groups of people. I found that couples in open relationships scored higher in almost every measure of internal happiness and happiness with their partner. I tried to broach that with Daniel once, but he flat out refused to listen, denying he ever cheated on me, the bastard..."

"So then what happened?" he asked, fully engaged in the story.

"So my plan was to keep doing my own thing, finish school, and wait until I was making good money before divorcing Daniel, but when I was nearly done with the program, he up and left me for one of his mistresses. Probably the point in time when I was hurting most financially—and that is when he chose to leave."

"Wow, sounds like a great guy!" James noted sarcastically. "What about the kids?"

He'd struck a nerve, and her eyes welled up with tears. "He hasn't seen the kids since," she explained. "He lost a ton of money when the housing bubble burst and the market was wonky. He owes me a lot of back support. He hasn't even attempted to see the kids, and I think it's because he's a failure, and he's embarrassed. They're old enough to understand that now."

James shook his head. "I don't know what to say, Sarah," he confessed. "I'm so sorry you had to go through that."

Sarah wiped away a tear and shrugged it off. "He was an asshole. I fell for him. It's just as much my fault."

"Don't say that," James argued. "What kind of man abandons his children? What kind of man doesn't want to know or see his children?" He took Sarah's hands into his own. "I know I'm not a father...yet...but I would want to spend every second I could with my kids."

Sarah saw an opening to shift the conversation away from her. *I feel exposed. I have shared too much.* "So...is that something you want? Kids?"

James's pupils expanded as if he were trying to envision his future. "Yeah, I suppose I do...someday."

Sarah nodded. "Well, you'll make a great father. Any kid would be lucky to call you dad."

His eyebrows shot up. "What makes you say that?"

It wasn't hard for her to elaborate on why. "You're smart, funny, good with my kids. Patient. Attentive...well, you are in person anyway..." She thought about his incommunicado spells, the dichotomy of his attention when they were together versus when they were apart.

Then her eyes trailed down his body, drinking in his muscular form. "And physically, you're quite a specimen. You'd be passing on great genes." She took a deep breath and added, "And because you have convictions. You believe in something...and you're willing to fight for it."

"I'm flattered." He laughed. "It's a high compliment considering what an amazing mom you are to Abby and Owen. You know what it takes better than I do."

"So," Sarah tested the waters, "I guess we just need to find you a woman worthy of having your baby!"

James smirked. "Yeah, know where I can pick one of those up?" He laughed again, and Sarah played along, still baiting him, gauging his response. "Well, I may know some-one, actually."

Sarah's heart began to pound against her ribs. *He doesn't realize I can't have any more children.* "Who's that?"

She fully expected him to play along. To say *her*. To throw her a bone.

"My high school sweetheart," James answered. There was an eternal pause before he added, "We've been back in touch."

Sarah was speechless but tried with every ounce of her

strength to stay calm, to dig a little deeper. "Oh?" she managed, a single, clear syllable. It felt like a gong ringing inside her head.

"Yeah," James said nonchalantly. "I saw her when I was back in Ohio for Christmas. She just got out of a relationship...no kids yet, though... She's a nurse. It was really nice to see her again."

Sarah's heart was in her throat, strangling her. "Uh...were you going to tell me?"

"I'm telling you now." His voice rang with defensiveness.

Her nerves were crying out like a million daggers stabbing into her. She felt the shock reverberating through her from her spine to her extremities. *Wanting to know more. Wanting to know nothing. Wanting to take back the entire conversation.* Her love of information won out: "Did you sleep with her when you were home?"

He nodded. "Yeah."

She got off the bed and walked across the room to the window. She stood, trembling, wondering if she could put one foot in front of the other and make it out of the room. *My clothes. I need to put my clothes back on.* She started to gather up her shirt and socks. *Where's my bra? Shit.*

He stayed on the bed, rubbing his temples with the tips of his fingers. "Why are you mad? You're fucking that Polish guy!"

"Which I told you about. BEFORE I fucked him." Sarah tugged on her socks with twice the strength required, anger welling deep inside. "This happened two months ago, and you're just now telling me?"

"I didn't think you'd care," James explained. Now he was silent, and his blue eyes looked dull and gray.

Fully dressed, she turned and looked at him, noticing a furrow in his brow for the first time, the precursors to crows' feet at the edges of his eyes. It was as if he'd aged ten years since the beginning of their conversation. "So what's going on with you two?"

James cleared his throat and stood up, still nude. He grabbed a towel off the chair near his bed and wrapped it around his waist. "I don't know," he said softly.

That's not what I want to hear. I came here intending to break up with him. Instead we end up making love and then I spill my guts about my failed marriage. Serves me fucking right.

What is wrong with me? He fucked another woman and didn't tell me? I don't need to know anything else. I just need to leave.

He watched her standing there, shaking with anger. He kept his distance but looked her straight in the eyes. "We broke up when I went off to Basic...then we lost touch when I married Becca. This fall she found me on Facebook, and we reconnected."

Sarah's dark eyes glared at him. "So?"

"We hung out when I was home. She came over to the house a few times. We reminisced. It was fun." His voice seemed small. Too small for his body. And now the tone was apologetic, not defensive.

He knew he was wrong not to tell me. "Still talking to her?"

He nodded.

Then she remembered what initiated this conversation. He revealed he may have found a potential mother for his children. *Something that I can't give him.*

All the feelings she'd had before about being his toy, a plaything—*someone to fuck and spend time with till he found a woman his own age*—came flooding back to her. *It explains everything.* Why he was so distant when they weren't together. Why everything had to be on his terms. Why she always felt she was yielding to him. She was stuck inside his Sarah Box.

I don't want to be in a box anymore.

"I have to go, James," was the only thing she could articulate. She could feel the tears burning the corners of her eyes like they were made of acid.

"What?" he seemed confused. "Why? I don't understand why you're so jealous."

Sarah shook her head, breaking a tear loose and sending it streaming down her cheek. "The fact you don't understand just further illustrates why I need to leave."

He tried to take her hand; she squeezed it for a moment and then let it go, watching it flaccidly flop back down to his waist. *He looks like he's in shock.*

"James, this kind of information is critical to your relationship with me. It's the type of thing we should have discussed before two months elapsed. You compartmentalize me. You don't want the different facets of your life to touch. And I get it; I do." She forced a tiny smile, her convictions rising. "But I'm holistic. Everything is connected for me, and I can't be boxed up like this."

"I've never promised you anything, Sarah. I thought I could do whatever I wanted." The defensiveness had re-emerged. There was no point in arguing; she could see he was firm. He didn't think he had done anything wrong.

"I guess not," Sarah said coolly. "Good luck with everything, James, and I mean that."

She picked up her purse and dug out her keys, exiting the room all at once, multitasking so she could distract her mind and carry her body away from that room, that house, that man. She was getting in her car, starting it up, and driving in reverse away from a giant cliff she had nearly driven off.

All the while, James remained in the same spot. Frozen.

16

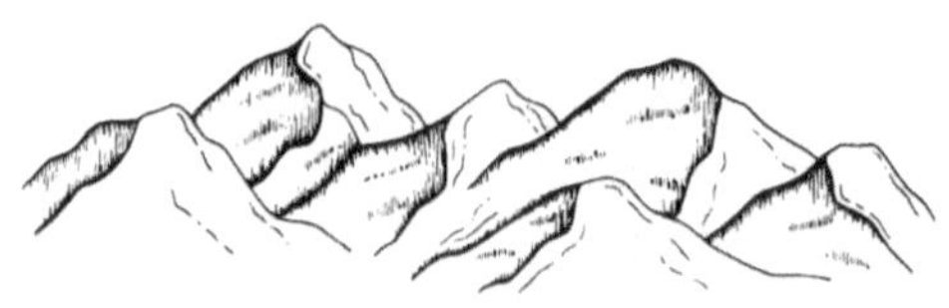

It wasn't just the plane lifting at take-off, it was also her soul. The past week had forced Sarah into survival mode: no sleep, hardly any food, harried packing for her trip, and avoidance of all modes of communication. She had a singular focus: her conference, with a secondary agenda of enjoying her homeland. Rachel had wanted to accompany her at the last minute, thinking she could make a few wedding arrangements with less hassle in person. Sarah had looked at her best friend, silence and desperation gripping her dark eyes, hoping to send the message that she needed alone time with every fiber of her being. She needed to heal.

Settling into her seat, her head back and earbuds cranking soothing tunes into her skull, she reviewed the events of the past week. Three days after she left his house, James had texted her: *I'm sorry. Can we talk?* She didn't respond. She knew she would only be reeled in again by his magnetic power over her, and really, there was nothing more to add to what she said before she left.

Two days after that, he tried calling but didn't leave a

message. And that was it. Two attempts at contact rejected, and now she could move on. *Too little, too late.* She switched The James Channel off for good.

My mountains will restore me. I'll feel like a brand-new person after this week away.

She sought solace and strength, so she'd left Maryland two days before the conference was slated to begin. She wanted a little extra time to enjoy her mountains and to put the finishing touches on her presentation. The weather forecast looked phenomenal for early March so her suitcase was burgeoning with both hiking gear and professional attire. *Nothing like going from hiking boots and flannel to three-inch pumps and a power suit.*

When she landed in Denver there was a text waiting.

Rachel: *James hunted me down. He really wants to talk to you. I told him you'd already left. He seemed devastated.*

Sarah: *When was that?*

Rachel: *Last night.*

And then:

Rachel: *Are you going to talk to him?*

Sarah felt a little stabbing pain as she considered the question. She didn't want to decide now. She didn't even want to think of him at all, but she should try to figure out why she fell so hard. *And closure, closure would be good.*

She texted Rachel three indefinite, but honest, letters.

Sarah: *IDK.*

She waited for her suitcase at the carousel and helplessly endured a slew of thoughts tossing in her head like laundry in a dryer. *Why am I so hurt? If I knew our relationship was doomed to fail, why did I let it go this far?*

She traced back over the six months since she'd first met James, and one thing resounded again and again: *he never felt for me the way I felt for him.* There were all sorts of reasons, all sorts of obstacles that could have gotten in the way: *my age, his age, my having kids, PTSD, not really knowing what he wants...*

And I can't change any of those things.

THE DRIVE to the hotel was jam-packed with snarled traffic. Sarah was starting to regret renting a car instead of relying on public transportation, but she wanted a chance to drive over to her hometown of Breckenridge to see her Aunt Sally, her mother's sister, and to drive down to Colorado Springs. She promised Rachel she'd take some pictures of three possible reception venues there since that was where the wedding was happening. After hitting nearly every red light in the entire city of Denver, she whipped the little black Nissan into the circular drive in front of the hotel and gratefully handed over the keys to the valet. She felt completely done. *I'm done with travel. Done with people. Done with thoughts. Wine and a bubble bath, that's all I want tonight.*

She checked into her room and lamented that it was only four o'clock local time. She was still on East Coast time and hungry for dinner. *Oooh, maybe I will order room service,* she thought indulgently. *The less I have to move tonight, the better.* She hoped she'd remembered to pack the novel she'd recently started reading. *Wine. Bath. Reading. Bed,* she itemized her agenda. *It sounds perfect.*

She noticed her phone was flashing with a text when she removed it from her purse.

Rachel: *All checked in? What room are you in?*

Grrrr. Leave me alone! But she responded,

Sarah: *914. Why? I'm going to bed.*

Rachel: *Isn't it like 4 pm there? Sorry, just wanted to know in case of an emergency. Don't worry, the kids are fine.*

Owen was staying at Rachel's house with Thomas. It was the kids' Spring Break, after all, and she didn't want them to sit around bored at Grandma's the entire time. She had also allowed Abby to stay at Chloe's house, although she was skeptical about trusting her to stay out of trouble. Rachel and Kathy were checking in with her at regular intervals, plus Sarah felt that Abby had matured a lot in the previous few months, so she was optimistic Abby wouldn't jeopardize the trust she'd gained.

She felt a little guilty about being away during their time off school, but she didn't have much control over when this annual conference was held. And getting a presentation accepted was quite prestigious. It would look wonderful on her CV.

Sarah popped two ibuprofen and went to find the ice machine. She felt at least fifty percent better having the wine on ice and starting a bath in the large oval garden tub. She was also feeling extremely grateful that she'd upgraded to a suite.

How often do I indulge myself? Oh, that's right, never.

I'm not going to feel guilty about this. I'm going to love every fucking minute of it!

She nearly squealed, she was so euphoric at the thought of her evening itinerary. She was always taking care of someone: Owen, Abby, Rachel, students, or even Pawel and James, to a certain extent. *I only want to take care of myself tonight.*

She carried the bucket, wine icily ensconced within, to the bathroom and set it on the tile next to the tub while she eased her clothes off. She had the bottle opener and a glass ready to go as soon as she'd soaked for a while and given the wine a chance to chill.

She caught a flash of her reflection in the mirror. She sucked in her stomach and struck a provocative pose, puckering her lips and sassily placing her hand on her hip. *I think I may have shed that ten pounds of holiday weight this week from not eating*, she thought, studying her image. *I look pale, though.*

Her skin was nearly translucent and streaked with turquoise veins under the garish lights. She scanned the wall for a dimmer switch and brought the lighting level down to where she could see well enough to climb into the tub and pour her wine but not much else. *Perfect.* She sighed, easing her body down into the bubbling cauldron wafting with the scent of jasmine and gardenia.

She slipped down to her shoulders, the heat penetrating her sore muscles like a magical balm. Leaning back against the cold edge of the tub, the ends of her hair absorbed the water and stuck to her neck and arms. *Ah, good, I left my phone in the other room. I'm sure the world can do without the ability to contact me for an hour or two. I forgot to text Pawel, but I'll do that later.*

The wine was still warm, but desperation forced her to pour a glass. She dropped a few ice cubes into the burgundy liquid and swirled it around before savoring the sweet but potent juice on her tongue. She relaxed and closed her eyes, her wine glass still in her hand.

"James who?" she said aloud, laughing into the half-lit emptiness, hearing a slight echo reverberate across the tile. She set the glass down on the marble floor and slipped her entire head under the bubbles. She baptized herself in the swirling waters, as if all of her pain would be washed away when she emerged.

She held her breath in the watery silence, feeling the negative energy escape her pores—until she strained to hear what sounded like a faint pounding. At first, she assumed it was the sound of blood rushing through her head. Then she heard the pounding become more insistent and jerked up out of the water to listen more carefully.

Sure enough, there was a persistent banging coming from the French doors at the front of the suite. *Oh, for fuck's sake. They picked a fine time to bring me the stupid extra towels I asked for.*

She drained the rest of her wine down her throat in one gulp and grabbed the nearest fluffy white towel to wrap around herself. She didn't even bother drying off; after all, she was getting right back into the tub. *With more hot water,* she decided, trying not to let the disturbance ruin her previous state of elation.

She left a trail of wet footprints from the bathroom tile, through the plush carpeting, all the way to the double doors. She didn't even bother looking through the peephole, throwing one of the doors open with her free hand, the other clutching her towel securely around her breasts.

The first and last thing she saw were his blue eyes.

HER HEAD WAS POUNDING. *Damn ibuprofen did nothing* was her first thought before opening her eyes. Everything was fuzzy. *Why am I so woozy?*

She felt a hand on her thigh and jerked herself awake. "Because you passed out," came the answer to the question she thought she'd asked in her head.

And there is James McAllister, sitting on the edge of my bed. My bed in Denver, Colorado. What the fuck is going on here? And then, with slightly more lucidity: *I hope I said that in my head this time and not out loud.*

"The room is spinning." She closed her eyes and gently shook her head, trying to make it stop.

"I bet it is," came his deep, soothing reply. "I'm sorry I couldn't catch you, but you only had the door half-open, and I would have knocked you to the floor even faster if I'd pushed it the rest of the way."

A vision of herself sprawled out on the carpet, still dripping from the bath, almost completely naked, with those little cartoon birds and stars circling over her head sprang to mind. *He must have carried me to the bed.* The towel was long gone; her hair was still wet, and she remained nude.

"What are you doing here?" she finally managed.

He smiled and unearthed her hand from under the white down comforter, folding it into his. "You wouldn't talk to me," he explained. "And, well, that just didn't work for me. So I took a few days' leave and came out here. I want to talk." He squeezed her fingers between his, his eyes wide and clear, his voice soft and imploring. "Please?"

She was still ridiculously dizzy. She didn't know if she'd passed out from shock, the wine, the heat of the bath water, the altitude change or the lack of food. But she was starting to believe shock was the most likely culprit, especially considering that having him this close to her was making her heart pound harder.

"I don't know what to say," was all she could muster.

"I don't want you to say anything now," James replied. "Get some sleep, and we will talk about it tomorrow. Your conference doesn't start till Wednesday, right?"

She nodded, still numb.

"What did you have planned for tomorrow?"

"Driving down to the Springs." She pulled the sheet up to cover her bare breasts, even though his eyes were pinned to hers and not roaming down her body. "Then home to Breckenridge on Tuesday."

This was surreal, him leaning over her, wanting her so badly, he flew over 1500 miles just to talk to her. *He knew I wouldn't be able to resist him in person.*

"Can I come with you?" he asked softly, his eyes filled with sincerity and a touch of hope.

She nodded. *I'm too weak to resist him right now.*

He got her a glass of ice water and returned to her bedside. "Here, I bet you're dehydrated from flying. Wine was probably not the wisest choice—and when was the last time you ate?"

She wanted to laugh; she wanted to cry. She would have never imagined this turn of events in a million years. *Surreal* was the only label she could think of.

"This morning in Maryland," she replied meekly. *I can't believe he's actually here.*

"I'm going out to get you something to eat," he announced. He placed the water glass on her bedside table and kissed her chastely on the forehead. "I'll be back in just a few."

This was not what I envisioned when I was considering room service.

The wooziness returned in a thundering wave crashing into her skull. In a flash, he was gone, and she was left wondering if it had all been a dream. She rolled to her side and snuggled deep into the down comforter, a smile faintly tugging at the corners of her lips.

I can't believe he's here...

"Why am I not surprised Rachel was in on this?" Sarah smirked as she steered the rental car deep into the mountains.

"Well, she cares about you a lot." James rested his hand on Sarah's thigh. "I know she's been absorbed lately with all the wedding plans, but she wants to help you. And I think you tend to shut her out. You're great at helping friends who need you, but I don't think you like to accept help yourself when you need it."

"What exactly is it I need help with?" she fired back, biting back another smirk.

James chuckled. "Me? I guess?"

Even after putting her in his Sarah Box, he really did seem to understand her. And what he said about Rachel was also spot on.

She shook her head and chanced a quick look at him, watching his lips curl up into his boyish grin. "How did you guys pull this off, anyway?"

"Rachel knows all your passwords, I guess, and logged into your wireless account. She searched all the numbers in your texts and phone calls until she figured out which one was mine—the only Ohio number, probably. Then she called me up and demanded to know why I didn't go after you. That was Friday," he relayed.

"So then she told you where I was staying. And that's why she asked what room I was in." Sarah huffed out a long, hot breath and rolled her eyes.

James was still chuckling. "I'd asked her if I should book

my own room. You know—what if you didn't let me stay? And Rachel said, 'She will.'"

"I don't know whether to yell at her or thank her," Sarah admitted.

"Well, I hope you'll thank her." James placed his hand on top of hers on the gearshift.

"I'll tell you after today."

After she finished laughing, she promptly changed the subject to her conference presentation, regaling James with details about her latest research study. He was engaged, posing questions about the methodology and the results. She loved how he was fascinated by the world around him: natural phenomena, the human condition, how the two elements interacted. *He is, in many ways, a philosopher, much like myself. No wonder I fell for him. I felt it from the beginning—our souls speak the same language.*

She watched the mountains flashing by the windows of the car and felt buoyant. There was something about her native land that gave her a different kind of energy, an intensity. She sometimes felt so beaten down by the demands and pressures of her job and family, but at that moment with the beautiful scenery whizzing past, she felt like a feather floating in the breeze. She looked over at James and sighed softly.

I still can't believe he's here. And how much I love him, despite everything. I guess I am going to have to see how this all plays out. It means I don't get to be in control. And I don't know if I can handle that.

When she turned down the road toward Garden of the Gods, the red rock formations rose before them. It never failed to stir feelings of awe deep in her soul. She felt like a tiny speck of nothingness when walking amongst such intense beauty; she was humbled by it. She'd visited there as a child, a little getaway her mother and Aunt Sally had arranged for her, Adam, and their cousins Emily and Jacob one summer. She remembered picnicking at the edge of Balanced Rock with the incredible vista of the snow-covered Rockies in the background. She had fallen in love with the place. Later, she met Rachel when they both lived in Denver, and it seemed fitting that her best friend had grown up in the city graced by this stunning beauty.

"I haven't been here since I was a kid." James's eyes were glued out his window, taking in the breathtaking sights. "It looks exactly the way I remember."

"It's timeless," Sarah agreed, pulling the car into a parking space near the Kissing Camels formation.

"I almost hear my mother's voice scolding me for running too far ahead and climbing up rocks I shouldn't have been climbing." His eyes scaled to the top of the formation where it looked like two camels were kissing, then brought his gaze back down to Sarah. "I guess we both have a past here. I didn't know if I'd ever see it again. Of course I hoped I would."

"The spirits of our child selves are running about," she noted wistfully. "I can feel them. Playing. Laughing." As she stretched out her arms, the golden sunlight captured the auburn highlights in her rich, dark wavy hair, casting a glow all around her, an aura of pure energy. She twirled in a circle, absorbing all the beauty surrounding her while James drank in her radiance, an earth goddess reconnecting to her terrestrial home.

He caught her in his arms. "So I finally see you in your element, Dr. Lynde." He smiled, stroking her hair that was flying in the breeze. "You seem like you belong here. Another timeless beauty."

Sarah looked into his eyes. "That may be the highest compliment I've ever been paid." She was stunned at how deeply it moved her. She was silent after that, still letting his words soak in.

They started down the trail hand in hand. There was much unspoken between them. She knew it would come out. It would all come out, but for now, she felt steeped in a shimmery peace and was happy sharing the big, wide, beautiful world with the man she loved.

AT LUNCH, the dam broke. They were perched near Balanced Rock, the site of her first picnic in the park nearly thirty years ago. *I would have never imagined as a little girl being here as an adult...with a man...having a grown-up conversation.* How simple her problems were at the age of eight, when she'd first visited. There was nothing simple about this: not her feelings, not James's desires, nor either of their actions.

"Here's what I want to know," Sarah began boldly. "What's her name?"

James made no attempt at being elusive this time. "Maggie," he replied. "Maggie Carson."

"Why didn't you tell me about Maggie?" Sarah questioned.

She could see him mentally organizing his words. "When I first started talking to her a few months ago on Facebook, it was almost unreal...just words on a screen at first," he explained. "I didn't know if I would ever see her, or if she'd even want to see me. She was pretty angry with me for getting married all those years ago. When I went off to Basic, we'd left things open-ended. We thought someday we'd end up back together. So she was hurt when I married Becca before I deployed."

"But then you *did* see her," Sarah interjected, bringing the topic back to his error of omission.

"Right." He dug into the red dirt a bit with his heels. "And it was weird at first. You know how it is when you see someone as an adult, someone you knew when you were growing up? It's like you have to get to know them all over again, but it's almost harder because you have all these memories of them, and you're always trying to reconcile the present them with the past them."

Sarah nodded. *At least he's being open. It's a step.* She started packing up their lunch leftovers and stuffing them in her backpack. "Let's walk."

They hiked down the path and crossed the road to the start of a new trail. He took the backpack from her and slung it over his shoulder. "So we talked about it," he continued, his feet pressing into the dusty trail.

She saw the impressions of his boots and the length of his stride. She couldn't bear to scan his body up to his face to see his eyes. She waited to hear what she knew he would say.

"About making a go of it, you know, marriage, family. All that. Like we had talked about when we were kids."

"But?" She was holding her breath on that one word.

"We're both...cautious. She just got out of a serious relationship. She never had kids; her ex was a jerk. You know about my experience. And, well, I'm getting ready to leave."

"Did you tell her about me?" She felt suspended, her heart cast out into the water, waiting for a fish to bite.

They were climbing now. She was following him up a rock that was slanted, and she watched the rust-colored dirt accumulating on the tread of his shoes. He had yet to answer her question. They continued to ascend, looping around and through another formation, the Siamese Twins this time, climbing again. There was a ledge, and he stopped to help boost her up on to it. In the distance, the clouds around the snow-capped Pikes Peak had dispersed just enough to give a glimpse of its icy spires touching the heavens. He sat on the cold red rocks and pulled Sarah down next to him.

"I told her I'm seeing other people," he said.

"So I don't understand what this means for us. If there even is an 'us.'"

He needed to pull off the Band-Aid. *The faster he tells me he's going to go make babies with his high school sweetheart, the faster I can reset The James Channel to something easier to watch. Something less painful.*

"I don't really know what any of it means," James said. "That's why I didn't tell you. Because I really don't know."

Sarah's fingers were trembling in her gloves, and not from the cold. Her eyes fell to her feet, wondering how they would carry her down this mountain. Wondering if she was strong enough for the descent. Wondering if the dirt could ever be removed. Her heart was somewhere near her throat, swelling to such proportions that it blocked her voice box from functioning.

"I'm sorry I didn't tell you," James's voice carried on the wind. "That was wrong. You've always been honest with me about your…other relationships. I just didn't know what to say."

"Do you love her?" her voice broke through the swelling. So fragile. Like a rose petal.

"I think I do," he said quickly.

She expected him to hesitate. He zigged when she thought he'd zag. No matter how well she thought she knew him, she didn't.

"Well, then you should be with her," Sarah concluded,

gaining strength, building her resolve. She shifted so she could get her legs under her and get back onto her feet.

He pulled her back down. "Sarah…" He lifted her chin so she was forced to look into his eyes for the first time in this conversation. The tears had already welled and would soon be past the point of no return. It never mattered how strongly she felt, she was rarely able to stop an in-progress cry. "I'm confused."

A tear broke loose and trickled down her cheek. "What do you mean?"

"I have feelings for you too." His eyes stayed locked on hers.

"What kind of feelings?" she pressed, still skeptical. She began reining in her heart, forcing it back down into her chest.

His eyes looked as clear and open as the sky that had parted to reveal Pike's Peak. "I care about you a lot. I love spending time with you. I don't know what that means, but I know I don't want to stop."

His arm was around her now, his hand spanning the small of her back. "When you left the other day…I stood there trying to imagine never seeing you again. And—" He took a breath. "—And I couldn't bear it. I didn't want to imagine it."

She allowed him to pull her into his arms. Their hips aligned, legs facing each other, feet still on the ground, but her face was buried in his chest, his fingers raking through her hair. She sobbed into his chest, wondering what all this meant, if his words were enough. If these feelings were enough for her, as amorphous as they were.

"Are you okay?" he whispered into the ear closest to his lips.

She pulled away and revealed her tear-stained face to him, her swollen eyes and nose, her heart exposed like a deer in the clearing with an arrow aimed straight at it. *This is the time; this is when I let it all out. If I don't tell him now, I may lose him forever.*

She found her voice: "I'm in love with you, James." The words fluttered out like snowflakes, so softly that they melted in his eyelashes.

Now it was his turn to be suspended, waiting for a "but."

She smiled, relieved the dam had finally burst; now the valley was about to flood.

"There's no 'but,' James. I just love you. I want you to be happy, and I know that might not be with me. I love you so much that it hurts... Sometimes you treat me like I don't matter to you. I feel like you put me in this box, and all I want is to matter to you. I don't want to be in a box. I just want to be important to you. All the time. Not just when you feel like it."

"You *do* matter to me, Sarah," he gasped, sounding incredulous that she didn't grasp the depth of his feelings. "Of course you matter to me. More than I probably even want to admit."

She looked up at him through watery eyes, the sun catching sparks of gold and amber from within the sepia depths. "Really?"

"I don't know how to explain it, but I feel love for you too. I don't know what else to call it," he admitted. "I guess I'm conflicted." She felt his heart grasping for an understanding that was just out of his reach.

"I believe it's possible to love more than one person," she assured him. "That's what polyamory is, after all. And there's nothing wrong with it. It's wonderful to be free enough to open your heart in multiple directions. I wish more people could."

"Your mind is beautiful." He smiled. "All of you is beautiful. How could I not love you? When you look into my eyes, I feel like you're staring straight into my soul. No one has ever looked at me like that before."

She squeezed his hand. Nearly as many questions remained as the ones that had found answers, like unmatched pairs wandering in the wilderness, waiting to find their other halves. But there was something, a tiny beam of light piercing the darkness, something to build on, something to nurture. It was the speck of hope she needed to believe in.

He covered her lips with his own, and she detected that he was now lighter, unencumbered, as if the burdens he'd been shouldering had disintegrated, shackles falling away. Nestled into his arms, she felt like they were soaring. Here they stood, on top of the earth, surrounded by her mountains. Their fortresses would protect this fragile love till it was strong enough to stand on its own two feet.

The moon casts just enough of a glow to highlight the contours of your shoulders and face as you shift your weight on top of me. I'm so wet from our last round that you slide into me with no resistance, making me gasp at the sensation of being filled by your hardness. You begin to move ever so slowly inside of me, shallow at first, and then increasingly deeper. You feel my back arching, my stomach tensing, my moans filling the room. Your mouth is close to my ear as you whisper, "No, wait for me, baby..."

I manage, "I'm trying..." Every stroke sends me an inch closer, hitting just the right spot.

Your arms around me, you're moaning, "Oh, fuck..." as I grip your cock deep inside me, trying so damn hard not to let myself fall off the edge.

I know you so well, every breath you take, every thrust, I know how close you are getting. My hands stroke down your back and you are so deep, reaching the core of me. It's taking everything I have to hold back, and feeling me approach the edge once more, again you demand, "Wait for me."

I can't even respond, knowing if I lose concentration I will explode around you. You're getting close. I can wait; I can do this. I want us to climax together. It needs to happen that way. In perfect solidarity. It's symbolic.

You're moaning all around me, your breath heavy and falling on my face, your muscles rigid and poised, and your cock growing harder. I am a vessel of your pleasure. Lying beneath you, feeling your weight on me, I love that I am the source of your ecstasy.

Finally, you whisper, "Now, baby, come with me," but I have already started shuddering beneath you, those last thoughts finishing me off. I'm still feeling my spasms around you as you release deep inside me.

You lie there, spent, your head on my chest until you become too sensitive and need to pull out. I feel your seed start to leak out onto my thighs as you shift beside me and pull me close to you, summing it up in three words: "That was intense."

And I have nothing to say except that I am yours. No holding back. Risks be damned, I'm all in.

17

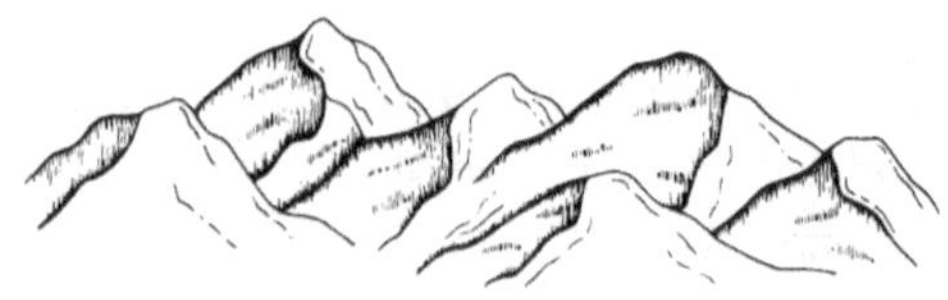

Spring began to unfurl its fresh green wings throughout the Mid-Atlantic shortly after Sarah returned from Denver. James had stayed through the first day of her conference and accompanied her to Breckenridge to visit Aunt Sally. Sarah's favorite aunt was practically her mother's twin, being only eighteen months her junior. Aunt Sally conjured up all sorts of embarrassing tales from Sarah's youth to amuse and entertain James. Sarah happily contemplated why this potentially awkward meeting seemed so familiar and comfortable. The conference presentation had also gone well, and Sarah exuded a strength and assurance she hadn't felt in months. She felt rejuvenated.

But nothing was better than coming home to James. After spending time with him in Denver, she sensed a closeness with him she had longed to feel for a man for years. She was blooming, just like the sunny yellow daffodils and indigo crocuses lining the stone-studded walk to her front door.

Their conversation on their last day together in Colorado rang through her memory:

"Just be honest with me, okay? Even if you think you

might hurt my feelings. Trust me to be able to handle what you need to say." She'd rested her hand on his chest, directly over his heart. "If this is going to work, we need to be open and transparent."

"Okay," he'd agreed, but she could see it wouldn't be easy for him. He was so used to boxing things away, compartmentalizing and repressing. She didn't know whether to blame his Catholic upbringing, military service, or the simple fact he was a man. In any case, she was slowly deprogramming him, positively reinforcing his openness and willingness to share, gently prodding when he seemed to shut down.

Rachel invited them over for a "welcome home" dinner shortly after the conference. Sarah watched Rachel give James a wink when she went to hug him as if to say, "We did it!"

That night at dinner, Rachel proposed a toast, "To Sarah and James, may your love grow and bloom, and may you find the happiness together that Jack and I have found." She turned to Jack and mouthed the words "I love you," as she clinked glasses around the table.

Then she pulled another rabbit out of her hat: "Sarah, your birthday is in a few weeks—and just happens to fall on a Saturday. You know what that means, right?"

"I don't," Sarah admitted, "and I'm a little scared to find out!" She scanned her best friend's face waiting for the answer.

Jack laughed; he obviously knew what the devious glint in his fiancée's eyes meant. "Which birthday are we celebrating this year, beautiful?"

"Thirty-seventh," Sarah replied, "which naturally requires no big celebration." She arched an eyebrow at Rachel, whose face was painted with mischievous excitement.

"*Au contraire*, my Little Pumpkin!" Rachel's devilish laugh filled the room. James was grinning in anticipation, and Jack was on the edge of his seat, waiting for the announcement he knew was coming.

"Alright, out with it!" Sarah demanded and, turning to James, questioned, "Are you in on this too?" He shook his head but then his laughter gave him away. She couldn't believe all three were conspiring against her.

"Two words," Rachel's smile almost split her face in half, "House Party!!!"

"Oh Rachel," she stammered, "you shouldn't have." She glanced at James and then back at Rachel, shooting her an uncertain look. *I don't think James is ready for that.*

"Too late, the invitations have gone out. And I get to give the birthday girl her first spanking!" Rachel exclaimed.

Jack looked on with approval. James was a little harder to read: *happy but blissfully ignorant?*

Three weeks later, she and James were en route to Rachel's for the birthday party, and Sarah was nervously reviewing all the etiquette with him. "Open doors mean you can watch. Closed doors mean don't go in. Always ask before you join in or touch anyone."

"Sarah," he gently placed his hand over hers on her knee, "I'm not going to leave your side. Don't worry; I'll be fine."

"Okay, okay," Sarah conceded. "I just don't want you to do anything you're not comfortable with, sweetheart. You'd tell me if you didn't want to do this, right?"

"Of course I would. Please stop worrying. I just want you to enjoy your birthday, okay?"

Sarah nodded, her heart fluttery. She'd feel better after a glass of wine. *Should James drink? Or not drink? Come to think of it, I have never seen him drunk. But his first house party is probably not the time for that.*

James pulled into Rachel's driveway and took the spot nearest her car, knowing they'd be blocked in by the other party guests. They'd already discussed spending the night. Rachel had insisted upon it.

Sarah burst in to find Rachel standing right beside the door. She held out a sparkly rhinestone tiara which she promptly affixed to Sarah's head. Jack swathed her in a sash that read in purple glitter: "Birthday Queen." Rachel smoothed Sarah's deep marine blue dress down over her bust and hips and then posed her and James for a picture. "Now kiss!" she commanded and captured the couple with their lips locked as well. It was the first time she and James had been photographed together.

Moments later, the guests began to arrive. Sarah hadn't seen many of their mutual friends for over a year. She'd been so busy with her summertime self-denial; then work, James, and family all fall and winter. She was humbled that so many people had turned out to celebrate with her despite her absence at an entire year's worth of events. There were also some new friends Rachel had made in her adventures with Jack.

Sarah worked the crowd as James observed her, witnessing her effortless transformation into the role of social butterfly. Her smile was broad, her eyes gracious, and she always gave warm hugs or kisses in lieu of handshakes. She introduced him as she went: "This is my boyfriend, James." No one used last names, only first names with this crowd. She never mentioned he was in the military. In fact, no one talked about their work.

Even though many aspects of the party seemed completely mundane—the eating, the drinking, the small talk about the weather—there was a different energy in this group. There was an openness, a sensuality, and a welcoming spirit that was palpable. Conversations they floated in and out of ranged from family life, to trips and vacations, to parties and clubs attended. Almost everything was upbeat, light, and suggestive—with plenty of innuendo.

Sarah gravitated toward one particular couple. The woman was a curvaceous redhead, a few inches taller than Sarah, with creamy white skin and piercing green eyes. Her husband had handsome features accented by dark, salt and pepper-sprinkled hair and a matching goatee.

As James finished his second beer, Rachel announced it was time to cut the birthday cake. He ambled over to see if she needed any help.

"James," Sarah called, motioning him back to her side, "Scott and Felicity are originally from Denver. I was just telling them about our trip there last month."

"Great city," James remarked, sliding himself into the conversation. Sarah watched Felicity's eyes sparkle as she scanned James up and down. "Can't wait to go back and visit."

"Are you both going out for the wedding?" Scott asked. "Maybe you can spend a few extra days? You should try whitewater rafting this time!"

"Oh," James replied, "that would be great, but unfortunately I won't be able to make Rachel and Jack's wedding. I'll be away on business."

Felicity twirled an auburn curl between her thumb and forefinger. "That's a shame," she cooed. "I was hoping I would get to see you again."

James smiled and glanced at Sarah for approval. "I know," Sarah lamented, "no one is more disappointed that he won't be there than me." Her face brightened a bit as she added, "But feel free to enjoy him tonight." She winked at Felicity and James's face flushed. She grazed his back lightly with her fingertips, stroking up and down from his neck to his waist.

Felicity beamed. "Oh, I would most certainly enjoy

that...but later... Looks like Rachel needs you for the cake cutting!"

Sarah moved toward the dining room where Rachel wielded the cake knife and a small black leather paddle. "Before we cut the cake, we need to give the Birthday Girl her spankings!" Rachel's piercing voice gained the attention of every guest. She handed the paddle to James. "I was going to do the honors myself, but I think you should get the first whack, right?"

"You bet." James smiled as he moved Sarah out in front of the table, putting her on display for everyone to see. He bent her at the waist and lifted her dress to reveal a lacy black thong dividing her smooth, round lily-white cheeks. He poised the paddle just above her right cheek and delivered a solid wallop that elicited a nice, tight, high-pitched cracking sound, coupled with a squeal from the birthday girl's lips.

"You've got to count them, Sarah," Rachel chastised her, the wicked grin still spread across her face.

"My bad." Sarah laughed, almost having forgotten her friend's sadistic streak. "That's one."

Rachel, Jack, Scott, Felicity, and the other guests each followed suit with Sarah counting each spanking. There were almost enough attendees to divide the spankings evenly, up to thirty-four. Felicity, Rachel and James took the last three, and James added one more "to grow on." Sarah's posterior was glowing bright red by the end of the exercise.

She straightened up and smoothed her dress back down. "I definitely deserve some cake after that!"

Rachel lit the candles and made a comment about what she wouldn't mind doing with the hot wax, but Sarah shot her a look that said *I've tried to be a good sport, but that's crossing the line.* The entire crowd sang a rousing, off-key rendition of "Happy Birthday," and Sarah filled her lungs with air to blow out the thirty-seven candles.

But first she made the traditional birthday wish: "I want James to be mine." She extinguished all the candles in a single attempt.

Felicity slithered through the crowd like a snake, and in a flash was by James's side again, her green eyes lusty and wanton. She was so close to him that her breasts were grazing his arm, and one of her hands had slipped around his waist as she whispered something in his ear. He nodded, and Sarah watched his eyes avert to her milky white cleavage.

But when Felicity started to pull him toward the hallway, he stopped. "We're bringing Sarah and Scott too, right?"

A barely discernible spot of disappointment eked its way across her face. "Oh, you only do same room?"

Sarah took Felicity's hand and drew close to her so as not to make a scene. "It's his first time full swapping," she said softly in her ear. Felicity nodded in understanding, then scanned the room for Scott and motioned for him to follow them back to the bedrooms.

James looked to Sarah for an explanation, but she'd already grabbed Scott's arm and was pulling him toward the guest bedroom. When they entered the room, she turned to James, cupping his face in both her hands, gazing up into his eyes wearing a serious expression.

"What's 'full swapping' entail?" he whispered as Scott and Felicity began to undress.

"When you swap partners," she coached. "Are you sure you want to do this? Because if you don't, it's fine."

He smiled. "No, no, I do. If you do." His lips brushed hers in a lingering kiss, drawing her body snugly against his.

"Everything okay?" Felicity questioned from the bed. She had one shapely leg extended and the other propped up, revealing her smoothly shaved sex crowned with springy auburn curls. Her full breasts topped by luscious pink nipples rested against her ribcage, begging for attention.

Sarah stripped off her dress, bra and panties and crawled across the bed, noticing her bottom was still tender from all the spankings. Her long, dark hair cascaded down her back as she kneeled, taking one of Felicity's nipples into her mouth, swirling her tongue around the rosy areola. James and Scott both took a seat on the edge of the bed to watch the show.

Felicity tilted her head back in ecstasy and moved her hand between her legs so she could touch herself. She leaned down and lifted Sarah's face to hers, their lips meeting as both murmured soft sighs. Her fingers slid in and out of her wanton pussy, and her other hand gently cupped Sarah's breast as they kissed.

James's eyes never left the sight of the two intertwined as he deftly pulled his clothes off and returned to his front-row seat, propped up against two pillows at the head of the bed. His erect cock pointed to his navel and his testicles had swollen, all aching to be touched.

His nudity had not escaped Felicity's notice as she broke from her kiss with Sarah to stretch her body across the bed, giving herself access to James's cock. She smiled up at him and licked her lips before her tongue darted out to tease the tip of his erection.

Sarah shifted off the bed and fell to her knees on the carpet between Scott's legs. His engorged member also begged for attention, and Sarah eagerly took it deep into her hot, hungry mouth, her hands on his hips allowing her to control the depth of his strokes. She bobbed up and down for several moments, then pulled back to watch James, his eyes reduced to slits, and his face clenched in concentration.

She returned her attention to Scott's cock, his hand guiding her head up and down his shaft. "I think you should go lick Felicity's pussy," he suggested.

"Mmmmm," Sarah sighed, not requiring much cajoling.

She slid back onto the bed and coaxed Felicity onto her side so she could still suck James's cock. The redhead propped one leg up, aiming her glistening mound of red curls directly at Sarah's face. Sarah lapped lightly at her pearly pink clit, which elicited a surprised gasp from the redhead's mouth, as if she didn't expect the sensation to be so intense from such slight pressure. Sarah began to taste her more fully, delving her tongue into the tight, sweet abyss.

She felt James's eyes on her as she parted Felicity's lips with her fingers and licked up and down her slit, just barely entering her pussy with the tip of her tongue during each pass. His expression had not changed when she glanced over at him; he was finding it a challenge to keep from climaxing in the redhead's mouth. His eyes shifted for a moment to a spot behind her.

As soon as she felt the hand on her ass, Sarah realized James had watched Scott move off the bed and to a standing position behind her, poised to penetrate her lovely backside with his long, hard cock.

She winced as she felt him spread her labia to enter her and the head of his condom-sheathed length crash hard into her cervix. She let out a cry as the pain reverberated through her body—a good pain, one on the very edge that lies between pleasure and discomfort.

A look of concern verging on panic clenched James's face, but she smiled and mouthed the words, "I'm fine," just as Scott thrusted again and took her breath away. Then Felicity reached for her, pulling her mouth back to her pulsating sex. She began to grind her hips into Sarah's face, urgently needing to feel her tongue again.

James stood up, grabbed a condom from the nightstand, and unrolled it onto his cock. He pulled Felicity's legs out from under Sarah's mouth and dragged her to the edge of the bed. She squealed in delight, and Sarah propped herself up on her forearms to watch James slide his thick, throbbing manhood into Felicity's passage, moistened with her own desire and Sarah's saliva. She rested her feet on James's broad, muscular shoulders.

"Uhhhhhh," he moaned, leaning in to get a deeper angle as he slowly stroked in and out of her while she cried out with each thrust.

Scott was clearly enjoying watching his wife's pussy being assaulted by a young, fit stud and began to intensify his own speed as he drilled into Sarah. The ladies' faces rested side by side, their bodies angled in opposite directions. Turning toward each other, they began to kiss again, their tongues exploring each other's mouths when they weren't thrown off course by the relentless thrusts.

Sarah reached her hand down to fondle Felicity's breasts while they kissed, feeling her orgasm build around Scott's skilled cock. The room started to spin—hands and tongues and bodies, all in motion, all grinding and writhing to the same impassioned, consuming rhythm, while moans and sighs of unbridled rapture filled the air with a symphony of ecstasy.

Sarah screamed, "Oh my god!" and exploded onto Scott's cock, the pressure requiring him to slow down so he could keep from following suit.

This time he took a cue from James and pulled Sarah's legs out from under her, flipping her onto her back so he could mount her, and soon he was back inside her pussy, stroking deep inside her. She wrapped her legs around him and turned slightly so she could watch Felicity gripped by her own orgasm, her eyes closed tightly, her mouth contorted and whispering, "Oh fuck, oh fuck, oh fuck," lightly under her breath, punctuated by squeals as James moved in time to her spasms.

Sarah watched the look of concentration on his face as he

waited for Felicity to finish and then pushed her up the bed so he could move in between her legs. *I'm impressed. Some guys have performance issues the first time they do a group thing, but he's taken to this like a duck to water.*

As if he felt her mind shift to thoughts of him, he looked down at her and smiled, reaching for her hand. He laced his fingers through hers, and she watched his ass cheeks clench as he thrusted his manhood into the very beautiful redhead beneath him. They locked eyes, and she knew they were sharing something very deep, very intense, and very rare.

Something she knew was called compersion.

"I'm so sorry I didn't get to celebrate your birthday with you," Pawel apologized as he handed Sarah a beautifully wrapped rectangular package.

"Oh, you shouldn't have!" She smiled, ripping into the gold paper and setting aside the green velvet ribbon it was tied with. She held up a copy of a small, leather-bound book. "Oh my god, Pawel, is this a first edition?"

He nodded, a wide grin spread across his cheeks. "I picked it up when I was in Europe, and I knew you had to have it."

"This must have been very expensive!" Sarah worried. "I can't even begin to imagine what you might have paid for it." She was calculating, based on her knowledge of the literary masterpiece, in the upper three digits, possibly four.

Pawel shook his head and drew his finger to her

lips. "Don't say another word. I'll be returning to Poland soon, and I want you to have something special to remember me by."

"First off," Sarah retorted, "this isn't special, it's practically priceless, and secondly, don't act like I will never see you again."

Pawel kissed the top of her head. "Tell me what you did on your birthday," he said, masterfully changing the subject.

"Oh," Sarah was easily distracted, "my friends Rachel and Jack threw me a birthday party."

Pawel's brows furrowed, clearly displaying his disappointment at not being invited. "Did you take your army guy?"

Sarah nodded. "He knows Rachel and Jack already," she explained, hating the sad look he wore. "Oh, Pawel, don't be jealous!" She added in a whisper, "Please?"

He patted her hand and forced his lips into a smile. "You're right, Princess. So, tell me about it."

"Well, it's funny the word 'jealousy' should come up," she began. "I've been thinking a lot about that word."

"Is that so?" He leaned toward her with interest. "I'm dying to know what this has to do with your birthday party." A laugh tumbled out of his mouth.

"Yes," she explained. "Do you know what the opposite of jealousy is?"

Pawel paused, then shrugged. "Not in English, anyway," he admitted, still smiling expectantly.

"Compersion. It's when you feel joy seeing your partner derive happiness or pleasure from another person," she elaborated. "I felt it at my party, with James."

"Oh, how interesting. So please provide some context for this feeling. What precipitated it?" He sounded like the academic he was.

"Well…" She wondered how much detail to give. "We

were...playing...with another couple. And watching him with her, well, I enjoyed it. I was glad he found pleasure in her body."

"That's wonderful, Sarah, and very enlightened." He put his arm around her and kissed her cheek. "I would like to think, given a similar circumstance, I would feel the same way if I watched someone else make love to you."

"Right," Sarah sighed, unable to picture that scenario for some reason. "I'm troubled, though."

"Why?"

"Despite my best efforts, I'm having a lot of trouble feeling compersion for James as far as Maggie is concerned." Sarah had already explained the whole situation to Pawel, once shortly after she and James had had their falling out in February, when James recommended she be patient while he sorted out his feelings, and then again after she'd returned from Colorado following their reconciliation. Pawel was not only familiar with the details, but he'd also been a good sounding board and source of support.

His angle was also remarkably different than Rachel's, which consisted of, "Get him to dump that bitch and devote himself to you."

Pawel understood why someone would want to maintain multiple relationships; after all, he had an agreement with his wife to do that very thing. And he understood how James's age and life experiences had led him to feel confused about what he felt and what he wanted.

"You're frightened," Pawel observed, a knowing expression narrowing his eyes, "and insecure."

Sarah didn't enjoy being called either of those things. "How am I insecure?" Negativity swiftly bubbled up against her carefully constructed shield.

"You feel insecure in the relationship," Pawel assessed. "He hasn't done enough to make you feel like he's fully invested in you. There's too much unknown, too much risk of heartbreak."

Much to her dismay, she found his position inarguable. "He's in Ohio this week for his mother's fiftieth birthday. He could be with her right now."

She hadn't seen an actual picture of Maggie yet, but her mind had already formulated an image of a tall, leggy blonde. *I could be totally off, though, who knows?* The thought of a beautiful young woman hanging on to his arm as they greeted all his family members, them fondly remembering her from their high school days, from prom pictures and yearbook photos, it stabbed at Sarah's heart. *I don't like it. No, scratch that, I absolutely loathe it.*

Pawel exuded empathy from his dark, bespectacled eyes. "When does he leave for Afghanistan?"

"June," Sarah replied. "I know I shouldn't expect him to have this figured out. It's not fair to force him into figuring out what he wants to do with the rest of his life when he's getting ready to go off to war. But I just feel...this pressure...a sense of urgency..." She sighed as her mind scrambled for the right words. "I don't know how to say it. I feel like I'm on the verge of losing him, and I'm angry at myself because I wish just knowing he loves me was good enough."

"Have you told him what you actually want?" Pawel asked.

Sarah shook her head. "I'm afraid to. I don't want to scare him."

She gripped Pawel's hands with her own as she let her voice finally give words to what her heart had been feeling for months. "I don't think I've ever felt this strongly about anyone. I'm just crazy about him. Meaning, he makes me crazy." She percolated a little sparkling laugh as she fully admitted how irrational her mind could be when it came to James.

"Oh, Sarah, I'm trying to feel compersion too," Pawel admitted, taking her into his arms. His voice had cracked a little, and Sarah realized how hard he was clinging to his sensibilities, and how hard he had fallen for her, despite trying to downplay it for the benefit of their friendship. The words were unspoken between them, and she knew it was because he didn't know if she could return the sentiments.

Not in the same way that he loves me, but I do love him. He's a beautiful man, so thoughtful, so sincere. He's deliberate and eloquent, so impassioned about his work. He listens and really hears what I'm saying, better than perhaps any friend I've ever had. I do love him, and I want to make sure he knows before he goes how much I care for him.

Then her thoughts turned darker: *but what if James only loves me in the way I love Pawel? What if it's just a deep, intense friendship and not really romantic?* She shook her head to drive away the marching tears threatening to flood her eyes at any time as she clung to Pawel's wiry frame.

But how do you explain the sexual chemistry? How do you explain the fact our bodies are drawn to each other like magnets?

It's so unfair. Why do we have to have such deep, irrational, uncontrollable feelings when they can't be returned? It's a cruel trick of nature that we're biologically wired to have these intense, profound desires.

All I want is James, and I'll never truly be able to have him. My whole body, not just my poor heart, is breaking over him.

SARAH WAS restless and desperately missing James by the end of his trip. She'd avoided making contact, trying her best to give him space and not expect much, if any, communication. As the days of silence passed one by one, all she could do was imagine the conversations, touches, embraces, and kisses he and Maggie were sharing.

I'm driving myself crazy with these thoughts. She felt so stupid for dwelling on something so out of her control.

Finally, it was the day he was scheduled to return to Maryland, and she could resist no longer, dialing his number early in the morning after a night of endless tossing and turning.

Her heart pounded as she heard each ring in succession, only half-expecting to hear his voice. She'd almost forgotten what it sounded like, it'd been so long. He seemed so far removed from Maryland.

What if he found what he was looking for in Ohio? What if he isn't coming back to me?

"Hello?" his familiar velvety sound smoothed its way across the line.

"Hi..." Her voice trailed off, her mind frozen and empty of words, her heart too constricted to beat.

"Sarah? Everything okay?" He sounded concerned.

She cleared the choke back down her throat. "Yeah, I...just miss you...needed to hear your voice. I wanted to know if you were coming home."

"Of course I am." He laughed. "I'm on my way now. I miss you too." There was a little drag of silence, a bit of static on the line where she tried to read more meaning into those few words.

"Things are fine; nothing has changed. I'll be home soon."

He'd offered the tiniest pearl of reassurance. That's all she needed to hear. At least for the moment.

18

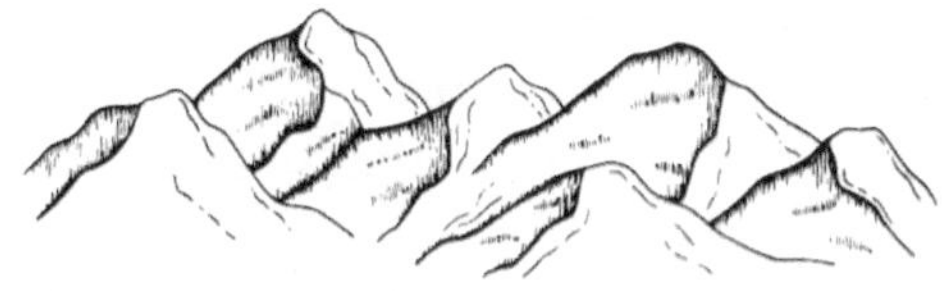

Sarah awoke with a start, struggling to get her bearings. Immediately, she felt his arm around her, his reassuring voice in her ear. "Come here," he soothed her, pulling her into his body, smoothing her hair away from her face and cradling her in the nook of his arm, her cheek on his chest.

Yes...this...here... She stumbled over her thoughts as he wrapped his leg over her hip and pulled her thigh through his so they were crisscrossed together.

That was a bad dream, she told herself. *Just a dream. I'm safe in James's arms, and nothing else matters.*

Her brain slowly woke up even as her body relaxed. She listened to his breathing slow and deepen, feeling the rising and falling of his chest gently moving her cheek up and down as she rode the waves his lungs made. She reviewed their reunion as if watching it on a film reel, as if it were two characters in a movie and not her and James.

First there was the embrace and the moment when their lips met. There was the small talk, the "how was your drive?"

and "how are the kids?" All the usual pleasantries were perfunctorily exchanged. They walked inside and found their spots on the sofa next to each other, surrounded by books.

"How's your family?" she'd asked him, studying his face like she was administering a polygraph. She needed answers. His body would give them.

He was relaxed, legs spread, back reclined against the cushion, pupils dilated in the dim light. "Great," he shared. "Mom was really surprised to see me. No one told her I was coming. I couldn't believe Patty and Allie could keep a secret that long."

Sarah smiled, envisioning her own fiftieth birthday...*only 13 years away now*. How could Owen not be there? What would it be like to see Owen go off to war? She couldn't fathom the worry James's mother had endured throughout her son's military career. And now she'd have to say goodbye again.

"Did you take Maggie to the party?" she asked, distracting herself from feeling Mrs. McAllister's pain.

James nodded, his facial features tightening. "Yeah, my family remembered her from when we used to date...back in the day."

"Right," Sarah replied a little more curtly than she intended. *Compersion, compersion, compersion*, she chided herself. "So, did you guys have a good visit?"

"Yes, we did." His whole frame stiffened. "We talked a lot about what we both want."

He isn't going to just give it away; I'm going to have to earn it. She felt like a paleontologist, taking months to patiently extract one tiny fossil. "And what is that?"

"Well," James replied, "you know, normal everyday stuff: a house, kids, good jobs, a happy family."

"And you think you can have that together?" She hated

the way her tone still sounded condescending, even when she'd tried so hard to pull back and be objective. She was unable to divorce her feelings from this no matter how hard she tried.

James shrugged. "Maybe." His eyes narrowed. "What do you want to hear, Sarah?"

"The truth," Sarah replied without hesitation. "I want to know if you're planning to marry her, to start a family with her. I want to know if she has any idea you have a girlfriend in Maryland you're spending every weekend with. I want to know what the hell all this means for you and me."

So much for playing it cool. She rolled her eyes, more at herself than at James. *Patience was never my strong suit, and I would have made a terrible paleontologist.*

He took her hands into his own, like he had done so many times before. "Look, Sarah, she knows about you. And the only thing I'm planning is to go to Afghanistan in June. Will I come home next spring and marry Maggie? Maybe. Will I come home and want to marry you? I don't know. Anything is possible."

Did he just say he might want to marry me?

He got up and moved across the room, clearly agitated. She wished it wasn't so difficult for him to talk about this.

If he's going to be in love with two women, it comes with a responsibility to keep the lines of communication open, to make both of us feel secure. He can't shut down every time I want to know what he's feeling. Does she ask him questions about what he's doing here? About what he feels for me?

"What does she know about me?" Sarah asked softly. "And please don't get mad, James, just tell me the truth. I need to know."

He nodded stiffly and returned to the sofa. "She knows your first name, that you're a professor, and that you have kids. That's about it. She really doesn't want to know anything else."

"But she knows you're sleeping with me?" *Why is that so important to me?*

He nodded. "She's not wild about the idea, but she realizes I met you before she and I got back in contact."

Sarah's cheeks inflamed. "Plus there's the whole you live here and she lives in Ohio thing."

James placed a hand on her knee. "Don't get defensive, Sarah. You're the one wanting to know all this stuff."

She cooled under his touch. "You're right." She scanned his face, searching for clues about what he wasn't saying, but she found nothing. "How's the sex?"

He looked down as if he couldn't believe those words had come out of her mouth. "Seriously?"

"Just tell me," Sarah coaxed him. "Please?"

"It's pretty good." James shook his head in disbelief that he was sharing an evaluation of his sex life with one partner with his other partner. "She doesn't have the...appetite that you have," he admitted. "And she isn't as responsive. Is that what you want to hear?"

I'm not going to get any more useful information. I've pushed him too far already. She suggested they grab some dinner, and his entire demeanor transformed as if the conversation about Maggie had never happened.

Sarah didn't mention her name again that night. After returning from dinner, they'd made love on the couch while a movie played, Sarah straddling James's thighs and bobbing up and down on his cock until she squirted all over him. He dragged her off to the shower, pushing her against the wall and taking her from behind while the hot water pelted their flesh.

Thinking about how intense their sex was sent chills up

her spine. *How could it be any better? It's me and James. It's pure magic.* She nestled into his arms and fell back asleep, begging her mind to create sweet dreams for her this time, rather than nightmares.

SARAH RETURNED HOME EARLY the next morning to get Owen ready for his soccer game. Abby stumbled out of bed and into the kitchen as she was making coffee. "How'd things go with James?" she asked, yawning.

"He's fine; he had a good trip to Ohio." Sarah didn't want to divulge the whole Maggie situation but was pleased her daughter was thinking of someone other than herself.

"Oh, glad to hear it." She sounded somewhat detached, poking her head into the refrigerator to look for the butter.

"I've got it over here." Sarah pointed to the plastic container by the toaster where she was making toast for Owen's breakfast.

"Got it, thanks," she replied, then added nonchalantly, "Oh, by the way, Tyler and I broke up."

Sarah felt a searing pain rip through her, a shock shooting down her spine. "Oh my god, what?! Abby, are you okay?"

She nodded slowly and shrugged. "Yeah, whatever. It's no big deal."

Sarah immediately pulled her daughter into her arms, holding her tiny frame against her chest. "Honey, you dated him for a long time. What was it, seven, eight months?"

"Eight months, one week, and three days," Abby enumerated, "but who's counting?"

Sarah examined her daughter's eyes. They were a little red, slightly puffy, but nothing else gave away that she'd just suffered a breakup. It almost looked like spring allergies. "What happened? If you feel like talking about it, I mean."

"I simply decided I didn't want to limit myself to dating one boy," Abby explained. "I'll be turning sixteen next month. I want to keep my options open." She looked so wise and mature standing there, one hand on her hip, her hair pulled back into a loose ponytail. "You know, like you do."

Sarah had to physically keep her jaw from dropping. "Uh...what do you mean, like I do?"

Abby tilted her head and thought for a second about how she wanted to elaborate on her comment. "You date more than one man at a time. Like right now, you have James and Pawel. When you were still married to Daniel, you saw Jonathan. And when we first moved here, you were sorta seeing Rick, Jason and Anthony."

A smile slowly crept across Sarah's face. *I don't know why I'm so shocked. She's my daughter, after all. Of course she's intuitive and perceptive. Of course she knows what's going on. I always thought Owen had inherited my empathic abilities, but let's face it, I raised both of these kids myself.*

"Well, Abby, I think that's a very smart decision. There's no reason to limit yourself to one boy when you're so young and just learning about yourself. Besides, you need plenty of time for your girlfriends too."

Sarah wondered if Abby was interested in girls? If she realized her mother was bisexual?

Abby nodded. "Chloe and I made a pact not to have serious boyfriends till we're seniors."

Sarah laughed. "Okay, well, whatever you two think is

best." She put the butter and milk away. "How did Tyler take the breakup?"

"Like a typical guy," Abby replied. "Told me he never really liked me that much anyway. Ugh, Mom, why do guys have to be such jerks?"

"If I ever figure out the answer to that one," Sarah promised, "I'll be sure to let you know!"

SARAH DROVE BACK over to James's house for a quiet evening of watching movies and vegetating, a reward for finishing up some work. She took some papers to grade and a bottle of wine she vowed not to open until seven papers were graded. James laughed at the little bargain she made with herself and promised not to interfere with her goal.

He was quite industrious, engaging in all manners of domestic tasks while she sat on his couch armed with her red pen. He dusted all the books and bookcases, started laundry, and was folding the clothes that sat rumpled in baskets during his journey to Ohio. What was even better—he was doing it shirtless. *So much for not interfering...*

She finally set down her pen and declared victory over the requisite number of papers. "Plus one more for good measure," she announced, catching James's attention on the other side of the room.

He laughed at her, making his way over to plant a kiss on her cheek. "You're such an overachiever."

"I need more than that," she complained, pulling him down on top of her on the couch.

As his weight sank into her, she wrapped her legs around his waist, feeling his cock grow hard in his sweatpants as he pressed against her pubic bone. "We're wearing way too much clothing though." She squirmed her way out from underneath him and started to pull her black yoga pants off. "Meet you in your room naked in two minutes," she suggested as she traipsed off to the bathroom.

She found him reclining on the bed, the sheet pulled up to his waist, flipping through channels on his television. "Really?" she questioned, "you'd rather watch TV?"

"No, but I didn't think you'd just be two minutes," he replied sarcastically.

"Your cock is a powerful motivator; what can I say?" Her eyes gleamed wickedly as she ripped back the sheet and climbed to a kneeling position between his thighs.

She proceeded to work him into a frenzy, his head thrown back, only guttural moans managing to escape from his throat as she licked and sucked every square inch of his manly parts. When she was satisfied he was ready for her, she climbed up his body and slid her wanton pussy down his shaft.

"Oh my god," she sighed, "you feel so fucking good inside me."

He mumbled something unintelligible and moved his hands to her hips, where he controlled her movements up and down. She propped herself on her wrists, slamming her body down with all her force as he pushed himself up, deeper inside her. His eyes closed, and she studied his face, wondering where his mind was, wondering when he might lock gazes with her.

He moved his hands behind his head and allowed her to take over. Obliging, she leaned down so that her breasts grazed his lips. Ordinarily he'd take her nipple into his mouth and gently chew on it, but his lips were firmly closed, expressionless.

She continued to grind her pelvis into him, a little more slowly, wondering why he was so distant. And then she realized he had lost his erection. She rose too far, and he slipped out from inside her. The wetness that had gathered on his cock turned cold against her upper thigh as she dismounted him. His eyes were still closed, but he pulled her into his arms.

"What's wrong?" she whispered.

He shook his head. "Nothing, baby, sorry."

She had dealt with performance issues in the past with other partners. *Stay calm, don't worry, don't assume,* she reminded herself of all the lessons she'd learned in the past. She stroked her hands down his chest, stomach and thighs. "It's okay," she said in her most soothing voice.

He turned on the movie, and they lay in silence. Sarah rolled onto her side and began to drift off to sleep. They both dozed for a few hours, and then she felt him press against her, his hand around her waist, pulling her bottom toward his hips. His erection strained against her flesh, buried in the cleft of her cheeks. He lifted her thigh to get the right angle to enter her, and, still drowsy, she jolted into lucidity, gasping as he filled her.

He moaned softly and started to move very slowly inside her. *I knew things would be better if we just waited a bit.*

He pulled out, pushed her over onto her knees and moved behind her. When his stiff cock slid into her, she groaned with pleasure and a sense of relief that his equipment seemed to be working as he firmly grasped her cheeks and began to stroke in and out. She tried not to worry too much about him and concentrated instead on the sensations radiating from her core.

Getting ever closer to climax, she pushed herself back against his driving hips, meeting each thrust with one of her own. His speed was increasing, and losing control was becoming a growing threat. He gathered her hair in his fist and wrapped it around his hand, knowing exactly which buttons to push to force her over the edge.

Damn, he knows me so well, she thought as she felt the first waves consume her. She felt suspended, her muscles spasming against him, tingling radiating out to her extremities and then back again toward her core.

James slowed down as she caught her breath. She laid her head down on the bed, angling her ass up, allowing him deeper access. She was silent for a moment, trying to read from his motions and sounds where he was, where he was going. He seemed to be slipping away again, both literally and figuratively. As he softened, she felt both his rising frustration and his desperation to push it below the surface.

She froze, wishing she could do something, say something to make it better. He withdrew. He fell to the bed, facing away from her, totally silent.

A tear stung at the corner of her eye. *Is this because of me? Did I do something wrong? Is it Maggie?*

All of her wise self-talk from two hours ago disappeared and was replaced with haunting insecurities. She curled her body to him, molding her soft flesh to his stiff, muscular frame. She draped her arm over his waist, resting her chin against his back. But she didn't speak. She listened to his breathing steady, his body spasm into sleep.

Then, realization dawned.

I'm keeping him from devoting himself to Maggie. He loves her and wants to be with her. To start a family with her. He's just confused because I'm here in the middle. I'm in the way. I need to go.

She silently left her warm spot in bed and gathered up her

things. He didn't even move. *This is for the best,* she thought as she got into her car and drove away.

IT WAS dark and a little foggy in the valleys of the curvy road Sarah traversed to exit James's housing development. The houses on the main road were spaced far apart and boasted thickets of trees and vegetation in between, making for a challenging drive in the pitch black, moonless night. She struggled to pay attention and stay awake, but her mind was tired and jumbled with sad thoughts and strong convictions that she was doing the right thing. She fought off her exhaustion, fueling her energy with desperate consternations, inventing all sorts of scenarios for how her relationship with James might play out.

She walked away with a broken heart in every single one.

This is a war I cannot win.

She cranked up the radio, but the song that blared out into the space around her ears spoke of unrequited love, and the singer's pain seared right through her. Her fingers trembling, she twisted the knob to turn it off; silence was more easily endured.

How did I get myself into this fucking mess? she asked herself for the millionth time.

She still had a few more miles till she reached the highway, but at least the main road was straighter and more brightly lit. In the distance she saw a pair of headlights veering back and forth on the straight stretch that lay before her, past where her own headlights shone. *Stupid drunk drivers.*

She slowed down and glanced at the glowing green numbers: *3:37. In the morning. On a Sunday morning.* Her mind traveled back to the last time she left James's house thinking it was the end. It was only two short months ago.

When her eyes went back to the road, the zig-zagging headlights were on top of her, shining through her, burning into her eyes. There was a jolt, an impact against the side of her car. A rush of energy bolted through her like a lightning strike, forcing her to veer sharply to the right to give the other driver a wider berth.

Her wheel struck the guardrail and flipped over it. In a swirling fraction of a second, her car rolled, then was back upright before crashing to an abrupt, head-jerking stop. Before she could panic, scream, or even think, the airbag shot up around her, enveloping her in a white cloud of sterile silence.

And then the white cloud went black.

THERE MUST HAVE BEEN DREAMS, millions of technicolor dreams, so vivid her mind and body ached from the continuous action, the clarity, the constant movement. And the sounds, the sounds had been so rich: the laughter of children, the crashing of waves, the squealing of tires, the screaming of sirens. And then there were the smells, searing through her nostrils, concentrated enough to make her sinuses explode: pungent cracklings of a campfire, gentle caresses of lilac blossoms, salty breezes wafting from ocean waves. But when her bleary eyes finally cracked open through swollen slits, all the colors, sounds and smells were stripped away. She heard only a low beeping and the soft, mind-numbing hum of machines, a disconcerting odor of disinfectant, and the dull, colorless gray of a clinical prison.

Where are my golden sun and purple mountains? Where is the sound of fall leaves crunching under my feet? Where is the smell of an apple pie cooling on the windowsill? Give me back my dream world, dammit, Sarah cried out into the caverns of her aching head.

But the only response she heard was, "Shhhhhh...don't try to speak."

She jolted at the sight of the nurse affixing the blood pressure cuff to her upper arm and at the feel of the paper-thin cotton gown clinging to her hip as the blanket was stripped away. She started to cough but then felt pain rip through her ribs like she was being stabbed in the lungs. *What the fuck?* She raised her fingertips to the pink-flowered gown and discovered that her chest was wound tightly in bandages.

"Your vitals look good," the nurse stated coldly. "You have some family here to see you. I'll go get them."

Well, isn't she Miss Personality?

Seconds later, the door pushed open, and Kathy and Rachel appeared, their eyes filled with concern and accented with dark purple circles underneath. Kathy sat in the chair nearest to her daughter's bed, and Rachel sat on the bed right next to Sarah.

"You're not family," Sarah managed a weak laugh.

"Her mind is fully intact," Rachel noted to Kathy, who smiled with relief. "I told them I'm your sister. Note the family resemblance." She pulled back her hair and turned to the side to reveal her profile, laughing.

"Where are Abby and Owen?" *I just want to see my kids. Oh, my god, I can't believe I'm in the hospital. What the hell happened?*

"They're in the waiting room with James." Kathy patted her daughter's leg through the blanket. "The nurse wanted to make sure you were okay before you saw anyone else."

James. Shit. The circumstances under which she left his house the night before crashed into her. "What's he doing here?" she asked. "Which hospital am I at?"

"You're still in Laurel," Rachel replied. "I guess you didn't make it that far from his house." She couldn't quite stop her next question before letting it slip out, "Why were you leaving his house in the middle of the night?"

Nausea and dizziness overcame her before exhaustion, a force stronger than she'd ever experienced, overpowered the nausea and dizziness. *I can't answer. My brain says no.*

Kathy recognized what was happening and shot Rachel a stern glare. "It's okay, honey, just relax. I think the doctor is coming in soon to talk to you. Save your strength for that."

She dozed until she felt adjustments being made to her cords, wires and tubes. A tall man in scrubs was standing at the foot of her bed, making notes in her file. "Well, good morning, Dr. Lynde," he said brightly when he noticed a peep of her brown irises show through the slits in her eyelids.

She still felt woozy but not bad enough to let the doctor's extreme handsomeness escape her notice. She scanned his name badge. *And hello...Dr...Russell. You're yummy!*

"You're a very lucky woman to have come out of that wreck with relatively minor injuries." Dr. Russell smiled at her over his clipboard. "You have a couple of broken ribs, some lacerations and contusions, and a concussion. We're going to keep you the rest of the day, just to monitor that concussion. And we're still waiting on the results of some tests. How are you feeling?"

Sarah noticed the clock read 9:13 AM. *How long have I been here?* So many questions flooded her mind, she couldn't grasp a single one; they seemed so slippery. She thought about all the x-rays and examinations she must have undergone while she was unconscious. *How many hands touched my body while I was out?*

Her next thought was of the other victim.

"Was that guy who hit me drunk?" she blurted out.

The doctor nodded. "And he's not doing as well as you. I can't release any other details though, I'm sorry." He said something fast and low to the nurse, who was busy changing the bag on Sarah's IV. "The police are going to be by soon to ask you a few questions."

The nurse wheeled the table closer to Sarah's bed. "You've got flowers," she announced, handing Sarah the card. "Do you feel like seeing your children now?"

Sarah turned the card over in her hand. Her face brightened at hearing the word "children," and she nodded happily. She set the card back on the table, unopened. She instantly thought of Pawel when she saw the flowers, thinking back to the time she got food poisoning at his house, and he sent flowers. *Wow, he's really on top of things. I guess news travels fast.*

Before another thought could squeeze its way to the forefront of her mind, she saw Owen's dark head peek around the corner and into her room. "Mom!" he squealed and ran to her, while Abby sauntered in behind him. He made a running leap to the bed, pushing the table with flowers out of the way and nearly tripping over her IV. Sarah felt a stabbing pain as he threw his wiry seventy-pound frame against her bandaged ribs.

"Oooooh, slow down there, baby," Sarah winced. "I'm still in some pain."

"Sorry, Mom." His eyes were wide with apology.

"I'm so glad you're okay, Mom!" Abby sat gingerly on the bed and tried not to stare too much at all the monitors her mother was hooked to.

"I feel so much better just having you both here with me," Sarah remarked as another party entered the room. It was a young, attractive state trooper. He smiled at the scene of mother and children on the hospital bed.

"Dr. Lynde? I'm Officer Chadd," he greeted her, shaking her hand with a firm grip.

"Can my kids stay?"

He nodded. "What do you remember from last night?"

She told him about the veering headlights, the car side-swiping her and sending her careening off the road. "Is the other driver okay?"

"He's in critical condition," Officer Chadd replied. "Young kid. Only twenty-two years old."

Sarah frowned. "Oh…I hope he isn't a UMD student. You probably can't tell me his name…"

"It's on the police report, so you'll be getting a copy of it for your insurance. Seth Zeliensky is his name," Officer Chadd reported.

The color drained from Sarah's face as vomit creeped up her esophagus.

"What's wrong, Mom?" Owen asked, laying his hand on his mother's arm with concern.

"He was one of my students."

A COUPLE OF HOURS LATER, Rachel tiptoed into the room as silently as she could muster, but still sort of loudly because she was wearing high-heeled boots. Sarah was dozing lightly but awoke enough to sense her best friend's presence and motioned for her to sit down beside her on the bed. "Did the kids go home?" Sarah murmured.

Rachel nodded. "Yes, your mom took them just after they saw you. They went to get something to eat too."

Sarah's head was pounding, and she realized it was time for another dosage of pain medication. They were giving her narcotics, and though she was a little loopy, she was starting to piece together the timeline of what had happened.

"I'm glad you guys came," she said. "I'd feel pretty lonely here all by myself."

"James is still here," Rachel told her. "He asked if you got the flowers."

Sarah sat up. "The flowers are from James? James is here?" The clouds cleared, and her head felt free, unencumbered.

"Yeah, he's been here all day. They called him first 'cause he came up as the last call you'd made from your cell. He called me, and I called your mom." She leaned in closer. "Sarah, he thinks you're mad at him and don't want to see him."

"I *am* mad at him," Sarah remembered. *He's been waiting here all day?* Her head was throbbing as she considered how he must feel knowing she wrecked leaving his house in the middle of the night. "No, I'm not mad. I just give up, that's all."

"What do you mean you give up?" Rachel questioned. "Since when do you give up on anyone or anything?"

"I think he should be with Maggie," Sarah admitted. "I can't make him happy. I'm holding him back from making a happy life with the woman he loves."

"Why don't you let him decide that?" Rachel asked sharply. "For fuck's sake, Sarah, you seem bound and determined to push him away as many times as you can. Why are you doing that?"

Sarah buried her aching head in her hands. "I wish I knew," she whispered.

"I'm going to go get him," Rachel announced and was gone before Sarah had a chance to protest.

Sarah reached over and grabbed the card that had been attached to the flowers off the table and slowly ripped opened the little envelope. It only said: *I'm sorry. James*

Sarah wanted to rip the card up. *What the fuck is he sorry about? Sorry we fought? Sorry he doesn't want to be with me? Sorry he's in love with two different women? Sorry he's leaving?*

Before she could postulate any other scenarios, she saw his broad frame in the doorway. "Are you sure you want to see me?"

Sarah nodded and watched him walk to her bedside. He remained standing. "Why did you leave last night?" He pushed the words out as if he couldn't take a step further without hearing her answer.

Sarah was silent for a moment as she studied his face. He looked tired, like he'd been up all night. His face was clenched with hurt and fear, his eyes gray with pain. She'd never seen him look so serious. Then his eyes traveled up the length of her body, encased in the white hospital bedding, tubes coming out of her arms and chest and nose. She witnessed his entire countenance soften as if her pitiful appearance drained all the concern about his own feelings out of his mind.

He grabbed her hand and bent to kiss her cheek. "Never mind," he said, his lips close to her ear. "It doesn't matter. I'm just glad you're gonna be okay."

She could almost hear his heart pounding in his ribcage

as he straightened back up and waited for her to say something. Anything.

"James, I had an epiphany last night," she finally spoke.

His eyebrows rose. "What's that?"

"I'm holding you back from being with Maggie," Sarah explained. "You're conflicted about what you want because I'm here, and I'm so accessible. But I know how much you want a traditional family and your own kids, and, well, I can't give you those things. I have to let you go. I have to let you go so you can be with Maggie."

James's face was blank, completely devoid of expression as he processed Sarah's words. Then he shook his head, and a little vein popped up in his neck she'd never noticed before. He cleared his throat. "No, Sarah, that's not what I want."

"Maybe not, but it's what needs to happen," Sarah replied adamantly. She pulled the blanket up to her chest, realizing the cold air and James's presence had caused her nipples to stiffen against the thin cotton material of the gown she wore. His mere presence was driving her completely crazy, despite her woozy head and injuries.

His eyes pierced through her as he slowly shook his head. "Please don't play the martyr, Sarah. Look, I know you're in pain, so I don't want to make things worse, but it's not for you to decide what is best for me. I don't know what I want right now, and I realize patience is not your strong suit, but I still want you in my life, Sarah. I only have a couple of months before I leave, and I want to be with you. I want to spend time with you."

Sarah had lost her ability to speak. Her ears were ringing with disbelief. Her eyes kept scanning his face, trying to figure out why he couldn't just let her go.

James continued, "Look, I don't know what's going to happen after I get back. I can't make you any promises, but I want the chance to see what happens. I'm sorry I had some issues last night. But I have a lot on my mind, and I'm getting ready to go off to war. It has nothing to do with you or how attractive or desirable I find you. It's just a lot of shit in my head that I don't know what to do with right now."

She nodded, the tears starting up again. "I wasn't mad about the issues you had. I just felt like maybe you didn't want me....and I don't want to keep you from pursuing what will make you happy..." Her voice trailed off before she weakly added, "...even if it's not me..."

In addition to the injury-induced pain, her body ached to touch him. As if sensing her need, he sat on the bed and took her into his arms, carefully avoiding the tubes and wires. Her head on his chest felt like home, despite the cold, sterile hospital bed.

"You make me happy, Sarah. God, I can't believe I almost lost you," he whispered, rocking her gently back and forth in his embrace. "I love you."

RACHEL DROVE Sarah home the next evening after she was released. Pawel was busy in her kitchen cooking a welcome home feast for her and the kids. Sarah was overwhelmed with gratitude and gave him a hug and kiss as soon as she saw him. He was very careful not to squeeze her around the ribs too hard.

"So you're out of commission for a while, right?" He gave her a little wink.

"Yeah, I suppose so," Sarah replied as if she hadn't made that connection yet. "Damn, that sucks."

"Tell me about it," he agreed, stepping back to take a look at her from head to toe. "You're still the sexiest woman I know, even in bandages."

Sex has been the furthest thing from my mind. How unusual. She smiled and mouthed the words "thank you," trying not to get choked up again. Crying and laughing were equally painful.

"Sarah, there's something else I want to tell you before the kids join us," Pawel said, his expression changing from bright to grave. Sarah looked at him expectantly. He took her hand into his and guided her over to the table where he motioned for her to sit down.

"I want you to hear this from me, before you check your email." Sarah nodded in understanding as he continued, "The university sent out a message to all faculty this afternoon," he explained. "It was about the accident. They said you were being released with non-life-threatening injuries. But the student who hit you..."

"What, Pawel, just say it... Did he...?" Her heart plummeted like a broken elevator car crashing down to the bottom of its shaft.

"He didn't make it," Pawel softly revealed. "I'm so sorry."

She shook her head as the tears took over. *An unspeakable tragedy.* He pulled her into his arms as the sobs ripped through her, the bandages tightening around her aching ribs. *He was so young...a senior...his whole life ahead of him.*

She remembered a paper he wrote for the research methods class she'd taught her first semester at UMD. How she'd met with him and helped him focus his research topic. She thought about his family, his grieving parents, his roommates, his friends. *Did he have a girlfriend? How is it that one bad choice could alter the course of history? Why is it that one split second can change the course of someone's life forever?*

If she hadn't been on that road, if she had been asleep in James's bed, maybe her student would have made it home safely.

Why is life so short and cruel? No wonder I want to fill my life with as much love as I can. Love is the only thing that transcends cold, hard reality. The only thing that matters.

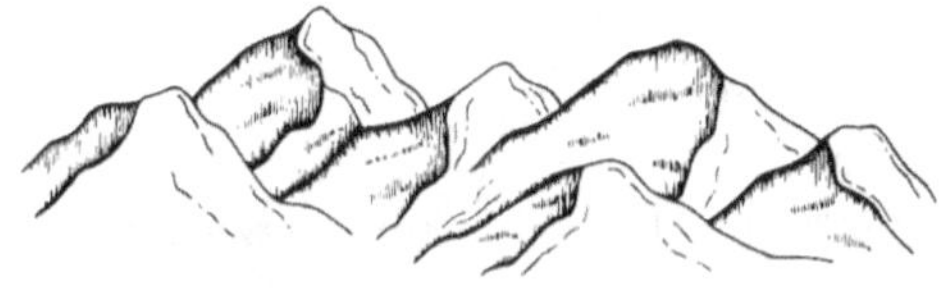

Sunlight sparkled on the rippling waters of the Chesapeake Bay as they crossed the four-mile-long bridge. The bay was dotted with white sailboats, and in the distance larger ships loomed gray and stalwart on the gently rocking waves. Sarah hadn't been over to the Eastern Shore of Maryland since the previous summer when she'd taken Owen and Abby to the beach. James had never been.

She watched his fingers grip the steering wheel as he concentrated on staying in his lane. *I'd almost think he is a little nervous to be driving over this bridge.* Sarah noted how fixated his eyes were on the gray pavement stretched before them. She glanced back at his thick, sturdy hands and remembered the night she met him, how imagining his hands caressing her body sent chills up her spine.

As they progressed down the highway, they took in the scenery of the Eastern Shore, the arched bridges over inlets and rivers, the flat rows of newly planted corn spreading to the horizon, the stately pine trees reaching toward the sky. Sarah was also reflecting on their last night together, when they'd celebrated James's thirtieth birthday. She'd surprised him by coming over midweek, a birthday cake and candles in tow. After she'd fed him cake and wine, she undressed him, stretched him out on his bed and sensually massaged every inch of his body with fragrant oils, underscored by flickering candlelight and soft music. He said it was the best birthday present he'd ever received.

And then she'd said, "I'm not done yet. I'm also taking you to the beach this weekend."

"The beach? What beach?"

"Assateague."

"Assa-what?" He'd looked at her quizzically.

She'd laughed, remembering her similar response when she'd first heard about the island on the Eastern Shore of Maryland where wild ponies frolicked on sandy beaches and grazed on sweet bay grasses. She thought the rumors must be greatly exaggerated till she saw the sweeping beauty of the marshes and the beach, and of the course the wild ponies, with her own eyes.

Her soul connected to the magic of the island the very first time she set foot on its sandy soil. She knew even then that someday she wanted to share its magic with someone she loved. It seemed a fitting place to take James to celebrate his birthday, as well as the end of the semester she'd narrowly survived, and of course, her recovery from the accident. She was blessed. Assateague was a good place to celebrate blessings.

They made it to the beach, where she helped James set up their tent in a small valley of sand dunes several yards from the water. There was a bit of shrubbery, but otherwise they were quite exposed to the wind and elements.

"Good thing it's not supposed to rain this weekend," Sarah remarked. "It's still going to get pretty cold at night, though, so you're gonna have to keep me warm." She winked at him as if she was issuing a challenge.

"It's probably better to come later in the summer," James replied as he surveyed the stakes and adjusted the tarp over the top of the tent.

"Well, you're not going to be here later in the summer," Sarah retorted coldly, hating to remind them both of that stark reality when she really wanted to have a peaceful, relaxing weekend.

Allow me just one more weekend of denial. This may be the last one we have together...ever. That last word rang through her mind like the tolling of a funeral bell.

He pulled her into his arms and kissed her softly on the cheek. "This place is beautiful, Sarah, and I'm glad to be here with you. Right here, right now, there's no place else I'd rather be." He bent to taste her lips, enflaming the heat between them even as the cool spring wind whipped around their embrace.

"It's relatively calm here now," Sarah said, "but later in the summer it's crazy crowded here on the weekends. Off-season is much nicer...it's just colder. But that means fewer bugs and more cuddling! Perks, if you ask me!"

"It's fine; it's fine. I'm sure we'll keep each other plenty warm." James grinned. "So what do you want to do first?"

Sarah's devilish laugh was lost in the wind, but she pulled James close to her again by the zipper of his fleece hooded sweatshirt and whispered in his ear a few deliciously lasciv-ious thoughts. He unzipped the door to the tent and pushed her inside, where he pulled her down and she tumbled on top of him, their laughter bubbling up all around them.

"We have to stay in here out of the wind," he said. "I don't see us recreating any famous beach sex movie scenes this weekend!"

"Where's your sense of adventure, Mr. GI Joe?" Sarah smirked, unfastening his pants while he pulled off his shirt.

Seconds later they were both nude, hands and mouths

exploring, words replaced by moans. The chill was quickly absorbed into the heat their bodies generated. She wrapped her legs around his hips as he pushed his cock deep inside of her, her pelvis grinding against him with every stroke. His lips never left hers as he took her over the edge only moments after entering her.

Afterwards she lay in his arms awash in contentment. "Do you think it's unusual that we still have this much sex after nine months together?"

James chuckled. "I've never had this much sex with *anyone* at *any* point in *any* relationship." He kissed her cheek. "You have the highest sex drive of any woman I've ever known."

"Really?" Sarah asked. "Exactly how many women have you...ahem...*known?*"

James's lips were still pulled into a smile. "Really? You really want to know a number?"

"Yeah, of course I do," Sarah replied. "It's not like I'm going to get jealous. Do you keep track?"

"Not really. I think about fifteen or twenty."

She mentally crunched that number, factoring in his age with the lengths of his deployments and the relationships she knew about, adding in Rachel and Felicity, the two women she'd watched him with.

"So I guess it's safe to say you've had some one-night stands," she surmised. "You're a very good lover—especially for having had so few partners."

"Twenty is 'so few?'" His eyebrows arched in surprise. "What about you?"

"Ohhhh." Sarah shot him a wicked smile, wondering how he would react to her admission. "I keep track."

"Oh yeah?" His eyes widened.

"I haven't been that active lately. I've only been with four men in the past year," she admitted, watching his eyes twitch at the word "only." She tried to keep her mouth from curling into a sheepish grin. "I have had much more...active...years though, in the past."

"So, what are we talking?" James questioned. "Fifty?" He watched her eyes shift upwards, indicating a higher number. "Triple digits?"

She laughed and playfully slapped him on the stomach. "No, not yet. I am pretty sure I'm in the sixties."

"So you've had three times more partners than I have," James calculated, "and you still think I'm a good lover?"

"Well, I've also had seven more years to fuck than you have," she teased him. "Maybe you'll be in the sixties, too, in seven more years?"

"Hey, I'm trying to be flattered over here." He shook his head as his lips pursed. "Maybe I just wanted to think I had some talent, alright?"

It was clear he was just joking, but she grasped his hand and leaned in close to his face. "Darling, you're not just good, you're the best I've ever had."

He was silent for a moment, humbled and awed by her assessment. His lips just inches from hers, he inquired, "What makes me so good?"

There were obvious skills like his breathtaking kisses and oral abilities—not to mention his amazing endurance—but she knew it ultimately boiled down to one thing and one thing alone: how much she loved him. She had never felt this connection, this passion for another partner before. She didn't even know she was capable of being this captivated, this drawn to another person. It was the interaction of their bodies, the intersection of their minds that created their magic.

She brightened as she discovered a way to explain it: "Do you remember telling me you were amazed by the way I always know just how, where, and when to touch you?"

He nodded slowly, his brows furrowed, apparently not

understanding what her recollection had to do with his love-making skills.

"Well, there's a simple reason why I'm able to do that. And why you're able to reciprocate. We have this connection that defies logic. Our souls speak to each other through our bodies. It's not just you; it's not just me... The sum is greater than its parts." She watched the understanding seep into his expression. "And I've never felt this depth or intensity with anyone else."

He said nothing, just held her tightly against him. She shut her eyes and listened to his steady heartbeat echoing through his flesh and bone. Her own heart was contentedly pounding away in her newly healed rib cage. Could she ever find the words that would make him want to hold her heart in his hands forever?

IN THE MORNING they witnessed the sun rise over the beach, which was deserted except for a dozen shorebirds strutting in the surf. "The ponies aren't even up this early," James remarked, glancing at his watch. "Not even 0600 yet. We must be crazy."

Dawn was a lady in pink and amber robes, spreading her flowing sleeves across the horizon and spilling a basket of gold onto the crests of faraway waves.

"You'll thank me someday." Sarah smiled, taking his hand as they strolled north. She had imagined walking like this with a lover, their feet pressing into wet sand while the surf crashed behind them, washing the record of their footprints away.

She breathed deeply as they walked, slowly acclimating to the paralyzing cold of the Atlantic that rippled over her bare feet with each wave. Her khaki pants were rolled up to avoid getting wet, and she zipped her navy windbreaker up to her chin while clutching on to James's arm for added warmth.

The sun will soon climb and warm the entire island. The cold won't last forever.

"I'm so lucky to be here, you know?" she let the words float out into the crisp morning air.

"With me?" he joked, squeezing her hand.

"Yes." She squeezed back. "And also to be alive…"

Only six weeks ago, she'd been in the hospital, grateful her life had been spared. It was the worst time of the semester, too. She got behind in grading, and then it was finals week, and she was still dealing with the pain from her injuries plus nightmares over her former student who perished in the crash. Her mother, the kids, Rachel, Jack, Pawel and James had all pulled together to make sure Sarah remained rested, fed, hydrated, caught up at work, and sane.

"Thank you again for all your help when I was recovering. I could not possibly have a better support system. I am blessed beyond measure," she told him.

"I know you'd do the same for me."

Despite her gratitude, she still wanted more. Here she was walking hand in hand with the man she loved, knowing he was going off to serve, yet she selfishly wanted him to stay and be hers. There was no promise he would come back to her, either literally or figuratively. There were no guarantees.

"What is it about Maggie?" Sarah regretted the words before they were even fully released. "What draws you to her?"

She felt him stiffen as he always did when Sarah spoke

her name. She knew how much he hated talking about Maggie, but she'd been preaching openness and transparency. She always preferred reality over letting her imagination create its own reality.

"She's..." he paused to choose his words carefully, "...smart and pretty, like you. But she is much more traditional. She understands my family and comes from a similar background as me. We share the same roots, you know?"

Sarah nodded. "What else? There has to be more than that."

"We want the same things. We share the same views. She was an army brat too, so we both grew up moving all over the place and landed as the new kids at our high school. That's how we met. In the school office...our dads were transferred there at the same time," James shared as if he were convincing himself as much as her. "She wants a family—and she's Catholic. She wants a traditional Catholic upbringing for her kids."

"Really?" Sarah was flabbergasted, never expecting faith to be on the list of Maggie's positive attributes. "I didn't realize religion was so important to you."

"Well, not in a fundamentalist, praying-all-the-time, going-to-confession sort of way, no," James explained. "But I want a religious foundation for my kids. Like what I had."

Sarah struggled to conceal her shock. She started to wonder about some of the things they'd done sexually and wondered how he reconciled those things with his beliefs. *Does he think I'm a sinner?*

"So, if I were Catholic—and wanted more kids—would you want to have kids with me?"

He looked at the ground as if he couldn't believe she was posing this question. "You know I haven't made any decisions about this yet, Sarah; I don't know why you keep pushing me." His voice was stern and closed-off.

"I just want to know what you like about her," Sarah admitted solemnly. "I want to understand what you want."

"The problem is I don't know what I want," he shot back rashly. "Look, I'm leaving in a few weeks, and I have to focus on that right now. I don't want distractions."

"Is that what I am? A distraction?" Sarah demanded. "Are you going to see her before you go?"

He nodded, ignoring the first set of questions. "She's coming next week to visit," he replied coolly. "And I'm going to Ohio for a week before I leave...to say goodbye to my family."

Sarah's heart felt like it was going to explode. *It's now or never. Put it on the line. Tell him what you want.*

They hiked down the beach far enough to reach the boardwalk leading to the dunes where their tent was. She sat down on the bench at the end of the wooden boards and emptied her shoes of the sand they'd collected. She scanned the ocean, which had turned blue under the rising golden sun. About twenty yards out, she saw the shiny steel gray of five dolphins jumping effortlessly into the waves as a pelican swooped down in their wake. She pointed them out to James, smiling. They watched them surface a few times before they were lost in the horizon.

She sat cross-legged before turning to face him. There were gulls crying on the wind as she took his hands into her own. "I know you're not in a position to make any decisions," she said. "I respect that. But I want you to know where I stand and how I feel. I can't send you off to war without you knowing what's in my heart and the depth of my feelings for you."

He nodded and let out the tiniest, nearly imperceptible sigh of agitation, and the sun caught his eyes as the light catches a prism, turning them a brilliant sapphire blue, a brighter color than she ever recalled seeing in the million times she'd looked into them.

Sometimes when I look at him, it strikes me all over again how gorgeous he is. Sometimes I'm nearly speechless from wanting him.

She knew how much was riding on the words she was about to speak, yet she struggled with the distraction caused by his piercing eyes, the masculine line of his chin, the broadness of his shoulders. *It would be so much easier if he wasn't so devastatingly handsome.*

He gazed at her expectantly, his eyes still aglow. "Everything okay?"

"James, I've been trying to talk myself out of this for months now. I've tried to tell myself that I can move on, that I can let go of you…that I can turn you loose. I know in the beginning I said I didn't want strings; I didn't want anything serious," she began, carefully gauging his reaction. "But I was wrong."

"Wrong how?" The agitation she sensed before had vanished. His body language was open, more receptive, his thighs parted, his eyes thoughtful.

"I didn't want to admit I was falling for you, that something was growing in my heart for you that I have never felt before."

He squeezed her hand, wordlessly urging her to go on.

She took a deep breath and let it all rush out: "James, I'm head-over-heels, one hundred percent, madly, absolutely, unconditionally in love with you."

Then she stopped to let him absorb her words. He looked like he'd fallen overboard without a life jacket.

I have not yet begun to fight, Sarah added silently, locking her eyes onto his. *Yes, I will fight for you. This is my last chance, so you better listen to what I have to say.*

It seemed like he needed to move his body to circulate the intensity of her words throughout his bloodstream. She had rendered him speechless. He stood, eyes still engaged with hers, his jaw fixed and lips moist with words he couldn't form.

She stood too, sliding her arms around his waist. "It's okay," she said into his chest, "I don't expect you to say anything. Just listen to me, okay?"

He nodded, still numb, as she continued, "I know you think Maggie is like you, and you can build a family with her, but I don't know if she can make you happy, James. I know I don't know her, but it's what my gut tells me...and if there is one thing I've learned in my thirty-seven years, it's that I have really good instincts about people."

She pulled back to watch his eyes again, to study his mouth for hints of what was churning in his mind before she continued to fling her desperate plea out to him like a life preserver.

"I would do anything for you, anything at all, to make you happy. If you want to have a family, then I would have your baby... We'd have to figure out the fertility stuff, but we could make it work. I've got a few years left. You want your kids to be raised Catholic? Then we will raise them Catholic, if that's what you want. I would move wherever your career took us. I can teach anywhere, really."

She was still clinging to him till the last sentence. He pulled away and took a few steps toward the shoreline. *I'm losing him.* The thought was a dagger stabbing her heart.

"But listen," she said, grabbing his wrist and pulling him back around to face her. "If you decide you want to be with Maggie... If you decide she can make you happier than I can, I will accept that too. I will be sad and hurt. But I will accept it."

Her eyes burned with tears at the thought of losing him to her, this tall blonde phantom who stood in the way of the one thing she wanted.

"I'm yours, James. I belong to you."

With those last words, she burst into sobs against his chest. He closed his eyes and rested his chin on the top of her head, her dark tresses whipping against his cheek in the relentless wind.

"The last thing I'd ever want to do is hurt you, Sarah." His lips pressed against her hairline before he pulled her toward the dunes and their tent. "Please give me some time. I just don't know right now. I love both of you for different reasons…"

He didn't say no. The tiny flame of hope was still alive.

It's the most I can ask for right now. At least I know he knows how I feel.

THAT AFTERNOON IT WARMED, and James and Sarah were able to explore more of the island unencumbered by sweatshirts or jackets and without shivering in the brutal wind. Sarah relished the heat of the sun boring into her pale, winter-ravaged skin, absorbing it into her shoulders which were bared in a tank top. They'd gone to the other side of the island, over to the Life of the Marsh trail, where the board-walk extended out into the bay. The long boards were littered with oyster shells and piles of horse dung, evidence of the wild ponies. They had yet to catch a glimpse of any of the beasts.

The trail angled through the marsh and then up a ramp and several stairs to an overlook. Across the bay, they saw huge houses rising from the water. "Imagine living there!" James stood behind Sarah, pulling her body back into his, his arms wrapped around her waist.

"Let's get a closer look." Sarah broke away, leading him down another set of stairs and around a bend lined with scrubby bushes and reeds. The boards ended in sand at the edge of the bay. She picked up a crab claw and moved its pincher back and forth like she was going to pinch James's arm.

He brushed her away, kicked off his boots and waded into the shallow water of the bay.

"How is it?" she asked.

"Warmer than the ocean," he answered, "which means it's almost tolerable." He laughed and motioned for Sarah to join him. In moments, they were submerged to their knees. He reached down and playfully splashed water up onto Sarah's light-colored tank top. The cool water instantly made her nipples erect.

"You're asking for it, Lieutenant McAllister!" Sarah giggled, scooping up two hands full of water and dumping it down the crotch of his baggy khaki shorts.

He chased her several yards deeper into the bay, which stayed shallow. They witnessed three kayakers go around the bend and out of sight before James grabbed Sarah and dunked her under the water. She came up sputtering and immediately jumped on his back, trying unsuccessfully to bring him down.

She screamed as he hoisted her up and over his shoulder, "Oh my god, put me down! James! Put me down!"

He carried her out of the water and laid her gently on the sand that was strewn with soft, dried sea grasses. In moments he was lowering himself on top of her, covering her mouth with his lips before she had a chance to protest. He stroked his finger down her cheek, then pulled her wet tank top up to reveal her hard peachy-pink nipples, eager for his touch. The languid tide of the bay lapped at their feet as his tongue darted over her breast.

"Oh god, James, that feels so good," she moaned, arching her back as her nipple disappeared into his hungry mouth. "But we can't do this here. There's bound to be more kayakers."

"But I want you now," he pouted, rolling off her.

"Let's go to the other trail and see if it's a little more secluded, okay?"

He nodded with a bit of disappointment and helped pull her to a standing position. They opted to drive the half-mile to the other trailhead, which was lined with huge pine trees.

This time the pine needle-covered dirt path wound its way through a forest that gradually gave way to more marsh. The boardwalk they traveled was flanked by clumps of phragmites waving their brown plumes in the breeze.

He stole a kiss around one corner and then froze. She opened her eyes and blinked, noticing she'd lost his attention. "What is it?" she whispered, afraid they'd attracted spectators.

He gently rotated her so they faced the same direction, right into the path of a beautiful chestnut brown mare, her sandy blonde tail calmly swishing back and forth as if she encountered humans kissing a hundred times a day. In the distance, past the reeds, were three more mares, a wobbly-legged foal and a stallion. They were all different colors and patterns of chestnut, white, and a darker reddish brown.

Sarah's heart soared to be sharing this moment with James. They witnessed the foal teeter over to its mother and begin to nurse. She clutched his hand, and he squeezed back, both mesmerized by the vision before them, the six wild horses framed by the windswept marshes and, in the distance, the gently rolling waters of the bay.

Only two months prior, she'd stood in Garden of the Gods with James, and now here they were experiencing a completely different type of coastal beauty. Like the mountains that reached the greatest heights and the oceans that stretched for unfathomable miles, their connection felt limitless, enduring. The jeopardy they faced...Sarah could scarcely believe it could all be coming to an end. It seemed as impossible as the mountains crumbling into the sea.

They continued on the path up a bridge that led to an overlook of the entire scene. The ponies were farther away now, but they could still see them grazing on the saltwater grasses, their tails happily twitching. The sun was starting to sink over the bay and casted a dusky glow over the water, rose giving way to amethyst toward the horizon, and due west, a fiery orange sun came closer and closer to touching the earth.

Now that the approaching darkness afforded them more of a cover, James climbed off the wooden platform and pulled Sarah down into his arms. They waded through the marsh to the spot where the thick supports for the elevated structure bore into the ground. He unfastened his shorts and slid Sarah's hands down into his boxers where she instinctively wrapped her fingers around his swollen cock.

He undid the buttons of Sarah's shorts, and she pulled them down and off, setting them gently on a dry spot a yard away. She couldn't believe she was standing there—in a national park—naked from the waist down, but glancing around, she saw no one but the ponies, and they didn't seem much like voyeurs.

James lifted Sarah up against the wooden pole, and she wrapped her bare legs around his waist. He held her ass cheeks in his hands and steadied her against the weathered-smooth wooden pole as he drove his erection into her eager wetness. She clasped her hands behind his neck, holding on for dear life as he continued to impale her.

He was totally silent except for the heavy breaths falling onto her neck. She muffled her own moans into his broad, muscular shoulders as her orgasm rocked through her body, making her shudder against him. That was enough to send him over the edge as he released his seed deep within her, his hands trembling and struggling to keep his grip on her as he enjoyed the last few spasms of his climax.

Walking back to the car, Sarah reviewed the day: a sunrise, a sunset, the miraculous sightings of dolphins and wild horses, amazing lovemaking surrounded by nature, and one heart completely bared, desperately awaiting its fate.

SARAH COULDN'T BELIEVE that the weekend was already drawing to a close. *What is it about the two of us that makes the time go so ridiculously fast? It's like we're in some alternate dimension when we're together!*

James's eyes focused on the ribbon of road stretching before them, and Sarah counted each little town they drove through as bringing them one point closer to home. *I don't want this to be over, though. We've come so far in the last two months. We've grown so much, and he will be gone in a matter of weeks. Why did we build this up just to have it ripped from our clutches?*

Her phone rang, jolting her thoughts away from James. She expected it to be Rachel but saw the incoming number had a Denver area code. She didn't like to accept calls from unfamiliar numbers, but it could be a relative or an old friend with a new cell phone number.

"Sarah?" came the voice.

She knew who it was before he said, "It's Daniel."

The color drained from her face. James sensed something was wrong and turned toward her, one hand gripping the steering wheel, the other gently rubbing her knee. She shook her head at him and said into the phone, "What do you want?"

There was an apologetic sigh on the line, and then: "I know you don't want to talk to me, Sarah, but please hear me out. I've spent the last three years getting back on my feet, and I am ready to see my kids."

"What makes you think they want to see you?" she asked coolly.

"They probably don't want to, and I totally understand why they'd feel that way," Daniel admitted. "I know I was a complete asshole, Sarah, but I've changed. I've spent the last three years getting my life back in order. I've paid my debts; I've gotten married; I have another child now. I have a great job, and I'm ready to be reunited with the missing members of my family."

"Well, I am happy for you, Daniel, but you don't get to decide one day you'll be a father, the next you won't, and then three years later decide you want your kids back. It doesn't work like that. I have to be a mother every fucking day, and I have done it totally on my own," she said as if ice water flowed through her veins.

James's grip tightened on Sarah's knee as he realized who was calling and what he was saying. "Just hang up," he advised. "Tell him to contact your lawyer."

Daniel's tone remained contrite. "I know you're coming to Colorado next month for Rachel's wedding," he said smoothly. "I would really like to see Owen and Abby and introduce them to their new brother while you're here."

Sarah was nauseated at the thought of being in the same room with him. "Abby is not your daughter, and that boy is not her brother."

"I am the only father Abby has ever known," he fought back, his tone sharpening ever so slightly.

"Better to not have a father at all than to have you in her life," Sarah retorted.

"Ouch." He was silent for a moment as if recalculating his angle. "I'm not surprised you're bitter. I assumed you would be." He took a deep breath and regrouped again. "Look, I am not trying to take them away from you or even change anything. I just want to see them. Just a few hours, Sarah, that's all I am asking for."

She stalled. *The longer he talks, the more likely his real motives will emerge.*

"Okay, how about this?" He tried yet another tactic, "Ask them if they want to see me. If not, then we won't do it. If they do, we will set something up."

Sarah slumped down into her seat, her knee twitching under the weight of James's palm. On one hand, she never wanted this man to reappear in her or her children's lives, but on the other hand, she didn't want either of the kids to someday accuse her of keeping them from their father, or father figure, as the case was for Abby.

"Fine. I'll talk to the kids and call you back."

She disconnected from the call and immediately buried her head in her hands, sending her dark locks cascading around her like a curtain. James's hand moved from her knee and began stroking down her back. "You gonna be okay?"

"That man has a definite knack for ruining things." As they made their way back over the Bay Bridge, she couldn't help but think it was an omen of other changes to come.

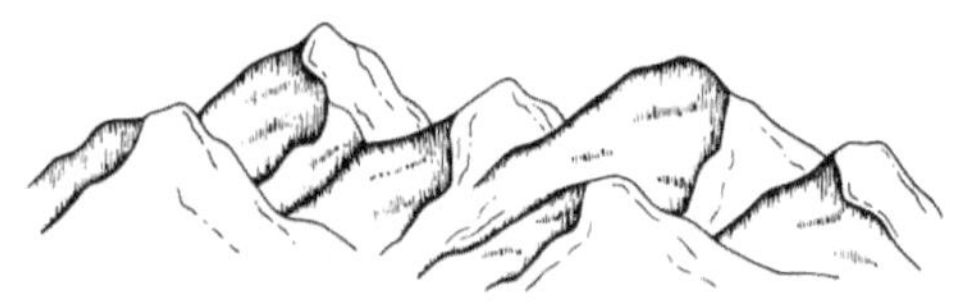

June brought its constant summer companions, heat and humidity, to the mid-Atlantic, which seemed to be having a pervasive impact on both moods and patience levels. Rachel was in bridezilla mode, and Sarah was scrambling to help her with last-minute arrangements. There were fittings to schedule and orders to review and RSVPs to count. On top of all the wedding stress, Rachel complained so much about Jack, that Sarah had to bite her tongue from blurting out that perhaps they should rethink this whole wedding thing.

Sarah was supposed to be enjoying her summer vacation from teaching, but in addition to playing wedding coordinator and maid of honor, she had also given herself an August deadline for getting her manuscript to the publisher. The edits were becoming tedious, especially when the early summer sun beckoned her outdoors into her garden.

Pawel was leaving at the end of the week to return to Poland, and James was leaving for Afghanistan via Ohio the week after. Beyond that, Sarah had returned from

Assateague still haunted by the phone conversation with her ex-husband Daniel.

"So do you think I should let him see the kids?" she'd asked her mother for advice.

Her mother was the wisest person she knew, and Sarah always gave her advice careful consideration. Kathy answered, "I think you need to see for yourself if he's changed—and if so, Owen should have an opportunity to know his father."

She'd also asked Rachel for her thoughts on the situation.

"I'd start by giving him a hearty fuck off!" her best friend had advised. "Oh, but wait. He owes you child support, doesn't he? Milk him for every penny you can!"

Sarah had another question for Rachel: "How do you think Daniel found out about your wedding?"

Rachel scratched her head. "No clue. But we still have so many mutual friends in Colorado, no doubt word got around to him, especially on Facebook. Did you say he was back in Denver?"

"He has a Denver phone number," Sarah recalled. "He said he has a son now."

"Are you going to tell the kids that?" Rachel questioned, her eyes wide.

Sarah nodded. "I guess so. Why wouldn't I?"

"Because if you ask them if they want to see their father and then mention they have a new brother, they'll almost certainly say yes. It sweetens the deal quite a bit, don't you think?" Rachel predicted.

She didn't like the idea of withholding information from her children, and she didn't like the idea of them missing an opportunity to meet a sibling. It had been over a week since Daniel's phone call, and he had already called again to ask Sarah if she had an answer yet. She needed to decide what to do. Soon.

That night after dinner, she lingered at the table after the meal was finished. "I need to talk to you two about something," she announced.

Owen looked at her inquisitively at first, but then solemnly guessed, "It's about Dad, isn't it?"

"Did he contact you?" Sarah demanded, afraid he'd violated their agreement.

"No," Owen replied with wide eyes. "I can just tell it's about him because of the way you said we needed to talk."

She'd nearly forgotten her son was as intuitive as she was. *If that boy ever learns to harness that power, he's going to make himself a fortune telling fortunes.* But her smile was quickly squelched by the topic at hand.

"Did he contact *you*, Mom?" Abby moved the conversation forward.

Sarah nodded. "He knows we're going out to Colorado for Rachel's wedding, and he's back there now. He has a new job; he is remarried, and..." She considered Rachel's advice again but decided it was better to tell the truth, "he wants to see you and introduce you to his new son."

Owen's face lit up like the sun, his dark eyes gleaming. "I have a brother?!"

Sarah couldn't help but adore Owen's excitement for nearly everything. It was a nice contrast to his sister's cynicism. Sarah studied her reaction to the news. Her expression was fixed, serious, with arms folded stiffly across her chest.

"Abby?" Sarah questioned, "what do you think about all this?"

"I don't trust him," she said plainly.

She glanced to Owen, whom she'd never known to hold grudges, and his face was still plastered with a huge grin, no doubt thinking of all the things he wanted to show and teach his little brother. *How can I deny him now that he knows?*

Abby placed one hand on top of the other on the table as

if delivering her final verdict on the matter. "I will see him, but I am not calling him Dad, and I don't trust him."

"Fair enough," Sarah agreed. "I will let him know we'll plan to spend a little time with him in Colorado."

She was already bracing herself for having to deal with this man who had been the source of so much pain. She called Rachel later that night to give her the news.

"I hope you know what you're doing," was what her best friend said.

"I am so much stronger now—on my own—than I ever was with him. I am a totally different person than when he knew me. We'll seem like strangers to each other," Sarah predicted.

"I can see that. I just don't want your kids to get hurt if he disappears again," Rachel explained.

But Sarah was still off on her philosophical tangent: "It's amazing how people come into your life and journey with you for a while, and then one or both of you outgrow each other, and you move on. There's a reason they're there and things happen the way they do, but sometimes you don't know what the reason is until much further down the road. Maybe I'll finally learn why Daniel came into my life...other than to give me my precious Owen."

"I think you just answered your own question," Rachel answered, a smile audible in her voice.

Sarah's lips curled into a smile too. "You're right. Daniel changed me. He made me grow up, find myself. I wouldn't be who I am today without the pain he put me through."

She couldn't help but think of James and Pawel, and what she would learn from knowing them. *Perhaps they were only meant to be with me during this short chapter of my life. Maybe relationships are meant to be temporary. It seems like destiny always forces people apart, forces us into short-term liaisons.*

Maybe nothing is forever.

ON THE NIGHT before his departure, Pawel insisted on taking Sarah out for dinner no matter how much she protested that she should have the honor of treating him. She scrambled around trying to find a parting gift that would appropriately convey her affection.

Nothing could match the Christmas or birthday presents he'd lavished on her, but she finally settled on two things. One was a photograph of her and the kids taken at Christmastime encased in a Maryland-themed frame that included the state flag, little blue crabs and a lighthouse. The other gift was a leather-bound journal in which she inscribed a poem she knew he'd love, followed by a few paragraphs expressing her deep and abiding affection and appreciation for his friendship and company throughout their short time together. She was afraid she wouldn't be able to do her feelings justice with a speech if she got too choked up during their goodbye; it was better to have it indelibly inscribed in ink.

The dinner conversation started out light and lilting. Pawel discussed his upcoming trip to Paris with his wife, which was meant to be a sort of second honeymoon.

"You know, since you won't come to live in Poland with me." He laughed, not intentionally trying to elicit guilt from Sarah, but she couldn't help but feel some anyway.

How simple it would be to marry a man like Pawel, someone so stable, so wise and mature. *No epic roller coaster like what I've been through with James.* But wouldn't it be boring? *Wouldn't I tire of all that...stability?*

She and Pawel had covered this territory the previous week when she spent the night at his house. He'd professed his undying love and devotion to her and promised her and her children a wonderful life if they'd relocate to Poland.

"But what about your wife?"

He had tilted his shoulders forward in the tiniest of shrugs. He never expected her to say yes. "Plus you're in love with that army guy of yours."

Sarah knew his heart was broken, and he was trying his best to accept that they could never have the relationship he wanted. And she understood exactly how that felt.

"I love you too, Pawel," she confessed. "I don't know what I would have done without you this past year. You've been my sounding board, my voice of reason; you've taken care of me. You're an excellent cook, an amazing kisser. You're kind and generous and so damn smart. You're very special to me, and I am going to miss you more than you will ever know."

Pawel seemed humbled by Sarah's words, as if they'd dulled the pain of her rejection. He had pulled her into a warm embrace and kissed her forehead chastely. That night, they had made love, a familiarity in their touch that Sarah knew she would miss.

Pawel was a gentle, giving, thorough lover. She wished there was a way she could give herself to Pawel the way she threw herself at James during their weekend on Assateague, but she knew it could never be. She just didn't have the same depth of feeling for him, no matter how much she wished she did.

She wasn't going to stay over on their last night together, and he'd insisted on taking a cab to the airport in the morning no matter how many times Sarah offered to drive him.

I think he's afraid it will hurt too much to know it's our last night. Then she wondered with a shooting pain how she would handle her last night with James.

It wasn't difficult for Pawel to see that she was distracted. "Oh, Sarah," he whispered after the waiter cleared away their plates. "I am so sorry you have to endure two goodbyes. I am overwhelmed with sadness at saying goodbye to you, but I'm going home to a wife who loves me, and my children, whom I've missed more than words can express. You're saying goodbye to me and James, and your best friend is getting married, which is always a goodbye of sorts. Are you sure you're holding up okay?"

The little dam Sarah had built to hold back her emotions cracked under the pressure, allowing a tiny wet tear to slide out before she could gain back control. "Well, I *was* okay." She forced a little laugh.

He studied her dark eyes as if he were searching for the right words to comfort her. "Sarah, you are one of the most amazing women I have ever met. I have a feeling you're about to draw in another amazing man, or maybe even two, who will fill these voids we're leaving. You are a magnet for strength, beauty and intelligence, my dear."

Another tear escaped as he continued, "You know, I believe people are placed in your path for a reason. They're either there for you to learn something from, or for you to teach. If you're lucky, it's both. I know you've taught me a great deal, and I can only imagine what all you've taught James. I know there is someone right around the corner who needs Dr. Lynde in his life—or *her* life." He punctuated that addendum with a wink.

"Oh, Pawel," she gushed, "I think it is I who have learned from you. It's hard to believe you're really going to be on the other side of the globe." She wiped her eye again, sopping up another tear.

He reached across the table and took her hand into his, squeezing it affectionately as his eyes danced between hers.

"Oh!" she exclaimed, hoping to lighten the tension a bit. "I wanted to give you a couple things. It's not much, but I knew you had a ton of stuff to ship back over, and I didn't want to burden your load too much."

He slowly untied the ribbons on the picture frame and smiled immediately at the familiar beaming grin of Owen, the half-smirk of the brooding Abby, and the gorgeous full-lipped smile of his beloved Sarah. "Not that I could ever forget you," he said graciously, "but putting this on my desk, I will be able to gaze upon your lovely faces every day."

He began to tackle the package containing the journal, his fingers nimble with the knot she'd tied. He turned the journal over and read the inscription, the poem and the words from Sarah's heart. Now it was his turn to choke back the tears.

He drove her home that night in near silence. The radio was low and humming with jazz, and the stars were just starting to peek through the indigo night. Sarah wondered if this would be the last time they saw each other, if this was really a goodbye or a "see you soon."

If I'm this choked up now, how am I going to say goodbye to James? I'm sending Pawel back to a wife and family who love him, who've missed him. I'm sending James off to a war zone.

They stood in Sarah's driveway intertwined for what seemed like hours. Pawel held her lush, curvy body close to his wiry frame, stroking her hair and promising her they would cross paths again, and sooner than she might think.

"You'll always have a special place in my heart, Sarah, always. I promise."

Those were the last words he uttered. He wiped a final, stray tear from her cheek, got into his car, and drove off into the starry night.

THEY HEADED to the bridal shop for the final fittings with a week to go. "How are you holding up?" Sarah asked her friend during the car ride to Annapolis.

"Good," Rachel assured her. "I think Jack is getting excited. I know we've been fighting a lot, but I think it's just because I'm stressed. I'm starting to see things fall into place now, so it's better. I'm feeling more in control."

Sarah patted her friend's knee as she took the exit toward the shop. "I'm really glad to hear that, sweetie."

"Listen, I know you're going through a lot right now."

Sarah glanced from the road into her friend's sincere eyes, surprised to hear those words come out of Rachel's mouth.

"I just wanted you to know how much I appreciate you," she continued. "I know it must be hard considering what's going on with you and James."

Sarah looked back down at her grip on the steering wheel. She felt her palms tighten around the leather. "I said goodbye to Pawel last night." Her gaze remained fixated on the road as she coasted to a full stop at a red light. "And next week I say goodbye to James. My heart hurts."

"I'm sorry," Rachel whispered.

"Maggie was here this week visiting him." Sarah confessed, "I just don't know what else I could have said at Assateague. I threw myself at his feet. I practically begged him to choose me."

"Hasn't he said a million times he can't choose anyone before he leaves?" Rachel clarified. "Why are you pushing so hard?"

Sarah shrugged. "I know him," she said. "I think he'll want to leave with some sort of resolution. That's what he did the first time he deployed. Even if he doesn't tell either of us which way he's leaning, I still think he knows what he wants in his heart of hearts."

"Can you even imagine going off to war?" Rachel asked. "I would be so fucking scared. Who the fuck knows what kind of crazy, irrational stuff I might do and say before I left?"

Sarah laughed. "You *are* going off to war. You're getting married."

Rachel laughed too and started to gather up her things while Sarah searched for a parking space. Before Sarah turned off the ignition, Rachel gave her a quick peck on the cheek and a hug. "I love you, Sugarlips, and no matter what happens, you know I'll be here for you, right?"

Sarah nodded, suppressing a tear. *At the rate I'm going with crying, I'm not going to have any tears left for when James leaves. Maybe that is for the best.*

TWO NIGHTS BEFORE JAMES DEPARTED, he visited Sarah's house to say goodbye to the kids. Rachel and Jack joined them, as well as Kathy, who'd met James when Sarah was in the hospital after her accident. Afraid it would be a somber affair, Sarah did her best to keep the mood light, playing happy music and trying to create a festive atmosphere.

Owen made a banner that said, "We're proud of you, Lt. McAllister," and he had his entire fifth-grade class sign it before school let out for the summer.

James walked in, took one look at the banner, and his hands flew to his mouth, covering up his shock. "He's so thoughtful," he told Sarah. "The apple doesn't fall far from the tree, after all." He gave Owen a salute and then a hug.

Abby made James a special dessert and got him a card. Rachel and Jack also got him a card and expressed their regrets that he wouldn't be joining them on their special day. Sarah presented him with photos of herself that he'd taken in Colorado as well as a Christmas photo of her and the kids. Then she played a special slideshow with pictures she'd collected throughout the time they'd been together. The slideshow ended with a view of Pikes Peak from the spot in Garden of the Gods where he'd first told her he loved her.

James seemed to be fighting his emotions. At one point in time, he excused himself to the restroom, and Sarah wondered if he was tearing up. She was certain he didn't want the kids to see him cry. She herself had never seen anything more than a tear collect in the corner of his eye, stubbornly refusing to fall.

When he returned from his brief sojourn, he was full of smiles and appreciation. He even gave a little speech about how he fully expected to Skype with everyone and promised to keep them all in the loop while he was away. "It's only nine months," he reminded them. "I'll be back before you know it."

"I have one more thing for you," Sarah said, withdrawing a wrapped package from the buffet drawer in the dining room where they were gathered.

"You've already done so much! What else could you

possibly give me?" he questioned. "Nothing else mushy, I hope!"

Everyone laughed.

"Just open it," Sarah said with a smile that lingered on the edge of wistfulness. He grinned back, then complied, his fingers ripping through the red, white and blue wrapping paper.

His eyes were wide as he studied the package. It was an e-book reader. He flipped the switch and saw it was pre-loaded with all of his favorite books plus a few of Sarah's favorites, ones she always said he needed to read.

"And as soon as my book comes out, you can add it too!" Sarah laughed.

James turned the reader over in his hands, which were almost imperceptibly trembling, and shook his head.

"What's wrong?" Owen asked. "Don't you like it?"

James was fighting that tear again. "Like it?" he echoed. "Owen, I absolutely love it. It's the best, most thoughtful gift I have ever gotten. Your mom knows how much I love to read. I couldn't have asked for anything better."

That night James crawled into Sarah's bed, and they fell asleep curled together but clothed. They didn't make love. Sarah had still not decided if she could bear to make love to him knowing it might be the last time.

I have less than twenty-four hours to decide.

SARAH STUMBLED into his doorway amidst a suitcase, two laptop bags, two grocery sacks full of books and miscellanea, and a huge canvas military bag. She felt nauseated seeing all his things lined up in the hallway.

He's really leaving. By this time tomorrow, he will be gone.

He came around the corner and startled at the sight of her. "Sorry, I didn't hear you come in," he admitted, taking her into his arms.

She carried the sacks of Chinese food into his dining room. She didn't want him to dirty any dishes, and she wasn't sure she could get through dinner in public without crying. She started to unpack the food while James grabbed paper plates from the kitchen.

Sarah was quiet as James handed her a plate. She scraped some rice and chicken onto it and sat hunched, mindlessly chewing.

I don't know if I can do this.

No, wait a minute, I need to feel this. I will regret this someday if I don't embrace the pain and let my heart feel the impact. That's the only way I will heal.

She took a sip of her soda, wishing she'd brought wine to dull this throbbing pain—or something even stronger. She didn't like these dark, ugly thoughts that had taken her mind hostage.

Is it that I worry about him not coming back alive, or I worry about him not coming back to me?

James was equally quiet and subdued, and he refrained from asking Sarah what was on her mind. It was as if neither wanted to know what the other was thinking.

He seems as distracted and out of sorts as I do. Maybe my being here is a mistake.

She'd hardly seen him or talked to him since Maggie visited the week before. When she'd asked how Maggie's visit went, he was fairly evasive, the Old James. Sarah tried to imagine her moving throughout James's house, stumbling over his laundry and inadvertently knocking over a stack of books. She tried to imagine her doing his dishes or combing her hair in his bathroom. She tried to imagine them domesticating.

Would she make him happy? Could she?

Her mind went even where her heart forbade. She envisioned them making love, James kissing her neck the way he kissed her. She wondered if they curled together like pretzels afterwards or if that was something special he only did with her.

Is there anything special between us, or are Maggie and I just interchangeable vaginas?

James looked up from his plate, his eyes looking tired and sad. "What's wrong with you tonight?"

She glanced up at him, her doe-like eyes meeting his as if to ask, *Seriously?* She stared past those blue irises, deep into the black abyss of his pupils, analyzing the pinpoint of white where the light reflected.

Don't you see this pain? Don't you see what you're doing to me?

He silently stood up and carried the remains of their dinner to the kitchen while she sat at the table paralyzed, too numb to move. No matter what the motivation was, no matter where her fears originated, there was no denying her heart was breaking from the potential finality of their goodbye. There was some intangible quality in the air that made her feel so desperate, so hopeless. She felt the pressing hand of time squeezing the breath from her lungs.

"Let's go sit in the living room," he suggested upon his return from the kitchen. He grasped her hand and pulled her up. She was weak and compliant in his grip, a rag doll. Listless.

His hand never left hers from the time he made eye

contact with her from their respective spots on the sofa until the end of his speech. She knew by the way he cleared his throat that what was coming would be a bomb detonating, destroying her hopes.

"Sarah, I have something I need to tell you."

Tell me, not ask me. She knew what was coming.

"I am going to ask Maggie to marry me," he said bluntly, not even waiting for the knife he'd stabbed into her heart to sink in. "We talked a lot about it when she was here last week, and I think it's what I want. She's going to move here and get a job while I'm away. She loved it here," he added with an accidental smile, twisting the knife a little deeper.

Her bleeding heart was in her throat. She forced some of her pragmatism to rise to the surface, to take over her speech. "I thought you said you weren't going to decide till you returned."

He nodded—it was a question he surely anticipated. "I thought so too, but I changed my mind." He paused for a moment, his gaze never faltering. "I love her...and when I get back, we want to start a family."

The throbbing pain gave way to anger, no matter how hard she tried to keep it at bay. "So nothing I said to you on Assateague matters? That I'd have a baby with you? Nothing I said made any difference to you at all?"

The desperate conversation on the beach where she'd thrown herself at his feet, promising him everything, surrendering her heart to him, echoed through her mind like the collateral rumblings of distant thunder.

His blue eyes were trembling, filling with tears like icy pools. She noticed the crisscrossing red streaks splintering through the white. *Red, white, and blue. How patriotic.*

"I thought a lot about what you said," he admitted. "I tried to picture it... I tried to picture us together like that."

Her eyebrows arched in a very easily interpretable question mark.

"I couldn't do it...couldn't picture it....and I don't know why. I have feelings for you, Sarah, but not in a family or marriage kind of way. I don't know why.... There's some sort of wall." He shook his head as if his being perplexed was all the explanation she needed.

"What do you mean, 'wall?'" she fired back. "You shouldn't have any walls when it comes to me. You can tell me anything; I want you to feel like you can tell me anything." She felt like she was pleading, begging for a chance. *Just a tiny golden chance.*

"Sarah, I don't know how to explain it. I know I love Maggie, and I can see us together. I can picture it. I've known her for a very long time. I pictured us together when we were still kids, even. She and I are from the same place, and we're at the same place in our lives now. You already have your kids, and you'd be starting over, and I..."

She stood up and moved to the window, studying the leaves swaying in the tall trees at the property line. *I've come so far, and I've fought so hard...but I've lost. I've lost him. Maybe I pushed too hard. And I didn't help him see what I see.*

Every nerve in her body was fighting her presence there. *I need to leave.* She headed toward the door, but he leapt up into her path.

His hands flew to her shoulders. "Please, Sarah, please don't be like this."

"So what happens now? What happens to me? Do I just fade out of your life? Do I just step aside and let you go off to war and pretend we never had this, that we never were together?" She was crying big fat tears, streaming down hot against her flushed cheeks.

He pulled her into his arms and held her so tightly that

her breath was limited to tiny gasps. When he released her, she saw the tears trickling down his cheeks as well.

Oh my god, he's crying. He's actually crying real tears.

"No, Sarah, that's not what I want." He stood just inches away as she folded her arms against her chest, hugging herself where his warmth had just been. "That's not at all what I want."

"Well, what do you want?" her voice echoed down the hallway, louder than she intended, more demanding.

"I feel close to you, and I don't want to lose that. You know me better than just about anybody. I can't imagine not having you in my life in some capacity," he explained, his voice soothing, drawing her back to him like he always did. She witnessed the corners of his mouth sneaking into a smirk, the trademark boyish smirk she had always been powerless against.

"So you want your cake and eat it too?" she accused him, renewing the anger he'd tried to assuage.

"Maybe?" He shot her an apologetic, boys-will-be-boys look, a lazy attempt to lighten the mood. But it wasn't going to work this time, and his patience for discussing anything of an emotional nature would soon wear thin, if their past history had any predictive value.

His tone grew rigid. "Alright, fine, Sarah, I'm sorry. I thought you'd feel our friendship was too strong and too precious to throw away." He stepped down the hall away from her, resigned. "Go ahead and leave if you want, but just remember this: I never made you any promises. I never said we'd end up together."

"No," Sarah agreed, "you didn't promise me anything, but you did say repeatedly that you wouldn't decide until you got back. You said you didn't know what you want."

"I changed my mind," he said coldly. "Are you staying, or are you going?"

Sarah wondered how hard he was fighting to convince himself that this was what he wanted. *Was this decision being driven by the same irrational forces that caused him to marry before his first deployment? Was this coming from fear, or was it really what he wanted?*

She looked at him standing there, his hand on his hip, his skin so smooth and his eyes so blue. His whiskers were beginning to shadow his jawline. She saw the outline of his chest muscles pressing into his t-shirt, the armbands of which gathered snugly around his biceps. Even in anger and despair she wanted to run her fingers down those muscles while he slid his eager cock into her soft, inviting sex.

This is my problem. He makes me crazy. Crazy with lust. Crazy with love. Just completely, undeniably crazy.

"What do you want me to do?" she asked breathlessly, knowing that no matter what, she belonged to him. Even if he didn't want her. She still wanted to make him happy, despite everything. Despite the rejection. And she didn't understand why.

He held out his arms to her. "I want you to stay," he said softly. "Please spend one more night with me."

The easy thing to do would be to walk away and accept defeat. The easy thing would be to block him out of her life for good and let her heart heal in his absence—to forget she ever knew him...loved him.

The hard thing to do would be to stay, to give him her heart in whatever capacity he would accept it, to pledge her devotion to him whether as a friend or lover. He was going off to war. He was putting his life on the line for the country. How could she abandon him now?

She was never one to take the easy way out. *I want to be strong. I want to be strong for him. For us.*

FOR A WHILE she stood in the hallway, collapsed in his embrace, until, without words, he pulled back and smiled at her, the lightness returning to his eyes. He dragged her down the hallway to his bedroom, which seemed empty now that so many of his possessions were packed up. Sarah immediately noticed a small burgundy box sitting on his nightstand and with a stabbing pain realized it was an engagement ring.

Seeing where her eyes were drawn, he went directly toward the box and moved it from the table. "I'm sorry. I didn't mean to leave it out."

"Can I see it?" her voice quivered. She knew not seeing it would be worse than wondering what it looked like. *The unknown is always worse than the known.*

He pulled the small burgundy velvet box out of the larger matching cardboard one and carefully flipped the lid open, revealing a half-carat round diamond encircled by smaller stones and set in white gold.

Here's the ring that I will never wear, she thought bitterly, the realization piercing her. She gently pulled it out of its velvet nest and examined it slowly, turning it over, watching how the diamonds refracted the light. Without asking or even looking at James, she slid it onto her finger, wishing it was hers. Wishing he was hers. *It fits.*

"It's gorgeous," she whispered, reluctantly returning it to its case.

He placed the ring in the top drawer of his mostly empty bureau and started to strip his shirt off over his head.

"What are you doing?" Sarah asked.

"I want you to come lay down with me," he said. "Please?"

"Oh, James, I don't know," she balked. She didn't know how to say no to him. "What about Maggie? I don't want to—"

He tossed the shirt aside and touched his hand to her lips. "She knows you're here. It's okay."

"But I—"

"Sarah, I still love you," he said. "I thought if anyone would understand being in love with more than one person, it would be you…"

She soaked in his words. He was right. She was poly; she should understand that making this choice was nearly as hard for him as it was for her. But society was the one who forced people to choose. To align with ancient customs and conventions—as a sociologist, she understood it all too well. She'd just never imagined James had the capacity for that. But he did. He had always been more than she thought he would be—in every way he'd always surpassed her expectations. *Except with texting me*, she thought with a smirk.

They were silent after that, their hands and speechless lips speaking the volumes of words trapped in the space between them. He pulled off Sarah's blouse, then she stripped the rest of her clothes away until she lay naked and exposed in the bed. He lowered himself onto her body so slowly, so carefully, as if she were made of glass. She felt that fragile too, as if she might crack into a million pieces at any time.

I've never had goodbye sex before. And that's what this is, right? I've never made love to someone knowing full well it would be the last time.

She couldn't find the words to protest; her body was already feverishly yearning for him, craving his touch, clinging to his kisses. Her hips arched toward him as his cock brushed against her swollen labia, so ready, blossoming open to receive him. He slid inside her like a hand into a glove, a perfect fit, so familiar and right that she ached knowing it would be the final time her sex yielded to him. She wanted to bottle the sensation of being filled by him, to open it up and experience it anytime she wanted. She imagined the first time she uncorked the bottle, the memory would be as strong as if it were the real thing, but over time it would slowly diminish like the final lingering notes of a fading perfume.

His strokes inside her were slow, steady, and deep; their bodies rising and falling in unison to a supernatural beat. *How could we have done this a hundred times, and yet it has never gotten old? How can he say he can go on without me, without this? Doesn't he realize this is a one in a million connection?*

She felt the building pressure of the physical sensations plus an avalanche of emotions suspended behind the wall of her orgasm. When the floodgates opened, both would be released. It would all explode and thunder, rushing around them like a hurricane.

Minutes later, she burst forth in every sense imaginable, from her eyes and her sex and every pore of her body, a cathartic baptism, redeeming her wounded soul. Her body shuddered so violently against him, his own release, which came on the heels of hers, was like a drop of water in a vast sea. She was the moon, and he was the tide.

In the aftermath, they lay quietly quaking and crying together.

THE NEXT MORNING, James whispered goodbye and placed a single, sweet kiss on Sarah's cheek. She turned over to meet his eyes in the early breaking light of dawn, just lucid enough to murmur, "I love you."

When she fully awoke an hour later, the ring was gone, all of the bags that lined the hallway were gone, and James was gone. She understood why he'd left when she was half-asleep. It was easier for him. Despite everything, she knew he cared. And she knew he was hurting too.

Alone in his house, she walked from room to room saying goodbye, weeping. She picked up a camouflage army jacket that lay, discarded and crumpled, on the floor of his closet. She smoothed out the thick canvas-like material, running her fingers over the name McAllister on the band above the pocket. She put it on and looked in the mirror, almost feeling his warmth around her, a tear rolling down her cheek. Still wearing the jacket, she locked the front door to his house on her way out.

She forced her feet toward her car, feeling empty and hollow inside. He had taken part of her with him, and she could never get it back.

Isn't this what I wanted? Didn't I push it all to this eventuality? I could have walked away so many times unscathed, but I refused. I knew the outcome, yet I stayed to watch it all come crashing down around me.

The mountain she'd wanted so desperately to climb lay in rocky rubble at her feet.

21

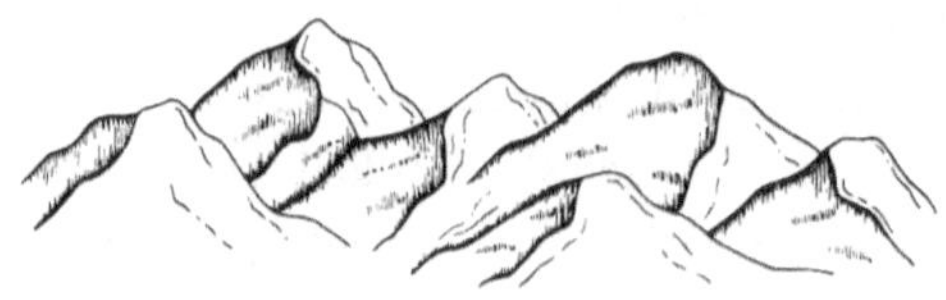

Packing for Colorado afforded Sarah a much-needed opportunity to distract herself from James's departure, although it still seemed surreal. The first morning after he left, she woke up thinking it was just a dream. By the second day, she finally accepted it wasn't a nightmare. Once she confessed to Rachel what happened the night they said goodbye, her friend had hardly left her side, making Sarah feel as though she were on suicide watch.

Folding her clothes into the suitcase, she was haunted by the déjà vu of packing for Colorado just a few months before, after she'd left James. Only this time she knew he wasn't going to pop up unexpectedly at her hotel. He'd be leaving for Afghanistan at the same time she was leaving for the wedding.

How can I even go back to that place now? Where am I going to find the strength?

There was no time to wallow in self-pity—mothers were rarely allowed that luxury. People were depending on her, plus it was hard to mourn when Owen and even Abby were so excited about the trip. They hadn't traveled as a family for quite some time. Sarah's mother was coming along too, and they were trying to talk her brother Adam into flying in for the weekend as well. It was going to be a regular family reunion with Aunt Sally driving over from Breckenridge, and, of course, their meeting with Daniel.

Sarah had displaced some of her sadness and regret about James with anger toward Daniel. But no matter how much resentment she tried to muster, she kept looking at Owen's face as he glowed with excitement at the prospect of reuniting with his father and meeting his stepmother and brother.

The flight was long and turbulent. The music and book Sarah brought to occupy her mind had failed miserably. Sleep had eluded her too. She felt her skin crawling with self-loathing.

I'm being a selfish bitch. I need to buck up and get through this, for Rachel, and for Owen and Abby. They don't deserve to put up with my miserable, depressing attitude.

Kathy reached across the aisle from her seat next to Abby and squeezed her daughter's hand tenderly, as if she knew exactly where Sarah's mind was and how much she was struggling. Sarah forced a smile of gratitude and remembered the advice her mother gave about enjoying every golden moment she had with James. She thought about rock climbing, their dinners out, winter hikes, movie nights and the wild ponies at Assateague, making love in a windswept marsh. *I did, didn't I? I cherished every single wonderful moment. And I will always have those memories.*

What about the memories James was building with Maggie? She couldn't escape the numerous curiosities she had about how his proposal had gone. Her mind was driving her crazy, constantly churning with questions she'd never get answers to.

Long flights mean too much time to think. She conjured up

an image of James, her mind dissecting his features: his striking eyes, his chiseled pecs, his delicious arms.

There was mass chaos at the airport in Denver. Her mother's bag was missing; Owen had just lost a tooth; Rachel was calling, and Abby needed to use the bathroom, but the only one they'd stumbled upon was closed for cleaning.

"First world problems!" Sarah laughed, relieved to be on the ground and finally able to turn her brain off. She tried to muster up as much positivity as she could and keep her brood in good spirits.

"My bladder is not a first world problem," Abby argued, heading down another hallway toward a different terminal.

"Text us to find out where we are," Sarah yelled after her. She left her mother at the airline's customer service counter and dragged Owen down to the rental car counter. She returned Rachel's call while she waited to be helped.

"Did you guys make it?" She sounded breathless and excited, her voice high-pitched and tremulous.

"Yes, getting the rental car now," Sarah replied. "Do I need to pick up anything for tonight?"

"Can you get me something for my stomach? I've been feeling queasy all day," she complained. "What's good for that?"

"Ginger," Sarah replied. "I'm sure it's just pre-wedding jitters. I'll get some tea. Anything else?"

"Nope! I can't wait to see you and go out tonight!"

Sarah had nearly forgotten she was taking the girls out on the town as sort of a makeshift bachelorette party. Rachel had really wanted to go to a swing club, but Sarah dismissed that idea because some of their friends in the area were much too conservative for that.

"I'm sure you'll still have plenty of opportunities for flirting and showing off," Sarah had promised. Rachel was trying to compete with the standard Jack set at his party the weekend before. They'd gone back to the club in DC and apparently had a pretty wild time. Sarah had not felt up to attending.

Everyone converged and piled into the rental car, all the confusion finally cleared up. Owen's tooth had stopped bleeding; Abby's bladder had been relieved, and Kathy's bag would be delivered to her by midnight. *Not ideal, but if that's the worst thing that happens, we'll be fine.* Her mind snapped—she hadn't thought about James for approximately forty-five minutes. *It's progress!*

The last time I drove from Denver to the Springs... No, she'd keep her mind occupied with telling her mother and Abby about their plans for the night. Owen naturally wanted to know why brides and grooms had bachelor and bachelorette parties, which Sarah tried to explain as delicately as possible. Then the entire car sang along to Journey's "Don't Stop Believin'" as their trusty rental car flew down the highway under Sarah's lead foot.

Rachel's complexion looked a little off when they first arrived, pale and sallow, but she brightened as soon as she saw everyone pile out of the car. She distributed hugs all around. "My mother is driving me nuts already," she whined.

Sarah shot her an empathetic look but couldn't help feeling relieved her own mother was as amazing as mothers came. Mrs. Brock was a tinier version of her daughter and twice as brazen and outspoken, as impossible as that seemed. She had a reputation for raising hell until she got her way, so much so that people generally acquiesced before her fury could be unleashed. Sarah always had the impression that Mrs. Brock was not particularly fond of her and blamed her for convincing Rachel to leave Thomas's father around the same time Sarah was getting divorced.

Owen and Abby went off to the den where Owen would be camping out on the floor with Thomas. Abby would take the small guest room off the den that shared a hall bath. She was already rolling her eyes at the prospect of being in such close proximity to the two pre-adolescent boys, but Sarah cast her a look that was widely known in their family as the "warning shot." It meant she had exactly two minutes to get her act together or suffer the consequences.

Sarah helped her mother get settled into their room, which had been Rachel's older sister's once upon a time. *It is still very...lavender*, Sarah mused, setting down her bag. "Do you need anything, Mom?"

Kathy smiled and waved her daughter off. "No, my dear. I just want to rest for a little bit."

Sarah opened the door, and Rachel was waiting for her in the hall. "Okay, I'll check on you later."

Rachel practically pulled Sarah's arm out of the socket dragging her into her bedroom. Her wedding gown hung from a plant hook in the ceiling, looking shimmery and white like an apparition in the light streaming through the half-open blinds.

Before she could say anything, Rachel clutched her abdomen and excused herself to the adjoining bath, where Sarah heard her expel the contents of her stomach.

Ugh. I hope it's not a stomach virus. Shit, I forgot the ginger tea! Damn!

Rachel returned several moments later and took a seat on the bed. "I don't know what my problem is." She sighed. "Maybe it was the eggs at breakfast?"

A moment of realization smacked Sarah across the cheek as she peered into her best friend's hazel eyes. *She's pregnant. Oh. My. God.* She didn't know how she could be so sure, but she was.

Rachel started to say something about Jack staying at a hotel clear on the other side of town, but the change in Sarah's expression led her to ask, "What?"

Sarah's eyes were wide as she patted Rachel on the knee. "You're pregnant."

She watched the rest of the color drain from Rachel's face.

"Oh...fuck!" was all she could manage.

Sarah watched her friend mentally calculating dates, reviewing a calendar in her mind.

"I got so caught up in the wedding stuff, I forgot I didn't start my period last week."

"Most brides are obsessive at keeping track of that shit." Sarah laughed. "You know, to avoid having their periods on their wedding nights."

"Yeah, yeah, well, that's never been a big deal for us," she explained. "Oh my god, Sarah, what am I going to do?"

"I'm going to go get you a test. And that ginger tea since I forgot it. And you are gonna have to reconsider your plans to drink tonight."

She left Rachel sitting on the bed in shock, a look of startled but happy wonderment spread across her face.

RACHEL CLOSED THE BATHROOM DOOR, test in hand, and Sarah waited quietly on the bed for the verdict. *She doesn't even have to take the test. I have no doubts.*

Further bolstering her confidence was the conversation she'd had with her mother when she was leaving for the drug store. She'd told her she needed to get Rachel some ginger tea for her upset stomach. "Oh, morning sickness already?" Kathy had asked with a sage smile.

"Wow, you noticed too?" Sarah had asked, not knowing why she was surprised. After all, she had inherited her uncanny ability to read people from her mother, even though she'd further developed her gift by studying human behavior for over fifteen years.

"It's written all over her face," Kathy replied. "I take it Jack doesn't know yet?"

Sarah flashed back to a visit to Rachel's hospital room after she'd delivered Thomas. Sarah had been only a few days away from her due date with Owen, and they'd discussed the merits of tubal ligation. Having her second child, Sarah was confident she should put childbearing behind her. Having her first child, Rachel wanted to leave that door open.

What if I hadn't shut that door? Would James have seen things differently?

She heard the door handle turn, and Rachel emerged, waving the test stick in the air. She was speechless. It took nothing short of a miracle to render Rachel Brock speechless.

"So I was right?" Sarah grinned, opening her arms to her best friend for an embrace.

The tears finally broke the dam, and Rachel collapsed into her friend's arms sobbing and laughing and talking all at once, "I got my IUD taken out in May. They said it would take months! Oh my god, I can't believe this! Jack is going to die!"

Her wheels were turning now as she began to realize how her life was going to change. "Gia and Thomas will be so excited!" And then: "Oh, fuck, I don't want to tell my mother."

Sarah laughed. "One thing at a time, honey. Just concentrate on telling Jack for now," she advised. "You have a wedding to get through!"

Rachel threw her arms around Sarah, squeezing her with all her might, then she looked at the test again. Sarah glanced down at the two parallel blue lines, thick and dark and unmistakably positive. She was fighting that ugly side of her, that dark, slimy green envy threatening to choke her.

She wanted to show nothing but support for her best friend, but she couldn't help but wonder why it wasn't her about to walk down the aisle, her pregnant with the child of the man she loved. Despite her efforts to conceal and submerge those nasty thoughts deep within her subconscious, Rachel's perception easily penetrated that façade. "Are you alright?"

Sarah nodded, biting her lower lip to keep the tears at bay. "I'm really happy for you, sweetie!" She smiled, still somewhat unconvincingly.

"I know you're happy for me, but you're also human," Rachel said. "You would have to be a robot not to be struggling right now. Please, just be honest with me. I'm worried about you."

Sarah grabbed a tissue from the vanity near the window. She blew her nose, flushing those threatening tears out of her sinuses. "You're right," she admitted. "I don't know why I think I always have to be in control, always perfect and altruistic. I guess, studying human behavior for a living, I must think I'm somehow above it all."

Rachel nodded in sympathy. "Have you heard from him yet?"

Sarah shook her head, "I don't expect to hear from him for a while, if ever, to tell you the truth." *After all, he wasn't a great communicator when we were together; I doubt us being thou-*

sands of miles apart is going to improve anything in that department.

Rachel looked surprised. "Oh, he will be in touch," she promised. "I know he cares about you a great deal. You can tell by the way he looks at you."

"I think," Sarah theorized, "he's so conflicted." She straightened up on the bed, her tone shifting into her Dr. Lynde voice, usually reserved for lectures. "On the one hand, he thinks he's this straight-laced, traditional military guy who wants the white picket fence, and the 2.5 kids, and the pretty wife who stays at home."

Rachel reconciled that with what she knew of James and Maggie. "Sure, that makes sense."

"But," Sarah continued, "I opened this whole new world to him that he didn't even know existed, you know: the lifestyle, polyamory…transparent and open relationships. I made him look into his heart and mind and challenge all his notions of tradition. But he still doesn't know if that's really him, if he can give up the ideals that've been drilled into him since he was a young boy."

"I think you have James McAllister figured out to a T," Rachel surmised.

Sarah nodded. "Nothing I say is going to change his mind though," she conceded. "He's just going to have to figure out who he really is."

Rachel hugged her again. "You're so smart, Lovechop! Only one of the million reasons I love you!"

Sarah smiled and hugged her back. "Enough about him," she changed the subject. "Let's go see what the kids are up to, and you can think about how you want to share the big news!"

THEY ARRIVED at the park a little before the scheduled meeting time. Owen's eyes had first bypassed the playground and fixated on the giant concrete circle with fountains of water streaming through the center of it.

"Oh my gosh, Mom, look!" he screamed, pointing. Children were splashing in the water of the pool that collected from the center of the structure, and their laughter carried on the summer wind throughout the park. Even Sarah marveled at the way the huge sculpture appeared to be a window to the mountains that served as its backdrop.

She motioned for Owen to head out onto the playground then took a seat on a nearby bench. Her skin was crawling with dread as she sat watching Owen run down a swinging bridge made of two by fours and slide down a metal pole on the other side of the suspended platform. Abby and Kathy flanked her as if she needed protection. *Weakest bodyguards ever*, Sarah mused glancing from her waify daughter to her frail mother.

Across the playground, sauntering through the gates opposite the huge fountain, she saw them. Daniel, shorter and stouter than she remembered on one side, and a petite redheaded woman on the other, swung a little boy with tousled red hair between them. She watched his feet lift off the ground, his jubilant face giving way to a fit of laughter as Daniel scooped him up and slung him onto his shoulders.

Sarah wanted to feel something stronger than what she felt, which was a mixture of apathy and detachment. She knew that man was Daniel, but it was not the Daniel she had known. The Daniel Taylor she'd known would not have walked through the park with her, a contented grin plastered on his face, swinging their son between them.

She was going to get through this, just like she did everything else.

His arms wrapped around her first, before he even acknowledged anyone else. He whispered in her ear, sounding sincerely filled with gratitude, "Thanks for agreeing to this, Sarah. It means a lot to us."

Before she could respond, he began to scan the playground for Owen. Then he introduced his wife to Sarah, Abby, and Kathy. "Everyone, this is Nikki." She waved a tiny, strained hello and stood back a little bit to draw attention to the freckled, blue-eyed boy who came up just about to Daniel's knees. "And this is Sam."

Just then, Owen came tearing across the playground and through the little opening in the fence. "Dad!" he shouted, his face radiating with joy.

Daniel picked Owen up and squeezed him against his chest in a display of affection Sarah couldn't remember him ever bestowing upon their son when he was small.

"Is this my brother?!" Owen exclaimed, turning to the little boy as soon as his feet touched the ground again.

The little boy bashfully clung to his mother's leg, and Daniel tried to coax him out of his shell. "Sam, this is your big brother Owen. He's eleven years old. Isn't he tall?" He turned to Sarah. "My god, he looks just like you."

Owen took Sam's hand and led him over to the smaller area for toddlers. Sarah was not surprised that he was so tender and gentle with the young boy. Daniel finally acknowledged Abby, asking her how school was and if she had a boyfriend. She answered his questions, and her mother squeezed her hand in a show of support.

Nikki was painfully silent, her face stretched into a fake-looking smile, as if she'd been coached to be an automaton. Sarah decided to engage her in conversation, following her as she moved closer to where the boys were playing. "So what do you do for a living?"

"I was a paralegal in the office building where Daniel worked when we met, but now I'm a stay-at-home mom," she gushed sweetly. "I also have my own business making cakes for all occasions."

"Oh," Sarah replied, "that's great!" She studied the young woman's features: a long, thin pointed nose, high cheekbones and thin lips. Her hair, which blew in the breeze and caught the sunlight in the lighter, strawberry blonde strands, was certainly her most striking feature.

"I think Daniel told me you're a professor?" she offered, trying to sound more interested than she likely was, but starting to seem more human than automaton at last.

"Yes, I teach sociology at the University of Maryland," Sarah answered. "I'm also about to publish a book."

"Wow!" Nikki exclaimed, now sincerely sounding impressed. "What's the book about?"

"It's about sexuality on college campuses and how it's transformed in the digital age," she explained.

Nikki's smile faded. It seemed like Sarah's research interests made her uncomfortable, and she scanned the playground, looking for a way to escape the conversation.

After the kids played for a while, Daniel gathered everyone and offered to treat the group to lunch. There were no objections so they caravanned to a pizza and sandwich shop only a few blocks away.

Lunch was casual and not nearly as painful as Sarah imagined. Daniel talked a lot about his new job, which was a normal, legitimate business and not some crazy, questionable scheme. Nikki chimed in about how great their neighborhood was and how they'd just fixed up their guest bedroom.

Oh, here it is; it's finally coming. The real reason for this visit.

"I know it's probably a long shot," Daniel began, "but we'd really love to have Owen, and Abby too, if she wants, out to visit us later this summer, or over Christmas break, or really whenever they want."

Sarah braced herself, took a deep breath and smiled sweetly. "Well, that's very generous of you both. I can't really give you an answer about that right now; it's something that will require careful thought and consideration," she replied as diplomatically as she could muster.

"Understood," Daniel replied warmly, and then he was off to the next topic, not even venturing in that direction again for the rest of the meal.

Later, on their way home, her mother remarked that she was proud of the way Sarah had handled herself. "Honey, you could have been really bitter, seeing him all happy and content with his new life and now wanting to come along and shake yours up. But you were gracious and generous, and I think you showed both him and your kids what kind of person you are," she praised her daughter.

Sarah sighed, thinking about what she had wanted to do and say. Sometimes she wished she could be brash and somewhat reckless like Rachel. But she was always controlled, deliberate, and thoughtful. She would have been angry with herself if she'd allowed Daniel Taylor to see her at anything less than her best.

THAT NIGHT WAS the eve of the wedding. Rachel was going nuts with rehearsal plans and stressing about her parents meeting Jack's parents for the first time. Sarah wanted to help calm her friend's nerves, but she felt weak, emotionally drained, and as if she had nothing left to give. She suggested that Rachel take a nap to conserve her energy for the rehearsal and dinner.

"You're napping for two now, don't forget!" Sarah winked at Rachel with what was the last shred of positivity she could muster.

Rachel's teeth gleamed between her lips as she clasped her hand over Sarah's mouth playfully. "I'm not telling Jack till our wedding night, so shhhhh already!" she warned.

Sarah made the universal gesture for zipping her lips and throwing away the key. Then she retreated behind the closed door of the bedroom she was sharing with her mother, who was in the den with the kids working a crossword puzzle. A sense of relief washed over her as she turned the lock and collapsed onto the bed. She felt as though she was lying on a bed of nails, each sharp point digging into her flesh. She curled onto her side and balled her body into a fetal position.

I don't know how much longer I can be strong for everyone. I'm falling apart on the inside.

She pulled the comforter over her head and buried her face in the mound of pillows under her head. *Losing James is the worst heartbreak I have ever experienced. The worst.*

I have never felt more rejected. And maybe I'm being a selfish bitch, but it seems like everything is wine and roses for everyone else in my life. Rachel is marrying the man of her dreams and having his baby. My ex has somehow transformed into the model father and husband and makes me want to vomit because his new life seems so idealistic and wholesome. And Maggie is going to ride off into the sunset with my man.

I should be happy for Rachel, and I should be glad that Daniel wants to be part of his son's life, but this all sucks. And I'm allowed to think it sucks, right? I don't have to be Miss Compersion and Altruism all the time, do I?

So why do I feel so fucking guilty?

She had clung to an eensy-weensy molecule of hope that he would contact her before he left, but her phone was dark and silent. She could nearly envision the tearful goodbyes, hugging his mother and sisters, kissing Maggie goodbye for the last time. They were sending their son, their brother, their fiancé off to war. Everyone in their lives would know they had a loved one thousands of miles away, in the path of ever-present danger, protecting and serving the country. Everyone would share in their pain, their worry, their missing him and praying for the best. Everyone would admire that they were sacrificing time with their loved one so he could answer the call of duty.

Where was her support? Where were the knowing glances and the hugs of solidarity? Where was the admiration for her sacrifice of time with the man she loved? *Oh, that's right, it doesn't exist. No one knows he's gone off to war and left me brokenhearted. I have to bear my pain and fear and missing him in desperate, hopeless silence because he doesn't belong to me anymore.*

And what's worse? As much as I wanted him, he never belonged to me in the first place.

SARAH HAD BEEN CHARGED with keeping the wedding day itinerary flowing smoothly, and she was grateful it prevented her mind from wallowing in the self-pity she'd indulged in the night before. She got everyone up in the morning, dressed, to their appointments with makeup artists and hairdressers, and to photo calls at precisely the right times. She made sure everyone was fed and hydrated, particularly the bride. She made sure everyone received the correct flowers and deftly juggled the caterer, the musicians and the officiant. And most importantly, she single-handedly prevented Mrs. Brock from ruining her daughter's wedding day.

Finally everyone was in place, the groom and groomsmen in their sharply angled line, looking so handsome and debonair. The parents of the bride and groom were seated along with all the guests. The bride, bridesmaids, and flower girl, Gia, waited in their positions for the processional to begin, Sarah inching ever closer to breathing a much-deserved sigh of relief. She could officially relax when the ring was on Rachel's finger—or maybe after the kiss. *Hell, better make it after the recessional just to make sure.* She knew what a wild card Rachel could be—and a pregnant Rachel was bound to be that much more unpredictable and volatile.

Finally the processional music started, which was "Canon in D," since Mrs. Brock had deemed "Here Comes the Bride" much too pedestrian for such a sophisticated affair. When Rachel had fired back with, "We're standing on a mountaintop, Mom, not in a fucking cathedral," Sarah knew it was going to be a long day. Not surprisingly, with a few more sharp-tongued exchanges, Mrs. Brock got her way, as usual. Sarah had gently suggested to Rachel that she choose her battles wisely.

Sarah swallowed to get the taste of that conversation out

of her mouth. *Just plaster a pleasant smile on your face and walk. That's all you have to do now.*

Her amethyst-colored gown twisted around her waist. It felt loose even though she'd just had it altered the month before. *I've lost weight since he left. He took my appetite with him.* She watched the silky material slide against the silver strap of her shoe with each step down the white cloth-covered aisle, slowly glancing side to side at the guests in their white wooden chairs, each row bedecked with fresh flowers.

Rachel and Jack had chosen the ceremony site from pictures they perused online. When Sarah had first seen the venue earlier that morning, she'd gasped. It was just fifty yards or so from the place she and James had hiked to after their picnic in March. Standing there four months later, Sarah heard his words, his admission that he loved her, echoing through the canyon. She begged the music to drown out that memory in her mind.

At last the bridesmaids, flower girl and bride were in place, and the officiant began the welcome and offered a prayer. *This day is not about me.* While everyone else's eyes were closed and heads bowed, she studied her best friend, who looked like a little cloud of white perched on the mountaintop, clutching her bouquet of pink and white stargazer lilies and purple irises against her stomach as if morning sickness had begun to plague her again.

She'd known this woman for nearly twelve years; they'd been through births and crumbling marriages and divorces and grad school and moves together. But today was their first wedding together, surely the first of many. *Someday in the not too distant future,* Sarah thought with a gulp, *we'll be watching Abby and Owen and Thomas and Gia walk down the aisle with the men or women they love. And the new baby too. And then we'll be watching our babies have babies.*

I just hope they will all find their happy endings, that they will love and be loved.

A soft sigh escaped Sarah's lips as she glanced from Abby to Owen, then to Thomas and Gia, trying to imagine them as grownups. She peered into her crystal ball at what their futures may look like. And then she looked back to the present and wondered if her mother would have dreamed this life for her when she was their ages.

Maybe this is my happy ending after all, just getting to be a mother and an academic and enjoying a life rich with beauty and intellectual pursuits.

She choked back a tear. She was truly blessed to have a loyal friend like Rachel, two beautiful children, and a mother who understood her and loved her unconditionally. Having an amazing man like James come into her life like a whirlwind, knowing from the beginning he would break her heart, but allowing herself to love him with every fiber of her being—despite her intuitions... *Well, maybe that is a blessing too. Maybe having loved and lost really is better than never having loved at all.*

I will never regret loving him.

She listened to her best friend's confident, bold voice carrying across the mountain as she recited her vows, looking deeply into the eyes of her beloved. She watched her slip a ring onto his finger and promise she would love him until death parted them. She watched Jack do the same, making her best friend his wife, vowing to love her and cherish her till the end of time. She watched them exchange their beautiful promise to each other and realized that just bearing witness to great love was a blessing. Knowing that two people desired for every part of themselves to be intertwined forever was a blessing.

Maybe I can't have that for myself again, but I can feel happy for those who do.

As the officiant pronounced Jack and Rachel husband and wife, Sarah scanned the range of Rockies in the distance, watching the lavender mist rolling in around Pike's Peak and remembering how James had looked against that same backdrop. She heard his voice in her head and felt his arms around her. He suddenly felt so close to her, as if his body was pressing against her.

Her eyes soaked up the distant snowy splendor of the highest ranges. The nearer red rock formations jutted into the sky, silhouetted against the darker gray mountains with their silver caps. She gasped for air as her lungs found themselves devoid of breath. Something beyond logic and reason was happening to her. Every cell in her body and mind began to resonate with a vibrant and melodic symphony that rose to the heavens like billowing clouds of smoke. She was enveloped in the chorus of a million voices from all throughout the universe ringing out with one, unified message.

As she began to grasp what was happening to her, a solitary teardrop slid down her cheek and onto the silky petal of a lily in her bouquet. Anyone watching would have thought she was moved to tears at the sight of her best friend in the world marrying the man she loved. But no...as happy as Sarah was for Rachel, this tear was something else. It was spawned by the ethereal anthem rising all around her.

She smiled through the tears that had joined the first one. *The rocks are crying out to me, and I believe...no, I know...he hears them too.*

As she focused her eyes on the exact spot where James first professed his love, she felt his presence and a renewed hope coursing through her more strongly than anything she'd ever felt in her life.

This isn't over. She trembled at the thought, her heart feeling like it was about to explode with love.

This mountain can still be climbed.

JAMES

He awoke with a gasp, his heart pounding against his ribs so hard he felt like they might shatter. Getting his bearings, he glanced around, finding himself on the plane, surrounded by his fellow soldiers on their journey halfway across the world. They were on a mission to promote freedom, but never had he felt more constrained. His mind struggled to get back to the dream he was having about a beautiful, voluptuous woman with long, dark hair and entrancing chocolate brown eyes.

Sarah...

No, he told himself. *I'm not supposed to be thinking about her.*

He tried to force his mind to dwell on his fiancée, Maggie, but it refused, stubbornly returning to that ivory skin, the full lips, the mouthwatering curves.

Yes, his cock was hard as thoughts of sinking into Sarah's wet, eager pussy filled his imagination. He swallowed, his Adam's apple bobbing in his throat as an overpowering hunger for Sarah consumed him.

It's just the sex I miss, he lied to himself, still trying to shake off the sensation, but his cock was not about to relent. *I'm in love with Maggie. She's going to be the mother of my children.*

You're a damn fool, his heart berated him.

You made a mistake.

His stomach twisted as he tried to arbitrate the war being waged between his heart, mind and cock. His entire body felt engaged in a battle he was sure he could never win.

Tell her how you feel, pleaded his heart.

I will, he decided. *If I make it out of here alive.*

358

TO BE CONTINUED...

Make sure to check out Book 2 of the Mountains Series, and the continuation of James and Sarah's story, Mountains Climbed.

ABOUT THE AUTHOR

USA Today Bestselling Author Phoebe Alexander writes #sexpositive #bodypositive erotic romance featuring compelling plots intertwined with passionate, fiery encounters. She believes that real, relatable characters can have even steamier sex than billionaires, rock stars, and the young and lithe-bodied. She also advocates for ethical non-monogamy through her writing.

Phoebe lives on the East Coast of the US with her husband, sons, and multiple fur babies. When she's not writing, she works as an editor and consultant for indie authors. She also volunteers her time running a 5000-member indie author support group. Her sexual fantasies have all been fulfilled, and now her single greatest fantasy is just having some damn free time.

Join Phoebe's newsletter at www.phoebe-alexander.com, Join her readers' group at www.facebook.com/groups/PhoebesAngels.

facebook.com/phoebealexanderauthor

instagram.com/authorphoebealexander

bookbub.com/authors/phoebe-alexander

twitter.com/eroticphoebe

amazon.com/Phoebe-Alexander/e/B00ANN43WK

ALSO BY PHOEBE ALEXANDER

Mountains Trilogy

Mountains Wanted

Mountains Climbed

Mountains Loved

Christmas in the Mountains

The Navigator

The Explorer

Mountains Transcended

Eastern Shore Swingers Series

Fisher of Men

The Catch

Siren Call

Sailors Knot

Turning the Tide

Spicetopia Series

Sugar & Spice

Virtue & Vice

Fire & Ice

Naughty & Nice

Dares & Dice

Loyalty & Lies

Alpha Bet Guys Series

A Hole

The Big O

Need the D

Hard F

Ride the C

The Playground

Project Paradise (The Juniper Court Series)
www.junipercourtseries.com

Rule Breaker

(the above standalones can be purchased together in the Wildhearted Women Boxed Set)